Praise for the Amanda Doucette Mysteries

A high-adrenaline plunge into the dangerous and murky waters
of homegrown terrorism.
— *Publishers Weekly* (starred review)

Masterly ... it's the wilderness that provides the story's passion.
— *Toronto Star*

A simply riveting read from first page to last by a master of the genre.
— *Midwest Book Review*

Readers of Tana French and Deborah Crombie may want to investigate.
— *Library Journal*

Launching a new series, Fradkin scores low for mystery, high for
wilderness adventure, and off the charts for her portrait of the bleak,
beautiful Newfoundland landscape.
— *Kirkus Reviews*

The book also leaves one wishing to know more about Amanda Doucette.
She is a plucky, adventurous, smart, caring person with an exciting,
globetrotting career and the potential for many great stories.
— *Ottawa Citizen*

If you want to get a real feel (and fear) of the woods, this is the book for you.
— *Globe and Mail*

A terrific read.
— *Winnipeg Free Press*

PRISONERS OF HOPE

Amanda Doucette Mysteries

Fire in the Stars
The Trickster's Lullaby
Prisoners of Hope

PRISONERS OF HOPE

An Amanda Doucette Mystery

Barbara
Fradkin

DUNDURN
TORONTO

Cover image: Shutterstock.com/Roy Boyce
Printer: Webcom

Library and Archives Canada Cataloguing in Publication

Fradkin, Barbara Fraser, 1947-, author
    Prisoners of hope / Barbara Fradkin.

(An Amanda Doucette mystery)
Issued in print and electronic formats.
ISBN 978-1-4597-3764-8 (softcover).--ISBN 978-1-4597-3765-5
(PDF).--ISBN 978-1-4597-3766-2 (EPUB)

    I. Title. II. Series: Fradkin, Barbara Fraser, 1947- . Amanda Doucette mystery

PS8561.R233P75 2018   C813'.6   C2018-901715-5
                                               C2018-901716-3

1 2 3 4 5   22 21 20 19 18

  Canada

We acknowledge the support of the **Canada Council for the Arts**, which last year invested $153 million to bring the arts to Canadians throughout the country, and the **Ontario Arts Council** for our publishing program. We also acknowledge the financial support of the **Government of Ontario**, through the **Ontario Book Publishing Tax Credit** and the **Ontario Media Development Corporation**, and the **Government of Canada**.

Nous remercions le **Conseil des arts du Canada** de son soutien. L'an dernier, le Conseil a investi 153 millions de dollars pour mettre de l'art dans la vie des Canadiennes et des Canadiens de tout le pays.

Care has been taken to trace the ownership of copyright material used in this book. The author and the publisher welcome any information enabling them to rectify any references or credits in subsequent editions.

— *J. Kirk Howard, President*

VISIT US AT

dundurn.com | @dundurnpress | dundurnpress | dundurnpress

Dundurn
3 Church Street, Suite 500
Toronto, Ontario, Canada
M5E 1M2

For my sister, Pam,
with affection and gratitude

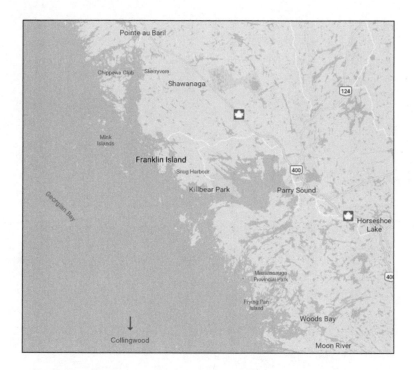

CHAPTER ONE

Amanda smiled as she watched the speedboat swoop playfully up the bay. Once it drew closer, she could make out the gleam of antique cedar and brass. A lone man sat in the cockpit, one hand on the wheel and the other trailing in the water. He leaned into the curves, grinning as the boat carved up the bay and left curls of froth and ripples in its wake.

She was sitting on a granite rock at the edge of the parking lot, and she rose for a better view as he pulled back on the throttle and aimed the powerful boat toward the nearest slip. Surely this wasn't George Gifford. She had pictured the kayak outfitter as a rough outdoorsman piloting a dented aluminum runabout. A beard, cargo pants, and khaki jacket with a half-dozen pockets and rings.

While she'd been waiting, there had been no such boat on the bay. In fact, it being late May, there were almost no boats at all. A few luxury yachts bobbed at anchor and a couple were tied up at the docks, but most of the summer cottagers' boats were still stored in hangars or under tarps inland, awaiting the summer cottage invasion.

Cottage season didn't truly hit its peak in Georgian Bay until the July 1st weekend, when cottagers and tourists poured in from the crowded cities farther south to set up stakes on the spectacular islands and bays that formed its coastal fringe. Over thirty thousand islands had earned the eastern coast the distinction of the largest freshwater archipelago in the world. Although it had once been overrun by the logging and fishing industries, most of it had now reverted to nature and provided an unspoiled getaway for kayakers, campers, birdwatchers, and hikers during the long, warm summer.

In May, however, the ice was barely out, and only the most intrepid were willing to brave the mosquitoes, blackflies, and chilly winds that still swept across Lake Huron from the west. Amanda was there on a scouting expedition for her family kayaking adventure in July. She had chosen the historic cottage village of Pointe au Baril as the rendezvous point with her outfitter because it was located in a deep, protected inlet near the midpoint of the archipelago. She and Kaylee had been waiting at the village dock for George Gifford for almost at hour, and she was beginning to wonder whether she'd been stood up. She'd thrown the dog's ball at least a hundred times, and her arm was growing numb.

On his website, George Gifford had seemed like a reliable man. His company wasn't big and flashy, but he was a fourth-generation Georgian Bay native who had thirty years' experience in the guiding and outfitting business. He had kayaked all over the world from the roughest Pacific seas to the most serene Ontario lakes, and he claimed to know every tree and shoal on the eastern Georgian Bay coast. She had been counting on him to help her choose the perfect itinerary for her group of eager but utterly inexperienced adventurers.

The man in the speedboat was standing now as he guided the boat into one of the slips and killed the engine. Morning sunlight glinted off his windblown hair, burnishing it to honey gold as he leaped cat-like onto the dock and tied up the boat. On the phone, George had the gravelly bass of an older man, and an internet check of his credentials had turned up a man with a steel-grey buzz cut.

Not George Gifford, then. Amanda felt a twinge of disappointment, which quickly changed to frustration. The man was nearly an hour late for their very first meeting, which didn't bode well for his reliability during the intricate coordination of the six-day kayak trip to the offshore islands.

She sneaked a peek at her phone. No messages either. And where was Chris? Even if he was late leaving Newfoundland, he should have texted his arrival details by now. Unless he'd gotten cold feet. Not that she would blame him. He'd expressed excitement about coming on this scouting expedition, and there'd been a palpable thrum of electricity between them, but what did she really know about him? No matter how much he was in her dreams, they'd spent barely two weeks together in the past eight months, most of it dealing with crises.

The stranger stood on the dock, shielding his eyes from the sun as he scanned the parking lot. He too glanced at his phone and frowned. Kaylee, delighted at the possibility of a new playmate and oblivious to his dark mood, snatched up her ball and bounded down onto the dock to drop it at his feet.

Amanda was about to call her back when the man's frown dissolved into a smile. "Well, what do you want?" he asked, bending to pick up the ball. Kaylee danced expectantly, and the man looked up at Amanda. "Can I throw it?"

"She'd love it!" Amanda exclaimed. The man curled back his arm and shot a beautiful high ball far up onto the road behind the parking lot. The little red dog was off like a shot, and the man laughed as he strolled up the dock.

"Beautiful dog," he said. "It's a Nova Scotia something, isn't it?"

"Nova Scotia Duck Tolling Retriever. Don't worry, no one ever remembers the whole name."

Kaylee came bouncing back to drop the ball in front of him. "Look at that focus!" he said. "Does she like the water?"

"Part mermaid! They're bred for it. I warn you, though, she'll retrieve until your arm falls off."

"This is my kind of dog," he said, bending to pick up the ball. "We just got a Lab puppy, but I think they left the brains out of the package."

Amanda laughed. "All puppies are like that." She tried to call Kaylee over so that she would not pester the man yet again, but the dog was too excited. "You have a beautiful boat. Is it an antique?"

"It is. It's been in the family — well, my wife's family — for sixty years. It's temperamental, but it's my favourite." He tossed the ball again and then looked up to scan the road behind the parking lot. His frown returned. "You haven't seen a woman and a baby anywhere around, have you?"

Amanda looked around. There was only one vehicle in the parking lot, an SUV from Michigan parked next to her lime-green motorcycle with its custom-built dog trailer. Most of the traffic that had driven by in the past hour had been contractors in pickup trucks.

"There's construction on the highway," she said. She'd been giving herself the same excuse for George Gifford's delay.

He grinned. "There's always construction on the highway." At that moment the roar of an engine and the squeal of tires heralded the arrival of a car. They both turned expectantly just as a silver Audi slewed into the parking lot and jerked to a stop. The door was flung open and a woman leaped out. Amanda noticed the skinny white jeans and the gold wedge sandals first before taking in the mass of platinum curls, the huge sunglasses, and the cherry-red lips. Not exactly a country look.

In that instant, Amanda felt every inch of her frayed jeans, baggy T-shirt, and flip-flops. In anticipation of Chris Tymko's arrival, she had washed her long, light-brown hair and pulled it into what she hoped was an attractive ponytail, but she'd clearly fallen well short of the mark.

"Her usual grand entrance," the man muttered before heading up toward the car.

"I'm sorry, I'm sorry!" Cherry Lips exclaimed. "The traffic out of Toronto was *insane*, and I had to stop four times because —" An outraged screech from inside the car stopped her short, and she clutched her head. "Omigod, Benson, he's been like that the whole time! He just won't settle! I tell you, you're a lifesaver. If it weren't for you, I'd be murdering the kid!"

Benson strode toward the car. "Well, let's get the little guy out." He opened the rear door and bent inside, crooning baby talk. The woman seemed to notice Amanda for the first time. Her gaze flicked over the baggy T-shirt, and a faint frown pinched her face. Amanda tried a sympathetic smile, which the woman ignored.

Benson emerged with a baby in his arms, now miraculously quiet. He tossed the little boy into the air and then buried his face in the boy's belly, making him burst into giggles.

"Benson, I have to go. I'm so late!" The woman opened the trunk and began to dump suitcases, half a dozen bags, a car seat, and a stroller on the ground. "If he gets colicky, push him around in the stroller."

"We'll take you for a motorboat ride, won't we, Tommy?"

"Thomas. It's Thomas."

Benson grinned at her, and Amanda suspected they'd played this game before. "Would you like to spend a few days with Uncle Ben? And all your cousins?" He tossed the boy again before tucking him comfortably in the crook of his arm.

"And if he won't eat, all the instructions from the doctor are in this binder here. His whole routine. He needs his routine."

"Candy, we'll be fine. Danielle is a miracle worker with babies. Don't worry, go!"

"I guess you can always get Kaitlyn to help out as well. If you can get her out of bed."

A frown flickered across his face. "She's only fourteen, Candace."

Candace looked about to contradict him but checked herself. She stood on tiptoe to kiss her son and then paused, her head tilted to gaze up at Benson. Her eyes softened as she touched his arm. "Thank you," she mouthed.

He bent his head to kiss her forehead. "Have fun. Get some rest."

Then Candace was gone with a squeal of tires and a little wave of her red-tipped fingers out the window. Benson turned toward his boat and paused to eye the mountain of luggage on the ground.

"I'll help you with that," Amanda said.

"Would you? That would be a great help. Actually, what would be an even greater help is if you'd hold the baby while I load the boat."

The baby began to scream the moment he left Benson's magic arms. Amanda could feel his rigid posture and his back arching away from her. She tried to coo and play as Benson had, but the screeching only grew more frantic. Finally, she went down to the dock, where he was loading bags into the boat. "He seems to be at the making strange stage," she said. "Maybe you should—"

"Oh, he's always like that. Anything new sets him off. I'll just set up his carrier in the boat, and then he'll settle."

Amanda paced the dock, trying to soothe the baby and remembering how the village mothers in Africa carried their babies everywhere in soft slings of cloth that moulded the baby to the mother's warm body. The infants rarely fussed unless they were hungry. Sometimes nature really did know best.

True to his word, Benson had all the gear stowed in the boat and Thomas strapped into his seat with a life jacket in no time. He started the engine and straightened to hold out his hand. "Thank you! I'm Ben Humphries, by the way."

He enveloped her hand in his gentle but confident grip, and she felt herself flushing like a fifteen-year old. "Amanda Doucette. Good luck!"

"Perhaps I'll see you and your beautiful dog around some day. Do you live in the area?"

"No, just planning a kayak trip. With Gifford Outfitters. Do you know them?"

His face lit. "Everyone knows George. Great guy. You're in good hands."

"I hope so. He's late."

With practiced ease he dropped down behind the wheel. "That's unusual. Maybe —" He broke off at the sound of a distant boat. They both turned to watch a small boat's progress up the sparkling bay. "That's probably him now," Benson said.

As the boat drew closer, Amanda could make out a sturdy aluminum skiff painted red in places and black in others, as if the owner had used whatever colour was handy at the time. A man sat in the rear. Sunglasses obscured his face, and a ball cap was pulled low over his eyes, but she could distinguish faded jeans and a tan windbreaker.

George Gifford at last?

"Yes, that's …" Benson scowled. "Oh."

"What?"

Benson shook his head and started the engine. "Nothing. My mistake. I've got to take off. Good luck with your trip!"

And with that he was gone, reversing away from the dock and then swinging the boat in a wide, graceful arc toward the open water. As the two boats passed, the man in the little skiff waved, but Benson made no response. Amanda had little time to puzzle over Benson's abrupt change of mood before the skiff swooped in to the dock. The man threw his outboard into reverse and came to a perfect stop against the side of the dock. He picked up the painter and wrapped it quickly around the dock cleat before jumping out. Hair bleached the colour of ripe wheat peeked out from under the ball cap. There was a youthful grace to the jump and a slight swagger as he walked up the dock toward her.

"You must be Amanda Doucette."

Doubts began to crowd in. The voice had none of the gravel she was expecting. When he pulled off his sunglasses, he revealed merry blue eyes, freckled cheeks, and a broken tooth that gave him a boyish, gap-toothed grin. The kid looked barely thirty.

Her heart sank. "I was expecting George Gifford."

"Well, you got his son, Ronny." He spread his arms teasingly. "Your lucky day."

This trip is going from bad to worse, Amanda thought as she transferred her duffel bags into the boat. *And it hasn't even begun yet.* Gifford Outfitters had been the enthusiastic choice of Frankie Montfort, the local social worker whose passionate and creative work with abused women had caught Amanda's attention earlier in the spring.

Georgian Getaway was to be the third in Amanda's Fun for Families adventures as she took her unique charity fundraising tour across Canada. In select locations along the way, she organized outings to give marginalized people a glimpse of the possibilities beyond the struggles of their daily lives. Each adventure targeted a different group in need and raised money for a related international charity, in this case Crossroads, a group dedicated to improving the lives of women and girls in developing countries. It had seemed fitting to choose abused women in this mainly rural part of Ontario, where options and escape routes were few.

Frankie had been the one to insist on including children. "We have to catch these kids early," she'd said, leaning across the table at the Tim Hortons in Parry Sound. "Growing up in an abusive home is terrifying, and by adolescence their reactions are entrenched. Girls in particular need to know that abuse is not their fault and they have a right to demand respect."

"But I want this trip to be a refuge for these mothers. An escape from the constant demands of nurturing. Plus I can't bring little kids on the open water. It's too risky, and everyone has to be able to pitch in." Amanda contemplated the trip she had in mind. Camping, paddling, strolling through forests and along granite shores. Stargazing, swimming, sharing stories around a campfire. It was to be a chance to laugh, to slip the bonds of their frightened lives and to find hope and confidence again.

All qualities she had tried to impart to the children and families she worked with as an international aid worker in Africa and Asia. She had loved the job and never imagined giving it up until a horde of jihadist thugs rampaged through the Nigerian village she was working in, torching buildings, slashing villagers, and kidnapping the children for their own brutal purposes. Amanda had managed to escape but had fled back home to Canada with her trust and her dreams in tatters.

Fun for Families rose out of those tattered dreams as a way to continue giving help and hope right here at home, while also raising money for overseas help.

"Nine- to twelve-year-old girls, then," Frankie had countered. "I was once one of those. They still have some fight in them."

Amanda smiled at the image of ten-year-old Frankie — fierce, raw, righteous — talking back to teachers, punching obnoxious boys in the head, getting suspended time after time. Teachers rolling their eyes and saying, "Well, what do you expect?"

Frankie was the kind of success story Amanda was aiming for, galvanized rather than defeated by her hardships and ready to take on any obstacle in her path. Fresh out of social work school, she had founded support services for abused women in the far-flung, sparsely populated Parry Sound District, including an emergency shelter, co-op apartment building, and counselling centre. Equally important, she was as adept at outdoor sports as she was at writing grant proposals and cajoling local service clubs.

Even at thirty, she still had the rebellious gleam in her eye that Amanda remembered so well from her own early years overseas. The belief you could change the world, and the energy to try. Amanda still felt that spark but now, in her midthirties, it sputtered and nearly winked out when fatigue, failure, or memories of Nigeria swept over her. Just being with this feisty young woman, with her ripped jeans, turquoise hair, multiple silver studs, and fringed leather jacket made her heart beat faster.

"Then let's include sons, too," Amanda had said. "Mothers with nine- to twelve-year-old children, period. Boys are affected by abusive men as well. They need to learn a different way to be a man."

Frankie was clearly not ready to forgive the male half of the species just yet, but by the end of the coffee meeting, they had hammered out the makeup and size of the group and a rough list of the activities. Amanda had come away with the name of the outfitter Frankie had recommended. "No one knows the islands like George Gifford, and he's also a huge supporter of our work. He sits on boards, organizes fundraisers, and talks to local clubs and bars. He's a guy's guy, and up here, that's everything. He hired me on as a cook one summer when I was a sixteen-year-old brat headed for jail. George is ..." Frankie paused, her eyes shining. "If any man can be a saint, he's one."

Standing now on the dock with George's son, Amanda wondered whether the sainthood applied to the son as well. He looked too young and brash, not yet tempered by the years. His eyes were impish and his movements jaunty and sure. He was sexy in an earthy, rumpled way, and Amanda suspected he knew it.

Not a saint by a long shot.

What was Frankie going to make of this when she arrived? Since she had worked with his father, did she already know the son? Amanda had only a moment to wonder before an aging Honda CR-V rattled down the road and jerked to a stop in the middle of the lot. Frankie yanked the emergency brake and leaped out. Silver studs glinted in the sun.

"Ronny!" There was no delight in her tone. "What the fuck are you doing here?"

Ronny grinned. "How ya doing, Flash?"

"George is apparently not coming," Amanda said, hoping to head off trouble.

"But he sent me."

"Oh, no, no, no. The deal was George. What the hell? He's dying to do this trip!"

"And he will," Ronny said. "He put his back out a few days ago, but it will be fine by July. I'm just here to work out the route and the supplies with you. I've been on hundreds of trips with Dad, and I know every shoal and eddy, all the secret camping spots and best hikes." He walked over to her car. "Let's call a ceasefire for now, okay, Flash? And get your gear in the boat. I'll even forgive you that kick in the balls in grade six."

Frankie's lips twitched. "I hope it did some good. But lucky for you, we don't need a ceasefire. I can't come. There's a crisis with one of the women. Husband found her and put her in the hospital. I've got to deal with cops and restraining orders. Again!" She pulled a handwritten sheet off her battered clipboard and held it out. "Here's the details on the group. If I can get things sorted out in a day or two, I'll join you. Otherwise ..." She shrugged as she climbed back in her car. "Sorry, Amanda. I thought George would be here."

This trip really is going from bad to worse, Amanda thought. What more could go wrong?

She didn't have to wait long to find out. The boat was loaded and ready to go when her cellphone rang. *Chris. Finally!* Her quiver of excitement faded when he spoke. His usually cheerful, teasing voice sounded tense.

"I'm still in Deer Lake," he said. "A situation came up, and Sergeant Knotts needs an extra hand. I think he's just being a jerk, but I better not argue."

"But ..." Her voice trailed off. What could she say?

"Sorry, I should have called earlier, but I didn't think it would take this long. But if I get a flight first thing in the morning, I should be able to get there by tomorrow afternoon. Will that work?"

Amanda's hopes sank. There was no point in arguing or pleading. Much of his current problem at work was her fault, and the tie between them was too tenuous for guilt or expectations. Suppressing a sigh, she turned to Ronny, who was playing with Kaylee.

"That your boyfriend?" he asked.

"He's not —" She checked herself. Ronny didn't need to know the complexities. With a vague shrug, she relayed the problem to him.

If he noticed her evasion, he gave no sign. "Tell him we're just going to Franklin Island for the night. There's lots to explore there, and it has cellphone coverage. I'll leave his kayak and gear at the marina in Snug Harbour, and if he gets here tomorrow, he can meet us on the island."

Amanda tried to keep the disappointment out of her voice. She'd been looking forward to this day ever since the phone call two months ago, when he'd finally committed to coming on the trip. She knew he was still wary, and their fragile relationship might crumble before it could really get started, but it was a step. He'd agreed to use some of his leave from his RCMP post in Newfoundland. Even with the others around, they would still have moments together. Chances to share the sunsets, the moonlight, the swims in secret lagoons, the tent at night....

This trip would give them a hint at their future. If any.

She relayed Ronny's suggestion to Chris and told him to keep her informed of his whereabouts by text. "Ronny says there is cellphone coverage on Franklin Island, so we can set up a rendezvous."

"Okay." His voice dropped. "Sorry, Amanda."

She gripped the phone and took a deep breath. "I'll miss you tonight."

For a beat he didn't respond, and she was afraid she'd gone too far. Until finally ... "Hold that thought."

CHAPTER TWO

Ronny gunned the engine, and Amanda grabbed Kaylee's collar as the boat bounced over the waves. Ronny laughed. "She's not fast," he shouted over the roar of the engine, "but she'll get you where you want to go."

"Where *are* we going?" she replied as he turned the boat southward to thread between two islands. "I thought we were going to explore by kayak."

"Yeah, yeah. We'll pick up the kayaks farther south in Snug Harbour. But you should see some of the coast before we decide on the route for the trip, and it's faster by motorboat."

All around them lay a maze of islands and wandering shoreline. Short, twisted pines struggled to find purchase in the polished pink granite of the water's edge. Red and green channel markers guided boats down the middle of the water-way, but Ronny slowed the engine and nudged the boat closer to land. In the lull, he pulled an iPad out of his pack and booted it up.

"Navigational app," he said with a grin. "It shows me water depth and the safest routes, takes most of the guesswork out of navigating. My dad says it takes all the fun out of it too, but I'm not taking any chances. This coast is full of shoals and underwater rocks. You gotta be careful, or they'll take out your propeller.

Dad knows every single rock, and I know most of them, but I like this high-tech stuff."

She glanced down at the map on the tablet. It looked a bit like a nautical chart, but a little blue dot marked their progress through the channel. Useful, but she agreed with George. Looking at the real landscape was more fun.

Ronny gestured to the shoreline as they passed. "Lots of cottages along here; not much public land for camping, but my dad wanted you to see it. These cottages are part of Georgian Bay's history."

The term "cottage" seemed like a gross inaccuracy. Some of the dwellings perched on the clifftops or sprawling across the manicured shore were more like palaces, with multiple decks and balconies, docks, boathouses bigger than most homes, and even floatplane hangars. There were gleaming wooden timbers, hand-hewn stone walls, banks of windows facing the sunsets. For her struggling single mothers, it would be a world as foreign and unattainable as Hollywood. She thought about the families she had worked with in Cambodia and Africa, living with six children in a one-room hut, trying to coax vegetables from a patch of dust outside.

Ronny must have seen her dismay, for his grin widened. "Different world, eh?"

"Who are these people?"

He shrugged. "Rich. These places can set you back well over a million. Some folks are from Toronto, but there's lots of Americans — Pennsylvania, Ohio, Michigan. They bought up the cottages during the war when Canada had gas rationing and they didn't." He swerved the boat just in time to avoid a pink rock that loomed like a whale beneath the surface. "But a few of the cottages are over a hundred years old and still owned by the original families. Most of them didn't start off rich. They came to work when fishing and logging were the big industries, and they built little cottages on the islands for the season. In a hundred years, you can make a lot of improvements."

"Improvements" didn't begin to describe the extravagance tucked into the inlets and perched on western points. As beautiful as some of the homes were, they didn't belong here.

Ronny seemed oblivious. "Think your group would like to see these?"

Her protective instincts kicked in. What was the point of rubbing their noses in their own poor luck of the draw? But that was being patronizing. Television had already shown them the unattainable world of the super rich. Advertisements seduced them with glamorous clothes, luxury cars, and homes that gleamed of stainless steel, marble floors, and crystal chandeliers.

"Maybe," she said, "but I don't see any place for us to land and explore." Most of the islands had private property signs prominent on the shore.

"Not here. This is millionaires' row. But there are public islands farther south, and we can make a day trip up here. Not much going on right now, but in the summertime, this channel is hopping. Speedboats, water skiers, floatplanes all zooming around."

As they rounded a point of land, another huge mansion came into view, with stone patios and gardens sprawling along the waterfront. Amanda stared at it in appalled fascination. It was stunningly beautiful, with soaring two-storey windows, square timber framing, and granite cladding. The sound of power tools whined above the low *put put* of the motorboat, and she could see swarms of men at work. Ronny drew closer, craning his neck to see through the trees.

"Construction season. This place is owned by some rich New York guy, Wall Street or something, just bought it last year. He's putting in a swimming pool."

"Swimming pool!" Amanda looked with astonishment at the sparkling waters of the strait. "Why on earth?"

He shrugged. "Heated. And some people don't like swimming with fishies and crayfish and zebra mussels. But they can build a whole Disney theme park if they want, as long as they bring jobs. I've worked on a couple of these mansions, and a buddy of mine is working on this one."

Amanda tore her eyes away and looked across the channel, where country estates peeked out from the shoreline of rocks and trees. "Is that shore all privately owned as well?"

His gaze flickered. "Mostly. It's a couple of big islands."

"Can we take a peek? They might be nice to paddle through."

He hesitated a beat before turning the boat and guiding it across the channel. He pointed to the tablet. "Zoom in on that app. Lots of tricky shoals for a motorboat around there. We don't want to end up at the bottom of the lake."

As they drew closer, she saw most of the homes were still boarded up for the winter, with boats tucked into boathouses and docks lifted from the water. One or two floatplanes bobbed in the water, however, and as they came around another point, a deep natural inlet sliced through the granite shoreline, protecting a sailing yacht from the open waves. In another slip beside the yacht, polished wood flashed in the morning sun. Peering closer, she could make out the familiar contours of an antique speedboat.

"Wait!" she cried. "Can you go closer?"

He glanced at his watch. "Our gear's waiting for us at the marina."

"Who owns that place?"

He turned the boat back toward the marked channel. "Been in the family so long, it's called Saint Clair Island. Toronto family made their money in mining and steel years ago. The old tycoon just died a couple of years ago."

She could see figures moving around the property, sweeping the patios and stringing up lights through the greenery. Others were cleaning the barbeque and setting glasses and plates out on a long table. Down at the dock, a lone handyman was hammering in some new planks. "Looks like they're having a party."

He shrugged. "Could be. Might be their big cottage opening weekend, but I don't exactly get an invite. Used to be they hired local people to work their parties, but now they bring in crews from Toronto." He wheeled the boat around and opened the throttle on full, apparently having forgotten the threat of hidden rocks. Soon they were carving between the buoys at the centre of the strait, the mansions just distant scars on the wild granite beauty of the shore.

Images of Benson stayed with her, his open delight with Kaylee and his loving touch with the baby. Yet he had ignored Ronny, and now Ronny was being equally evasive. *Was there a story there?* she wondered idly. Was it just a clash of two solitudes, resentment over the loss of local jobs, or something more personal? Benson, for all his playful warmth, came from privilege and clearly enjoyed his luxuries. As Ronny himself said, different values.

She shook herself. *Down, girl. Your prejudices are showing. Just because he has money, that doesn't automatically make him a bad person.* Even in the developing world she had known wealthy people who were extraordinarily generous and kind, and if his money had been in the family for generations, he could hardly be blamed for it anyway.

A fluke of fate, she thought, putting the mysterious encounter behind her.

As Ronny had assured her, the kayaks and gear were waiting for them when they piloted up the inlet to Snug Harbour. He had packed food for four days, and once they'd transferred their personal and group gear to dry sacks, Ronny explained the intricate process of packing the kayaks.

"You gotta balance the weight in the front and back hatches," he said as he stuffed the first dry sack deep into the front hatch. "Otherwise it won't float level. And you gotta keep your emergency kit in easy reach. You don't want to be trying to open a hatch when your boat is upside down in the water."

"But we're staying in sheltered bays, right?" Amanda said. "We've got kids and novice paddlers with us."

"Yeah, yeah, but you never know when a storm will blow up. Even the quietest water can turn ugly. Better to overprepare than underprepare."

Amanda could almost hear his father's voice in the warning. She eyed him with new respect and relief. He might be young and cocky, but he appeared to know his job. The kayak she was packing was wider and heavier than the sleek craft he was using, because she had to fit Kaylee in the cockpit in front of her. She had done some paddling with Kaylee earlier in the month, and the dog was not thrilled with the cramped quarters, but Amanda hoped she would get used to it. In any case, the group would mostly be hopping from one island to another in short stints, because she doubted ten-year-olds would be any more patient than Kaylee.

"Why four days? I thought you said we needed three."

"Always plan for a wind day. If we get stuck on the outer islands, you'll be glad of the extra day's food."

Amanda's phone buzzed. A text from Chris. *Finally got the time off. Flight to Toronto crack of dawn tomorrow! Can you wait for me?*

She felt a rush of mixed feelings, thrilled that she'd soon see him but frustrated that it might delay them another day.

"We can't wait for him," Ronny said when she told him. "We'll stick to the original plan and camp on Franklin Island. We'll send him the coordinates and he can meet us there tomorrow."

"But —"

"It's not far, and it's all pretty sheltered paddling. I can't just fart around here for a day. I got a fishing group later in the week."

So they set off down the broad inlet, paddling directly west toward a red-and-white lighthouse at the entrance to the harbour. Kaylee sat between Amanda's legs and peered out over the top of the cockpit, excited by the waves lapping the bow, the gulls wheeling overhead, and the shoreline slipping by. She snapped at the waves, and Amanda had to remind her frequently to stay still. Hordes of blackflies swirled around them, luckily kept at bay by Deep Woods Off.

"Please tell me the bugs aren't like this in July," she said as she spat out a blackfly.

"They aren't." Ronny laughed. "The blackflies will be gone in a week or two. And out on the islands the wind keeps them down. You'll see."

Up ahead the sun blazed a swath of gold across the water, silhouetting the lighthouse against the open bay beyond. When the inlet widened, the breeze picked up, slowing their progress as they ploughed against it, but true to Ronny's word, it chased away the mosquitoes and blackflies.

Ronny turned right before the lighthouse and led them into a narrow, protected channel behind an island. The sun beat down and they swished through the water. Paddling abreast of her, he kept up a running chatter about the surroundings and his choice of route.

"It's usually calm in here," he said. "No wind and waves to fight against, and motorboats have to slow to a crawl. This will be a perfect time for your group to practice their skills, learn to stop and turn and lean from one side to the other. By the time we reach the end, they'll be ready to cross the open channel to Franklin Island."

The four leaders would be in single kayaks, whereas each mother would share a tandem kayak with her child. That way if a child became tired, the group could still continue.

"Do you know rolls and rescue techniques?" Ronny asked as they approached a deep, narrow channel carved between steep rock faces.

Amanda had learned emergency manoeuvres in calm water, but she knew that wasn't where they'd be needed. Heaven help them if a tandem kayak capsized.

"We'd better not get into a situation where they're necessary, Ronny," she replied. "At the first hint of rough water, we'll go ashore."

"That's always the plan," he said. "But the bay can surprise you. I need to know what you can do."

The next turn proved his point. The wind hit her full force as the channel opened up to reveal an expanse of white-capped chop. Across the channel lay a low-slung stretch of land. "We have to get across this, for example," he said, digging in his paddle. "That's Franklin Island up ahead."

The sun was still warm, but the wind churned the water into frothy waves. Her kayak began to rock as the waves slapped the hull, and Kaylee's ears flattened in alarm.

"Luckily, it doesn't look very far," she shouted, steadying her boat into the waves.

"It's not, and on a good day, it'll be no problem. We'll time the crossing for the morning, when the wind is down. And this spot" — he pointed to the rugged granite point — "will be a perfect place for a midmorning break. But today we'll head due west across the channel and then hug the shore around the southern tip. There's this fantastic campsite I want to show you."

They paddled in silence, sticking close together and keeping their bows pointed into the wind. Once she found the right rudder setting, Amanda's boat sliced effortlessly through the water, and she let her thoughts roam. In these rare times, she felt almost healed, able to stay in the beauty of the moment without being dogged by a formless sense of dread. She was in Canada, enjoying a blissful sunny afternoon out on the water, far from the smoke and seared flesh, the screams and guttural shouts, the dark, racing shadows backlit by orange flame.

And all the children, gone.

Unbidden, the memories crowded in of her frantic search through the compound, of the burned-out bunks and empty huts. Of her friends and colleagues running headlong into the night, lungs seared and eyes streaming from smoke and tears.

She stopped paddling and shut her eyes. *Don't fight it*, she told herself. She let the waves buffet her as she rode out the surge of fear and rage. With deep breaths, she took stock of herself. Of each sensation and thought. Sometimes she remembered certain details, sometimes others, and sometimes nothing but the dark dread. But here, she told herself, on this serene Georgian Bay afternoon, with the waves slapping and Kaylee's head in her lap, it was all half a world away.

Ronny's shout pulled her out of her reverie. She'd blown backward while he had forged quite a distance ahead. He was frowning as he swung around. "I want us to stick together," he shouted. "Always. At least on an open crossing like this."

Amanda dug in her paddle and felt the kayak leap forward to close the gap. She felt a surge of elation, not only at her speed and power but also at her triumph. She had ridden out the fear.

Not beaten it back or outrun it, but gone with it and let it run its course. A success.

This time.

They reached Franklin Island and meandered around its rocky points and grassy inlets, enjoying the afternoon sun. A few powerboats roared by farther out in the channel, but for the most part they had the idyllic waters to themselves. Lush green shrubs and grasses dipped into the water's edge. They surprised a great blue heron fishing in the reeds and a row of turtles basking on a log in the sun. The water was clear enough to see the multicoloured pebbles on the bottom and the small fish darting away. Amanda smiled. The children were going to love this.

The wind hit them again when they left the lee of the island to paddle around the tip to the western side. The land grew more rugged and the pines clung to the crevices, bent and sparse. Up ahead she saw a broad expanse of flat rock, its multicoloured swirls burnished gold and pink in the sinking sun. Sunlight winked off the whitecaps, and they had to fight to keep the kayaks from blowing onto the rocks. Her arms ached from the effort, and she was grateful when Ronny finally aimed for a small inlet and slipped his kayak aground.

"Perfect place for our camp," he said as he clambered out. "Big enough for half a dozen tents, nice flat terrain, awesome sunsets, no bugs, and" — he pointed triumphantly to a sign nailed to a tree — "a thunderbox! All the comforts of home."

Amanda laughed as she tucked her own kayak in beside his. When Kaylee leaped up, thrilled to be free, Ronny grabbed her collar.

"One thing I forgot to warn you about. There are a few rattlesnakes around here. They're very shy and they won't attack, but they'll defend themselves against an aggressive dog. Best keep her on a leash."

Amanda felt a prickle of fear. From her years overseas she was no stranger to poisonous snakes but had forgotten that Eastern Canada had one poisonous snake, small and rarely fatal to humans but potentially so to small pets and children. Ronny found a photo of the snake on his phone and showed her the fat, blotchy brown specimen.

"They'll make themselves scarce now that we're here, so we'll be fine at the campsite, but when we do our hikes, wear shoes and watch your step."

Amanda hugged Kaylee close. The inquisitive little dog would certainly get the wrong end of that encounter. "What else should we be on the lookout for?"

"Bears. They're good swimmers and hop from island to island looking for food. They'll have their cubs with them, and they like to check out campsites at night." He pointed to a rope-and-pulley system strung between two trees. "This site is well set up to hang our food. Another reason I like it."

The huge orange sun hung just over the open water to the west, lighting the surface in rippling gold and pink. They set up camp quickly and sat on logs enjoying their dinner while nature put on a glorious scarlet show.

Afterward, as the western sky and water shimmered in lilac and rose, Ronny fished a harmonica out of his pack and blew a quick, jaunty riff. He grinned.

"I can't fit my guitar into my kayak, but this does the trick. Whaddaya think? It'll be great for campfire singalongs with the kids." He shut his eyes and played a rollicking blues tune, tapping his bare toes on the rock. Amanda found herself tapping in concert.

"You're good."

"I used to play in a band in high school before most of the guys moved away. We had some good times."

Amanda had a memory flash of Chris bent over his guitar, playing Ukrainian folk songs at a village kitchen party in Newfoundland. Another man full of surprises.

Later that night, as she lay in her tent listening to the echoing calls of whippoorwills, images of Chris roamed through her mind. His crinkly blue eyes, his ski-jump nose, his long, gangly limbs that seemed to have a mind of their own … every inch of him adorable. Kissable. She sighed and wrapped her arms around Kaylee. She was finally drifting off to sleep when the soft music of a cellphone woke her. Not hers, Ronny's. She heard his muffled voice, murmuring, reassuring, concerned. Almost tender. "Don't worry, I'll be there."

A girlfriend, probably. At midnight, who else?

CHAPTER THREE

The morning dawned calm and clear. Tendrils of mist lifted off the glassy lake and drifted slowly inland. As they sipped their morning coffee, Ronny studied the open water through binoculars.

"You heard from Chris yet?"

She shook her head. "He's probably in the air."

"What time does he land in Toronto?"

"I don't know for sure, but I assume late morning."

"And then he's got to drive up here." He jiggled his leg restlessly. "We got the whole day then. What are you up for?"

Amanda looked at the woods behind them. "Maybe we could check out some of the inland hikes on this island. That would be a good break for the kids on one of our days."

Ronny glanced at his phone. "The bugs would be brutal. The weather is so calm, I think we should make a run for the Mink Islands instead." He pointed to a string of dots barely visible on the horizon.

She breathed in the crisp air. The scene was so peaceful that she never wanted to move. When she made a face, he grinned. "You should at least check out the paddle so you know if it's too hard for the group or not. The Minks are a chain of small islands, some of them bare rock and others big enough to explore and camp on. Lots of birds and other small critters, awesome sunsets, plus shipwrecks and a lighthouse."

Amanda eyed the open water doubtfully. "How far is it?"

"It's about five or six kilometres across, depending which route we choose. If we leave now, we'll have the whole day to check it out and figure out whether it's worth seeing."

"But what about Chris? He's supposed to meet us here on Franklin Island this evening."

"We'll be back before supper."

"Is there cellphone reception out there?"

He hesitated. "Some. But don't worry, we'll be back."

She glanced around at the polished rock and inviting paths. "I don't think I want to subject these families to five or six kilometres of open-water paddling. There are plenty of interesting things to explore on this island alone."

Ronny was already packing his kayak. A frown flitted across his face, quickly replaced by his easy, gap-toothed grin. "Sure, but it would be fun. Even for us. You'll love it."

She wavered. The Georgian Getaway trip was planned for six days, which gave them plenty of time to play with. It might be worth it to know all the options. "Did you check the morning's forecast?"

Ronny didn't look up from his packing. "It's all good."

Barely half an hour later, their gear was fully packed, including their tents.

"Why so much gear?" she asked as she watched him stuff one last huge dry sack into his hatch.

"In case we have to stay over," he said nonchalantly. "Like I said, always be prepared."

As before, they packed their emergency gear close at hand. Kaylee had decided she didn't like the constraints of the cockpit and opted to lie on the front deck instead. She didn't like her life jacket either.

"That's not negotiable, princess," Amanda said as she strapped it on. In the early morning, the water was still peaceful. Only a slight breeze ruffled the surface, and far out over the Mink Islands a few fluffy clouds hung over the horizon. Kaylee was a strong swimmer, but if bad weather sprang up, five kilometres in rough water would be too much for any dog.

The crossing took a little over an hour, and soon they were cruising between slabs of pink and grey rock. Cottages peeked out between the pines on the larger islands as Ronny led them farther north, but the smaller islands were empty. He wove through the shoals with an expert hand, passing by several inviting rest spots that Amanda eyed longingly. Kaylee too was alert and poised to leap off the deck to explore. Only Amanda's firm warnings kept her in place.

Ronny finally guided his kayak ashore in a sheltered inlet of an island near the centre of the chain, large enough to have grasses, stubby trees, and a bulbous hill in the middle. The rock formations at the water's edge were fascinating. Multicoloured stripes of rock, polished smooth by the centuries, formed undulating patterns and swirled into circular holes. Wildflowers grew in the crevices.

They spread their towels on the flat granite shore. Kaylee found a stick to be tossed and leaped gleefully into the water again and again, her eyes shining, her tongue lolling, and her paws dancing with anticipation. The sun was hot, the rocks baking, and the water looked so inviting that Amanda peeled off her outer clothes, waded out onto a flat slab of rock, and plunged in, expecting silky bliss.

The cold froze her breath in her lungs. After a moment of gasping and flailing, she scrambled back onto shore.

Ronny was laughing. "Kinda takes your breath away, don't it? It's still early in the season. The Great Lakes take a while to warm up."

"No kidding!" Amanda sputtered, snatching up her towel. "Another reason not to risk a capsize in the middle of the lake."

As they unpacked their lunch, the breeze picked up, and more white fluffy clouds piled up in the west. Amanda frowned. "What's the weather forecast for the afternoon?"

Ronny shrugged. "I didn't check this morning, but yesterday it said clear. No small craft warnings."

She gaped. "You didn't check?"

"No worries. I been paddling these waters since I was two. The wind will be behind us going back."

"Still tricky, especially with Kaylee on the front. Do you think we should head back now?"

"We haven't had lunch yet, and there's a great hike I want to show you to the top of that hill. Awesome view." He pointed to the outcrop covered in spiky pines. The granite knob at the top was polished clean by glaciers and storms.

Amanda could see little danger in the playful clouds and teasing breeze, but she was no expert on Georgian Bay. Ronny had spent his youth out on these waters, and he was already opening a beer. He held another out for her and gave her his biggest gap-toothed grin.

"What's the worst? We wait till evening."

She thought of Chris, who should be touching down in Toronto at this very moment. But it would take him a few more hours to get to the campsite on Franklin Island. *Go with the flow, Doucette*, she told herself as she took the beer.

By the end of lunch, the playful breeze had become a strong wind, and waves were lunging at the rocks. Gulls wheeled in the azure sky overhead, eager for fish.

In the sheltered cove, the sun baked the granite shore. Ronny stripped off his shirt and stood in his ragged jeans, show-ing off his tanned, rippling chest. Tattoos of musical notes curled around his biceps and one of a stylized guitar peeked above his waistband. "Fantastic. I love the water when it gets sassy."

"But ..." Amanda began uneasily.

"It's nothing but convection winds. They always increase on a warm afternoon. We'll wait it out and paddle back at sunset." He stretched, catlike, and checked the time. "I'm going to take a short paddle over to another island. I promised I'd check out the winter damage on my buddy's cabin. Fifteen minutes tops. Just chill out here, and when I'm back, we'll take that hike."

The wind snatched at his words, and the sibilant roar of the waves blurred all sound, but a faint shriek drifted in on a gust of wind. Kaylee's ears pricked up as she stared out across the water. Another plaintive cry. Gulls? Amanda's gaze tracked Kaylee's, but she could see nothing but bobbing waves and flashes of white caps.

"Where are the binoculars?" she asked.

Ronny handed them over, and she trained them on the waves, twirling the focus and sweeping back and forth. Another cry, and in the water, a flash of red, riding on the crest of a wave before dropping back out of sight. She sucked in her breath as she waited for the next wave. Lifting it up.

The bow of a boat.

"There's someone out there!"

Ronny grabbed the binoculars. He took only a brief glance before he began to drag his kayak down to the water's edge.

"I'm coming too," Amanda said. "We don't know how many are in the boat, and my kayak is bigger."

Ronny frowned, as if sizing up whether she'd be more of a liability than a help, before nodding curtly. Together they clipped ropes and paddle floats to the kayaks, stuffed some emergency flares into their life jackets, and tied an outraged Kaylee to a tree. Within a minute both kayaks were on the water.

Ronny's kayak sliced expertly through the water, but Amanda fought the wind and waves with each stroke and bounced around like a cork. Ronny rapidly outpaced her as he barrelled out over the open water. Waves sloshed over Amanda's bow. Anger took hold. This little midafternoon breeze was not going to get the better of her! She braced and leaned and punched forward until her boat, sluggishly, reluctantly, began to obey.

They had lost sight of the red boat. Had she imagined it? Or had it sunk? Just as she began to doubt the sight of her own eyes, an orange, plastic bailing bucket bobbed by. Farther over, a coil of plastic rope. Ronny gave a shout and pointed to a yellow PFD floating in the water, aimless and abandoned.

Amanda began to fear the worst. She scanned the waves. Ronny was still powering ahead, and a few seconds later, his shout carried over the wind. "Over here!"

Amanda dug her paddle in. Ronny was bobbing on the waves, leaning over in his kayak to reach for a dark shape in the water.

"Raft me!" he shouted as she paddled alongside. "Come up beside me and lean across to stabilize both boats."

Amanda started to paddle around him.

"Not that side!" he shouted. "You'll crush her."

Belatedly, her water rescue lessons came back to her. She drew her boat alongside and leaned across both boats. Beyond Ronny's boat, she could make out the shape in the water. The woman lay on her back, motionless, dressed in black pants and yellow windbreaker. A PFD cushion was looped uselessly through one arm, and waves lapped over her face. Her long, dark hair spread around her, and her eyes were rolling back in her head.

Every second counted. Ten minutes ago, this woman had still been calling for help, but hypothermia and exhaustion were taking their toll. Ronny leaned far out of his kayak and slipped his paddle under to lift her head. Immediately, her eyes flew open and she began to flail. She clutched the paddle and began to pull toward Ronny's boat.

"You're all right!" he shouted. "Just relax! We're going to get you up onto one of the kayaks, but I need you to let go of the paddle."

She continued to clutch at the kayak, which rocked. Amanda leaned over farther, trying to keep them both stable.

"What's your name?" Ronny asked.

She merely shook her head. He asked her again. "Sophia," she stammered through blue lips. Amanda could see that her grip on the paddle was weakening. Ronny unclipped his extra life jacket and held it out.

"Sophia, let go of the paddle. Take this instead."

She took the life jacket, and he coaxed her through the motions of slipping it on. Then, exhausted, she stopped thrashing and lay limp.

"Amanda, do you think your cockpit is big enough to fit her in front of you?"

Amanda made a quick guess. The woman was petite, even smaller and more delicate than she was. "Absolutely. Just tell me what to do."

"Bring your kayak around to her other side, bow facing her. Then get your rope ready and make a big loop. We're going to get her up on your front deck first."

Amanda released his boat and fought the waves and the chop created by the rocking boats as she brought her own boat around.

Without her stabilizing grip, Ronny's kayak was pitching wildly and his face contorted with the effort of keeping it straight.

"Sophia, we're going to give you a rope, and you're going to roll over onto your stomach and pull yourself onto the deck of Amanda's kayak."

No response. "Sophia! Can you hear me?"

Her eyes fluttered open. She turned her face toward Amanda. "Sophia, take the rope! Loop it under your armpits."

Sophia let out a wail and lunged for Amanda's boat, which nearly capsized.

As Amanda fought to control her kayak, Ronny tried to talk the terrified woman down. "Sophia, listen to me. You'll be safe in the kayak, but you have to do exactly what I say. Loop the rope around you."

This time, perhaps because she was too exhausted to panic, Sophia took the rope. "Good. When I count to three, you're going to kick your feet and Amanda's going to pull. I'm going to lift."

"I'm — I'm cold!"

"I know you are, Sophia. But we're only a few minutes from shore. Let's get you on the kayak. Ready?" Her teeth chattered and her limbs shook, but she managed a nod. When he tried to lift her, however, she clutched him and nearly pulled him over. The kayaks rocked. Amanda saw anger flash across Ronny's face, but when he spoke, his voice was soothing. "Sophia, remember, just kick. We'll do the rest."

This time, they managed to hoist Sophia onto the front deck of Amanda's kayak, face down and hanging onto the deck ropes. The kayak's bow sank and the stern rose, catching the wind. Sophia shrieked, and it took all Amanda's strength to keep her kayak level.

"You're fine," she murmured. "This kayak is tough as nails."

Ronny grinned at her in thanks. "Now, Sophia, swivel around to face the other way until your feet are in the cockpit."

"The-the what?"

"The hole. Amanda will guide you and pull you in."

Bit by bit, Sophia slithered and pushed until she slipped into the hole and landed in Amanda's lap. Amanda ignored the searing pain that shot through her hips. She pulled the thermal blanket from behind her seat, draped it over the woman, and rubbed her back. She had stopped shivering, which was a bad sign. "Lean forward over the deck and lay your head down so I can paddle," she whispered.

Once they were all stable, Ronny looped his tow rope to Amanda's bow. "Good work, gang! Now to shore and a warm fire."

Amanda's boat lumbered and pitched as she tried to paddle over Sophia's head, but with the aid of the tow rope, they were soon on shore. Ronny sprinted up and laid a sleeping bag on the rock in the sun. Sophia stumbled as she clambered out of the boat and required Ronny's steadying hand to make it to the sleeping bag. As he bent over to check her pulse and temperature, his voice was soft and his touch tender.

"You're okay," he murmured. "This sun will warm you up big-time. We have some tea, but I don't think we need a fire."

"What happened?" Amanda asked as she poured tea from her thermos.

Sophia had still barely uttered a word. Now she clutched the sleeping bag below her chin and rocked back and forth. "The boat ... I hit a rock. Made a hole, lost the engine."

"Was there anyone else in the boat?" Ronny asked.

"No, no. No one."

"Where were you coming from?" Amanda asked.

She didn't answer. She had light-brown skin, long, thick hair that hung about her in sodden black ropes, and the broad, high cheekbones of Southeast Asia. Her accent was hard to place, but the slight lilt of Spanish suggested Filipino.

Amanda handed her the cup of tea, which she cradled in shaking hands. "Thank you," she whispered. She looked in dismay at the water all around. "How will I ...?"

Amanda was already rummaging for the VHF radio she'd seen in Ronny's daypack. "Ronny will radio the marine OPP and get a rescue boat out."

Her head jerked up and her eyes flew wide. "No!"

"The accident should be reported," Amanda said.

"No. I'm okay. It's too much trouble for police to come." When Amanda frowned in puzzlement, she put her hand on Ronny's arm and pasted a smile on her face. "Please. I don't want to be trouble. I can go back with you."

"No," Amanda said. "Ronny's kayak is too small, and I can't paddle five kilometres across open water with you and my dog in the cockpit."

Ronny had been strangely quiet, but now he squinted out over the water, which was still churning. "We can't go anywhere yet. It's too rough."

"I need to go! Someone is waiting."

Amanda quietly studied the woman. Something didn't add up. The woman had almost drowned, so perhaps her fear was understandable, but it was the mention of the police that had driven it over the top. Amanda had seen that kind of fear before, in places in the world where justice was arbitrary and where the authorities were not always your friend. Amanda had thought Sophia was from the Philippines, which had its share of police abuse, but there were other, more oppressive countries in Southeast Asia. Could her fear simply be a hold-over from her homeland?

She took out her cellphone. "Ronny, maybe your dad could come out in the boat and pick her up." She frowned at her phone. "No signal."

Ronny nodded to the hill. "You should be able to get one up there."

She held out her phone. "Why don't you call him?"

Ronny squirmed. "Maybe better if the request came from you. I'll stay with Sophia."

His discomfort seemed peculiar, but she had no time to waste on the subtleties of father-son relationships. Even if she reached George, it might be several hours before he could get out here. Amanda leashed Kaylee, and the two of them set off, picking their way through mossy bogs and stunted pines. *Just like a Tom Thomson painting*, she thought as she looked up at the jagged pines silhouetted against the puffy clouds. Kaylee led the way, nimble-footed and happy, her nose to the ground as if following some invisible scent.

Midway, Amanda paused to check her phone, which still showed no signal. Frowning, she scanned the horizon. *Our luck*, she thought. *There is cellphone coverage along most of this coast now, but there must be some hill between here and the tower.* Farther up the trail, the trees gave way to prickly juniper, moss, and lichen-covered rock that crunched underfoot. Amanda stood on the tallest rock. One bar. Not enough. She waved her phone with her outstretched arm, hoping to snatch a signal from the ether, before glancing at the phone in disgust. *We could be here until tomorrow*, she thought.

She made her way through a scrawny copse of trees to the lee side of the hill, already formulating alternate plans. If necessary, she would ask Ronny to double up with Sophia in her larger kayak while she took his. Kaylee would have to squeeze below deck.

As she swept aside the last pine branches and stepped into the clearing, Kaylee gave a short bark. Far below, in the open water between the island and the distant shore of Franklin Island, she spotted a splash of red.

"Hey!" she cried, rushing toward the drop.

A second shape came into view behind the first, this one yellow. "Hey!" she shouted. "Help!"

The two kayaks didn't turn. If anything, the lead kayak seemed to surge forward as if to escape. Paddles thrashed the water, and scraps of shouting could be heard over the gusts of wind. *What the hell?* Amanda thought. *Those look like ... our kayaks!*

"Goddamn!" Amanda yelled. "Ronny! Stop!"

The kayakers leaned into their strokes, powering away from the island. Furious, Amanda spun around and began to race across the hilltop. This made no sense. Maybe a crisis had occurred. Maybe he'd left a note or some clue as to his plans.

She and Kaylee slithered back down the hill as fast as they could, grabbing saplings and boughs to break their descent, and reached the beach within minutes. The two kayakers had long since disappeared beyond the neighbouring islands on their way to the open water.

Dumped on the shore where the two kayaks had been was some food and camping gear. Had Ronny emptied the kayaks to make them lighter for speed, or had he been trying to leave her some supplies? She pawed through the piles, but there was no note, no clues, no apologies or explanation of any kind.

What the *hell*! Why would he take off, unless Sophia was in distress and needed help immediately, in which case why not use his VHF radio to call for help?

That thought caused her to search once more through the gear. No radio, no flares, no compass, and no maps. Not even a mirror or shiny pot for signalling. Nothing but binoculars and a useless cellphone. She glanced around the deserted island. This was deliberate. Ronny had left the first aid kit to ensure she was safe but had removed every means by which she could summon help. That sneaky, manipulative bastard! Why?

She turned the puzzle over and over in her mind. When she'd first headed up the hill to get a cellphone signal, he'd been fully supportive of asking his father for help. Even in retrospect, she could see no deception in his manner. Yet something had happened shortly after she left. Something had changed his mind about the urgency of the situation or the need for secrecy. Otherwise why not wait for her to come back down and explain to her that he was going to take Sophia ashore and would send help for Amanda as soon as he got there? She might not have liked the idea — indeed would have argued for doubling up on one of the kayaks so all three could go back — but she would probably have agreed.

Instead, however, he had sneaked off and left her no means to call for help, thus making sure that he and Sophia got a good head start before anyone else got involved. Ronny was young and impulsive, maybe even overconfident, and she had a sense he could be a practical joker, but he was not reckless. He never forgot the dangers of the lake. He'd been eager to prove to his father that he could handle the trip. So what had happened to change his mind?

Sophia.

Sophia had begged them not to call the police. She had claimed she didn't want to be trouble, but she had seemed afraid. What could she possibly have told Ronny to convince him to leave? Amanda thought about the scraps of shouting she'd heard as they left the island. The splashing paddles. An argument? Had Ronny been trying to stop her?

Wind gusted across the open bay, whipping up whitecaps. Waves foamed over the rocks. Memories of her days lost in the Newfoundland wilderness crept in, of surf spewing high into the air and wind gusts spinning her little boat around like a toy top. Fear clogged her throat, fear of being helpless out on the water, but even worse, fear of being left alone. Just her and Kaylee perched on this tiny island in the vast, relentless water.

She hugged Kaylee as she beat back the racing panic. She was not helpless. She was not abandoned. She was only a few miles from civilization. She had supplies and shelter. Ronny might send help any minute. Chris might even track down where she was, but in the meantime, she had to prepare for a night on the island.

CHAPTER FOUR

Chris glanced at his cellphone one last time before pulling off the highway in Parry Sound. No texts. No response to the last four he had sent since arriving in Toronto three hours earlier. He stopped off at the crowded Tim Hortons for a much needed coffee and toasted BLT before continuing down toward the harbour. The Town of Parry Sound was nestled at the end of a long, deep inlet, its harbour protected from the open lake but big enough for large cruisers, yachts, floatplanes, and even a couple of cruise ships.

He parked his rental truck at the dock and unfolded his tall, lanky body from the driver's seat, stretching to ease the pain and stiffness in his back. The gesture reminded him of his father after a long day on the tractor, windblown and roasted by the prairie sun. He pushed the thought away with disbelief. He was thirty-five years old and ruggedly fit from hiking the mountains around Gros Morne National Park. Surely at the peak of his prime.

With longing, he eyed the floatplanes buzzing in and out. It was over a year since he'd flown, and although he'd considered renting one to speed up this trip, he knew the cost would be prohibitive. *There's a lot of money around here*, he thought as he watched the planes and cruisers come and go. Even in this sheltered harbour, the wind was strong, bobbing the yachts in the slips and clanging the rigging against their masts. Clouds were piling in from the west, threatening to turn the blue sky leaden.

Was a storm on the way?

Immediately to the right of the docks, the Ontario Provincial Police station sprawled along the water's edge. As he debated dropping in to check on possible weather alerts, two OPP officers burst out the door and hopped into a police Interceptor. Before he could approach, they had peeled out of the parking lot and headed up the road.

Although he knew he'd always be extended a brotherly welcome, he had no friends in the local OPP. He did, however, have a buddy in the Coast Guard whom he knew from Newfoundland. There were no guarantees he'd be on duty, but the Coast Guard was the more appropriate place to ask about weather warnings and general marine conditions.

Checking his GPS, he followed its route to the Coast Guard base up the street, amused to see a squat little red and white lighthouse guarding the front gate. He felt right at home. He parked on the street and walked through the open pedestrian gate unchallenged. As he was heading for the main building, he spotted a flurry of activity down by the dock, including an ambulance with its back doors open and a couple of paramedics loading gear into a sleek, steel Coast Guard boat. Parked next to the ambulance was the police Interceptor he'd seen leaving the OPP station earlier. The two officers were down on the dock conferring with a man Chris recognized as a Coast Guard captain from his uniform and insignia.

The three men and the paramedics loading up the boat moved with an intensity that gave Chris pause. Was this a routine assignment or was there some emergency? He was debating approaching them to offer assistance when one of the OPP officers noticed him.

"Can I help you?" he snapped as he approached. With one arm outstretched, he tried to herd Chris back toward the gate.

Chris identified himself, but the officer seemed unimpressed.

"Is there any way I can help?"

"Everything's under control, Corporal," the man said, still herding.

Recognizing the practiced cop stonewall, Chris abandoned the effort and made a show of turning to leave. Out of sight, he ducked inside the main Coast Guard building, startling the clerk seated behind a bank of computers. He identified himself again and gave his folksiest grin.

"It's beginning to blow out there," he said, "and I'm wondering if I should be going out in my kayak. What's the weather like out on the bay? Any alerts or warnings?"

The clerk nodded. "Small craft warning. Winds from the north, twenty gusting to thirty knots. You don't want to be out in a kayak."

"If it's anything like Newfoundland, you folks get lots of tourists and city folk who get themselves in trouble out on the water."

"Oh yeah."

"Is that what all that activity is about down at the dock? A distress call?"

The clerk's eyes flicked to her screen, and she frowned.

Chris tried again. "Sorry, I know you're busy. I'm worried about my companion, who is already out on the water. Have there been any distress calls?"

The woman shook her head. "No, it's not that. I hope your friend has the sense to wait it out on land."

"Is it going to get worse?"

The clerk adjusted some controls and spoke into her microphone to confirm some order. As an afterthought, she glanced at Chris. "Excuse me, sir, but you shouldn't really —"

"But my friend—"

"Check the marine forecast," she said impatiently. "We've got a couple of rough weather days ahead. Not a time for a paddling holiday."

Chris thanked her and went back outside. Clouds roiled angrily across the sky. The clerk was right; it was not a time to be out in a kayak. But where the hell was Amanda? Why had she not answered her texts or phone?

He loved her independence of spirit, but sometimes it drove him crazy. He'd grown up in a large, boisterously close-knit Ukrainian family who never let a phone call or email go unanswered. But he knew Amanda sometimes went weeks, even months without talking to her parents and saw her brother only once or twice a year at obligatory family holidays. She had dozens of friends cultivated in her years overseas, but except for Matthew Goderich, there was no one she could call on in a crisis and no one she felt an obligation to. Until Chris came along.

She was probably fine and having too much fun to give him a second thought.

He climbed back into his truck and drummed his fingers on the steering wheel, tamping down his frustration. Damn it, he couldn't simply wait for word. At the very least he could go to Snug Harbour where he was to pick up his kayak and see whether the marina there had any news.

The trip took him half an hour, even navigating the narrow, twisting road down to the harbour at near-reckless speed. He was surprised to discover both launching areas bustling with activity as boaters came in off the lake in anticipation of the storm. Pickup trucks and boat trailers jockeyed for position at the shore. He caught sight of an OPP SUV drawn up at the marina boat ramp, backing its boat trailer and Zodiac into the water. Another pickup truck with a kayak on top was parked on the grass, the name

"Gifford Outfitters" displayed in modest blue letters on its door. A grizzled middle-aged civilian was down at the water's edge helping the two OPP officers guide their Zodiac into the water.

Chris parked his truck beside Gifford's and strolled down to lend them a hand. "George Gifford?" he asked the civilian, whose skin was like leather burnished from years of wind and sun. When George nodded, he extended his hand. "Chris Tymko. I believe you're waiting for me?"

"Yeah, I'll get you your gear in a minute, soon as I finish here," said George in a voice as weathered as his skin. Only his deep azure eyes looked youthful.

"Any word on the party?" Chris asked. "Amanda Doucette isn't responding to my texts."

"I haven't heard from my son since yesterday," George grumbled as he signalled to the OPP officer to back up farther. "Silly boy wanted to do this trip, insisted he could handle it. I hope he's not trying to be a cowboy."

"Is that usual? I mean, for him not to be in touch?"

"He's a capable kid, I'm not saying he's not. But it's part of our protocol. You check in every day. And he knows how special this trip is. I wanted to give him the chance, but sometimes ..." He shrugged. "You know kids."

Chris studied the sky uneasily. The water glistened coal-black, and even in the sheltered marina, the wind was rocking the boats against the docks. "The weather doesn't look good."

"Yeah. He should have contacted me to tell me if they were heading in or waiting it out on shore somewhere."

Chris gestured to the OPP Zodiac. The officers were at the back of the trailer, unhooking the cables. "But this ... it has nothing to do with them?"

"Oh, no, no. This is a call from one of the island cottages. Some kind of medical emergency."

The Zodiac floated free of the trailer, and Chris and George leaned in to hold on to it while the officers parked the cruiser. They came down to the water's edge with armloads of emergency gear, including cameras and crime scene bins. Chris's curiosity spiked, but George fell silent the moment they approached. Within minutes the Zodiac was clear of the docks and accelerating out toward the open water. Chris turned back to George as they walked back up the boat ramp.

"Crime scene?"

George shrugged. "I don't know. I just know the OPP is throwing everything they have at it. Rich Toronto family, probably they're afraid of a bunch of pushy city lawyers." He waved a dismissive hand. "The gossip chain will be buzzing with it soon enough, but for now, let's have a look at your gear. Although if you'll take my advice, you'll stay right here, grab a room at the resort next door, and wait for the weather to lift."

"When is that? The Coast Guard said it could be days."

"Could be. But bay weather can turn on a dime."

Chris squinted out toward the open water to the west. The surface of the harbour was choppy but not impossible. He knew the passage to Franklin Island was partly sheltered, but there was a stretch across the open channel to the island. He was used to sea kayaking in the rugged North Atlantic, and he doubted this inland lake could put up a similar fight.

"Do I have a couple of hours before it gets really bad?"

George shrugged. "Depends on your definition of bad."

"Newfoundland-coast bad."

George laughed. "Yeah, you got a couple of hours. But take the inside channel and hug the shore where you can. The minute the waves get too much for the kayak, get the hell to the nearest shore."

———

The wind hit him the minute he rounded the end of Snug Island and entered the open strait. Up ahead lay the sprawling expanse of Franklin Island. He knew it wasn't far, but as the wind fought his every stroke, the island seemed to shimmer farther out of reach. Waves slapped over his bow, threatening to swamp him. The lake kayak bounced around like a toy. He was used to an ocean kayak, which was longer and heavier, with a high bow designed to slice through waves.

He bent his head, leaned into the wind, and powered forward. He had to keep paddling, because every minute he stopped to take stock or catch his breath, the wind blew him back over the hard-fought metres he had gained.

The opposite shore inched closer, and eventually the wind and waves eased up as he entered the lee of the island. He drew up to shore and wiped off his map, grateful for its plastic sheath. Amanda had said they were planning to camp on the western side, which meant they'd be open to the elements. Would they have changed their mind and sought better shelter inland?

He scanned up and down the shore with his binoculars. No pair of brightly coloured kayaks. He ate a quick snack and shoved off again, hugging the shoreline as he worked his way south. The wind tore at the pine trees and churned the water, masking all other sound, but nonetheless he shouted Amanda's name at regular intervals along the way. Only one boat roared by in the main channel, and there were no birds or animals foraging for food in the sheltered inlets. *Wise creatures*, he thought.

He worked his way south and was just paddling around a flat, scoured shelf of granite at the island's tip when the wind hit. It had gathered strength over five kilometres of open water, and now its full force blew him onto the rocks. His kayak rose on a swell and slammed on the bottom with a loud crunch. *Fuck!* Chris poled with his paddle to push himself farther out. In that moment he glimpsed a flash of yellow moving in the shallows of a narrow crevice. Each wave tossed it back and forth. He approached cautiously, bracing his paddle on the rocks ahead to prevent a collision.

As he drew closer, he could make out its square shape. He released his spray skirt, clambered out of the kayak onto the slippery, algae-covered rock, and leaned in for a closer look.

It was a waterproof foam paddle float. How long had it been there, and where had it floated from? The strong winds regularly blew bits of rope, water bottles, fishing tackle, and other detritus across the open lake until they landed up against the shores, but this float had no visible damage from the sun or water.

George had lashed Chris's paddle float to the back deck of his kayak, and although a powerful wave could knock it free, it was unlikely. Chris felt his first prickle of alarm. Had there been a capsize? Had someone lost their paddle float in a failed rescue attempt? With his binoculars he scanned the open water to the west. Nothing but whitecaps. The shoreline up ahead wove in and out in points and inlets, but he could see no traces of human activity.

He secured the paddle float to his kayak and set off again up the coast, keeping a sharp eye out. Even if the group had camped inland to avoid the wind, they would have left their kayaks pulled up on the shore.

He had travelled about fifteen minutes up the shore when he came upon a large, well-maintained campsite. He had passed a few smaller ones along the way, all of them deserted. If Amanda and Ronny had gone ashore to wait out the storm, this looked like the most likely spot. He threaded his kayak into a narrow opening and ran it up onto the soft sand.

After he'd climbed out and carried it up out of harm's way, he scanned the area. To his disappointment, it looked empty, but perhaps they had gone farther inland for added protection against the elements. He called out. Nothing. Checked his phone. Still nothing. Stretching his cramped muscles and rubbing his back, he began to scout the area. A clear path led from the rocks back into the shelter of the trees, and as he followed it, he caught sight of flashes of colour ahead. He began to jog, and soon the colours took shape.

Two kayaks lay overturned and stacked against each other under the camouflage of the trees. Stencilled on the hulls were the words "Gifford Outfitters." He glanced around, but there was no sign of tents or settlement, although the soft pine needle floor would have been ideal.

He rolled the top kayak over and checked the hatches. The water pump and bailer were both clipped on, but the hatches were empty. However, in the second kayak he pulled a dry sack out of the rear hatch and emptied it onto the ground. Clothing and personal gear tumbled out — toiletries, quick dry shorts and shirts, rain suit, and rain boots. He held them up. Far too big to be Amanda's. The tour guide's? Why had he left his gear in the kayak while Amanda had not? And where were the tents and emergency gear?

He rummaged through the pockets of the clothing, finding nothing but two crumpled receipts, one for gas in Parry Sound and the other for a large Tim Hortons coffee and doughnut.

"Hello!" he shouted. "Amanda?"

Nothing came back to him but the distant hiss of surf rushing up the granite shore. He checked his cellphone, which had a weak but adequate signal. Still no response to his texts! He dialled Amanda's number, but it went straight to voicemail. Turned off or out of range? What was the woman doing?

"Amanda!" he snapped into the phone, trying to keep the frustration out of his voice. "I'm on Franklin Island, and I think I found your kayaks. Where are you?"

As he spoke, he began to explore farther inland. The grass was flattened along a narrow path leading into the woods. Perhaps an animal trail or one of the many routes to the interior campsites and lakes on the island. Had they gone farther inland to seek better shelter?

Buoyed by that hope, he began to trot up the path, scanning the woods on either side for tents or camping gear. The path led through copses of trees, marshy grasslands, crusty rocks and ponds, and back into more trees. Along the way, he spotted several flat, sheltered spots to pitch a tent. Why would they have ignored those? Where were they going, if indeed they had taken the path at all?

As the wind lashed the first splatters of rain against his face, he cursed his own stupidity. He'd left his rain gear in his kayak. At the same time the path petered out on an expanse of rock and tufted grass. He cast around in a wide circle, trying to pick up the trail on the other side, but to no avail. He shouted. Phoned Amanda again. This time he let loose his frustration and alarm.

"Please call me! I need to know you are safe from the storm!"

He retraced his steps to the beach, harbouring the faint hope that he'd missed them and they were back at their kayaks. But the two boats lay as he'd left them. By now, bruised clouds smothered the sky and waves battered the shore in an angry black chop. Huge raindrops splattered the rocks and stung his cheeks. He dragged his dry sacks up under the meagre shelter of the pines and fished out his rain gear. He had hoped to share Amanda's tent but as a precaution had brought his own small tent just in case things didn't progress as he hoped. The baby pup tent would be dubious protection against a powerful storm, but at least it was easy to put up.

Within minutes he was huddled inside, coaxing a flame from his tiny butane burner so he could make some hot tea.

The temperature had dropped at least five degrees. Once the tea spread its warmth through his core, he began to consider his next move. The storm had come earlier than predicted and was gathering power. The sky was almost as dark as twilight, and although his watch displayed only 7:00 p.m., darkness would be upon him soon enough. There was no time to waste. From his own police experience in Newfoundland, he knew it was better to incur the anger of the local police than to leave it too late.

He phoned the OPP in Parry Sound. The officer on the desk sounded harried. When Chris explained his location and his predicament, she fired off a few routine questions. "Are you in a safe situation? Do you have shelter, water, and food?"

"I'm not worried about me," he said. "I'm an RCMP officer myself, and I don't like what I see. I can't reach my friend. I've found her and her companion's kayaks, but there's no sign of them."

"Have you searched farther inland?"

"Of course I have," he snapped before drawing a deep breath. "They are very overdue for a rendezvous and not responding to my calls."

"The signal can be unpredictable there in a storm," she said. "Are they experienced in the wilderness?"

"Yes. One of them is a local outfitter."

"Who?"

"Ron Gifford."

"Oh." There was a pause. "And he's with your girlfriend?"

Chris bristled at her sceptical tone. "Yes."

"Well, maybe ..."

"What?"

The woman giggled. A most unprofessional giggle. "You're right, Ronny knows his way around these parts. I'm sure they're just waiting out the storm."

"But —"

"If they haven't turned up by morning, call again."

"Will you at least take my name? And notify me if you hear anything?"

"We're pretty busy here...."

"Just take my number, will you? Call it cop instinct, but I don't like what I see here."

There was a long pause. He could hear paper rustling and radio chatter in the background. Finally, she came back on. "Very well."

CHAPTER FIVE

Amanda's anger came in waves as the afternoon wore on. She walked every inch of the little island, looking for the clearest views across the channel in the hope of spotting Ronny. Surely he would come back for her once he'd delivered Sophia to safety. Or he'd send a rescue boat. The *bastard*! He could have left her a note or waited until she'd come back down the hill. At the very least, he could have left her some flares. The fact that he'd wilfully jeopardized her safety was the most infuriating thing of all.

As the clouds massed overhead and the wind whipped the open water to a frenzy, alarm began to take over. The water was now too rough and the wind too strong for even the most skilled kayaker. He couldn't come back, and she was left to weather the storm on this tiny, exposed island. Far out in the open water to the west, she could see ships steaming north and planes droning overhead, but none came close enough for her to signal.

When the rain began to lash the island, even the boat and plane traffic was no longer visible, and she realized no one was going to come before tomorrow. A grim determination took hold. She turned off her cellphone to preserve its battery and found a small patch of flat land tucked under the pines on which to pitch her tent, making sure to tie it firmly to the surrounding trees. Even so, it trembled in the wind and rain.

She dragged all her gear inside, pulled on her rain suit, and set off to devise some SOS signals. Perhaps Kaylee sensed her anxiety, or simply the dangers of the storm, for she clung to her side, tail between her legs.

Although a fire on the open shore was the most obvious way to signal for help, the flames would not last five minutes in the rain. Brightly coloured fabrics would have to do. She lugged her yellow towrope up the hill and tied it between trees in a large "H" on the flat, barren top. Not great, but perhaps a plane would spot it.

Back down on the shore, she hung her red-and-orange dry sacks on the trees and arranged rocks in the shape of an SOS on the open slab of granite. As a final effort, she hung her white camp sheet from the tip of a scrawny pine. By now, darkness was gathering and both she and Kaylee were chilled and starving. She herded them both into the tent. In the morning, if help had not come, she would light a fire on the shore. Hopefully, by then Chris, or at least that little prick Ronny, would have reported her missing, and the search-and-rescue crews would be out looking.

After drying off and feeding Kaylee her kibble, she inspected the food supplies Ronny had left her. The cold can of beans was unappetizing, but at least it appeased her hunger. Afterward, she curled up with the dog in her sleeping bag and lay listening to the roar of the wind and the lashing of the rain. The little tent shook and flapped, but it held. She willed herself to sleep.

The nights always haunted her the most. Images leaped up, of screams and flames and stench. Of guns spurting, machetes flashing ... of hiding in dusty ditches and in broken, abandoned towns. And for a year after the terror, of huddling behind the bed in her Quebec cottage, unable to separate then from now.

Turning on her flashlight, she pulled her notebook out of her pile of clothes. She had brought it to make notes of potential destinations and adventures, needed gear, and points of caution. In the past, on the recommendation of her therapist, it had also served as a sounding board for her personal fears and doubts. Her journey toward recovery had been recorded there, vivid and raw in the staccato language of her thoughts.

I expect to be rescued tomorrow, she wrote after the date, *but if the storm is really bad, it may be a few days. I am safe, I am dry, and Kaylee keeps me warm. We have plenty of water and food for at least three more days. But if something goes wrong and no one finds me, this is a record of what happened.*

She hesitated, her pen tracing doodles on the page as she pondered how to frame her experience. *Yesterday we picked up a woman who had sunk her boat. She said her name was Sophia but gave no further explanation. She seemed afraid. Ronny Gifford deserted me in order to take her to the mainland, an extremely unprofessional thing to do, and if he does not send someone back to rescue me, he should be charged.*

Her anger welled up again, but with it an eerie calm. She was not fleeing for her life across hostile terrain; she had been abandoned by an inconsiderate prick who had no business being a guide. No matter what else, she'd see him pay for that.

But the more she replayed the scenario over in her mind, the more she thought perhaps Ronny had been trying to stop Sophia, and having failed in that effort because he had the heavier, more cumbersome kayak, he had opted to go with her to shore. But if that were the case, why had he not sent someone back to rescue Amanda, and why had he taken away all her means of signalling for help?

The little pup tent swayed and shuddered in the wind, and rain hammered against the flimsy nylon shell. As darkness descended,

Chris ate the remains of his trail mix and scurried down to the water's edge to filter more drinking water. He had come prepared to meet up with Amanda, not to spend a night on his own. He had a flashlight but was reluctant to squander battery power, so he huddled in his sleeping bag and tried to sleep. Visions of Amanda, lost, wet, and scared as she'd been in Newfoundland drifted through his head. Questions crowded in. Why had she not contacted him? And why had they left no message with their kayaks?

His watch read 6:00 a.m. when he awoke, stiff and sore. *Who do they design these things for anyway?* he thought as he jackknifed his tall frame out of the tent and scanned his surroundings. The wind had abated but a cold, steady rain slanted down, blending sky with lake in a grey wall. The granite rocks were slick, and water dripped from the pine branches and soaked the forest floor. He squelched down to the water's edge and peered up and down the shore. Nothing. The chop was still strong but probably manageable with a decent powerboat.

Back inside his tent with fresh tea brewing, he phoned George Gifford. Judging by the sound of his voice, gravel raking across steel, he suspected he'd woken the man up. But George was clearly used to the unexpected and to the prospect of trouble, for he snapped to attention with a gruff, "Yeah, Gifford here!"

Chris identified himself. "Has your son shown up?"

"Not that I know. Where are you?"

Chris explained about the campsite and the abandoned kayaks. "But there's no sign of them, and Amanda is still not responding to her cell."

"Yeah, well, in this weather ..."

"I know all about weather, George. And crappy cell coverage. But I've just spent a miserable night freezing in a tent and starving, so I'm running out of patience."

George grunted. "These kayaks, any ID in them?"

"Your name, one red, one yellow."

"That's them."

"I called the cops last night, but they were pretty dismissive. Maybe I should call again."

There was a pause. "They pretty much got their hands full with a death up on one of the islands. Let me give Ronny a call and get back to you."

Barely two minutes later, George called back. "Still no answer. They could be out of range. Where are you? I'll come out and pick you up. Give me time to pack up some supplies."

Chris read off his GPS coordinates, grateful that someone was finally taking him seriously. The OPP had not phoned him back, and he debated bugging them again, but decided to wait until George arrived. The man had not sounded alarmed, but his quick assessment of potential danger was reassuring.

It was past seven thirty when the faint drone of an engine penetrated the steady drum of the rain and waves. As it grew louder, Chris emerged from his tent and waded into the water to guide George's battered aluminum boat to a safe landing. George tilted the motor and poled the boat in with an oar. As it ground ashore, he leaped from the bow with an agility that belied his weather-beaten age. The hand that gripped Chris's was gnarled and rough, but strong.

"Any word?" he said as he headed up the shore to inspect the kayaks. "Yep, these are the ones. Ronny's gear too. Why the hell wouldn't he take his gear? She took hers."

He raised his head and pushed his rain hood back to search the woods. "Tents are gone. They must have gone inland, left their kayaks properly protected, so they weren't in a rush. Maybe just taking a hike to explore the island."

Chris felt a chill. "Could they have been injured on the hike? Fallen off a cliff?"

"You can always slip and fall, but two of them? No, I think they're just camping out of range. Did they know what time you were coming?"

"I don't know. It depends whether Amanda got my texts."

"Well, then they'll probably come back to the shore when they wake up this morning. That's Ronny for you. Not one to worry."

"But Amanda wouldn't leave me hanging."

George cast him an appraising glance, but whatever his thoughts on relationships — or women — he kept them to himself. "Lots of inland campsites. I brought coffee and breakfast, and if they haven't shown up by the time we're done eating, we'll check out the campsites."

As soon as the strong, smoky coffee coursed through him, Chris's spirits revived. George was right; Amanda hadn't known his arrival time, and if they were out of range, she might not have received his follow-up texts either.

The rain continued, reduced now to a fine mist that soaked the landscape. After pouring fresh coffee into two thermoses and storing all their gear under tarps, they set off. George had a detailed map of the island, which showed all the hiking trails and inland campsites, but he did not appear to need it as he strode up the trail.

Chris left a clear message for Amanda tucked in the shelter of his kayak, asking her to sit tight until their return. It was eight thirty. Surely she and Ronny would come walking back any minute.

It had been a long night. Each gust of wind jolted her awake, and by morning Amanda could feel every twig and rock beneath her. Daybreak did not bring new hope but instead a drenching wall of mist that blocked all view of the lake. She ducked out of the tent and went to scan the open water. Her heart sank. Not a peek of sun or blue sky. Another day marooned. Another day of damp and cold and fear.

Just as she was making her way back to the shelter of her tent, she heard the drone of an engine. She rushed to the water's edge and peered through the mist. Sound was deceptive, but it appeared to be coming from the open lake to the west. Slowly a white shape materialized, blurry at first but taking the form of a large cruiser as it drew closer. It was barrelling northward so fast that Amanda knew she had only moments to catch its attention.

She snatched a yellow tarp and raced up and down the shore, screaming and jumping. Within seconds Kaylee joined in the chaos with excited barking.

The boat continued north. Drawing opposite, it was close enough that she could make out the railing around the prow and the sleek white cabin on top. Amanda grabbed her life jacket and hurled it high into the air, again and again.

The boat slowed, turned its nose toward her, and seemed to hover uncertainly. Amanda renewed her frantic waving until mercifully the boat headed for shore. It approached cautiously, pitching and tossing in the waves, until finally the engine stopped altogether. A small figure in a fuchsia raincoat with large white polka dots emerged from the cabin and went to the rear to lower the anchor. Amanda's relief was short-lived, for there was still at least seventy feet of roiling water between the boat and the shore. What did the skipper think she was going to do? Swim?

The figure stood on the front deck shouting at her. Although Amanda could only hear snatches of sound, she could tell the skipper was a woman. "I'm stranded!" she shouted back.

After several moments of futile shouting back and forth, the woman unhooked a back hatch and hauled out a large yellow object, which she quickly unfolded into a self-inflating dinghy. The little yellow boat looked impossibly fragile as it bounced around in the waves. Wielding tiny oars, the woman climbed into the boat and began to row. Amanda smiled with relief as she waded into the frigid water to greet her. She could see a scowling face peeking out from the oversized rain hood and recognized the cherry lips and sodden platinum hair.

"Hello!" she exclaimed as she helped to guide the dinghy onto the beach. "Thank you so much! I've been waiting since yesterday —"

"I don't have much time!" the woman snapped. "Get in."

Amanda turned towards her tent. "I'll just grab —"

"Get in!"

"Okay." Amanda called Kaylee and snapped her leash on.

"Not the dog! I won't take the dog on my boat."

Amanda stared at the woman in dismay. She wore the same impatient, harried look she'd had the first time Amanda had seen her in the parking lot at Pointe au Baril. "I'm sorry, I can't leave my dog. She's seen me through thick and thin, she's more a guardian angel than a dog."

"Oh, for fuck's sake."

"I'll keep her glued to my side. She'll be no trouble."

"I have white leather seats."

"I won't let her on them."

The woman shook her head and glared out into the storm. "This isn't even my boat; it's my friend's. If she scratches anything, you're paying."

Gratefully Amanda grabbed her backpack, held the leash tightly, and scrambled aboard the wobbly dinghy. The woman looked more at home in the gardens of Rosedale, but to her credit, she knew how to handle a boat. She guided it easily through the chop and within minutes had them all aboard and the cruiser fired up again. She wasted no time on small talk as she gunned the motor north.

The grim set of her mouth suggested she had things on her mind, so Amanda wisely kept her own small talk to a minimum. She perched on the edge of the immaculate white leather bench and kept Kaylee pinned at her feet. Beneath her, the powerful boat throbbed.

"You can just drop me off at the nearest cottage or store that has a cellphone signal," she said.

"Not much open this time of year."

"There's a signal on Franklin Island."

"I'm not headed that way."

"Okay, any place along the way would be fine. I really appreciate this. I didn't relish being stuck for days. That island was getting awfully small."

The woman cast her a sidelong glance. "You forget to tie your boat up?"

How to explain? She remembered Sophia's fear the day before. Who knew what her story was, but it was not Amanda's to tell. "Long story. Something like that."

Now that the boat was slicing full throttle through the open water, the woman dropped into her seat and rested her head on the wheel.

"Can I get you anything from the galley?" Amanda asked. "You look done in."

The woman raised her head. To Amanda's surprise, there were tears in her eyes. "You look familiar," she said.

"I'm Amanda. We met ... well, not exactly met, but our paths crossed at Pointe au Baril, when you were meeting your —" She paused, unsure of the relationship. "Benson."

The tears spilled over. She dashed them away. "He's dead. That's where I'm going. My sister called me in a panic."

Amanda felt a stab of loss. She remembered the hand-some man striding up the dock to greet her, tossing the ball for Kaylee, and laughing aloud at the dog's response. So vibrant and full of joy.

So young.

"I'm sorry," she exclaimed. "He didn't look sick."

Candace whipped her head back and forth. In the shelter of the cabin she had pushed back her hood and now her unkempt, wet hair flew in all directions. "No, he wasn't sick. My sister says … they don't know how he died. The cops were called."

Amanda sucked in her breath. "What happened?"

"I don't know, I don't know! All I know is she called and said they found him yesterday morning, dead in the library. I —" She faltered. "I didn't check my messages until this morning. My sister is in a state."

"But it could have been a heart attack or something."

"The place is crawling with police, and they won't tell her anything." Candace shook her head. Shadowy islands loomed ahead in the mist, cluttered with cottages and docks. She slowed the boat to navigate between them.

"I'm sorry I've put you to this trouble," Amanda said. "There are houses along the way here where you can let me off."

Candace was on her feet, steering ahead with a stony gaze. The tears had dried on her cheeks. "And give these bitches some-thing more to gossip about? We're almost at Janine's place. You can call from there."

A large island loomed ahead. Amanda recognized it from the boat trip with Ronny. Had that only been two days ago? At the time, only a yacht and some power boats were tied to the docks, and a few canoes and kayaks were stacked on a rack, but now the entire shoreline was bristling with official-looking boats. Police in uniforms and white coveralls could be seen through the trees. Candace forged ahead at full throttle, aiming for one of the larger docks, and only cut the engine back at the last minute. A barrel-chested officer in an OPP uniform hurried down the dock and tried to wave her off, but she ignored him.

"Excuse me, ma'am, this is a restricted —"

"Oh, fuck off, Neville!" she snapped as she grabbed the bowline and tossed it to him.

"Sorry, Candy," he said, meekly tying off the boat. "I didn't recognize you. It's been a while."

"Yeah, well, it's Janine's place now, isn't it? Where is she?"

"I'll take you to her." The OPP officer tried to take Candace's elbow, but she shook him off. As an afterthought, she flicked her hand in Amanda's direction. "This is Amanda. She'll be going soon, she just has to call for a ride." With that, she headed up the stone stairway toward the mansion perched on the hill.

As the OPP officer turned to follow her, he glanced at Amanda, and his scowl returned. "Don't touch anything, don't get in our way!"

Amanda stood on the dock, keeping a tight hold on Kaylee. Thus dismissed, she took in her surroundings. The grand old house commanded a stunning view of the lake from its perch on the hill. Built of stone, with massive square timber beams darkened by age to a rich mahogany, it seemed to command views from every room, as well as from decks and stone patios staggered at intervals down the slope. Two equally luxurious guest houses were visible through the trees.

There's real old money here, she thought as she switched her phone back on. Money, death, plus a hint of sibling jealousy. And a frightened stranger fleeing southward in a dilapidated old boat.

She glanced at her screen and saw a dozen missed messages from poor Chris.

CHAPTER SIX

Amanda walked over the flat granite rocks along the shore until she was out of sight and hearing of the police and other officials. Tucked in behind an overhanging spruce at the water's edge, she dialled Chris. He picked up before the second ring.

"Amanda!" he shouted, and the unbridled joy in his voice sent a thrill through her body. "Jesus! Where are you? We've been looking everywhere!"

"I'm fine." She lowered her voice. "Who's we?"

"George Gifford and I. We found your kayaks but —"

"Where?"

"On Franklin Island. We figured you must have gone inland to escape the storm."

She heard muffled voices as Chris spoke to someone else in the background. "Two kayaks?" she asked.

There was a pause. Doubt in his voice. "Yeah. Why?"

"That's not me, Chris. That's Ronny Gifford and someone else. Ronny left me and Kaylee stranded on an outer island while he took some woman to the mainland."

"What the hell? Who?"

"I don't know. Sophia Somebody. She cracked up her boat off the island where we were exploring."

More muffled voices. "Where's the island? We'll come get you."

"No, I got a lift to an island cottage up near Pointe au Baril." Amanda heard voices nearby and glanced past the tree to see two officers poking along the shore with long poles. Gripping Kaylee's leash, she moved farther away.

"Are you okay?"

"Yes, I'm fine," she whispered, "but Chris, something is going on. The owner of this cottage was found dead here yesterday. There are cops everywhere."

"Yes, we saw them."

"I think he may have been murdered. The woman we found yesterday seemed in a desperate hurry to get away. I think that's why Ronny took her to the mainland. I don't know the connection — she seemed foreign — but I do think there is one."

"You should tell the cops."

"I will, but ..." Amanda tried to sort through her feelings. "She seemed really scared. Panicked, in fact. I don't know if she witnessed something or was just afraid she'd be under suspicion. She didn't seem dangerous."

"And you know that means nothing." He paused, and she heard him talking to another man, presumably George. "They must still be on the island here. The water is too rough for kayaking. If you like I'll call it in, since this is where they are. So the cops can at least get the search started."

She felt her tension ease. Having a cop around came in handy. "Thanks."

"George and I will come pick you up as soon as we can get there."

"How long?"

"I don't know. George knows the property where you are, but we have to walk back to our boat. Hang tight."

Her heart was buoyant as she hung up and gathered Kaylee's leash. Chris was on his way! "Come on, princess, let's go exploring."

She was just climbing up the bank under cover of thick shrubbery when she heard nearby voices again. The two officers were still examining the shoreline.

"This is impossible," one said. "The rain washed everything away."

"But she must have dragged the boat over here somewhere. She had to sneak away without being seen."

"It's pretty dark out here at night."

"But there are motion-sensor lights on the dock. Set those off and someone would see."

Amanda peered through the elderberry. The two officers were staring back at the dock. "We don't know when she left. Could have been in the morning."

"The dog was barking in the middle of the night. About four a.m., according to the wife."

"Hardly reliable. Judging by the booze bottles all around, most of the household was down for the count."

The first officer grunted. "Well, we'll keep going, but I think she's long gone. They'll be lucky if they catch her before she hops on a plane out of the country."

"That cook knows something. Shifty eyes. And they stick together, don't they?"

"Oh come on, she's probably just scared. They're all scared."

Amanda ducked low as they trudged by below her, wielding their poles to search the reeds and shrubs along the way. There was obviously a manhunt on for Sophia. Chris had said he would call in the report, but maybe she should track down that scowling cop after all.

As she clambered up the slope toward the main house in search of him, she heard a baby wailing and a dog barking inside. Several voices were raised in shrill frustration.

The French doors flew abruptly open, and a woman burst

out. She was dressed in a pink nightgown that plunged low over her breasts and barely covered her crotch, but she was wrapping a man's yellow raincoat around her body. Her face was blotchy and wet. Tears or rain?

Her only make-up was yesterday's smudged mascara, and the long hair tumbling in disarray down her back was copper instead of blond, but the resemblance to Candace was unmistakeable. The grieving widow.

"Candy!" the woman shrieked. "Where the fuck are you?"

Candace materialized in the doorway behind her, holding two cups of coffee. "Janine, come inside. It's disgusting out."

Janine ignored her. "You have to get rid of that puppy. I can't stand it. It was his dog, anyway, and he promised I'd never have to lift a finger. Well …!"

"Jesus, Janine. The puppy is the least of our problems. We've got four kids to take care of, cops roping off half the house, fingerprint powder everywhere, a cook who won't come out of her room, and a goddamn nanny who's disappeared!"

"Not to mention my husband, who's fucking dead!" Janine shot back. Through the open doorway, Amanda heard the renewed screaming of small, cranky children. Since it looked as if neither of the sisters was equipped to address the chaos, Amanda stepped up onto the patio. "I'm sorry to interrupt, but maybe I can help."

Janine blinked. Her eyes narrowed. In the harsh daylight, Amanda could see the beginnings of crow's feet around her eyes. Older than she'd like to be, Amanda observed randomly. "Who are you? The girl from the village?" Janine's eyes fell on Kaylee, and her voice rose a few decibels. "With another goddamn dog?"

"No, I'm Amanda. I'm —"

"A friend," Candace said hastily. "I picked her up on the Mink Islands. She's waiting for a lift out."

"And you brought her here? Now? With a dog?"

"I will tie the dog up out here," Amanda said. "And I can help. Get the children some breakfast, for example."

Janine shook her head weakly. Her anger, so quickly roused, died just as fast. "Whatever," she muttered, turning back toward the door, "I can't face this. I can't even ..." She stumbled as she groped her way back inside. "Please handle this, Candy."

Amanda looped Kaylee's leash through the railing on the patio. "Point me to the kitchen," she said. "My ride will be along soon, but meanwhile I can take this off your hands."

Candace vacillated in the doorway. Her eyes searched Amanda's, perhaps seeing some reassurance in their depths, for her bleak expression softened. "Thank you. We're ... well ..." She lifted her shoulders in a helpless shrug.

"I know."

She found three of the four children in the main room, a spectacular showcase with intricate mahogany wainscoting, a floor-to-ceiling stone fireplace, polished oak floors, and a wall of windows overlooking the channel. But in sharp contrast to the majestic setting, chaos reigned. Two curly-haired blond girls, whom Amanda judged to be twins about four years old, were tumbling on the floor, screaming and clawing each other, while a large black puppy bounced around in circles, barking like a demented wrestling fan. A chubby boy of about two was crying in a playpen, both fists crammed into his mouth.

Amanda swooped him into her arms. "Okay, kids, I'm Amanda, helping cook. Who knows how to make pancakes?"

The twins stopped to stare at her as if she'd grown a horn.

Amanda feigned shock. "You've never had pancakes?"

One of the twins curled her lip in a sneer. "Of course."

"Then you're helper number one! Come show me where the kitchen is."

"Cook doesn't like us in the kitchen."

"Well, then, Cook will have to kick us out, because I need all the helpers I can get." Amanda turned in place and pointed jokingly out the patio door. "Where's the kitchen? That way? No. This way?"

The sullen twin rolled her eyes. "You're silly."

"That's my name! And who are you? Willy and Nilly?"

A reluctant giggle. Within minutes, the sullen twin, who announced her name was Taylor and her sister Teagan, was leading the way to the back of the house. When she stepped into the kitchen, Amanda's jaw dropped. The room was bigger than her entire Laurentian cottage and gleamed with quartz and stainless steel. The walls were lined with cupboards of antique white and glass, displaying enough copper pots and china to rival Buckingham Palace.

"Oh, goodie, a treasure hunt!" she said, keeping the boy propped on her hip as she randomly opened doors. "What do we need for pancakes? Let's put everything on this ping pong table."

Taylor laughed. "That's not a ping-pong table, it's a counter."

"Is it? Wow. Can you find me the eggs?"

She sent both girls scurrying around the kitchen in search of ingredients while the little boy helped her choose the best pan from the rack on the wall. Then she stood the girls on stools and slipped the boy into a highchair, all clustered around the work station. "I need three helpers — a mixer and a measurer and an egg breaker."

The little boy was designated the mixer, a task he undertook with glee, and soon the counter, their hands, and their hair were covered with flour. The puppy bounced excitedly underfoot, hoping for errant food. As Amanda ladled batter into the frying pan, Taylor watched her solemnly.

"My daddy's dead."

"I know, sweetie." Amanda paused to give her a hug.

"Danielle killed him."

"Who's Danielle?"

"Danielle!" Taylor looked at her in disbelief. "Our nanny."

The side door beside the pantry flew open, and a middle-aged woman peered out. "Don't you talk like that, you hear, Taylor? We know no such thing."

"That's what Mommy said," Taylor shot back. Her face was reddening and her chin quivered.

"Nobody knows. The police don't even —" Belatedly, the woman seemed to register the chaos. "What are you doing to my kitchen?"

"We're making pancakes," Taylor said. "I broke the eggs."

The cook — for that's who Amanda assumed her to be — swung on Amanda. She looked like an aging bulldog guarding her domain, but behind the ferocity of her glare, her eyes and nose were red. "And who are you?"

"I'm Amanda, a friend of Candace's. I'm helping out for a few minutes."

"Not in my kitchen you aren't!" She strode across the slate floor to snatch a bowl from under the little boy's nose. "That's the wrong bowl. He'll scratch it."

It looked like an ordinary stainless steel bowl to Amanda. Predictably, the boy shrieked and hurled the mixing spoon across the room.

"Right!" the cook snapped. "Out! Everyone out!" She flicked her hand at Amanda. "You can entertain them in the playroom while I fix this mess. And get that dog back in his crate!"

"It's okay, the pancakes are almost finished," Amanda whispered as she ushered the reluctant children out.

The playroom was cluttered with every conceivable toy — blocks, dolls, and stuffed animals — as well as laptops, iPads, and a huge TV mounted on the wall. To Amanda's dismay, the twins flounced down on the floor and went straight for the iPads. In the background she could hear the cook slamming cupboards in the kitchen and then Candace's sharp voice.

"Edith, keep calm! Have some respect for what Janine and the family are going through."

The cook muttered something unintelligible. It might have been an apology, but Amanda wasn't betting on it.

"She meant well. And if you'd done your job this morning ..." Candace broke off as if a wiser second thought kicked in. "Please. Prepare Janine some toast and tea. Let Amanda finish the pancakes. I'll see if I can get Kaitlyn to help you."

Amanda heard her retreat down the hall, leaving the cook to mutter in quiet outrage about pigs flying. Reluctantly, Amanda put the puppy into his crate and slipped cautiously back into the kitchen to check on the pancakes.

"I cared about him too, you know," Edith grumbled as she slapped a loaf of homemade bread on the counter. "We all did. He was such a ... nice man. Far better than she deserved, you ask me, and I don't know if I can stay on. Not after this."

Amanda flipped the pancakes. "You've been with the family long?"

"Since I turned sixteen, longer than you've been alive. Duncan Saint Clair — that's her father — took me on for the summer. That was back in the days when he hired local help instead of bringing in his staff from Toronto. I never planned to stay. His girls were a handful, and on weekends there were parties all summer long. Too much money for nothing, I always told my husband; may he rest in peace." She shot Amanda a sidelong glance as she arranged a flowered teapot and cup on the tray. "After he died, I had no place else to go. Mr. Saint Clair had promised to build me my own little place here with a garden." Her face fell. "Well, that never happened, did it. After he died, Janine inherited and said it was a waste of money. I had a beautiful room right here in the main house, she said, with my kitchen just steps away. Well, take a look for yourself." She waved her hand at the side door by the pantry. Then with an effort, she squared her shoulders. "No point carrying on about it. Janine is not her father, and with Mr. B gone now too, there will be nothing to stop her. And I don't care if you do tell Candace that. I'm going to quit."

"Is there just you and the nanny, for this whole place?"

"Most of the time. At least Mr. B brought in a man for spring clean-up. Someone he knew from Toronto. Foreigner. Hard-working fellow, though. Janine paid him a pittance of what a local would get. It was different when Mr. Saint Clair was alive. Plenty of locals got full-time summer work here on the island."

The kettle whistled, and Edith poured hot water into the teapot. She busied herself with the tray, her movements sharp and angry. "Don't pay no attention to what little Taylor says. Danielle didn't kill Mr. B. A sweeter, gentler girl you'll never meet. She just wanted to get away from here. Stuck on this island all summer with three little kids and a puppy, and then Candy dumps her own brat in her arms so she can spend a week with her latest man. Candy needs a break, Janine said, but would Danielle ever need a break? Janine wouldn't even hire a local teenager to help. I suggested my niece, but oh, no, not qualified enough. In other words, no dumb locals near their precious genius kids."

"Who's Kaitlyn? Candace mentioned getting her to help."

Edith blew out a puff of air. "When hell freezes. Janine's daughter. Sulky little thing."

Amanda stacked the cooked pancakes on a plate and ladled more batter into the pan. She threw the question out casually. "Why do they think Danielle did it?"

"Because she took off. I don't blame the silly girl. She knew she'd never get a fair break — a foreigner in a house full of rich folks from the city? Everyone knew she wanted to leave, and they kept her passport and documents locked up in the library. Everyone heard the huge fight between Janine and Mr. B that night, right in the middle of the party. He wanted to help Danielle, but Janine refused to give her the papers. Next morning Mr. B's dead on the floor of the library, Danielle's papers are gone, and so's she."

It sounded pretty damning, Amanda thought, except for one crucial detail, which Edith herself supplied in a parting shot as she headed out the door with the tray. "But what's the motive? Mr. B was on Danielle's side. If I'd been her, I'd have gone after Janine!"

CHAPTER SEVEN

Amanda peeked in on the children. The girls were engrossed in a cartoon, and the little boy was asleep on the floor. Mercifully, Candace's baby, Thomas, was nowhere to be seen, but the puppy was pressed against the front of his crate, whining in soft defeat. His tail thumped with renewed hope at the sight of Amanda.

She stroked the puppy's nose, slipped him a pancake, and set the plate of pancakes on the table beside the twins before tiptoeing away. She needed to get down to the dock because Chris and George would be arriving soon. There was enough toxic grief and recrimination in the household already without her unwanted intrusion. She thought about Danielle, stuck in the middle of it, burdened with all the care of four children and a neglected puppy.

From her work overseas, Amanda knew something about the plight of domestic foreign workers who came to Canada on temporary visas with the stipulation that they live in their employer's home for two years before they apply for permanent resident status and ultimately Canadian citizenship. Many of them left husbands and children behind, clinging to the hope of sponsoring them to come to Canada once they themselves had become permanent residents. This was the prize that made it all worthwhile.

In theory, there were laws and legal recourses as well as a contract spelling out their rights and benefits under the employment agreement, but the reality was sometimes very different. Coming from countries with dubious systems of justice often biased in favour of the wealthy, isolated in a strange country, and dependent on their employer for both pay and references, they were often afraid to speak out.

Overwork, long hours, threats of retaliation, and withholding of identity documents were sometimes the least of their problems. Who knew what other personal and sexual demands took place in the privacy of the respectable homes where they worked? Danielle had clearly been asked to do more than was fair and felt trapped enough to head out into the open lake in a flimsy boat. Was that all, or had something more sinister been happening on this remote, private island?

The police were already looking for her, and Amanda had no doubt their efforts would double once they learned of her escape with Ronny. What chance did a lone, foreign woman have against the resources of the state? Amanda hesitated on her way out. She had planned to tell the scowling OPP officer what she knew, but now she wondered if she should just stay out of it and leave it to Chris, who'd already said he intended to report the woman's presence on Franklin Island.

When she went outside to retrieve Kaylee, she was surprised to see a young girl kneeling at the dog's side, stroking her soft fur. Her head was bent, and tears dripped silently down her cheeks.

The girl jumped to her feet when Amanda appeared. "It's okay, it's okay," Amanda said, holding out a soothing hand. "My dog is good company when you're sad."

The girl said nothing but didn't run away. Amanda tried to fit her into the household. In her skinny jeans and cropped leather jacket, she was tall and lithe, her teenage body just beginning to develop curves. She had dark hair pulled into a haphazard ponytail and the same slanted blue eyes and full lips as Janine. *Come-hither lips*, Amanda thought, even though the girl looked barely fourteen.

"Hi, I'm Amanda," she said, taking a guess. "Are you Kaitlyn?"

The girl bobbed her head in a wary nod.

"I'm sorry for your loss, Kaitlyn. This must be awful."

She shrugged and swiped her hand across her cheeks. "He wasn't my father."

"It sounds as if he was a nice man, though."

"Lotta good that did him." She backed away, as if the sympathy was too intense for her.

From inside the house came a distant shriek. "Kaitlyn, where the fuck are you?"

Kaitlyn flinched but made no move to reply. Instead, she hovered, as if she wanted to say more. Amanda nudged her on. "I heard the nanny did it. What was she like?"

A frown of suspicion flitted across Kaitlyn's face. "She had the poor-little-me act down pat ..." Kaitlyn cast her a look beneath her lashes. "Especially with men. She had Ben conned, acting like she was so overworked. And not just Ben. She was planning this escape for days."

"How do you know?"

"I heard her on her phone, talking to someone."

"Who?"

"Some man. I didn't get it all because she kept switching languages, but I could tell enough. She was talking about getting a boat to pick him up."

The patio door burst open. "There you are!" Candace exclaimed. "Make yourself useful. The twins are tearing the place apart!"

"Isn't Mom there?"

Candace grew red. "Your mother just lost her husband. And the girls just lost their father."

"I lost him, too, you know," Kaitlyn mumbled.

"Yes, but he wasn't *your* father!"

Kaitlyn's face collapsed. As she turned to flee, she cast one last salvo over her shoulder. "Tell Mom to deal with her own spawn!"

Candace deflated as she watched the girl disappear down the hill. "I guess that was harsh. But just this once, I wish that girl would show some heart."

Amanda heard the drone of an approaching engine and looked up as a boat streaked into view. As it rumbled to a stop and drifted into the dock, she recognized the tall, reedy man standing in the bow, painter in hand. She hadn't seen him in almost four months, but her heart jumped and a thrill rushed through her.

She stooped to untie Kaylee. "There's my ride. Thank you so much for your help." She paused. "This is a difficult time for everyone." She left the woman still standing on the patio. Regretting her words or reluctant to return inside? Death had left the household in chaos, but perhaps no one more than the young teenage girl who'd been denied the right to grieve. Amanda considered the latest tidbit of information Kaitlyn had let slip in her bitterness. Was it worth passing on to the police?

Something else to talk to Chris about, she thought as she ran down the slope to the dock. *Right after I give him the biggest hug he's ever had.*

Pressed against the cold damp of his raincoat, Amanda had little time to savour the hug before the police descended onto the dock, snapping orders. Restricted zone, they said. Move along.

Their tone changed when the scowling cop, whom Candace had called Neville, recognized George.

"Sorry, George, we can't let you dock. There's been an incident —"

"I heard," George said, leaping off the boat without a hint of back pain, Amanda noted. A quick recovery ... or had Ronny been lying? "This is Corporal Tymko of the RCMP. Neville Standish."

Standish frowned. "RCMP? You guys involved already?"

"Nothing official," Chris replied, disentangling himself from Kaylee, who was whirling around his legs. "I'm mainly here to pick up Amanda."

Standish's frown eased. He even managed a handshake for Chris and a smile for Kaylee.

"We may have some information for you, though," George said. "Don't know if it's related, but could be. My son Ronny picked up a woman out of the water off the Mink Islands. Her boat had swamped. Ronny and her paddled over to Franklin Island, leaving Amanda stranded ..." George shook his head in disbelief. Anger reddened his face.

Standish snapped alert. "Where are they now?"

George shrugged. "Don't know. Ronny's not answering his phone. Chris and I found their two kayaks pulled up on Franklin Island, and we searched for them but with no luck."

Standish swung on Amanda. "When was this?"

"Yesterday morning, maybe eleven?"

"Did you see the woman?"

Amanda hesitated only briefly before nodding. She bristled at his accusatory tone, but the police needed to know the facts.

"Description?"

Amanda gave a quick description of the woman and her clothing. "She gave her name as Sophia, but I think she may have been the nanny here."

"Danielle Torres? We have a BOLO out on her." Standish strode over to one of the Coast Guard boats and unfurled a large waterproof topographical map of Georgian Bay. They all bent over the map while Amanda figured out where Danielle's boat had swamped. It was out in the open lake beyond the shelter of the many islands but on a clear path toward the cities and towns of the populated southern shore. Standish tapped his finger on their present location, which was marked Saint Clair Island, and then traced the route south past the Mink Islands.

"Looks like she was making a run for Midland or Collingwood. Right, now George, where did you say you found the kayaks?"

George peered at the map. "Pretty much straight opposite this Mink Island, on the western side of Franklin. Can you get a more detailed map of that?"

"Yeah, I can pull one up on the computer, but let me call this information in to Regional HQ. We've got to update the search."

He disappeared out of earshot, leaving Amanda studying the map with Chris and George. Amanda saw George sneak a peek at his phone. "What the fuck is Ronny playing at?" he muttered. "This doesn't make any sense!"

"The water was extremely rough when they took off," Amanda said. "Maybe they considered themselves lucky to get across at all and didn't want to try going around the island. The wind could have blown them onto the rocks."

Chris had been studying the map. "Or maybe they crossed the island by foot. Look, it's only a couple of kilometres wide at this point. They could have caught a boat on the other side and been in Snug Harbour or Parry Sound in no time."

George straightened, the lines of worry and anger easing on his face. "Ronny has a lot of buddies in the area. Everyone's got a boat. He could have phoned one of them. And if the little bastard is helping this girl escape, it explains why he hasn't been in touch yet."

"Is that like him?" Amanda asked. "To help a perfect stranger?"

"Yeah, if she was young and pretty."

Amanda was silent, replaying the brief exchange between Sophia and Ronny on the shore after the rescue. Had he recognized her? Before she could make up her mind, Standish reappeared with a couple of OPP officers in tow. "Right. Incident Command wants you to take me to those two kayaks, George."

When they all moved to climb on the boat, Standish stopped them. "George will do. We don't need the whole gang, including the dog."

"But how will we get back?" Amanda asked.

"We'll take George in one of our boats."

"Take mine, Chris," George added. "I'll get it back from you later."

Chris turned to Standish. "Do you need us for anything further?"

"I'll need your contact info, especially Ms. Doucette's. The investigators from GHQ will need to take a formal statement from you. But for now ..." A smile twitched across his thin lips. "You're free to go. Carry on as planned."

"This is not exactly what we planned," Chris murmured as they approached the rustic front door of the little lakeside cottage. It was one of five scattered along the shoreline of a sheltered cove north of Snug Harbour, but because it was not yet high season, only one other was occupied.

"He's out fishing by six a.m., so he won't bother you," the resort owner said with a grin as she unlocked the door. They followed her from room to room as she showed them the amenities, which were few. But the greatest amenity of all was the spectacular view across the broad channel from the mainland to Franklin Island. The rain had stopped and the sun peeked through a sliver in the clouds, spreading gold and peach across the sullen pewter lake. The rain-washed grass sparkled and the wind had dropped to a soft breeze that kept the mosquitoes at bay.

Even better, two red Muskoka chairs sat on the slab of rock in front of the cottage, beckoning. Once the owner had left, Amanda walked down and sank into one with a sigh. Now that they had retrieved her motorcycle and his rental truck, booked a cottage, and bought a few groceries in Parry Sound, now that the drama and fear and anger of the day was over, an exhausted peace descended over her. Thinking she couldn't move another limb, she'd left Chris to unpack the groceries.

Peace hadn't descended, of course. Ronny and Danielle still hadn't been found, and out on Saint Clair Island just a few kilometres up the coast, a family was still locked in the turmoil of grief and suspicion. But she and Chris were out of the maelstrom, safe to enjoy the next few days and maybe salvage the planning of her kayaking trip.

Kaylee, fed and watered, seemed content to curl up at her feet, ignoring the call of the sticks and the water. Amanda reached down to stroke her fur and willed away the memories of the day. Behind her, the screen door creaked open, and footsteps on the grass behind her brought a smile to her lips. Chris held a glass of wine in each hand. He handed one to her, and set the other on the arm of his chair as he sat down. He groaned as he stretched out his long legs. They sat in silence awhile sipping wine and savouring the sunset. Gulls wheeled overhead, and the whine of a distant boat drifted in on the breeze.

He reached out and twined his fingers through hers. "How are you doing?"

"Better." She tilted her wine glass toward him. "Thank you."

"You're welcome. I'll fire up the barbeque in a minute."

She tightened her fingers in his. "Not yet. I've been thinking ..."

He brushed his lips to her fingers. "Mmmm?"

"Not that."

"Uh-oh."

She laughed. The wine was flowing through her in a warm flush. "There's more to this story. Ronny's behaviour was odd. Little things. He insisted on going out to the Mink Islands yesterday, even though the wind was picking up and the islands weren't on my agenda anyway. He told me the marine forecast was fine, but I checked and it wasn't."

"What are you thinking? That this was all planned?"

She shook her head. What *was* she thinking? "Probably not the swamped boat. That would be too dangerous. I don't know if anything was planned, there are just these weird pieces that hint at something. The victim's teenage stepdaughter told me she'd overheard the nanny making arrangements on the phone. The first night, on Franklin Island, Ronny got a phone call in the middle of the night. And earlier, when Ronny and I were in his motorboat going along the coast from Pointe au Baril, he was pointing out all the cottages, who lived in them, and their history, but when I recognized Benson Humphries's boat on Saint Clair Island, he didn't want to go for a closer look. He steered away, in fact." She groped for the elusive threads of connection. "It was like he didn't want to be seen."

She shifted in her chair. Straightened. "Another thing. I may be reading too much into this. Ronny said he didn't know the nanny, but when she said her name was Sophia, he got a funny look. Just for a split second. He recovered fast, and I thought he was just reacting to her. She was terrified."

"She'd almost drowned."

"Yes, but this was a different kind of terrified, as if she were running from something."

"We now know she was."

"Yes. She was. But it makes me wonder, what did Ronny know? He looked startled when she gave a fake name."

"What do you want to do about all this?"

"Nothing. Not yet. It's all just impressions." She tilted her head at him playfully. "And you cops don't deal in impressions, do you?"

"No, we don't."

They grinned at each other in silence. Coral light was spreading across the water, and the first mosquito of the evening whined in her ear. He stroked her fingers. She felt the heat of his touch spread through her. He turned his hand in hers.

"Are we …?" he whispered.

Her voice almost gone, the fear and yearning so great. A whisper back. "Yes, we are."

CHAPTER EIGHT

She awoke to the gentle caress of his fingers on her arm and the soft press of his lips on her shoulder. It was too early. She feigned sleep, but her lips curled.

"I see you," he whispered, nuzzling her neck.

Her smile widened. She felt the warmth of a morning sunbeam across her back and the tangle of sheets cocooning them. It had been a night embraced in pleasure, urgent at first and later languid and sleepy, both of them giggling as Kaylee tried to wriggle between them.

"What time is it?" she murmured, still not opening her eyes.

He nibbled her ear. "Who cares?"

As she arched her back, a cold, wet nose shoved itself against hers. She shrieked and her eyes flew open. Inches away, Kaylee's eyes were fixed on her. Now the dog leaped onto the bed, tail wagging.

"So much for the tender moment," Chris said.

"She's never had to share me before. You could always feed her and put her out," Amanda murmured, reaching down to squeeze him. "I'm surprised you have anything left in there."

"I've been saving up for months."

"Hold that thought. But for now, the perfect tender moment would be a fresh cup of coffee in bed."

He clambered out of bed, grabbed some pants, and padded out of the room with Kaylee bouncing at his heels. She listened as he rustled around the kitchen, filling the coffee pot and feeding the dog.

"You and I have to come to some sort of agreement, princess," he was saying to Kaylee. "You can't hog the bed. Not always. In fact, sometimes you should withdraw discreetly to the other room. And staring is a no-no."

Amanda stifled a laugh. This was going to be new ground for all of them. She stretched and pulled the quilt up against the morning chill. What wonderful new ground it was! She was just imagining the delights of his return to bed when the throaty rumble of an engine drew near and tires crunched on the gravel outside. Kaylee started to bark.

Amanda peeked through the window to see George Gifford swinging down from his truck. Behind the truck was a trailer carrying two kayaks and a boat. Hastily, she began to pull on clothes just as he hammered on the door.

"Sorry to disturb you two lovebirds. I brought a couple of double-doubles and a dozen Timbits."

Amanda entered the kitchen as Chris was setting the Tim Hortons coffees and doughnut holes down on the table. She handed him his shirt, which he accepted sheepishly.

"Any news?" she asked George.

George shook his head. Amanda could see a pinch of worry on his face beneath his studied casual air. "No word from Ronny yet either. I've called around, talked to his friends. No one's heard from him, and he didn't call any of them to pick up him and the woman either."

"Does he have a lot of friends?"

"He gets around. He's lived here all his life, and he's always been the friendly sort."

Amanda pried the lid off the coffee and took a doubtful sip. She preferred her coffee akin to rocket fuel, but she was grateful for its warmth. Chris had not progressed beyond filling the pot. "Did he know Danielle?" she asked.

George had selected a chocolate Timbit and paused in mid-bite. A frown flitted across his brow. "Why would he?"

She shrugged. "Just wondering if maybe they planned something."

"Like what? Smashing up in the middle of the lake?"

"Of course not. But I'm trying to make sense of things. Ronny received a phone call the night before, and I overheard him say 'I'll be there.' The next morning he was really insistent on going out to Mink Islands. He also said he was going to check on a friend's cottage there."

"What friend?"

She shrugged. "Something about checking for winter damage." She replayed Ronny's explanation in her head. "He said he'd only be a few minutes. I remember thinking it was a bit weird."

George looked doubtful. "I don't know any friend of his out there. Did you tell the cops any of this?"

"Not yet. There is nothing firm, just funny coincidences."

George sighed. He sat back in a kitchen chair, looking weary. "I don't know if he knew her. But it's possible. She was here with the family last summer, and if she brought the kids to any activities at the Chippewa Club, their paths might have crossed. That's a community club on an island up near Pointe au Baril. He was a boating and diving instructor out there. The cops are nosing around, and you can bet if Ronny and Danielle so much as said hello, they will uncover it."

Chris leaned against the counter, his long legs crossed. "So they turned up nothing in the search of Franklin Island?"

"Some footprints on the inner beach where they might have caught a boat. The ERT unit may bring K9 in today, but they're talking like they think Ronny and Danielle have already left the area."

"They're just covering all the angles. That's what we do."

George set his Timbit down, half eaten. "But it makes no sense that he wouldn't contact me. He doesn't always think things through, but he knows I'd worry. I can see him helping out this woman. He always had a soft spot for the ladies — as they had for him — and it's got him into trouble sometimes. A couple of bloody noses, mostly. That's how he lost that tooth. But why would he not send word? I'd even settle for a goddamn text! *Everything good, Dad.*"

"Maybe he will once she's safely away," Amanda said. It was a lame excuse, but it was all she could come up with.

"It makes him look guilty," George continued as if he hadn't heard. "The cops already think he was part of this. Not that he killed Ben Humphries, of course, because he was with you, but they're talking accessory after the fact. And maybe conspiracy to plan the crime and the get-away."

The small shreds of coincidence did point that way, but Amanda kept her concerns to herself. "That's a lot of planning. And a lot of dots to connect to prove it."

"Unless they can prove he had a prior relationship with her," Chris said. He was looking thoughtful. *You're not helping*, Amanda wanted to say.

"Well, he does know the wife. Known her for years, since they were both kids."

"What wife?" Amanda said. "You mean Janine?"

George nodded. "They haven't been close for years, but one summer they were a hot item. The talk of the Chippewa Club."

"When was this?"

"Years ago, when they were teenagers. Ronny was in a high school rock band, noisy punk stuff, mostly, and they were hired regularly to play at the club. And at local bars in Parry Sound. He thought he was pretty hot stuff, he got the girls going with that Elvis hip thing. And Janine ... she's always been a wild one. Her father couldn't corral her even if he tried, and he didn't. Just laughed. Let her turn that island into party central all week while he worked in Toronto. And when he died, the whole cottage and island were hers."

Amanda's mind was already racing ahead to possibilities. Picturing Ronny and Janine having a secret affair, Janine tiring of her wholesome husband and no longer needing him now that she had her father's money. She remembered Benson's reaction to Ronny that first day. Was there something there? "Did she continue her wild ways even after her marriage?"

George's eyes flickered, as if he'd just seen the implication behind her question. "I never paid much attention. But she moved on from Ronny years ago. He was nothing but a flash in the pan for her, a local plaything. She'd have her pick of better meat in the city."

Amanda didn't say anything. It didn't matter what Janine felt for Ronny. It was his feelings that mattered, and if he had continued to harbour a secret yearning for her, Amanda could easily see Janine exploiting it. Her brief encounter with the woman had been enough to tell her that. Making the unsophisticated country boy commit crimes for her would be sport.

"Besides, he hasn't gone off with Janine," George added with more conviction in his tone. "The police think he's run off with Danielle. Where's he going to go? What's he going to do? Run off to the Philippines? The boy's never been out of Ontario."

George hung around awhile, helping them to unload the kayaks and put the motorboat in the water before he ran out of excuses to stay. Amanda sensed he was at loose ends, unable to focus on the routines of his day while his missing son occupied his thoughts.

As Chris and Amanda watched his truck wend its way toward the road, she linked her arm through his and laid her head on his shoulder. "I have a bad feeling about all this."

"You and me both. But the most obvious answer is usually the right one. Danielle killed her employer and somehow co-opted Ronny into helping her escape."

Amanda tilted her head to study him. "That doesn't sound simple. That sounds very devious. She didn't strike me as devious, just scared."

He slipped his arm around her. "Amanda, just look how she's made you feel. Like she's vulnerable and needing protection. And you met her for all of half an hour. Imagine what she could do to a gullible young man."

The inconsistencies of the past few days nagged at her. Ronny's avoidance of Saint Clair Island, his unexplained phone call that first night, and his insistence on paddling out to the Mink Islands and checking on his friend's cottage. His shocking desertion of her, which seemed out of character with the nice, responsible — albeit playful — man she'd thought he was.

But most damning of all, his continued silence about his whereabouts, even to his father.

She sighed as she headed back inside. In the kitchen, she cracked a couple of eggs into a skillet. "I admit the whole thing looks suspicious. But I heard the cook's opinions, and I met Janine. There was a lot going on in that household, a lot of anger and resentment. I wonder if the police have been able to determine what he died of."

"The body would have been transported to the Forensic Pathology Unit in Toronto, and the post-mortem will probably be done today or tomorrow. But if there's no clear cause of death —"

"Apparently nothing obvious like a bullet hole or bashed-in skull," Amanda replied. The aroma of butter and fried eggs filled the kitchen. "There was a party with a lot of drinking. I saw booze bottles and glasses all over the place. A simple thing to slip something into his drink."

"Or to get the drinks mixed up." He fed four slices of bread into the toaster. "Everything will have been bagged and sent for analysis, including possible DNA, to see who drank what."

She rolled her eyes. "That will take weeks."

"And if it was poison, it may be untraceable, so ..." He cocked his head. "Do you know if anyone in the household would have access to poisons? Pharmacist, physician, nurse?"

She laughed. "I didn't get that far in my eavesdropping. But it's a good bet a nanny and a local outfitter's son wouldn't be high on the list."

"The cops will figure that out, honey."

The word slipped out so naturally that she wondered if he even realized it. Then he busied himself with the toast, red creeping up his cheeks. "We're not that dumb, you know."

"Far from it. But that forensic evidence won't come back for weeks, and meanwhile the police will be focussing their efforts on Ronny and Danielle, because they've taken off." She turned into his arms. "After breakfast, do you fancy a motorboat ride up the coast?"

"Where to?"

"Oh, maybe Pointe au Baril. Or the Chippewa Club. If Ronny and Danielle met before, that would be the place."

"What about scouting for your kayaking trip?"

"That too. We can have a picnic lunch on one of the islands on our way back."

Two hours later, the sun was high and sparkling off the bay as they set out. Amanda let Chris drive the boat so she could sit up front to navigate the channel and keep a sharp lookout for underwater hazards. Kaylee balanced on the bow, snapping at the waves that splashed up.

As they passed the waterfront mansions along the way, most of them still shuttered, Chris's eyes grew wide. He pointed to a dilapidated, two-storey boathouse sagging into the water. "The mother-in-law suite?"

As they neared Saint Clair Island, Amanda waved him closer. He cut the engine and they drifted forward. In contrast to yesterday, the place looked abandoned. Crime scene tape still fluttered in the brisk breeze, but all the official boats were gone, as well as Candace's white cruiser.

Chris was staring up at the house that sprawled in decks and patios and wings over much of the slope. "The older daughter got all this?" he murmured. "That would make one pissed-off younger daughter."

"Yeah, and I think she had ways of extracting revenge. Like getting them to babysit while she went for adult R&R. But I can't see her bumping off her brother-in-law. That wouldn't get her any closer to the family money chest, and from what I saw of them together, she thought he was one of the good guys."

"How good?"

She replayed the brief dramatic interplay between Benson and Candace. Had there been any intimate undertones? Only the faintest hint, maybe not even there at all. "No, not that good. More like he was sympathetic to her. So she had no reason to profit from his death and perhaps a lot to lose."

He laughed and leaned forward to ruffle her hair. "You got me playing 'what if' too, Sherlock!"

"I can't say I blame the family for leaving," Amanda said. "It must have been awful to be stuck here, looking at the spot where he died. Do you want to go ashore, just to check?"

"Check what?"

She shrugged. "Just to get a sense of where he died."

His smile faded. "No. It's private property."

"There's no one here."

He nodded toward the house. "There will be surveillance cameras."

She snorted in dismissal.

"Amanda, I'm a cop."

She studied his set features in silence. "I think I lost an earring here yesterday. I'll just check …"

His lips twitched in spite of himself. "You? An earring?"

"Hey! I've been known to dress up on occasion. In fact, I own a whole box of earrings from all over the world. All with sentimental value."

Still he didn't move. They had drifted up to the dock, and Kaylee unexpectedly leaped out. Amanda made a half-hearted attempt to grab the leash but in the end had to clamber ashore. She stood on the dock a moment, expecting to be challenged by a police guard, but heard nothing beyond the sibilant whisper of waves.

"Amanda …" came Chris's warning voice.

She held out the leash. "You stay here with her. I won't be a minute."

Before he could react, she spun around and scrambled up toward the house. As she'd expected, it was locked up tight. She worked her way around the perimeter, trying every door without success. She peered around the window and doorframes and examined the patio door, not surprised to find everything barred from the inside. The place was like Fort Knox. There was likely some valuable art and electronics inside, and with cottages in the area sitting empty most of the year, security would be state-of-the-art. She glanced up at the eaves and spotted a video alarm system. She ducked down in dismay then realized she was probably already on Candid Camera.

Cautiously, she pressed her face to a nearby window. Inside was a library with floor-to-ceiling bookshelves, comfortable easy chairs, and a massive antique desk. The scene of the crime! All the empty bottles, glasses, party trays, and other detritus from the party had been removed, but the desk chair lay upturned, and a pool of something slimy stained the floor. Although it was too dark to be sure, it looked too viscous to be alcohol. Her pulse quickened. Blood? Had he been stabbed or hit after all?

She tried the window, and to her surprise the sash lifted. She lifted it farther and slipped one leg in, imagining Chris's outraged protest. *Just a peek*, she promised him silently. If Benson was poisoned, that pretty much guaranteed premeditation, but if this was blood ...

She clambered over the sill, steeling herself for the shriek of an alarm, but instead was immediately assailed by the stench. Death and decay mingled with other bodily smells. She pressed her hand to her nose and breathed shallowly as she tiptoed into the room.

She recoiled at the sight. The room was crammed with memorabilia, like a ghoulish, overcrowded museum. Stuffed fish and animal heads were mounted on the walls between the books, not just the usual deer and moose heads, but bears, leopards, antelopes, and other animals she recognized from Africa. Wooden carvings and stone sculptures from around the world cluttered every surface, and even the furniture was heavy, ornately carved art. A trophy hunter's room from a bygone era. Was this Janine's father's work or some earlier Saint Clair ancestor's?

She tore her eyes away from the lion's head that was mounted behind the desk and focussed instead on the pool of fluid on the floor. It was dry and crusty at the edges, and she could see scrapes where the forensic team had removed samples, but it still had an oily sheen at the centre. The colour was a putrid yellowy orange, not the deep red of blood. She bent closer and risked a sniff.

Vomit.

Making a face, she backed away and began a quick patrol of the room, trying to avoid the many tragic eyes gazing down at her. The desk was empty, the contents likely taken by the forensic team for further analysis.

Nearby was another stain, clear and shiny against the rich oak floor. It too was scraped. Wrinkling her nose, she bent over it and caught a whiff of urine. She studied the two stains. It looked as if the poor man had fallen here, vomiting and voiding his bladder before he died. She felt a twinge of sorrow as she thought of his last moments. He had been such a happy, vibrant man. There were no blood smears or drops. Whatever killed him, he had probably ingested it.

Fingerprint powder was still evident on many of the surfaces, doorknobs, and windowsills. Who had touched what? She raised her head to search the room for a safe or a locked drawer. Danielle's papers had been locked up in the library, and they'd disappeared along with the nanny. Amanda was just going to check the desk drawers when she heard a short, sharp bark in the distance. She rushed to the window to peer down at the dock. Kaylee was on alert, staring at something through the trees. When Amanda dived out the window onto the patio, a flash of lime green at the shore caught her eye through the trees. She squinted. A kayak.

A figure was scrambling toward it. At the water's edge, it grabbed the kayak and turned to glance back up at the house. Amanda gasped as she ducked out of sight. She had managed only a brief glimpse of the figure but enough to make out the familiar cropped leather jacket.

CHAPTER NINE

Chris remained tight-lipped as she clambered back into the boat.

"Do you want to know what I found, or would you rather not?"

He said nothing for a moment as he steered the boat back out into the channel. Then he sighed as if in resignation. "Not what you did, but I guess ..." He shrugged. As she filled him in on her discoveries, his head tilted with interest in spite of himself.

"Poor bastard," he said when she described the urine and vomit. "There are a lot of lethal drugs out there these days, and it doesn't take much. They sound like a partying crowd."

"But why the huge police response? And why all that forensic analysis? Do the police know something?"

"That's standard operating procedure. Just crossing all their *t*'s and dotting their *i*'s. Especially since there's big money involved, and with that, big press coverage." He paused. "And big lawyers."

She fell silent, pondering the implications. Who would inherit? Who stood to benefit when so much money was at stake? Benson didn't own the island but presumably had his own assets. As they motored farther up the channel, they passed a couple of *For Sale* signs on the island mansions.

"I wonder what these would set you back," she said, attempting to lighten the mood. She pointed to a ramshackle old cottage tucked on a granite chunk of rock so small that there was barely room for its deck. "Oh look, there's one we can afford."

His wide crinkly-eyed grin spread across his face. "That might be under a million."

As they rounded the point, a sprawling old inn came into view on the island ahead. It had the sweeping covered veranda and ornate turrets typical of Victorian grandeur, but a jumble of more modern outbuildings was spread out on either side. Docks, boardwalks, and beaches rambled along the water's edge. A trio of workers was painting the outdoor trim.

"Wait!" Amanda said. "Maybe that's the Chippewa Club. George said Ronny ran activities there for kids and teens, and he might have met Danielle there. Let's check it out."

"Isn't it a private club?" Chris asked dubiously.

Amanda shot him an exasperated look. "It's not open for the season yet, but these workers probably know him."

Chris guided the boat into the dock, and Amanda jumped out with Kaylee. One of the workers glanced their way before returning to her work. Now that they were closer, Amanda could see the workers were not local men from the area but middle-aged women dressed in mismatched, paint-smudged clothes.

Amanda approached, pretending to be enchanted by the historic old building. "Do you need any more help?" she asked casually.

One of the women paused, a paintbrush in one hand and a paint can in the other. She had a plain but kindly face and looked to be in her late forties, a good age to know some of the past secrets of the club. She frowned quizzically, as if trying to place Amanda.

"We're new here," Amanda said. "Actually just thinking of buying that little island down the way. The realtor told us about this gorgeous place! It looks as if it's seen a lot of history."

"It has. Including being allowed to almost fall down."

"And the community bought it?"

The woman nodded, her wariness fading as pride took its place. Amanda extended her hand. "I'm Amanda, and this is Chris."

"Venetia Lawless." The woman laughed ruefully at the paint on her hand before returning the handshake. Kaylee joined in the greetings, distracting them all before Amanda got her firmly back on leash. The trim paint was blue; not a good colour on an orange dog.

Amanda returned to the task at hand. "And all the property owners around here can use it?"

"We have a paid membership roster, and everyone chips in on maintenance. Don't be deceived by the quiet. During the summer, this place is hopping. We have beach parties, regattas, picnics, and if you have children, there are wonderful children's programs."

"Yes, we ran into Ronny Gifford a few days ago. Seems like a friendly, capable guy. He said he ran activities here."

A flicker of disapproval crossed Venetia's face. "Yes, Ronny is a ... popular fellow."

Amanda laughed. "Uh-oh. That sounds ominous. He *is* a flirt, I'll give you that. I imagine he leaves a few hearts broken in his wake."

The other two women had stopped their work to listen. Amanda heard a ripple of laughter. "Very astute of you," said Venetia. "Just between you and me, I suspect he won't be hired back this summer. Too many ..."

She broke off as if thinking better of it, but one of the other women was less circumspect. "Hormones," she said. She had flaming red hair that would be visible halfway across the bay. The streak of blue paint wasn't a good look on it either.

Amanda glanced at Chris, who was playing the strong, silent type at her side. "Didn't we hear that he ran off with that nanny who killed Ben Humphries?"

It was a bold move, and Venetia's eyes widened in surprise. "Nothing stays secret in the country, I guess. And people make up what they don't know." She cast a warning glance at the woman beside her, who had looked about to pitch in again.

"Oh?" Amanda said. "It's not true?"

Venetia shook her head. "No. Yes."

"Make up your mind, Venetia," said the redhead. "Yes, they ran off together."

"I mean, I don't think that poor girl killed Ben." Venetia hesitated as if reluctant to speak ill. "There are a lot of people in that family I'd put ahead of her. If Ronny did run off with her, it was probably because he knew she wouldn't get a fair shake."

"So they were friends from before?"

Belatedly, Venetia put her paintbrush back into the can and leaned against the side of the building. The others followed suit, clustering around Amanda.

"I don't know about friends," Venetia ventured before the redhead jumped in.

"Oh yeah, he met her last year. She'd bring the holy terrors — pardon me, the twins — over to play on the beach. They were a handful, and she was run ragged." The woman laughed. "Ronny was his usual charming self to a pretty young thing in distress."

"So this was her second year with the family?"

"Yeah, she should have been nearing the end of her mandatory two years," the redhead continued. "Frankly, I'm amazed she hung in. Working for that bunch must have been hell."

"You mean the husband was difficult?" Amanda knew she was pushing her luck, so she tried to keep her voice as casual as possible. Just a woman enjoying a bit of salacious gossip.

"Oh no, Ben was a sweetheart," Venetia said. "Poor man. It was Janine…." She shook her head.

Once again the redhead burst in. "Janine first, last, and

always. She was given the world on a platter, but she thought she was owed the whole universe. And if she didn't get it, boy, she could be nasty."

"Now Peggy, you're going to scare off Amanda," Venetia said. "We're not all like that. It's a nice, peaceful, friendly community."

"I can see that," Amanda said. "We love it! But still, who knows what goes on in the privacy of those islands, eh? Jealousies, marriages on the rocks, secret affairs. Maybe it was Ben who was planning to run away with the nanny."

Venetia looked as if she'd been slapped. "That's a leap."

Amanda covered her false step with a laugh. "I met Ben the other day. Seemed like a really nice guy, and talk about gorgeous! I bet he has lots of women chasing him."

Venetia drew her lips tight. "He was crazy about his kids, and Janine would have cut off his access —"

"Not to mention his balls," Peggy said.

Venetia continued as if Peggy hadn't spoken. "She's got the money and the connections. He didn't come from money, and he loves what it can buy. Loves the lake. He's out on that boat all the time with his photography and watercolours. And he's become quite an accomplished racing sailor."

Peggy leaned in, not to be outdone. "Janine now ... she's more likely to grow tired of him. He's not enough of a party animal for her, so she'd be the one to stray."

Amanda digested this while she tried to figure out what to ask next. She'd already pried out far more than she'd hoped to. "I can see how having three little kids could cramp her style."

"Oh, hardly. That's what the nanny was for. But now, the nanny was getting close to the end of her term, and she couldn't wait to get away. She'd already started the process of getting her permanent resident status and bringing her husband and son over here."

Venetia looked at Peggy in surprise. "Who told you that?"

Peggy flushed and looked at her toes. "I shouldn't have said anything. She was in Walt's office last week, asking. Ronny brought her —"

Amanda hid her surprise, but before she could query further, Venetia cut in. "Then it makes no sense she'd run away now."

"Except Walt told her it might take two to four years to process because of government backlog. She was really upset. Two more years of working for Janine, and her own son will hardly know her!" At that moment something out on the water caught Peggy's eye, and she frowned. "Oh, dear, look who's coming."

All eyes followed hers. A lime-green kayak was making its way toward shore. "Poor lamb," Venetia muttered. "She always gets forgotten in all the fuss, but she's going to miss Ben most of all. She took a long time to let him into her heart, but he treated her better than all her blood relatives combined."

"He's not her real father?" Amanda asked, counting on Peggy. A risky question, but she had no time for subtleties. Kaitlyn was clearly visible in the cockpit now, her hair blowing in a straggly tangle around her.

True to form, Peggy snorted. "Janine got around. I'm not sure even she knows who that is. Or cares."

They fell silent as the girl docked her kayak and disembarked in one fluid move. As she approached, she shot Amanda a quick, puzzled glance before Venetia stepped forward and enveloped her in her arms.

"Oh, sweetie, I'm so sorry. What an awful, awful thing."

Kaitlyn remained rigid, her eyes closed. "Can I stay with you, Aunt Venetia?" she murmured finally. "I can't stand ... I just can't be around them right now."

Matthew Goderich was scurrying past all the rainbow displays of fabric in the fashion district of Queen Street West when Amanda phoned. It was a glorious spring day in Toronto, and the locals were flooding the streets, window shopping, sunning themselves on park benches, and sipping lattes at sidewalk tables. The younger, more energetic ones were jogging in the latest designer attire. In that fleeting interval between icy winter and hot, muggy summer, late May hit the perfect note.

After years of reporting from war-torn and impoverished corners of the world, Matthew was relishing every moment of being back in Canada, with its blue skies, clean air, neatly tended parks, and polite people. He figured after spending years bringing the struggles of the developing world to the attention of the West, he'd earned a little luxury. He'd even found the perfect job; running Amanda's country-wide Fun for Families charity still allowed him to keep his hand in the fight for global betterment, but from the comfort of his homeland. He loved raising awareness, money, and enthusiasm for the causes she chose, and despite having lived his whole life on a shoestring, he found he had a talent for raising money. He had networks of big donors all around the world, but he'd also discovered the value of social media crowdfunding. Amanda's work touched the hearts of ordinary people who wanted to help even if they only had ten dollars to spare.

Now he was on his way to a late lunch meeting with the president and CEO of a local IT start-up who had expressed support for women's causes. He had deep pockets, but more importantly, he'd grown up in Georgian Bay.

Horns were blaring and streetcars were screeching. A distant jackhammer made the din so loud that he almost didn't answer his phone, but when he glanced at the name, he couldn't resist. He hadn't heard from Amanda in several days and was getting restless. It would also help his appeal for money if he could provide the CEO with specific details on her planned itinerary.

And if he were honest with himself, he was also curious, and not a little jealous, to know how she was getting along with her spit-polished Mountie.

Ducking into a side street and blocking his other ear, he answered. "How's the trip going? I hope the weather is co-operating. We had the mother of all thunderstorms yesterday."

"So did we." Amanda's voice sounded distant. Tinny. "And the trip is ... well, it's taken a detour."

He waited.

"I'm with Chris in Pointe au Baril," she said. "But there's been a death — possible murder — on one of the islands."

His fear spiked. "Are you okay?"

"I'm fine. We're fine. But it's a long story, and I need your help."

He listened while she described rescuing a nanny from the lake, only to have her disappear with the tour guide, leaving Amanda stranded on a remote island. Overcoming his outrage, he refrained from interrupting, his years as a journalist having taught him to give people time for the story to emerge.

"The police seem to have decided that Ronny and the nanny are guilty and are trying to flee the country. Perhaps already have. But I'm not so sure."

He rolled his eyes. How like Amanda to charge in single-handedly to defend the innocent. "It sounds like the police have this well in hand, Amanda," he said. "They do have a shitload of resources and intel at their disposal."

"But sometimes, as we know, they are wrong," she countered. "I've been talking to people, and there are plenty of reasons she would flee besides being guilty. She's a foreign national here on a temporary visa. She has run afoul of influential, old-money Toronto wealth. She has no one to back up her side of the story."

"Which is?"

"Well, I don't actually know."

"Uh-huh."

"That's what I want your help with."

He sighed. "What do you want me to do?"

"Do you have connections in the Philippines?"

He riffled through his memory. "Possibly. Why?"

"See what you can dig up on her. I'm not naive, Matthew. I know she may be guilty, and I also know she may be using Ronny. Apparently, she consulted a lawyer about getting her husband and son over here once she gets permanent residence status. I want to know if that's true. Specifically if there even *is* a husband and son. I assume he'd be in the Philippines."

He pressed his finger into his ear. Had he heard her correctly? Did she expect him to track down some guy halfway around the world in a country of nearly a hundred million people?

"Matthew?"

"I'm here. I'm just wondering how the hell …? It's a needle in a haystack. Less than a needle. A speck of dust."

"That's your specialty. It will be like the good old days. You used to be able to find out anything!"

"I was younger then."

She laughed. "Don't go all stodgy on me. Use your contacts. Use your charm."

He was silent a moment as he tried to think up more arguments. "You got a name for this alleged husband? And a place of residence?"

"Not for him, but the nanny's name is Danielle Torres. Try Manila and work your way down."

"How old is this Danielle Torres?"

"I'd guess mid to late twenties. She has a son, and she's been here almost two years."

"Do you know how many Filipino nannies there are in Canada?"

"I know. Thousands."

"About twenty-five thousand, actually."

Amanda groaned. "But she would have come over in the summer of 2016. That narrows it down."

"And is she properly certified?"

"I have no idea, but I suspect the Saint Clairs would demand the best." She paused. "I know it's a needle in a haystack —"

"Speck of dust."

She didn't miss a beat. "And I will try to get more details on her for you, but I don't know how much nosier I can be."

"You? Nosy? Never!"

She laughed again. How he loved to hear her laugh, a sound so rare in recent years. "Okay, I'll be nosier if you promise to do the same."

When he hung up, he shook his head in frustration. Why did he always end up promising her the moon? He knew why, of course, but that made him feel even more the fool. He was never going to compete against the man with the halo.

Reaching the little bakery café five minutes late, he was relieved to see that his potential donor had not yet arrived. After ordering an espresso to keep his brain cells cranked up, he chose a table on the side patio and scrolled through his contacts in Southeast Asia. Some had been made years ago, and he had no idea whether they were still valid. People in the diplomatic, trade, and media fields rarely stayed put for long.

But he did uncover three promising leads; an aging, burned out British journalist friend who had retired to Hong Kong with his Asian wife, and two local media hacks in Manila. He glanced at his watch. Both Manila and Hong Kong were twelve hours ahead of Toronto, which meant it was the middle of the night there. Not the best time to be calling out of the blue to ask about specks of dust in haystacks.

He drummed his fingers on the table, not happy at the prospect of waiting at least six hours before he could initiate the search. Amanda might be getting herself into trouble again, unable to resist the urge to solve someone else's problem. Of his three contacts, the one least likely to hang up on him was his fellow journalist in Hong Kong. In the fine balance of favours they'd traded over the years, Dave Walters owed him. And he knew Amanda. He might even care.

By the miracle of mobile technology, the call went through on his first try, and within seconds he heard the round vowels and swallowed consonants of North England. "This better be good, whoever you are."

Matthew could hear music and laughter in the background. He had not dragged his old friend out of bed. "Dave, it's Matthew Goderich."

The voice rose above the clamour. "Who?"

"Matthew Goderich!"

"The fuck you are."

"Yours truly. It's been a while."

"It has that. Where the hell are you?"

"Back in Canada. How've you been keeping?"

There was a pause, and the background noise receded as if Dave had moved to another room. Matthew heard the click of a door closing. He tried to ease into his request with a bit of small talk, but Dave cut him off. "What's up, Goderich? I've got people here. Can we do this memory lane tour another time?"

"Right. Absolutely. Listen, I've got a favour to ask."

"Of course you do."

Matthew waited. He knew Dave's curiosity would get the better of him. It only took five seconds.

"Wha'?" Dave asked.

"This is the short version. I'm trying to track down the whereabouts of a Filipino man, probably living in Manila, who is married to a temporary foreign worker over here in Canada." As he articulated the request, he realized how absurd it was. He didn't even have the man's name, let alone his date of birth or address, and in Metro Manila alone, there were over twelve million people.

"What's the longer version? Why?"

Matthew provided a sketchy outline of the nanny's involvement in a possible murder, as well as the husband's possible role. "I want to know if he's trying to get into Canada."

"And you want this for a story?"

"No, I'm just verifying the nanny's story." He hesitated. "Amanda Doucette has gotten herself mixed up with this nanny, and you know Amanda."

Dave chuckled. "I do. How's she doing?"

"She's doing much better." Matthew spotted a man striding across the street toward him, dressed in casual jeans, a T-shirt, and sandals. He looked barely thirty, but he radiated power. "Look, I won't keep you now. The nanny's name is Danielle Torres. She's been working in Canada for almost two years, so she may have got her work visa in Manila in the summer of 2016. Her husband's name may be Torres as well. And there may be a young son with him too."

"Lots of maybes, Goderich."

"I know. Just see if you can dig up anything on him. Even a phone number. I can take it from there."

"I can't promise anything. It might take a while too."

"I'll owe you."

"Uh-huh. When do I collect?"

"You know my door's always open." Matthew laughed as he hung up just in time to greet his lunch companion. The fact that he'd almost never had a door to call his own was a small joke between them.

Fortunately, Ian Macintyre was a busy man with no small degree of ADHD, so within an hour they had finished their meals and Matthew had secured a hefty donation to the Fun for Families initiative. Just as Ian was pulling his credit card out of his wallet, Matthew took a shot in the dark.

"Amanda's there right now mapping out the trip. Unfortunately, there was a possible murder up there —"

"Yeah, I heard."

"You probably didn't know the dead man. They were cottagers up near Pointe au Baril. I know you're from Parry Sound —"

Ian laughed. "Yeah, the other side of the tracks. No, I didn't know him, but of course I knew the Saint Clairs. Everyone did. They've been fixtures up there for nearly a hundred years. Duncan Saint Clair died two years ago, but he was very involved in the community, as were earlier generations. He used to bankroll boat races, hunting parties, and fishing derbies. You name it, he was in the thick of it."

"A popular guy?"

"It's amazing what a pile of money will buy. But I don't see that continuing with his daughters running the show. The old man understood about giving back to the community. Hired locals, funded activities in the area. The daughters used that island as a party venue and little else. I worked a summer party there once while I was putting myself through university, and I tell you, you couldn't pay me enough to go back! But —" he shrugged "— who knows, maybe Janine's grown up. Duncan Saint Clair must have seen something in her."

The waiter materialized with the card machine, ending Matthew's chance to extract more gossip, and afterward Ian leaped to his feet. Matthew stayed behind, nursing another espresso while he considered his next move. He didn't expect to hear from Dave Walters until the next day, but in the meantime, he could do some informal sleuthing of his own.

So he opened his laptop, ordered another espresso, and hooked up to the café's Wi-Fi. A quick Google search yielded the address of Janine and Benson Humphries; where else but in an exclusive enclave in the heart of Toronto. Neighbours loved to gossip, and in genteel, well-heeled Rosedale, he suspected they might have a lot to say about the scandals of Janine Saint Clair.

CHAPTER TEN

Before he ventured into the field, Matthew knew he needed to arm himself with as much background detail as possible about his subjects, so he entered the name "Benson Humphries" into another Google search. He scanned the hits, noting that although the major news media had reported extensively on his death and the police investigation, there was no mention of homicide or even cause of death. The coroner had ruled the death suspicious, but the lid was tighter than a drum on the details.

Dr. Henry Benson Humphries was a neurologist on staff at one of the big downtown Toronto hospitals as well as the University of Toronto Medical School. Judging from his list of publications and presentations, he was a well-respected rising star in his field. He was thirty-six years old, born in Saskatoon the son of local schoolteachers, but he'd been educated first at the U of T Medical School and later at the prestigious Johns Hopkins Medical School in the United States.

Matthew ploughed through all the professional accolades and achievements in search of personal insight into the man beyond his modest roots, but it was only when he Googled Janine Saint Clair that he learned more about their private life. The Saint Clairs were identified as one of Toronto's pre-eminent old-money families. Janine had attended an exclusive girls' private school and later Queen's University, but she had never held a job in any normal sense of the word. She was on the boards of numerous foundations and charities and was frequently the spokesperson for worthy social causes.

Janine had met Benson at one of her hospital foundations, where it appeared both of them were on the board. It had been a fast romance, culminating four years ago in an extravagant wedding up at the country house in Georgian Bay. Duncan Saint Clair had hired an entire cruise ship to bring the guests up from Collingwood and to put them up for the weekend.

Twin girls had been born six months later and a boy two years after that. Shortly before the birth of the twins, they had moved into their current Rosedale home, a wedding present from her father. So Daddy had bankrolled not just the super-wedding but also the super-house, Matthew thought. What was he trying to buy? A steadying hand for his wild child? A shot at respectability? The good doctor had brought impressive genes, ambition, and work ethic to the table, but little else.

Matthew Googled Duncan Saint Clair and was greeted by an avalanche of hits even greater than his daughter's. The family had originally made its money in mining and steel up in the Parry Sound area, but had long since diversified into mining and real estate holdings all over the world. Duncan had been a man of enormous energy and appetite. He travelled everywhere on business and played as hard as he worked. There had been a string of liaisons, but only one wife — the mother of his girls — who was reputed to be mentally unstable. Years ago he had banished her to a life of secluded luxury and round-the-clock care in the Cayman Islands. He'd raised his daughters alone, albeit with a large domestic staff who no doubt did most of the grunt work.

Duncan Saint Clair's death two years ago had been widely reported, and eulogies had poured in from global high-flyers.

He had died in a sailing accident in the Fiji Islands, where he was vacationing with a group of friends. He was only sixty-six years old, a man struck down at the top of his game, according to the friends who were with him.

To the delight of Toronto's people-watchers, his will had caused quite a stir. He had left the island mansion and much of the control of his portfolio to his older daughter, leaving his younger daughter Candace with his city house — worth millions — and a generous monthly investment income. Her share of the portfolio, however, was mostly tied up in trust for possible off-spring. It seemed Daddy trusted her taste in men even less than Janine's.

Matthew was so absorbed in his note-taking that he failed to notice the server hovering until the woman discreetly slipped his empty coffee cup onto her tray. "Can I interest you in an afternoon tea, sir, and perhaps a pastry?"

Matthew glanced at his phone in surprise. It was nearly five o'clock. Too late now to stir up some gossip in the Rosedale neighbourhood. Families would be readying for dinner and their evening commitments. Rosedale gossip would have to wait for another day. With a smile, he headed to the pub across the street for a beer and some spicy wings and settled down to Google Danielle Torres.

Chris and Amanda had returned to their cottage, packed a late picnic lunch, and taken out the kayaks George had left them. They passed such an enjoyable afternoon puttering among the coastal islands that Amanda barely gave the murder and the fugitives a moment's thought. Much of the land was unspoiled First Nations territory, where the only human presence was the occasional fishing boat trolling down the channel. The sun was warm and the water so serene that it was difficult to imagine only two days earlier, a painful, ugly death had occurred.

They returned to the cabin as the sun was slipping behind Franklin Island, and Chris headed for the kitchen. When she pulled out the bag of potatoes, he poured her a glass of wine and shooed her out.

A girl could get used to this, she thought as she took her mystery novel outside and settled into one of the red Muskoka chairs to enjoy the sunset. Only after they had finished Chris's delicious meal of steak and barbequed vegetables did her thoughts drift back to the tragedy of Benson Humphries's death. When the mosquitoes drove them back inside, she used her phone to create a hotspot so she could check for news on the investigation.

"Oh!" she exclaimed. "Matthew has sent me a whole pile of background notes on Benson and Janine."

He came to sit beside her as she read. Matthew's notes were point-form, full of abbreviations and non-sequiturs, but the gist was clear.

The information about Janine's charity work took her by surprise. Amanda had regarded Janine as a spoiled, self-indulgent socialite born into a wealthy, privileged life who had never known hardship, but it seemed as if she'd embraced the philanthropic role that wealthy society ladies had performed for decades, perhaps even centuries.

"Maybe she's not such a bad girl after all," Amanda said.

Chris rolled his eyes. "She gets all the spotlight and all the credit. I bet everyone else does all the work."

Amanda nudged him playfully. "You cynic, you."

"Occupational hazard."

They returned to the notes. "Well, well, well," she said a few moments later. "Janine was three months pregnant when they got married."

"Hardly shocking these days. Friends of mine had their daughter as their flower girl."

"I know, but when that much money is involved ... and it means they didn't have much time to get to know each other and make sure they were really suited."

Chris read over her shoulder. "Looks like her father was the one really pushing for it."

"Judging from what we've learned about Janine, I bet Benson was a big improvement over the previous men she'd dragged in."

"She sounds like a chip off the old block, though. I've known guys like Duncan. The world is their playground, and they leave a swath of broken hearts wherever they go. Proud of it, too."

She made a face. "In a perverse way, maybe that's why he left her control of the estate. He thought she'd be as wild and ruthless as he was."

Matthew was deep in the middle of a sexy dream and loath to leave it when his cellphone's ringtone blasted through the boozy fog of sleep. He groped for the phone, squinted at the caller, and groaned.

"Gotcha!" Dave Walters crowed.

Matthew deciphered the time: 3:45 a.m. "This better be good. Epic, in fact."

"A little respect is due. I've found your nanny's husband."

Matthew struggled upright in bed. The blind that hung crooked over his bedroom window was no match for the neon restaurant sign across the street, and an eerie red and green glow lit the room.

"I'm impressed," he said. "I Googled Danielle Torres and got sixty-four thousand hits. Realtors, actors, and who knows what. So I ordered another beer and called it a night."

"Danielle *Rodriguez* Torres, that's the name you want. She was born in Manila on June 2, 1988. On December 24, 2010, she married Fernando Peña Torres, and on January 4, 2012, they had a son, Raoul. The Philippines has a good education system and good literacy rates, but their pay is crap compared to the west. Danielle had been working as a school teacher in Manila, but in February 2013 she took a job making three times that much as a nanny in Dubai —"

"When her son was barely a year old?"

"Yeah. Not uncommon in the Philippines, which exports more nannies around the world than any other country. It's a big part of the country's GDP, and the workers support whole families back home. Dubai is a huge employer of foreign workers. She tried for three years to get a position in Canada and got her visa to work for the Saint Clairs in May 2016."

"What were her husband and son doing all that time?"

"According to my sources, until recently, living with her mother in Manila."

Five years separated from her son, Matthew thought. *Almost all her kid's life.* "Any word on him moving to Canada?"

"I'm getting to that. Unless you're footing the bill for me to fly to the Philippines, I have to rely on dubious local sources. People are nervous to talk. Nobody trusts this new government, and they don't want to draw attention to themselves or get their friends in trouble. And in Fernando's case, even more so. Last month his brother was shot in the street by police in one of the regime's so-called extrajudicial executions. Apparently he'd never used drugs a day in his life; his only crime was being poor."

Matthew grimaced. In an effort to rid the country of drugs, the Philippines' president had sanctioned the shooting of suspected dealers without bothering with arrest and trial. Over ten thousand had been killed, some of them innocents caught in the crossfire. "That would ratchet up Fernando's desperation, for sure."

"Yeah. Word has it that Fernando's been in hiding ever since, possibly living in that squatters' village in the big Manila cemetery. I did manage to reach his old supervisor at work by pretending to be a Canadian visa officer. The supervisor was surprised I was calling. Fernando already has a visa, he said. His wife is waiting for him there, and she's made lots of money. He'll make a good Canadian, this supervisor assured me. Honest, works hard, wants a better life for his son."

"Did you happen to find out how he got this visa? And what kind it is?"

"Well, that was going to be tricky, since I was the visa officer. I did ask him if he knew when Fernando applied and whether it was online. I said something about getting our wires crossed. He said Fernando just told him two weeks ago. Came in all excited to quit his job, said it had cost him lots of money, but he'd found a lawyer who helped him sort out all the confusing paperwork."

Matthew's heart sank. A "lawyer." Right. Probably one of those scammers who masqueraded as immigration consultants and charged hundreds of dollars for fraudulent or inaccurate documents.

"Did he know whether Fernando had already left the country?"

"Well, my good man, for the vague promise of 'My door is always open,' this is all you get. I think it's pretty damn brilliant. I haven't lost my investigative edge, even after two years of sloth."

"And I'm duly impressed. I mean it, Dave. We should get together. Escape that crazy skyscraper hell you call home and come to Canada. We've got wide open spaces, skies that are still blue, lakes you can swim in ..."

"All that clean living. My body couldn't stand the shock! In any case, you can take up the trail from here. The man and his son were winging their way to your clean paradise. You can find out if they got there."

"Can you do me one last favour?"

"Jesus, Goderich! I give you the moon ..."

"Can you email me a photo of this man and his son?"

Amanda stretched languidly, curling her toes and reaching her arms over her head. The sheets were a sweaty tangle scented with musk and sex. She took the coffee Chris held out.

"A girl could definitely get used to this," she murmured.

He chuckled. "Which part?"

"All of it. All of you."

He slipped in beside her, balancing his own coffee. "Kaylee is still reserving judgment."

Amanda propped herself up on her pillows and snapped her fingers at the dog, who eagerly left her perch on the windowsill and jumped up on the bed to snuggle between them.

"We'll make it up to her," she said. "I'm thinking of a hike in Killbear Provincial Park today."

He glanced at her, and his expression of wary hope made her laugh. "Even if I was tempted, there's nothing we can do until Matthew finds out about Danielle's husband." On her bedside table, her cellphone rang. She glanced at it. "Speak of the devil."

"I hope I didn't wake you up," Matthew said, sounding amazingly wide awake for such an early hour.

Amanda cast Chris a mischievous smile. "We're on our morning coffee."

"Okay, good. Did you read the notes I sent you last night?"

"They were very enlightening."

"Well, I've got more."

She listened while he relayed the information from his source in Hong Kong. "They may be on a plane heading over to meet up with her as we speak."

"Part of it jives with what the daughter Kaitlyn said she overheard," Amanda said. "Danielle spoke to someone on the phone a few days before Benson's death." She paused to sip her coffee, savouring the delicious jolt of caffeine. Strong and smoky. This man was definitely a keeper. "Can you use one of your contacts to find out whether they've arrived in Canada?"

Dead silence. Then a chuckle. "Darling, I love you, but do you know how many flights come into Pearson Airport every day? More than a thousand, from dozens of airlines."

"I know. I just thought maybe you had some friends in border services or the police. You seem to be able to pull the most amazing information out of your hat."

"Even I am not that much of a magician." He sighed. "I can just see my epitaph: 'Last seen stationed outside the arrivals gate at Pearson International, clutching a tattered photo of a young Filipino man.'"

"Now you're talking!" she exclaimed. "Seriously, Matthew, I do appreciate all that you've done. At least we know he and Danielle were in touch, and she was intending to meet up with him. So she may have been on her way to the rendezvous when she cracked up the boat, rather than running away from the murder. It gives me some leads I can follow up here."

Chris had gone into the kitchen, where the sizzle and fragrant aroma of butter and eggs arose, but now he returned to stand in the bedroom doorway, scowling.

"Amanda, don't," Matthew said. "Just don't. Much as I hate to say this, just enjoy your time with Chris."

"They're not mutually exclusive."

"Neither are murdering your boss and going to meet your husband."

"I don't like the sound of this," Chris said once she'd reported Matthew's latest news. They had taken their breakfast outside, and, with the help of lavish bug spray, were enjoying another spectacular Georgian Bay morning. A few boats puttered up the channel in the distance, but otherwise the lake was peaceful. "It sounds like they've given up going through legitimate channels. The poor man probably bought a fake visa. He might be turned back before he even gets on the plane."

"It might not be completely fake," she said. "More likely the charlatan sold him a visitor's visa, which to the average Filipino who's never travelled before might look perfectly valid, but it won't let him stay in the country. He needs Confirmation of Permanent Residence, which he can only get after Danielle has her own permanent resident papers and applies to sponsor him. Danielle at least knows that, because she consulted a lawyer. So she knows he's going to be in the country illegally."

"You know how many foreign nationals with expired or incorrect documentation are floating around our country?" Chris asked. "The government doesn't even know, because it doesn't keep track of who has left, but possibly as many as half a million. A lot of them are in Toronto. The government has no resources to police this unless someone reports it. Very likely Danielle and her family will just go into the underground Filipino community, where they can live for years without trouble."

"But what about health care? And school for the son?"

"Fake documents. There's a whole underground economy, and once you're plugged in, there are plenty of employers happy to hire undocumented people because they get hard workers willing to do crap jobs. Plus they don't have to pay decent wages and benefits or conform to labour laws."

"So she will continue to be exploited."

"As long as they stay under the radar, it's probably still better than their life in the Philippines."

Reluctantly, Amanda had to admit he was right. Even apart from the Philippines' lethal war on drugs, she'd seen the desperate working conditions in much of the developing world. The long hours, the near-slave wages, the complete lack of benefits, and the unsafe conditions even for ordinary jobs like factory work. All for pittance in pay. She also knew who benefitted: consumers in the West demanding ever cheaper goods.

Kaylee was ranging over the shoreline chasing the tiny fish that collected in the pools. Amanda watched her idly for a moment, lost in thought, and then looked up to study Franklin Island across the channel. "I wonder where Ronny fits into all this? He and Danielle were obviously close enough that he helped her with the lawyer's appointment and her escape from the island. And I've been thinking about him. He was trying his best to do a good job for me, and he knew his safety standards."

"Amanda, he left you stranded in the middle of a storm!"

She nodded. "I know, and that still makes me mad. But I don't think he would have ditched me unless he had a really compelling reason."

"Even if he did, he could have sent help for you afterward!"

"Unless he thought I could call for help from the top of the hill. He may have been buying him and Danielle time to get to the mainland. Maybe all the way to Toronto."

"You're giving that asshole more credit than he deserves."

She knew he was right but couldn't shake the niggle of worry at her core.

Chris stroked the nape of her neck. "If he helped her travel all the way to Toronto, she'll probably ditch him as soon as her husband shows up. I'll bet he'll turn up back here in a few days, probably with his tail between his legs, depending whether his original motive for helping her was…."

"Lust?"

Chris laughed. "Yeah."

The niggle wouldn't go away. Ronny had plenty of opportunity to send a reassuring word. Even a simple text to his father. "But he needed a boat to get them at least to Parry Sound, where they could catch a bus to Toronto. His father says none of his friends lent him one. George is trying to act cool, but I think he's worried sick."

"More than that, the cops have interviewed all his friends, and no one has heard from him."

"At least that they're admitting to the cops."

Chris grew sober. "Amanda, I know you don't want to admit Danielle might have killed Benson Humphries, but the whole scenario is looking more and more suspicious. Because if she did kill him, then all this other stuff, including Ronny hiding out, makes sense."

She set her cup down and jumped to her feet, startling Kaylee, who raced up the grass with a stick. *Ever the optimist*, Amanda thought as she threw it.

"That's something we can do," she said. "We can look harder for that boat."

CHAPTER ELEVEN

After losing his way in the crescents and twisting streets of Rosedale and stopping to puzzle over his phone GPS several times, Matthew finally stumbled upon the right street. He cruised down it, peering at the brick and stone mansions set discreetly behind leafy trees. The street numbers were often hidden on door transoms, carriage lanterns, or ornate porch pillars. The implicit message seemed to be, *if you don't know where you're going, you have no business being here.*

Number 16 was a gabled red-brick fortress with a two-car garage at the rear and a low brick wall across the front that encased an immaculately trimmed garden. Even the peonies were well behaved. Daddy's little wedding gift. The place looked deserted; the window blinds and curtains were closed tight, and if there were cars, they were parked inside the garage.

The neighbours' houses looked equally unwelcoming. Nearby, a group of professional gardeners was trimming and mulching and fertilizing the budding greenery. They shouted back and forth in a babble of languages, but Matthew doubted he'd have any luck with them even if they spoke English. He parked his car down the block and strolled up the street. Two houses down from Number 16, his luck changed. Behind the Audi in the drive, he spotted a woman kneeling in the rose garden below her bay window. Blonde hair peeked out from her wide-brimmed straw hat, and her oversized rhinestone sunglasses didn't look as if they came from the dollar store. An old, baggy man's shirt covered most of her clothing, but her sandals looked designer issue as well. Her skin was porcelain pale. A cup of coffee sat on the stone step beside her.

He strode up the driveway. "Hello," he said cheerfully. "I'm Matthew Goderich with Associated Press." That had once been true, and he still had an ID to prove it. He gestured in the direction of the Humphries house. "I'm putting together a background piece on Benson Humphries, and I'm trying to verify some information I was given. I hope you can help me."

The woman stood up slowly, wincing as she straightened her knees. Matthew sympathized. He could see now that she wasn't as young as she was aiming for. Grey hair blended with the blonde, and there were deep lines around her lips, which were painted rather imperfectly in bright rose.

She held herself ramrod straight, but a faint scent of alcohol wafted from her. At ten in the morning, what luck! From behind her sunglasses, she appeared to be sizing him up. For the occasion, he had dressed in a tan sports jacket and grey slacks, and he had polished up his black Italian shoes. All knock-offs from the Vietnam street markets, of course, but they did the trick.

"Have you some identification?" she asked in careful private school diction.

He produced his AP card, but before she could examine it too closely, he launched into his spiel. "I understand Dr. Humphries was a respected physician but had personal struggles."

"I have no intention of contributing to baseless gossip."

Matthew nodded his understanding. "Nor do I. That's why I want it verified. I want to ensure the piece is fair and sympathetic. Some of the tabloids are preparing to publish some unsavoury things about him."

She kept her lips pursed shut, but he sensed her wavering. Curiosity drew her forward.

"I'm told in his personal life he had a dark side."

A frown deepened the furrows between her brows. "Who told you that?"

He smiled. "I keep all my sources confidential, I promise you. Is it true he had a violent temper?"

"That's nonsense. Benson was the nicest man you'd ever meet."

"I'm told he was only after his wife's money, and there were violent fights in the house."

"Whoever told you all this is just trying to stir up trouble. Maybe the stepdaughter. I wouldn't put it past her." She studied him shrewdly.

He filed that tidbit away but pretended to be uninterested. "I've also been told Janine is ..." He searched for a neutral-sounding word. "Quite outgoing and loves to host parties."

The woman snorted. The movement unbalanced her, and she reached for the wall to steady herself. "Outgoing is an understatement. Wild is more like it. Always has been."

"Oh, you've known her a long time? Before they moved here?"

"Since she was a little girl. Daddy's little girl. Goodness, he spoiled her. He had her installed on boards and foundations, even though she hardly ever came to meetings. If there was a photo opportunity, she'd be front and centre, but don't expect her to do any work."

"Yet Dr. Humphries must have seen something in her."

"She's a beautiful woman, I'll grant you that, and she could be charming. In the beginning, that charm could be infectious. However, I think recently ..." She chewed her lip as if debating how far to speculate, then shook her head.

He nudged. "The charm was wearing off?"

She wavered. "I think he'd begun to realize he'd made a mistake. But he adored his children. Poor man."

"What do you mean?"

"Nothing. Just, it's a bit of a trap, isn't it?"

A car drove by, and her gaze flicked uneasily to it. Sensing her discomfort, he changed the subject. "The nanny has apparently disappeared. Did you know her?"

Her lips tightened. "Yes, she's been with them a couple of years. Before that they went through nannies like a revolving door. I've heard the rumours, but I can't imagine Danielle had anything to do with Benson's death. He was all that stood between her and Janine."

"What do you mean?"

"Janine wanted a maid, a cook, a housekeeper, and, God knows, probably a personal dresser, too. I'd hear the poor girl up at all hours of the night with the baby and then at six thirty getting the twins breakfast. Janine was raising those twins to be as spoiled as her. They'd order Danielle around, scream at her if their egg was too runny." The woman waved her arms in exasperation. "I think that's one of the reasons Ben was starting to worry."

"Was he thinking of leaving Janine?"

"Oh no, he —" She shook her head and wobbled again. "I didn't mean to give that impression. I've probably said too much. I've been so upset, you see. The poor man. Never mind. I should —" She shook her head again, picked up her coffee, which Matthew suspected was laced with Bailey's, and headed for the door without so much as a nod goodbye.

Despite her abrupt departure, it had been a good haul. Matthew tucked his folder under his arm and continued down the street in search of other neighbours. The file folder was mostly a prop to support his cover story as a reporter. He didn't expect to find anyone else so willing to talk, although Janine had clearly not inspired loyalty in the community, but after wandering aimlessly down a few blocks, he spotted a children's playground tucked beneath majestic, leafy trees. Preschoolers were chasing each other about, clambering on structures and pushing trucks in the sand under the watchful eye of adults. He knew as a man alone he'd be viewed with suspicion in a playground, but he hoped to find some of Janine's friends. If indeed she had any.

Several of the adults appeared to be nannies, however, and one threesome was gathered on a bench under the trees, laughing and looking at their phones. His hopes rose, for they were chattering away in Tagalog. He cooked up another impromptu cover story as he approached.

"Do any of you know Danielle Torres?" he asked. "I called at the house but there's no answer."

Blank stares.

"I'm her lawyer, and we were to get some immigration papers signed today."

More stares, now laced with suspicion.

"Sponsorship papers for her husband and her son."

"She's not here," one of the women said.

"Where is she?"

"She have your number, she will call you."

"But she doesn't know these papers need to be signed today." He brandished his folder for good measure and hoped that none of the women knew the glacial pace of sponsorship applications. There was no such thing as a day's turnaround. More like two years. "Can you get in touch with her for me?"

"I don't know where she is."

Another woman fired off some words in rapid Tagalog, and they both eyed Matthew with even greater suspicion. "My friend says there are no papers. You lie."

He sighed and settled down at the end of the bench. The trio edged away. "Look, I'm not here to cause her trouble. I know there are people who pretend to be lawyers or immigration consultants. They take your money and they cheat you. I think Danielle's husband hired one of those in Manila. I don't know how much money he spent, but I do know the papers are no good. That's why I'm here. To try to get her the right papers. She came to see me in Pointe au Baril."

It was a nice touch. There was another flurry of Tagalog as the women argued, presumably over whether to trust him or not. Finally the first woman, who was older and the unofficial leader, said, "Danielle don't need your help now. Her husband and son, they are already here."

"Oh? Where?"

The second woman interrupted and wagged her finger at him. "No, no, no. They are all fine, sir. You take your papers away. I don't think Danielle ask you."

"She's going away," the first woman said. They argued again and seemed to settle on a story. The older woman waved her hands in a shooing motion. "They all go home. Canada is not good for them."

And with that, they collected up their jackets and strollers and headed across the park toward their charges.

As he made his way back to his car, Matthew pondered his next move. He wasn't convinced Danielle and her family had actually left the country, for it seemed a convenient lie to get him and the authorities off her tail, but the women had let slip a useful tidbit that was probably true. The husband and son were already in Canada. Whatever visa he had bought, it had worked well enough to get him into the country. The husband's next step would be to reunite with Danielle. Where? In Toronto, where they could easily slip underground? Or up in the Georgian Bay area?

Even he as an experienced investigator was no match for the thousands of escape routes they could have taken in Toronto. However, if the husband had travelled to Georgian Bay to connect with Danielle, the trail would be much easier to pick up. As a stranger in Canada, with limited English and even more limited funds, he would probably take the train or bus. That narrowed down the search considerably!

Back at his favourite coffee shop near his apartment, he ordered an espresso with a *pain au chocolat* and booted up his laptop. A quick internet search narrowed down his options even more. Only three trains a week passed through Parry Sound, all of them in the dead of night. By contrast, three buses a day went from Toronto to Parry Sound.

He could start at this end by asking questions at the impossibly busy Toronto bus terminal on Bay Street, but the chances of the husband and son being noticed and remembered were far better at the much smaller station in Parry Sound. He pulled out his phone.

"George was already by yesterday asking the same questions," the marina owner said. Chris and Amanda had been visiting marinas and boat rental places all morning, working their way along the coast, and they were down near the bottom of their list. This one was a tiny, ramshackle operation that offered boats for rent or sale as well as fishing equipment, permits, and guiding services. It was tucked into a narrow inlet south of Parry Sound, and its fleet appeared to be two sorry-looking aluminum runabouts turned upside down on the reedy beach.

"I'll tell you the same," the owner said. Greasy strands of white hair draped his shoulders, and a droopy lip gave him a permanently hangdog look. If he could afford to retire, Amanda suspected he would have ten years ago. "I ain't rented a boat yet this season, not to Ronny or nobody else. But I'm helping George spread the word. George got a lot of respect in these parts, and if he's worried, we all are."

"Has he heard from the police?" Chris asked, waving away the bugs. There was barely a breath of breeze in the marshy inlet, and the mosquitoes and blackflies were ferocious. Amanda was already yearning for the truck.

"Dunno. The police are not Ronny's friends in this. They think Ronny got himself involved in that murder, and he's taken off. Along with the nanny."

"Do you think that's possible?"

He shrugged. "Ronny's a good kid. Big heart. Gets that from his dad. But when it comes to pretty women ..."

After thanking him, Chris and Amanda climbed back into the truck. Despite their best efforts, a dozen insects followed them inside.

"I don't like the sound of this," Amanda said as Chris navigated the truck over the potholes. "I think Ronny has been set up to be the fall guy. Everyone says he's got a big heart but a weak spot for women."

"He's a big boy, Amanda. Don't underestimate him."

"I'm not! He's been a jerk. But he's naive. Living up here, what does he know about the illegal underground world? Once Danielle connects with her husband and son and she doesn't need him any more, she'll cut him loose. She'll disappear and he'll be the one left facing all the questions."

He glanced at her. "I thought you believed she was innocent, too?"

Amanda sifted through her feelings. "But she was up to something. We know that from the phone call that Kaitlyn overheard a few days earlier."

"And the documents she stole from the murder scene."

Amanda focussed in on a mosquito to deliver a carefully aimed swat. In that instant, her phone rang and the mosquito flitted away.

"Amanda!" Matthew sounded excited. "Any word up there?"

"No. We've been looking for the boat Ronny and Danielle must have used to get off Franklin Island."

"There's been a new development. I've been snooping around Rosedale, where apparently Benson was next to sainthood but Janine is more like Marie Antoinette. As in 'let them eat cake.'"

Amanda laughed. "That's more or less the same verdict up here."

"She treated the nanny like her own personal servant —"

"Slave?"

"Close. Anyway, Danielle's nanny friends are a protective bunch who close ranks against outsiders, even a nice, helpful guy like me, but they did let slip that the husband and son are already in Canada."

"Oh, dear."

"That's not official confirmation, but I'm thinking one step ahead. If they're going to reunite with Danielle, it's going to be by bus. Either they take the bus up to Parry Sound or she takes the bus from Parry Sound to Toronto."

Amanda was tempted to interject. There were numerous other, equally plausible choices besides those two. If Ronny and Danielle had a boat, they could head straight down the bay toward larger towns such as Collingwood or Midland at the south end. In fact, by heading west into Lake Huron, they could get all the way to the United States.

But she sensed Matthew had a proposal to make, and since they couldn't cover every possibility between here and Michigan, they might as well start somewhere.

"The police hunt is on for her up here," she said. "It would make way more sense for them to disappear in the big city."

"But it would be much easier for us to find them in Parry Sound. I'm on my way to the Bay Street bus station now, but you know it will be a zoo. Dozens of buses and potentially hundreds of passengers."

Amanda took aim at the mosquito again. "I'm pretty sure the cops have already canvassed up in Parry Sound."

"For her and Ronny, yeah. But not for the husband and son. I'm sending you their photos. If you ask up there and I ask down here, maybe we'll get to the bottom of this mystery."

She chuckled. He sounded like the old Matthew she had known years ago. "You're enjoying this, aren't you?"

"I'm trying to help you out, Amanda." He sounded hurt.

"And it's a good story."

"It's an *important* story. Abuse of temporary foreign workers, the impossible roadblocks they face trying to get permanent residence, the desperate decision to go illegal. Oh, and in this case, the terrified escape from Duterte's killing squads."

She sobered. He was right. She had been so focussed on the minutiae of the case — on Danielle's phone call, her deception of Ronny, and her role in her employer's death — that she'd forgotten the bigger picture. That desperate people were forced to make desperate choices.

And that much of the world was desperate.

When Matthew sent the photos, she sat for a moment studying their faces on her phone's small screen. The husband's photo was his passport headshot. Despite his sombre expression, Amanda could see a sparkle in his dark, slanted eyes and a wide, generous set to his mouth. He had a sweep of thick black hair that added a rakish air. An attractive man, she thought. He was listed as five feet, six inches and one hundred and forty pounds;

a small, delicate man like his wife.

The little boy grinned out at her from his photo, his black eyes twinkling like his father's and two mischievous dimples framing his smile. Black hair curled around his ears. He looked like a child well loved, yet he was growing up without his mother while she worked to make a decent living for them thousands of kilometres away.

Amanda smiled. The hunt had become personal again. These two were about to be swallowed up by the underground of illegals, fugitives through no real fault of their own. Always on guard, denied access to the services and benefits Canadians took for granted, and forced into the lowest paid, poorly regulated, under-the-table jobs.

"Turn around, Watson," she said. "We have a new assignment."

CHAPTER TWELVE

The Parry Sound bus terminal was in Richard's Coffee in the commercial outskirts of town just off the main highway. The parking lot was busy, but inside, the only customers were a table of retired old-timers who looked like regulars. The server flashed Chris and Amanda a broad, welcoming smile as they stepped up to the counter. Her thick, straight, black hair was stylishly cut into a bob that swished as she moved, and a row of silver earrings curled around her ears. Her high cheekbones and deep chocolate eyes suggested Indigenous heritage.

Amanda scanned the menu board of breakfast sandwiches and lunch specials. "Way past breakfast," she said, glancing at the clock overhead. "Let's grab some lunch."

The so-called bus terminal was a wicket adjacent to the serving counter. When Amanda wandered over, the same server glanced over from assembling their order.

"Can I help you?"

"Is it possible to talk to someone who works in the bus terminal?"

She laughed. "That would be me. Do you want to buy a ticket?"

"No, we want to ask about a couple of passengers."

A wary frown flitted across her face.

"It's about the death up near Pointe au Baril," Amanda added.

"Are you cops?"

"I'm RCMP, but off-duty," Chris said reassuringly. "Just following up."

Amanda hid a smile. How quickly her straight-as-an-arrow cop was slipping into the spirit of things. "We'll take our food to the table, and when you have a moment to chat, come on over."

Chris and Amanda were halfway through their soups and grilled cheese sandwiches when the waitress finally flounced down beside them. Her nametag said "Lily." She looked to be in her midtwenties, compact and muscular from all the miles she put in at the restaurant.

"I don't know what I can tell you. The OPP already came by twice, and George Gifford too, asking about Ronny and the woman. I didn't see them, and Rena didn't either — she works the other shift. But if they bought their tickets online, they could have got on the bus outside, and I'd never have seen them." She paused. "That's what I would have done."

Chris nodded. He was grinning, and Amanda could see him turning on the folksy charm. "This soup is amazing."

Lily beamed. "We've been number one on TripAdvisor. We get repeat customers all the time. Folks on their way to Sudbury get off the highway just to eat here."

"Is that right? We're actually interested in another man who might have gotten off here from Toronto in the past few days. He would have had a young boy with him."

When Amanda showed her the photographs, her face lit up. "Oh yeah, I remember them! The kid was crying, so I gave him an extra special big chocolate chip cookie." She laughed. "He was still eating it when they left."

"What day was this?"

She frowned. "One day pretty much blurs into another, you

know? It was the two twenty, that much I remember. Saturday, maybe?"

Amanda did a quick calculation. Saturday was the day Ronny and Danielle disappeared and the day after Benson Humphries's murder.

"Could have been Sunday, though."

"Did you talk to them?"

Lily shook her head. "They didn't ... at least, the little boy didn't seem to speak English." Her eyes widened in comprehension. "Oh, wow! Do you think they're related to that nanny? They looked kinda Asian."

Chris stepped in. "Did you see where they went?"

"Yeah, well, they were with Larry. Came in with him to grab some food for the ride."

"What ride?"

"They went off in his truck. Larry's, I mean. He was on the bus, too."

"Do you know where Larry lives?"

"Just outside the Shawanaga reserve, that's north of here. Maybe half an hour?"

"Does Larry have a last name?"

"Yeah, Judge, but you don't need it. Everyone knows Larry. His place is on the road going into the village. He's a fishing guide. Just look for the place that has boats and engines and trailers all over the yard."

Kaylee was clearly disappointed that they were on the move again with nothing but a short pee break on the nearest patch of scrubby grass. She balanced between them on the truck console, her long tongue lolling with excitement as they followed the winding road. Trees and rocks meant an off-leash run.

Shortly after leaving, Chris pulled off the road and took out his phone. "We probably should have George with us for this. People know him and trust him, and in the country that goes a long way."

From her years overseas, Amanda knew exactly what he was saying. The RCMP had no such trust, particularly among the First Nations. Chris gave George only the briefest explanation, but it was enough to galvanize the worried man to action, because when Amanda and Chris arrived at the grey clapboard bungalow near the village, George's truck was already parked outside and he was sitting on the porch with half a dozen locals.

"This is Larry," he said, gesturing to a massive, battered man with a huge belly and hands the size of dinner plates. They were gnarled and scarred by years of work, and when he reached forward to offer Amanda his hand, she noticed one of his fingers was missing.

"Now what's this about?" His voice was honeyed with age and surprisingly soft for a man his size.

Amanda held out her phone. "I understand you gave this man and his son a lift from the bus station last Saturday."

Larry's face shuttered, and he took a step backward.

"You're not in trouble, Larry," George said. "We're just trying to find Ronny, that's all."

"Yeah, I did. He was a stranger in these parts, didn't know the area. I figured I'd help him out."

"Where did you take him?"

Larry looked surprised. "Here. The man wanted a boat. Said he was supposed to get one." He gestured toward his front yard, cluttered with canoes and boats, some painted bright turquoise. "I rent them out sometimes."

George barrelled in, impatient with excitement. "You rented them a boat? Where did they go?"

Larry shrugged. "I took them down to the landing. He asked the way out to Franklin Island, so I gave him a map. I told him stick to the channel markers, warned him it was easy to get lost. And he wasn't a very good skipper. Drove too fast near the shoals. I saw him racing down toward Parry Sound later in the day."

"What time was that?" George demanded.

Larry squinted. "Don't pay much attention to time. Maybe five o'clock? I was down near Killbear, too far away to be sure, but it looked like my boat. Painted them all turquoise last summer."

"I saw that boat!" George exclaimed. "I remember the child in the bow with a woman. But I didn't think … I didn't connect … I thought they were a family from the reserve."

Larry grunted. He didn't say anything, but Amanda guessed what he was thinking; to a white person, all brown people looked alike. "No, it was this guy. Ripped me off, too. Said he only needed the boat for the day, paid cash. He never brought it back."

"Now I'm really worried," Amanda said as they headed back up the road. George had said there was a woman in the boat but not Ronny, and immediately upon learning the news about the Filipinos, he had raced for his truck.

"Time to light a fire under the OPP's ass," he'd shouted as he peeled out of the Larry's yard.

"Let's go back to Franklin Island," she said. "Start from where we know Ronny was last."

Chris shot her a quick glance as he wrestled the truck down the road. "That would take up our whole afternoon. Besides, the cops have already searched the island."

"I know, but maybe they missed something."

He didn't answer, but she could tell by the set of his jaw that he was annoyed. He maintained his silence through the rest of the trip back to their cabin, where she began to change into shorts, T-shirt, and sunhat. Chris opened a beer and retreated to sit outside and toss the ball for Kaylee.

Amanda came outside with life jackets for her and Kaylee hooked over her arm. "I can go without you if you prefer."

"I know you can." He twirled his beer and swung on her. "This is what I mean, Amanda. You just can't let these things go, can you?"

A retort was on the tip of her tongue, but she checked it. He was right; she couldn't let things go. Not when someone she knew could be in trouble. Ronny had been a jerk, but something was wrong.

"It's bad enough you think all cops are incompetent —"

"I don't —"

"But this was supposed to be our holiday. Planning your trip, enjoying this amazing countryside." He paused. Looked away. "Getting closer."

"And we have been doing that." She fought her irritation. He was right on all counts, and she had to learn to control her obsession. She had to learn she couldn't fix everything.

"Barely," he muttered.

She walked over, ran her fingers through his short, fuzzy hair, and kissed the top of his head. "Can I make you a deal?"

"It had better be good."

"We have those trout filets in the freezer. We could pack them up with salad, asparagus, and wild rice, and take the kayaks over to Franklin Island. Barbeque, sunset on the beach, tent under the stars …" She nibbled his earlobe. "Sound like a good deal?"

He chuckled. "Keep going."

"Well, imagine …"

"And when do we fit in the search for clues about Ronny?"

She smiled. Even she was getting into the spirit of the evening. "In the morning."

He caught her hand. "Promise?"

She nodded.

"Deal."

The wind had died down to a ruffling breeze by the time they launched their packed kayaks into the water. They dug their paddles in to power over the open channel to the island and then enjoyed a more leisurely meander around the tip to the western side, dodging rocks and tiny islands. Chris led the way, and Kaylee, from her perch on the front deck of Amanda's kayak, kept a sharp eye out for wildlife. Amanda searched the shoreline for signs of Ronny. Anything. A backpack, a pair of flipflops, the ashes of an old fire.

The island was deserted.

Amanda was tired and hungry by the time Chris signalled that they had reached the bay where Ronny and Danielle had stashed their kayaks. Sunset burnished the rocks a brilliant pink. The kayaks had been removed, presumably as evidence by the police. She was grateful for the long, warm solstice evening that allowed them to cook at nine o'clock at night while the sun painted sky and water in extraordinary swirls of coral and mauve.

As the sky grew dark, they sat under the blanket of stars, picking out constellations and meteor showers. The call of distant whippoorwills drifted across the water. Afterward, they passed a luscious, playful night in the little tent, but worries crept back over her in the morning, waking her just after dawn. She leashed Kaylee, pulled on her bug shirt against the morning assault, and leaned over to kiss Chris.

"I'm just taking Kaylee for a pee. If you get up, coffee would be nice."

She intended to explore only a short distance to clear her head, stretch the kinks out of her body, and exercise Kaylee, but the morning was magical. Birdsong filled the air. Mist rose in tendrils off the lake and clung in shreds to the trees farther inland. To the east, the sky was a rosy blush through the trees. Outraged crows cawed and flapped in the pines as they passed beneath.

She and Kaylee walked inland along the path over rocky knolls, around ponds, and through scrubby pine. Dew shimmered on the slender tips of grass, soaking her shoes, and the air had the loamy, faintly fetid scent of marshy woodland. She became lost in time and was surprised when she came upon a large inland lake. Its flat granite shore invited swimming. She remembered Ronny mentioning it as one of the activities her group might enjoy. She could still hear his excitement and see his gap-toothed grin. The purest, most pristine water on the planet, he'd said. He was so proud of his home.

She stood on the granite shore, sweaty and hot from her hike. Kaylee tugged on her leash, whining softly and lifting her nose in the air.

"You want a swim, girl?"

Kaylee whipped her head around, and Amanda leaned down to unsnap the leash. "Let's do it. But no rattlesnakes, you hear?"

Kaylee took off along the shore while Amanda stripped off her clothes and stepped into the water. The cold snatched her breath away. *Do I really want this?* she asked. But the mosquitoes, delighted by the banquet of bare flesh, descended en masse, forcing her to plunge in. She gasped and flailed as she waited for her body to adjust. Gradually she eased up and began a slow, sensuous breaststroke out into the lake. The water flowed like silk over her bare skin. Heaven.

In the distance, Kaylee barked. Amanda scanned the shoreline, but there was no sign of her. "Chris?" she called.

Another bark. A whine. More barking. *Don't you dare find a bear or porcupine*, Amanda thought as she scrambled out of the water. *Or worse, a snake.* She yanked some clothes over her wet body as she raced in the direction of the sound.

Around a bend in the lake, up a steep ridge, and onto a well-worn trail, a whiff of decay reached her nostrils. Kaylee was barely visible at the bottom of the ridge on the other side, but Amanda could hear her whining.

"Kaylee!" she shouted. "Leave it! Come!"

The dog glanced up but didn't come. Overhead, crows flapped and cawed.

"Damn it, don't you dare," Amanda shouted as she plunged down the steep slope. The stench of decay grew stronger, and she noticed the hum of buzzing flies. At the bottom of the slope, Kaylee was rummaging in a pile of branches jumbled and tossed about.

Amanda's breath froze. She rushed forward, pushed the dog away, and lifted the top branch. Then another, and another, until a stockinged foot poked through.

Oh no. No, no, no. She waved the flies away and tore at the clumps of moss and reeds that lay beneath, whimpering with panic and horror, until Ronny was exposed, laid out on his back with his hiking boots set neatly at his side, his arms folded, and a makeshift wooden cross placed over his chest.

CHAPTER THIRTEEN

After hanging up, Chris walked back to Amanda, who sat on a rock at the top of the ridge, gripping Kaylee's leash and fighting the nausea that surged from the pit of her stomach.

"They're sending police Zodiacs up from Parry Sound," he said as he pointed to the slope of lichen-crusted granite rising to the east. "They'll land in a small bay just to the other side of that hill, and the cops will hike in."

Her teeth chattered. "When?"

"Half an hour or so for the first responders. Meanwhile, they said don't touch anything or disturb the scene."

"Disturb the scene?" She glanced around at the leafy forest floor and the rain-washed rocks. "The cops have already been trooping through here. George too. Why didn't they find him?" The image of Ronny's partially buried face was seared into her memory. Puffy and green, crawling with flies and maggots, torn off in strips by the creatures of the forest. "Poor kid. How long do you think he's been dead?"

Chris looked down the slope toward the body. "The maggots have got a good start, and it's beginning to bloat, so four or five days. The forensics guys will be able to pinpoint it, but my guess is he died the day he left you. It looks like the killers tried to bury him, but they obviously didn't know much about burying remains in the wild. The crows, foxes, and other scavengers will scatter the body all over the place."

She shuddered, loath to face the obvious: that the killers were almost certainly Danielle and her husband. She rose and slithered partway down the slope for a closer look, oblivious to the branches whipping her legs.

"Amanda, don't. We're supposed to sit tight."

"I can't just sit tight. It's better if I ..." *Keep busy*, she added silently. *Find a problem and focus on solving it.* "I won't go close. I just want to see how he died."

Ignoring the damage the animals and the passage of time had done to what had once been a handsome young face, she studied his body from afar. There were bloody scratches on his arms and legs, but they were superficial and hardly lethal. Pressing her shirt to her mouth and nose against the stench, she squinted at the maggots seething on his head, noticing details she had failed to see in her initial horror.

A deep, ragged gash ran the length of his left temple. She looked up the steep hill. Could he have slipped on the wet ground, fallen down the hill, and hit his head on some rocks? Could he have been pushed? Or had this been a violent blow delivered with the intent to kill? She scanned the ground around him.

"Amanda ..."

"If he was killed here, there might be signs. A scuffle, gouges, a sharp rock, or the murder weapon."

"Which the police will find, and they have the evidence kits and protective gear to do the job right. If you contaminate the scene, you might ruin all chance of bringing the killer to justice."

Reluctantly, she retraced her steps up the slope. She knew he was right despite his linear, cop-like thinking. It was that approach that had failed Ronny in the first place and left him rotting in the bush for days while the police searched airports and issued nationwide warrants.

As if he understood her mood, he softened and drew her into his arms. "I know it's terrible," he whispered.

She let herself relax against his chest, not trusting herself to speak.

"We should go to meet the cops so we can show them the way," he said eventually.

She drew back and tilted her head to look into his eyes. "You go. I want to stay with him to keep the crows away."

He said nothing, but his gaze flickered.

"I'll sit tight, I promise. But I feel ... it's the least I can do for him."

He kissed her forehead, and she watched as he headed up the trail. Once he was out of sight, she glanced around. The misty, idyllic morning was gone. Dark shadows and menace had stolen in. The hoarse cries of the crows were full of threat, and the tendrils of fog coiled ghostlike along the forest floor. At the periphery of her mind, the old memories massed. She shivered and half rose to follow Chris.

Keep busy, she told herself, focussing on the terrain near the body. Everywhere were signs of disturbance — branches broken off, small shrubs uprooted, and moss ripped up — damage likely caused by their efforts to bury him. It was impossible to tell whether a deadly fight had happened here too.

Standing on the trail, she tried to put herself into their shoes. The small bay where the police boat was going to land was only a short distance due east. If Ronny and Danielle had been crossing the island to get to the mainland side, as she and Chris surmised, they would likely have been heading along the trail to the same bay, which Ronny would have known well. But the trail ran along the top of the ridge as it skirted the lake rather than coming down into the dense brush where the body lay.

Perhaps up here, somewhere along the top of the ridge, was where Ronny had died.

She put Kaylee on her leash, retrieved her walking stick, and picked her way along the edge of the rocky trail. She wasn't sure what she was looking for — a blunt weapon, a loose slide of rock, gouges in the slope — but she kept a close eye on Kaylee as she went. The dog, with her infinitely better sense of smell, might detect something Amanda couldn't, like traces of blood or residue of human contact.

Amanda didn't plan to go far. She reasoned that the fight or attack would have been close to the burial site, because it would have been extremely difficult to move the body any distance through the densely wooded terrain.

She had made it only a few yards when a scrap of red caught her eye, snagged on a jagged spur of rock at the edge of the trail. She bent for a closer look. Red cloth. The same red as the shirt Ronny had been wearing. Her heart hammered as she backed away and scanned the ground for more signs. Now, with her newly tuned eye, she spotted small scuffs, overturned stones, and broken branches at the edge of the trail.

Had Ronny been dragged along here? The path had probably been disturbed by numerous feet since the killing; she and Chris had been along it, as had George and the police. Nonetheless, in order to minimize disturbance, she continued on tiptoe along the edge. Kaylee snuffled the ground intently, pausing to bury her nose in an interesting scent. Amanda pulled her away. If the dog detected traces of blood, the forensics cops would not appreciate her nose print in the middle of sensitive evidence.

A few yards farther on, Kaylee swerved abruptly off the trail. The low-lying shrubs and forest mulch looked untouched, but Kaylee plunged her nose into the middle of a bush.

"Wait!" Amanda yanked her back in case the murder weapon or some piece of key evidence had been tossed into the bushes. Or a snake lurked there.

Carefully, she parted the shrub with her walking stick and peered down. There, nestled in the deep leaves, was a small, rectangular shape. She knew she should leave it for the cops, but curiosity got the better of her. Just a quick peek.

Covering her hand with her sleeve, she used two fingers to fish out the object. A cellphone. She recognized the clear, waterproof case. Ronny's cellphone.

Chris is going to kill me, she thought. But what if Ronny left any last-minute clues that could explain what happened to him? Any texts, messages, or phone calls? If she was really careful, she could check without contaminating evidence.

She knew she didn't have much time. The police would be arriving any moment, and she would have to turn the phone over to them.

To prevent fingerprints, she laid the phone on the ground and turned it on, relieved to see the screen light up. Four days in the bush, a torrential rainstorm, and the battery still functioned. Even better, Ronny hadn't bothered to activate the password lock function.

She bent over it to check his text messages. Nothing but a series of incoming texts from his father, demanding to know where he was. She tapped his browser and was surprised when it opened to a Flickr page of photos by H.B. Humphries labelled "Springtime on the Bay." Odd that the last thing Ronny had searched on the internet was an album of photos taken by a dead man.

Why?

Quickly, she typed the link on her own phone — Chris was absolutely going to kill her — before moving on to his phone calls. Ronny had received a phone call from someone that first night of their camping trip. Who?

When she accessed the list of recent phone calls, she was astonished to see he had made two calls on May 22. That was the day he'd died! The last was at 2:16 p.m., which, if her and Chris's calculations were correct, was only a short time before.

She copied the two numbers into her phone. She would check them out as soon as she had more time. The next number was an incoming call the previous night at 12:31 a.m. That would have been the mystery call he hadn't wanted her to overhear. She entered that number in her contacts list as well. Scrolling back through the phone calls, she saw this same number repeated five more times over the past two weeks, but not earlier. The number had no name attached, so she would have to do more sleuthing to uncover who the caller was. But she had a strong suspicion: Danielle Torres.

Danielle would have probably arrived at the summer home within the past two weeks, and Amanda knew she'd connected with Ronny at least once to set up the lawyer visit in Pointe au Baril. The first call had originated two weeks ago, followed by four calls during the week before Benson died.

Plenty of time for them to have set something up, but what? Her escape or Benson's murder?

Gingerly, she parted the shrubs and set the phone back into the nest of leaves exactly where she'd found it before stepping back to study the surrounding brush. Several branches were broken, and one small shrub was flattened. Something violent had occurred here. A fight? An assault? Had the phone slipped out of Ronny's pocket, unnoticed by his assailant, or had he tossed it into the bushes in a last-ditch effort to send a message?

The path was full of jagged rocks that he could have fallen on, but the ferocious rain had washed away all visible traces of blood. Only Kaylee's keen interest in the ground suggested there might be traces of human residue.

She retreated along the trail toward the lake, peeking under bushes and ground cover in the hopes of finding more clues. About fifteen feet farther, Kaylee lifted her head sharply and stared over a steep drop at the edge of the trail. The cliff was almost vertical, falling away to thick brush about ten feet below. Kaylee's nose twitched. It could be anything — a chipmunk, a vole, even a rattlesnake — but Amanda had learned to trust her dog's senses. Keeping a tight rein on the dog and a close eye out for snakes, she circled farther over to avoid disturbing the scene, and worked her way back toward the base of the cliff.

Thick shrubs and grasses grew in the loamy soil. Even with the insect repellent, mosquitoes and blackflies swarmed around her in delight. Flailing at them with one hand, she used the other to part the leafy canopy with her stick as she walked. Was this a fool's errand? Had the dog found some dead animal or other treasure?

Up ahead, in the shadow of the granite cliff face, she spotted broken branches and flattened grass. In the centre, a lichen-crusted rock protruded through the grass. Sunlight dappled the lichen, and flecks of iridescence glinted in the cracks. What was it? Dew? She peered closer. Her pulse spiked. No, not dew. Not clear.

Rust red.

The drone of an engine penetrated her focus. The police were nearly there. She scrambled back toward the trail. She had mere minutes to get back to the body, but before she did that, she wanted to phone the last number Ronny had called just before he died. Once word got out that he was dead, she would lose the element of surprise.

The engine stopped, and shreds of male voices drifted on the breeze. Fending off the bugs, she pulled out her phone.

It rang a long time, and Amanda was just beginning to wonder whether the owner was screening unknown numbers when the call was picked up. After a few seconds of ragged breathing, a harried woman's voice came over the line.

"Who is this?"

Amanda analyzed the voice. Familiar. Where had she heard it? "Hello, it's Amanda Doucette."

"Who?"

The voice was sharper now. More impatient. More imperious. Janine! "Amanda Doucette, Janine. I was at the cottage yesterday with your sister."

"What the hell? Why are you calling me? Candy's not with me!"

Amanda scrambled for a credible cover story. "I'm calling about Ronny. We're very worried about him. He's disappeared, and we can't find him anywhere."

"Ronny's a big boy." Her voice chilled, and Amanda noticed she hadn't even asked who Ronny was.

"He hasn't even called his father. But I know he called you a few days ago. I'm hoping he told you where he was going." She held her breath. If Janine asked her how she knew about the phone call, she'd have no plausible explanation.

Fortunately, Janine was not functioning on all cylinders. Lack of sleep, sedatives, or simple grief? After a long pause she came back on the line, her voice low and sad. "He just called to say he was sorry about Benson. He didn't say where he was."

"But how did he find out? Your husband's name hadn't been released back then."

"Well, I imagine straight from the horse's mouth — that nanny he's run off with. And if I had any clue where the two of them are, trust me, the cops would be the first to know."

The line went dead. Janine had hung up. Her bitterness had sounded sufficiently raw that Amanda suspected she was telling the truth about Ronny's disappearance. Unless she was an Oscar-calibre actress, Janine did not know that Ronny was dead. But Amanda was less sure about her claim that Ronny had phoned to offer condolences. She replayed the fateful afternoon's scenario. Ronny and Danielle were hiking across the island, presumably en route to a rendezvous with Danielle's husband and child. Why would Ronny stop in the middle of that hike to make a simple condolence call? That made no sense.

When she and Ronny had rescued Danielle from the lake, she had been nearly incoherent, but she'd made no mention of Benson's death. It's possible that she told Ronny during their hike across Franklin Island, but that was still hardly the time for a condolence call. What made much more sense, Amanda thought as she spotted Chris and the police contingent striding over the rise, was that Ronny was puzzled by Danielle's panic and her refusal to involve police, and he'd called Janine to find out what had happened at the mansion. After all, Janine and he were long-time, albeit estranged friends.

But that raised more questions. Had Janine told him about Benson? About the nanny's involvement in his death? If so, was that the reason he'd had to die?

Amanda pulled the blanket tighter and snuggled more deeply into the crook of Chris's arm. "I have a confession to make," she murmured.

"Mmmm?" He kissed the top of her head, but his voice had a wary edge.

They were curled up on the sofa in their rental cabin, wrapped in blankets against the evening chill off the bay. Two tumblers of the finest single malt the Parry Sound LCBO had to offer sat on the coffee table, and a fire roared in the wood stove.

It had been a long day with the police while they waited to be questioned and Amanda showed them the phone and the possible bloodstain she had found. Once the police had finally let them go, they had to retrieve their kayaks and paddle back to the mainland. The effort had demanded every last ounce of her energy. Back in their cabin, it had taken her more than an hour and two shots of Scotch to finally stop shivering.

"Ronny's phone …" she began.

He waited.

"I looked at it before I put it back."

Still he waited.

"But I put it back exactly as I found it."

Silence, but she felt him draw away ever so slightly.

"I was looking for clues."

"Spit it out," he said finally. She told him about the phone call she had made to Janine and Janine's implausible explanation.

"The police are going to find out you handled his phone and called an important witness, and they're going to be pissed."

"Not necessarily. Since Janine lied to me, she may not want the conversation revealed."

"The cops will find out. They'll be looking at phone records."

She felt his suppressed anger, but she steeled herself to continue. She needed him to know what she had discovered. "I know you're mad, but this is important. Ronny was looking at photos taken by H.B. Humphries on Flickr. I assume the B is Benson. I didn't look at them, but I copied the link, just in case."

She could see that despite his disapproval, she had piqued his curiosity. The wary frown eased as he leaned toward her. "Photos. That's strange."

"Shall we check them out?"

She set her laptop on her lap and accessed the collection labelled "Springtime on the Bay." The collection had been created only a week before his death but already contained over a hundred photos.

Chris tilted his head to see more clearly and ran his finger along the sidebar. "It looks like he's got a whole bunch of collections, dating back four years and mostly of Georgian Bay. So it's possible Ronny's just been following his photos for years."

She shot him a skeptical look. "Uh-huh. And just happened to look at them as he was rushing across the island." She clicked on the latest collection and watched rows of thumbnails fill the screen. She scrolled through them, entranced. Close-ups of dewdrops shimmering on leaf buds, a chickadee at the feeder, a lone kayak heading out into the bay. Sweeps of granite shore, silhouettes of ragged pines, reflections of cloud on a glass lake.

The photos captured the many moods of the bay, from dark, sulky clouds, swollen creeks, and angry whitecaps to the serene reflections of sky and fresh-leafed shore. "What an artist's eye!" she exclaimed.

"He wasn't big on people," Chris observed.

"This was his relaxation. Maybe he got enough human drama at the hospital."

As if to defy them, a series of candid family shots came onto the screen. Danielle playing hide-and-seek with the twins and picking up pebbles on the beach with the baby, Janine on the deck painting her toenails. Photos of workers balanced on ladders, raking the gardens, and trimming deadwood.

"Did you see any of these guys?" Chris asked.

She nodded. "Ronny and I saw them when we went by in the boat, but they were all gone when Candace brought me to the island."

Chris nodded. "The cops would have shut down all work, taken statements, and sent everyone home."

"Janine and Benson were having a cottage opening party, so they brought in staff from Toronto." She cocked her head. "Ronny wasn't pleased. There are lots of local people needing work."

The next photo was of Danielle standing at the bottom of a ladder, steadying it and looking up at a young man removing an old bird's nest from the eaves. "Looks like they had their nanny doing double duty on yard clean-up," Chris said.

Amanda studied Danielle's face, which was tilted up into the sun. She looked amused rather than angry. The next photo was a close-up of the two of them standing in the shelter of the cottage wall, their heads bent toward each other as if in intent conversation. In this photo Danielle did look angry and the young worker thoughtful. One of his hands rested lightly on her shoulder.

Amanda sucked in her breath. "Omigod! Do you suppose Danielle had an accomplice?"

"This photo was taken with a telephoto lens," Chris said. "Not unusual for a nature photographer, but it makes you wonder if he was deliberately spying." He enlarged the photo with his fingers. "Did you see this man at all?"

She studied the close-up. The man was wearing a Blue Jays baseball cap and sunglasses. He looked small, compact, and dark-haired, but much of his face was in shadow. "Certainly not her husband. I think he was the guy working on the dock."

"What was she up to? And I wonder when this photo was taken."

"Probably shortly before his death. We know they had only been at the cottage for two weeks." She tapped the photo. "We have to find out who this guy is."

"The police will be on it, Amanda. They'll be checking out all the workers."

"But they might not know there was a secret relationship between him and Danielle. Maybe no one knew."

"Except the dead man."

A knock on the door startled them both. Chris opened it to find George standing on the doorstep, ragged and limp. He managed to utter one word, "Fuck," before Chris grabbed his arm and drew him inside.

"You need a strong drink, my man."

CHAPTER FOURTEEN

Three drinks later, slumped on the sofa, George began to talk. "There's only ever been the two of us for near thirty years. His mother died when he was a baby — a snowmobile accident — and I ... well, I wanted to keep things simple after that. Maybe a mistake, since Ronny chased everything in a skirt. Might have been what got him killed."

"For what it's worth, George," Amanda said, "I think Ronny was killed because he was trying to help. Maybe he trusted someone a bit too much, that's all."

"Yeah, well, that was Ronny. Never saw the bad in people. Got himself used more times than I can count." George shook his head as he took a sip of Scotch, spilling some down his shirt without seeming to notice. Or care. "Not by the local people. Growing up, every woman around took a turn at mothering him, and I was happy to let them do it. Maybe that's why he grew up without the sense to say no to them."

Amanda laid a hand on George's arm. She felt him flinch as if the tenderness hurt. "You can never love a child too much."

He stared into his drink. "I never strapped him, you know? Not even in his wild years with the band, the parties and drugs, the fast cars. The girls. People thought I didn't care about those things, but I did. His mother died driving her snowmobile too fast. I lectured her till I was blue in the face, and all it did was make her go faster. Maybe if I'd ..." He took another sip. "People do what they're going to do, right?"

His hands shook so much that Amanda suspected he was only a few sips away from total emotional collapse. She moved to avert it. "What was there between him and Janine Saint Clair?"

"Well, those were the people that used him, eh? The summer people? They'd hire him to play at their dances and teach their kids kayaking. They even all played together at the club as kids. But he was never one of them. Not when it came to fancy parties or sleepovers or invites to the city. Especially when he got to be a good-looking lad with a charm the daddies didn't like." He slammed his glass down and struggled to his feet. "I'm sorry, didn't mean that. Duncan Saint Clair was a decent man, always supported the community. He was just blind where his girls were concerned."

Chris blocked his wavering path toward the door. "George, you're in no shape to drive home."

"Gotta go home in case the police have news."

"They have your cellphone number. I'm going to fix you up in the spare bedroom."

George lurched forward. "I should go home."

Amanda threw subtlety out the window. "Did the police tell you Ronny phoned Janine the day he died?"

George clutched the doorframe. Blinked. "He hasn't spoken to her in years."

"Why not?"

"You don't need to know that. Chris, where's that bed? I need to lie down."

He collapsed across the spare bed before Chris could even lay a sheet over it. Chris pulled off his boots, drew a blanket up, and cracked open the window for some fresh air.

It was the next morning before he emerged, red-eyed and slack-jawed, and headed for the bathroom. Five minutes later, purged and shaky, he sank into a rickety chair at the kitchen table and accepted the cup of coffee Amanda poured him.

"He got her pregnant. At least he thought it was his. She said it wasn't. But the dates fit. It all fit. And when I look at Kaitlyn, more and more as she grows up, I see Ronny's mother in her. But ..." He shrugged, wincing as pain shot through his head. "The Saint Clairs banded together, said it wasn't his, lawyered up, and refused to even let him near the kid. That's what I can't forgive that bitch for. He wasn't trying to shake them down, he didn't want their money, and he sure as hell didn't want Janine! But he was excited to have a daughter. Every summer he watched her grow up, worried if she seemed too moody, too alone, too wild. He would have loved to teach her things. Kids love Ronny, and it would have done no harm."

The sound of sizzling butter filled the silence as Chris tossed eggs into a frying pan. Both he and Amanda said nothing as George gripped his coffee in two hands and took a shaky sip.

"So there. That's the story you didn't need to know. Except maybe it explains why he fell for Danielle's sob story. He knew what the Saint Clairs were capable of. And the chance for a little payback would be nice too."

"Does Kaitlyn know?"

George shrugged and looked with dismay at the scrambled eggs Chris put before him. "Who knows what story they fed her? But she's a smart young lady. And rumours around here never die. But I'll tell you something. The time for the Saint Clairs to run the show is over. I've lost my son. Now, by God, I'm going to claim my granddaughter."

By the time they had restored George sufficiently to steer him into his truck, the morning sky had turned bruised and angry. A cold wind blew off the lake, and a few raindrops lashed the ground. Chris stood in the cabin doorway and scowled at the curtain of rain advancing across the channel.

"Our last day. What a bummer. What should we do with it?"

"I need to round up another outfitter," Amanda said. "George is in no shape to do it next month."

"I think you should give him the option. He might welcome the distraction."

"To take care of a bunch of mothers and their kids?" She grimaced. "That would be the worst kind of reminder."

"But let him be the one to say no. Give him a few days."

She leaned into his arms, relishing his practical calm. He was right, of course. Rushing headlong into fix-it mode wasn't always the best. "I wonder what he's going to do, how he'll handle the Saint Clairs. He seemed ready to roar over to the island and demand his rights."

"He wouldn't have much luck with that," Chris said. "They've all gone back to the city to plan for the funeral."

"Oh God, not all. Not Kaitlyn, remember?" She thought back over her encounters with the girl. Sneaking up to the island, seeking solace in the arms of her Aunt Venetia. And most strikingly, that first time when she pretended not to care about Benson's death, while tears dripped down her cheeks onto Kaylee's fur. All children seek a connection with their parents, none more than those who don't have them. Adopted children, no matter how much they love their adoptive families, harbour dreams, hurts, and hopes about their birth parents. Fatherless children filled the void with fantasies.

If Kaitlyn had any suspicion that Ronny was her father, she might have watched him secretly for years, just as he had her.

She might have built up a relationship in her mind and fantasized about the moment of their union. It was bad enough that she had lost her stepfather, who by all accounts had been a supportive, loving man, but if she had heard about Ronny's death, she knew her fantasy father was gone too.

And into this maelstrom of teenage anguish, George would charge with his own desperate need.

"We should probably stop him," she said, pulling away from Chris and turning to the cabin. "In case he's heading straight out to look for Kaitlyn. In the mood he's in, now is not the time for either of them."

"Don't meddle, Amanda."

She was already pulling on her raincoat. "I won't meddle. I'd just like to ..." She stopped. What *would* she do? "I don't know. Get to her before he does." She grabbed Kaylee's leash, called the dog to her, and headed out the door. "Coming?"

He muttered a curse but yanked his jacket off the peg. Once they were in the truck, he glared at her. "Where are we going?"

"Let's start with Venetia, the woman we met at the Chippewa Club. Even if Kaitlyn is not at her place anymore, hopefully she will know where she's gone."

"And where's Venetia?"

She ignored the sarcasm in his tone. "We'll ask in Pointe au Baril. It's a small place, so someone will know where Venetia Lawless lives. Not too many with that name."

In fact, the first person they asked, a contractor loading lumber onto his steel barge down at the dock, knew exactly where Venetia lived. "Venetia? Yeah, follow this road around the shore, keep right, and right again, hug the shore, and it's the little green house up the hill on the left. Can't miss it."

They did miss it, twice, as they followed the twisting shore road around the points and bays, peering at the various possible turn-offs. Dark, brooding clouds sulked overhead, but the rain had eased up to a drizzle. Some of the waterfront homes were extravagant, hidden behind screens of cedar or lushly blooming lilac, while others were older and more decrepit, with assorted vehicles, sheds, and woodpiles cluttering the yards. The little green house was perched on a rocky outcrop across the road from the lakefront, its roof sagging and its paint peeling.

"If Venetia is a blood relation, she sure drew the short straw in the family inheritance lottery," Chris observed dryly as he navigated the truck up the steep, rocky drive. "Have you figured out what you're going to say to her?"

"The truth," Amanda said. "Venetia seems like a straight-up woman, and we don't have time to butter her up anyway."

Chris parked his truck behind an aging Subaru on the patch of gravel that passed for a drive, and before they could even climb out, the screen door banged open and a large black Lab puppy tumbled down the steps. Venetia was on its heels, shouting. Her commands fell on deaf puppy ears.

Kaylee leaped out of the truck, and the two dogs began racing around the vehicle. Venetia watched for a moment before shrugging in defeat and turned to Chris and Amanda with a quizzical frown. "Hello again."

"You've got the puppy!" Amanda blurted out.

Venetia looked startled. "Yes. I've only had him a couple of days, so ..." Her eyes narrowed. "What do you mean, *the* puppy?"

Amanda spoke quickly to head off the woman's outrage. She explained about being with Ronny when they picked up Danielle and about going to the Saint Clair cottage with Candace. She apologized for their earlier deception at the Chippewa Club and admitted that although they were indeed taken with the little island cottage for sale, it was not their main reason for being in

Georgian Bay. But none of that was as important as the news they brought today.

"Ronny Gifford has been found murdered," she said bluntly. "In fact, Chris and I found the body yesterday on Franklin Island."

Venetia had crossed her arms across her chest as Amanda explained their deception, and the expression on her plain, lumpy face remained stony. Not a flicker of shock or sorrow at the news of Ronny's death. Did she already know? Amanda wondered as she rushed on. "But the reason we're here now is that George Gifford is on a mission." She glanced through the screen door into the darkened cabin. "Is Kaitlyn here?"

Now Venetia's expression changed. Hardened. "No," she snapped.

"George thinks Kaitlyn is his granddaughter. Ronny's child."

"That's ridiculous."

"Is it?" Amanda waited, letting the question sit in the silent space between them. Venetia could have filled it with protests, but she did not. Instead, she watched the dogs, who had stopped for breath, tongues lolling. "Does Kaitlyn know?"

Venetia pressed her lips together. Emotions warred across her face. "I don't know," she said finally. "She may suspect. She used to ask who her father was until Janine flat-out told her it wasn't important. *He* wasn't important."

"Which is like telling a child half their life story is blank. What a terrible thing to do to a child."

Venetia hesitated, her gaze wavering. She snatched a ratty sweater from a peg on the wall and gestured to three old wicker chairs grouped on the porch. "You might as well sit down."

The chairs were wet, but Venetia seemed oblivious as she sank back with a sigh. "I did tell Janine it was a bad way to handle it, but Janine only thinks what she wants to think. And to her, Ronny was erased from her life."

"Why?"

"Because …" Venetia shrugged. "Because he didn't fit her image of the Prince Consort. Because her father wouldn't have it, because he accused her of slumming. Apparently, only the male members of the family are allowed to do that. I should know." She shook her head sharply. "Not that any of this matters now. What is George Gifford planning to do?"

"He wants a relationship with his only remaining flesh and blood."

"Now? Today? Is that why you've come racing over here?"

Amanda felt a twinge of annoyance. "I don't know what he's planning, and you can do what you please with the information. But in his mood, I thought you should be prepared. Does Kaitlyn know Ronny is dead?"

Venetia dropped her gaze and fiddled with her large, knobby fingers. "Maybe," she muttered. "She's always on that damn phone, so if there was anything on the news.…"

"Or on someone's Instagram or Facebook." Amanda turned on her phone and scrolled through the latest local news alerts. On Twitter she found a tweet about his death with a link that opened into a memorial Facebook page already filled with photos and reminiscences. Ronny, gap-toothed and goofing around on a skateboard, strutting on stage, paddling white-water. The last photo, posted a mere half hour ago, showed Ronny posing on a dock that Amanda recognized as Saint Clair Island. He was tipping his baseball cap playfully at the photographer. There was no caption, but the poster was Kaitlyn Saint Clair.

"Damn," Venetia muttered when Amanda showed it to her. "She rushed out of the house about an hour ago."

"Where to?"

She pointed up the hill behind the house. The dogs had

resumed their chase and now looped wide circles around the yard. "She probably took her kayak. It's in the back creek on the other side. Not many other places to go around here."

Amanda wondered whether Kaitlyn was headed out to the island to finish what she'd been trying to do when they'd spotted her two days earlier. "It looks as if she and Ronny had a friendship of sorts," she said. "His way of getting close to her. Did you know he also kept track of Benson's photos online? Maybe also as a way of keeping tabs."

"Janine would never tolerate a friendship. He wasn't even allowed on the island. So this ..." Venetia tapped the photo. "This was behind Janine's back."

Amanda took the phone back and accessed Benson's photos, scrolling through them until she came to the one of Danielle and the construction worker. "Do you know who this guy is?"

Venetia squinted at the poorly defined face. "That looks like Julio."

"Who's Julio?"

"A handyman who's been working on the cottage, just seasonal repair stuff. With an old cottage, there's always something. He's not local. Benson brought him up from Toronto."

"Was he staying over on the island?"

"No, he's staying at one of the Saint Clair cottages across the channel on the mainland. I sometimes saw him paddling over to the island in the morning."

Amanda tried to keep her voice casual. "From the looks of the photo, he and Danielle know each other. Did you ever see them together?"

"I don't get out to the island often." She grimaced. "Actually, not ever. It's not big enough for Janine and me."

"Has Kaitlyn mentioned him?"

Venetia shook her head. "But he'd only been there for a week or so. And Kaitlyn hasn't been talking about much of anything since she came to stay here."

While Amanda's mind raced ahead along this track in search of more questions, Chris leaned in. "Where is this place he's renting? Far from here?"

"In Skerryvore. It's not far by canoe out the back route behind here." She gestured over the cottage in the same direction Kaitlyn had gone. "But it's very roundabout by road."

"Amanda, let's head over and see if he's there. I have a couple of questions for him." He had put on his cop voice, and even his shoulders seemed to straighten as he unfolded himself from the chair. "I think it's better if Venetia handles Kaitlyn — and George, if he shows up — her own way."

Amanda was startled but followed him without protest, calling Kaylee to get into the truck. Chris had something on his mind. She waited until he had turned the truck around before asking. "Okay, what gives?"

They lurched down the rocky lane with Kaylee sprawled on the console between them, panting. "This guy Julio is a loose end," Chris said. "We've got nothing but fragments of the puzzle. He's up from Toronto, Benson hired him, and Benson obviously saw Danielle talking to him, because he took a picture of them. Could be innocent. But I want to see if he's still there or if he's taken off like Danielle."

She liked the thrill of the chase, but she sensed an unusual urgency as he accelerated around the twisty curves. She hung on to the dog with one hand and the shoulder strap with the other. "But that's not all, is it?"

He shrugged and made an effort to slow down. "Call it a cop hunch."

"What hunch?"

"The guy could be back in Toronto by now, especially since he couldn't have continued to work at the cottage."

She studied his intense profile. "But Kaitlyn headed off somewhere in a kayak an hour ago. And you're thinking … him?"

"Like I said, nothing but a bad feeling."

"But why would she go to him?"

"She's hiding something. Why would she try to sneak back on the island? And why would she leave Venetia's place right after learning about Ronny's death? What if she knows something? Saw something? And what if she thinks this guy is involved in Ronny's death? Her *dad's* death?"

CHAPTER FIFTEEN

The drive to Skerryvore stretched on forever through dense forests and rocky clearings. They passed only two other vehicles, both pickups of indeterminate age and colour. Once again, they were guided only by vague directions, although Venetia had given them a street address, which they punched into Chris's GPS.

"But it's not much of a road by then," she'd said. "More a track. Look for the smallest cottage at the end of it. It's an original log home. The Saint Clairs own it and sometimes use it if they're stuck on the mainland by bad weather."

The small community of Skerryvore occupied a peninsula surrounded by water, so there was little chance of getting lost. The modest cottages were tucked into the trees and scattered along the waterfront, creating a relaxed, natural feel. There were almost no vehicles in sight. They looped along the gravel road until it petered out, and at the end they found tire tracks continuing on through the mud.

Chris stopped and leaned out to eye the track dubiously before announcing they would walk from there. As they climbed out of the truck, he put a restraining hand on Kaylee. "I want her to stay in the truck."

"She'll have a fit."

"We don't know what we're facing. I don't want her to bark and warn them."

"Okay," Amanda said, reluctantly shutting the truck door and pulling her hood up against the chill. "But I can't promise she won't howl."

Chris grinned. "Just like her mom. Has to be in the thick of things."

True to the prediction, Kaylee began to howl the minute they left but fortunately stopped once they rounded a bend out of sight. Ahead of them was a rustic log cabin with a dock overlooking the sullen grey water of the bay. Islands were sprinkled about, obscuring the view across the main channel, but Amanda suspected Saint Clair Island was directly opposite.

The cabin stood cute and proud on its rock, commanding the bay. It was in good repair; the winter's debris had been swept off the deck, the windows sparkled, and a pair of freshly painted Muskoka chairs sat on the deck. Two kayaks were overturned side by side on the shore, and a small runabout was still under a tarp beside the house. Despite the tire tracks, however, there were no vehicles parked in the lane.

Chris was studying the ground. "One vehicle. Big tires. The tread is thick and new. I'm guessing a big SUV or truck, new or at least with new tires." He straightened to follow the track toward the back. "But today's rain has partially washed the tracks away, so they're not fresh."

Amanda tiptoed up to peer in the cottage windows. Deserted. But through the screen of cedar she spotted a third kayak pulled up on the shore beyond the point. A familiar lime green. *Damn, she's been here*, she thought. *The silly girl*. She headed for a closer look. The kayak was haphazardly pulled ashore, still half in the water and bumping in the waves. The paddle had been tossed nearby and farther up the life jacket, as if she had shed things as she moved.

"Amanda!" Chris's call was sharp with alarm. She rushed back to find him by the rear door of the cottage, bent over a figure splayed on the ground. The girl's arms were flung wide, and her honey-coloured ponytail was sodden in the mud. Chris was feeling for her carotid pulse.

With a cry, Amanda rushed to help. "Is she alive?"

He nodded. "Barely."

Amanda pulled her cellphone out of her jacket pocket, praying there was a signal. Hallelujah! "Let's hope they have 911 service here," she said as she dialled. Within seconds she had the 911 operator on the line and reported the emergency. Once the operator had dispatched the EMS team from Parry Sound, she came back on the line for further information.

Chris was already assessing her vital signs and calling out his observations. She was breathing, her airways were clear, and there was no visible sign of bleeding or injury. Her pulse and breathing were slow, however, just nine or ten respirations per minute, and she was snoring softly. Pupils were pinpoint. He tapped her shoulder and called her name. No response. He picked up her flaccid arm and pushed back her sleeve. Her skin was smooth but bluish and cold, possibly from the cold rain, but her nails were even darker.

"She's not getting enough oxygen," he shouted toward the phone. "It looks like an overdose. Tell EMS to bring naloxone, just in case. Lots of it. I'm going to do rescue breathing and CPR to get her oxygen up."

He rolled her onto her back, checked her airways again, and tilted her head back to blow air into her lungs. He worked like a pro, focussed and calm as he watched her chest and counted the seconds. Every few moments he checked her pulse.

Time crawled by. The girl lay clinging to life by a gossamer thread. The EMS were coming by road, but even at breakneck speeds it would take at least half an hour. A long time to sustain a life by CPR or rescue breathing. Amanda had stayed on the phone to provide updates, but once the ambulance took over communication, she handed the phone to Chris and relieved him to do CPR.

They worked in tandem for some time, alert for the sounds of an approaching ambulance. Even as Amanda focussed, questions tumbled through her mind. Was this an accidental overdose, sadly all too common even among recreational users now that fentanyl and other super-opioids had hit the streets? Was it a deliberate overdose brought on by despair? Had Kaitlyn been overwhelmed by a sense of loss, not only of her stepfather but also the father she secretly yearned to know?

Had it been something in between? Had she been so desperate for temporary oblivion that she didn't care if she ever came back?

Or had the overdose been more sinister? Had someone else handed her the fatal drug, promising her nothing worse than a mind-blowing high? For Amanda had no doubt that had she and Chris not stumbled upon her, Kaitlyn would be dead by now.

She looked up at the back door of the cabin. It was ajar, as if Kaitlyn had stumbled outside before collapsing. In a desperate attempt to escape? To get help? When Chris began his shift on CPR, she stood up to stretch her back and flex her arms.

"I'm going to look around inside to see if I can find any drugs or drug paraphernalia. There may be some clues that will help the paramedics and doctors."

He glanced up. "Good idea. But try not to touch anything. If this goes south ... the cops will want some answers." He nodded to Kaitlyn's arms, which still lay flaccid at her sides. "Unless she's hiding her track marks, she doesn't use needles. Most likely she snorted or ingested something."

Amanda slipped through into the darkened interior, which was neat and spartan. Clean dishes sat in the draining board, and the kitchen table was bare. A narrow hallway off the main room opened into three tiny bedrooms and a bathroom, each closed off by curtains in the doorway. Two beds were stripped, but the bed in the largest bedroom had sheets, pillows, and a duvet, all neatly made.

She returned to the main room for a closer look. Colourful throw cushions were lined up on the sofa under the window, but the rocking chair in the dark corner looked used. It had been jammed up against the wall, and its cushions were creased and crooked. On the table beside it was a small plastic baggy. She peered closely. Specks of pale bluish powder clung to the insides of the bag and dusted the tabletop. Nothing else. No flat surfaces or residue of powder lines. Had Kaitlyn taken the entire contents of the baggy and put it up her nose? Or had it been in pill form?

Amanda backed away, her eyes tuned to subtler details. One corner of the braided rug was flipped over, and a framed photograph of Georgian Bay had fallen over on the table. Had Kaitlyn done that as she stumbled to get outside, or had there been a struggle?

Chris's shout penetrated her concentration, and she rushed back outside to find him agitated and breathless. The girl's colour was worse.

"I've lost her pulse," he said. "Do chest compressions while I continue the breathing."

Amanda knelt at her side to begin CPR while he redoubled his efforts.

"Hang in there, Kaitlyn!" he gasped. "Hang in! Help is almost here."

Through her fear, Amanda heard a distant bark from Kaylee, and she prayed that Chris was right.

"You folks always seem to be in the thick of things," Sergeant Neville Standish remarked. "If I were the suspicious type …"

"Yeah, this is just what I want to be doing on my hard-earned time off," Chris grumbled. "Nothing better to do around here."

They were sitting in Standish's office at the OPP station in Parry Sound. Sandwiches and coffee had been brought in, although at this point Amanda thought a glass of Scotch wouldn't go amiss. It was nearing the end of a long, long day. Chris was scheduled to fly back to Newfoundland the next evening, but instead of sharing a bottle of wine and watching the sunset on the beach outside their cottage, here they were, sitting in plastic chairs in a faceless grey cubicle, facing a tight-lipped, florid-faced cop. Through the one tiny window, all she could see was the tarmac of the parking lot.

Kaitlyn was in intensive care at West Parry Sound Health Centre, still unconscious but alive. Amanda knew she should feel relief and pride that she and Chris had a hand in that, but she could only feel a sense of dread. Whether the poor girl would ever be whole again, either mentally or physically, was another question. Half an hour without adequate oxygen could kill off a lot of brain cells.

Janine and Candace were on their way up from Toronto, and Amanda was not looking forward to that drama. Could Janine summon the motherly instinct to put her daughter first for once? Amanda doubted it. She hoped at least that she and Chris could sneak off back to the cottage before the two sisters arrived so they could salvage some of their last night together.

They salvaged three hours. They barbequed the last of the trout, made it through most of a bottle of Sauvignon Blanc, and were relaxing in the Muskoka chairs hand in hand as the last lavender blush of sunset faded over the bay. The distant rumble of an engine and the stutter of tires on gravel made them groan.

"I hope that's not for us," Amanda murmured.

They both turned as a white Lincoln Navigator lurched to a stop inches from their cabin, spewing gravel. The door flew open, and Janine leaped out. In the days since her husband's death, she'd had her hair freshly cut and coloured and new gel tips on her fingernails. The effort was probably for media coverage, but the cosmetics couldn't hide the crazed eyes and the bony angles of her face. She waved away mosquitoes as she stomped over, fear and accusation in her eyes.

Amanda headed her off at the pass. "How's Kaitlyn?"

"She's terrible. Still unconscious."

"Shouldn't you be with her?" Chris said. *Cops*, Amanda thought. Subtlety wasn't their forte, but for once she was grateful.

"The doctors don't know when — even if — she'll wake up. What am I going to do, sit there and hold her hand?"

That would be a start, Amanda thought. Even Janine seemed to recognize her misstep, for she dropped her voice. "Candy is with her. She'll call. But I have some questions for you!" She pointed her gel fingertip at Amanda. "Who are you, and what are you playing at?"

Amanda tried for the short answer. She was here scouting locations for a trip and had become involved when Danielle swamped her boat off the Mink Islands.

"Bullcrap," Janine said. "Candy saw you with Benson in Pointe au Baril. Then you just happened to be there when Danielle swamped, you just happened to find Ronny's body, and according to my cousin Venetia — who I admit wouldn't tell the truth if a lie would do — you were snooping around the Chippewa Club asking questions about us. And now you just happened upon Kaitlyn in the middle of fucking nowhere!"

"Can I point out we saved your daughter's life?"

"Yeah, and I bet you want a big fat donation to your little charity for that."

Amanda hid her surprise. The woman had researched her and knew a lot more than she was letting on.

She was about to shoot back *that would be nice,* but Chris was on his feet. "That's enough. Go back to your daughter, and when you're ready for a civil conversation, come back."

Janine wasn't used to being ordered around, even by an extra tall Mountie who crowded into her personal space. She stared up at him. "Just stating the facts. Sir."

"Who's Julio?" Amanda asked.

Janine's gaze flicked to her. "Who?"

"The man your daughter went to meet. She was at his cabin."

"No, she was at *our* cabin. The Bat House, Benson used to call it, because before we renovated it a few years ago, that's all that lived there."

"But Julio was staying there."

Janine frowned and widened her eyes in theatrical surprise. "Oh, you mean the handyman Benson hired? Is that his name?"

"What's his relationship to Kaitlyn?"

"Well, you'll have to ask her. I don't keep up with all her friends." She paused. "But she was bored and lonely on the island — believe me, I've been there — so maybe she talked to him."

"So did Danielle."

"Well! The little Mexican gets around!"

"Mexican?"

Janine waved a dismissive hand. "Or whatever. He's from somewhere down there. I don't pay much attention to the workers Benson hires."

Amanda cut through the contempt. "Was he supplying drugs?"

"What are you, the cops? Oh I forgot, he *is* the cops, just out of his jurisdiction. I have no fucking idea if he supplied drugs, but that's a good basis for a relationship with Kaitlyn." She put air quotes around the word relationship. "So are you going to tell me what you're really doing snooping around my family? Even Neville thinks it's weird."

Amanda noted the first-name basis with the OPP sergeant. She had to remember the Saint Clairs had deep roots in the community and probably shared secrets and alliances she knew nothing about. "Most of it is coincidence," she said, trying to keep more bridges from burning. "But I did care about Ronny, and even more, his father George. George believes Kaitlyn is his granddaughter."

Janine blew a puff of air. "George and Ronny have been trying to weasel their way into our lives — and our bank accounts — for years. He can believe what he wants."

"But what if Kaitlyn believed it? And thought her real father was dead?"

Janine spun back toward the Navigator. "Kaitlyn has a big imagination. Did I mention bored and lonely? I don't want you visiting her, or talking to her, or putting stupid ideas in her head. Or anyone else's head. If you so much as peek into her room," she paused on the running board in a dramatic flourish, "you'll find yourself in court!"

It was so theatrical that Amanda almost laughed. "That went well," Chris said as the SUV took off in another spray of gravel. He slipped his arms around her waist. "But she's given us the perfect reason to butt out, leave this whole mess in Neville Standish's hands, and get back to our last night together."

She tickled his side. "I've got one last thing I want to do."

He tightened his embrace. "It better involve a handsome young Mountie with a —"

"It involves a pudgy, middle-aged journalist with a devious mind."

He dropped his arms.

"I want Matthew to see if he can get hold of the coroner's report on Benson Humphries. I want to know if they've confirmed cause of death as a drug overdose. Specifically something laced with fentanyl."

CHAPTER SIXTEEN

Matthew Goderich began to work the phones early the next morning, calling in favours and resurrecting contacts he hadn't used in years. He sat under the shade of a patio umbrella in what had become his favourite haunt. The coffee shop on Queen Street West brewed an exceptional four-shot espresso and served *pain au chocolat* still hot and oozing from the oven. After a month of living in Toronto, he'd already had to loosen his belt a notch.

The morning clientele was mostly business people engrossed on their laptops and a few coffee klatches of mothers with babies in strollers at their sides. No one paid him any attention as he surfed between laptop and phone.

From a former colleague now on staff at the *Star*, he'd learned that all information related to the Humphries investigation and post-mortem was being withheld at the request of the family.

"We know the police investigated," the man said, "and we know the investigation is closed and the coroner has released the body to the family. Funeral's tomorrow, in fact."

"Closed," Matthew said. "As in *there's nothing to see here, folks*?"

"Probably as in *there's nothing we want you to see here*."

"I guess money buys a lot."

"Yeah, everyone at the top is pretty cosy with each other, so the word came down to respect the family's privacy. The party line is 'The medical community mourns the loss of a well-respected neurologist who died at his family's country home in a tragic accident.'"

"Accident. What does that mean?"

"Well ..." the reporter lowered his voice, "the word being whispered around here is accidental drug overdose. Sadly, not much of a story anymore, even among the rich and privileged. I hear the Saint Clair country house has quite a reputation for wild parties."

"But was Benson Humphries a regular user?"

"I don't know. But you know with the opioids on the streets these days, it only takes once, and sometimes the user doesn't even know it's there."

After thanking him and promising to steer any useful tidbits his way, Matthew hung up and fiddled with his coffee spoon. The OPP had closed the investigation. Closed the book on Benson Humphries's death. But had they simultaneously opened another investigation into illegal drug dealing up in the Georgian Bay area? A man had died, after all. He could hear Amanda's outraged shriek all the way from Parry Sound.

Before he called her to report, he wanted to find out two more details. First, was Benson a user, and if not, who was, besides his stepdaughter Kaitlyn? Secondly, was fentanyl the cause of his death? As usual, going the official route would probably be a waste of time, for neither the medical nor police personnel were likely to give a crumb of information. He needed some back-door sources. The tipsy next-door neighbour? A street-level drug dealer?

In the end, he decided to go straight to the horse's mouth after all, using a plausible combination of truth and artful lies.

He tracked down Sergeant Neville Standish at his desk at the West Parry Sound detachment.

"I work with Amanda Doucette, managing her tours and finances, trouble-shooting problems. Chief cook and bottle-washer to an amazing woman and proud of it. I try to —"

"What can I do for you, Mr. ... ah ... Goderich?"

"She's planning a trip for some very vulnerable mothers and children next month, and she's stumbled on quite a mess —"

"Barged into it is more like it."

"Well, that's Amanda, but it doesn't change the facts. That there are drugs up there and young teenagers are overdosing. I need to know how big a problem drugs are up there."

There was a chuckle. Matthew held his breath. "I'd say your mommies and kids are more at risk in their own emergency shelters and group homes than they are out in kayaks on the bay."

"Agreed. And that could be a concern as well. How are the drugs getting in? Local labs and suppliers, or ...?"

"Drugs are getting in, for sure. Cottagers bring them up from the city more often. But with the locals, alcohol is still our number one concern, and should be yours too."

"Right. But we can search their bags for that. Drugs like ecstasy, acid, and fentanyl are so small they're easy to smuggle. Has the fentanyl problem reached you guys up there yet?"

"Some. We expect an increase when the summer folk arrive."

Matthew took the plunge. "I'm told fentanyl killed Benson Humphries."

There was silence. Standish didn't even grace that with an answer. Matthew pushed further. "And nearly killed Kaitlyn Saint Clair. It seems to me you already have an epidemic up there. And a local supplier."

"I can't comment on ongoing police matters, Mr. Goderich."

"Oh, come on! You've got a mess up there. A respected doctor dead, his stepdaughter hanging by a thread, a local tour guide murdered. I'm wondering if we should be going up there at all."

"Perhaps not," Standish replied calmly. "I'd be happy to have Doucette out of my hair anyway." With that he hung up.

Well played, Goderich. But Matthew had managed to learn fentanyl was not yet a big local problem and had more likely been brought in by outsiders. Standish had also implied, obliquely, that at least the drug investigation was ongoing.

The truck was loaded, Amanda's motorcycle was secured in the back, and Kaylee was already in the driver's seat as they locked the cabin door. Amanda took one last look out across the bay. Rain clouds were massing on the horizon again, and blackflies formed clouds around their heads.

"It was a nice place," she said, waving away the flies. "Even with the bugs."

He grinned. "Mother Nature, reminding us who's boss."

He climbed into the truck, shooing Kaylee over. As Amanda moved to join him, her phone rang. Matthew sounded apologetic as he filled her in on his meagre discoveries.

"How could they close the investigation so fast?" she demanded.

"They seem to have concluded he took the overdose by accident himself."

She thought of the vibrant man she'd met on the dock at Pointe au Baril. Confident and in charge. She thought of his photos, which showed a finely tuned artist's eye and a love of light and colour. To reach their conclusions, the police would have relied on statements by the family, any one of whom might have had something to hide.

"But …."

"It happens, Amanda, even to the most careful user. Dealers mix fentanyl with ecstasy or cocaine to give that extra little edge of euphoria, and sometimes the user doesn't even know. We know the Saint Clairs had wild parties. We know drugs were available. Being a doctor doesn't automatically make you more careful with your own health."

She pictured Benson in the middle of the floor amid pools of vomit and urine. It looked as if he'd been trying to get to the door. To get help? And why the vomit?

"Do you know how he took the stuff?"

Matthew said he didn't.

"He vomited. Maybe he ate a cookie or a brownie, and he didn't even know it was laced until it was too late."

He was silent, but she sensed his skepticism.

"What if he was trying to induce vomiting, Matthew? What if, in those last few seconds, he realized he was about to die?"

"We'll never know. And even if the police had concluded that, it doesn't mean he was forced. With drugs freely available at the party, the police would never be able to prove malicious intent."

Yet something strange was going on. Kaitlyn had obviously been distraught about something. She had tried to sneak back on the island, she had fled to her Aunt Venetia's house to escape her family, and upon learning of Ronny's death, she had gone to see Julio — where she had nearly lost her own life. Would have done if Amanda and Chris hadn't found her.

Amanda felt a chill as the potential implications sank in. Kaitlyn was in the thick of things. Was she in danger?

Amanda thanked Matthew hastily, asked him to keep digging, and hung up. Chris had been driving in silence, his eyes focussed on the road, and now he turned onto the main highway.

"On our way back," Amanda said, "can we stop by the Parry Sound Hospital? I want to check on Kaitlyn."

He pursed his lips. "Remember what Janine said."

"I don't give a fuck about Janine. I can deal with her."

"She said she'd sue you."

"Let her try. She'd have to air all her dirty laundry."

He looked at his watch. "I'd like to get to Toronto before rush hour. That can be a nightmare around the airport."

"Chris! Half an hour, that's all. I just … I need to … I'm worried."

He sighed, but he must have had his own concerns, or heard the edge in her voice, for he nodded. The West Parry Sound Health Centre was a sprawling modern hospital carved into a jagged rock face above the main street. Kaitlyn had been moved from ICU to a private room, which Amanda took to be a good sign. They wandered the halls for a few minutes before they found George pacing the small waiting room down the hall from her room. He looked haggard and dirty, as if he'd been in the same clothes for days. After learning Kaitlyn was asleep, they led him outside onto the terrace, and Chris went to buy him a coffee and a sandwich from the cafeteria.

George yanked back a patio chair and flung himself down on it. "Janine has slapped a no-visiting order on her and won't tell me anything!"

"She's being protective," Amanda said, "but you can hardly blame her."

"Protective, my ass. She's trying to keep a lid on the story. So far she's persuaded the doctor not to let the cops talk to the girl. And she's making plans to move her back to Toronto." Pain twisted his face. "Away from me, from Venetia, from anyone who really cares."

"Did she wake up? How is she?"

"She woke for a bit, but she's confused. I don't need to talk to her, I just want her to know I'm here."

"Did she say what happened?"

"If she did, Janine is not sharing it. I got friends on the force, so I know they're looking for this guy Julio, and they're analyzing the drug residue found at his house. But really ..." He lifted his shoulders in a weary shrug. "It's not the first time she's used drugs. Venetia tells me she and her friends get high most weekends in the city. Mostly just the feel-good, lovey-dovey stuff like marijuana, mushrooms, and ecstasy. It's at all their parties and even in the back corners of their school. The cops think she probably brought the stuff up from Toronto herself."

Chris returned with the food and cast Amanda a warning look, which she ignored. "Really?" she said. "But what about Julio? She was at his place."

George picked up his cup and lifted it to his lips with shaking hands. He took one sip and grimaced. "Barely waved over the coffee beans," he muttered. "Neville Standish can't get a lead on Julio. No address, no contact info. There are dozens of Julio Rodriguezes in Toronto, so without an address it's a slow process. Benson hired him under the table, cash, no paper trail. That's pretty standard up here. Nobody likes giving the taxman money. Not that Neville cares about that. Let Canada Revenue enforce their own rules. But finding one Mexican in a place the size of Toronto ... I think Neville figures it's a waste of time. He passed the name on to the OPP drug unit and the Toronto cops, but don't hold your breath. Pretty small potatoes for them."

Amanda sighed in frustration. "But there's a bigger picture here! We know Benson died of a fentanyl overdose, which might have been slipped into his food or drink —"

"Amanda," Chris said, "we don't actually know that."

"Humour me. On the night he died, there was a huge fight over the nanny's documents, which were locked in the room where he died. Conveniently, she was then able to steal her documents and escape from the island in a boat. We know she was acquainted with Julio. We know she, and someone else — maybe her husband or maybe this guy Julio — killed Ronny and escaped in another boat toward the south. Goddamn! The cops can't be giving up on Ronny's death so quickly!"

George had been listening intently. "Of course not, but Ronny's case has been taken over by major crime detectives from OPP Headquarters in Orillia. I hope they're connecting all the dots between Ronny, Julio, Danielle, and her husband, but Neville's not sure Kaitlyn's overdose is connected to it. Janine is pretty insistent that the girl is just unstable."

Amanda fell silent, but her mind seethed. Kaitlyn *was* connected, she was sure of it. The girl was tormented by something. Had she bought the drugs that killed her stepfather? Did she know how he died? And if she already had the drugs herself, why had she rushed to see Julio the minute she learned of Ronny's death?

It was a sinister, tangled web, and in the background was Kaitlyn's mother, blocking contact and inquiry at every turn. Protecting her daughter, or herself?

Through the window she spotted a familiar figure with angular turquoise hair and a fringed leather jacket striding through the cafeteria. A hand-tooled leather computer bag was slung over her shoulder, and she juggled a take-out coffee and sandwich container with one hand while texting on her phone with the other. Frankie looked like a woman on a work mission, but when she saw them, she veered over.

"George!" she exclaimed, plunked her food down on their table, and reached across to him. "I'm really sorry about Ronny."

When he remained rigid in her embrace, she drew back to scrutinize him. "What a terrible, terrible accident. Do the cops know what happened?"

"Not an accident, Frankie. Those people killed him. He's dead because he was trying to help them, and they killed him for it." He flushed, his whole body vibrating.

Frankie laid her hand on his arm. "Then I hope they catch them. Ronny was one of the good ones. I know we fought, but we were like family."

He seemed to deflate. After a pause, he gave a faint nod.

"How's Kaitlyn Saint Clair?" Frankie asked. "Is that why you're here?"

George raised his head to study her quizzically. Despite the studs and the tattoos, her smile was tender. "Ronny sometimes talked to me about her when he was worried about her drugs."

"She's okay. Her mother is going to put her in rehab in Toronto."

"That's a good thing, isn't it?"

He shook his head. "How's that going to fix anything? The poor kid's adrift, like a boat with no anchor. She's been adrift for years. The drugs are new, maybe this last year. But there are drugs in the house and that mother ... well, some people shouldn't have kids. God knows I made a lot of mistakes raising Ronny, but at least I tried, and there were lots of people around here to set me straight. Down in Toronto, who will Kaitlyn have? Especially now that Benson's gone."

"Maybe her mother will step up to the plate."

George gave a dismissive grunt. "Yep. Kaitlyn will have more luck getting attention out of poor old Edith Doherty. At least Benson did stuff with her. I'd see her out in the boat with him taking pictures together."

Frankie pried the lid off her coffee and blew across the hot liquid. She seemed to be stalling. George looked at her. "What?"

"Her idea or his?"

"I don't know. I think it was an escape for both of them. Why?"

She set her cup down. Shook her head. "No reason." With that she picked up her food and shoved her chair back. "You know me, George. Nosy Parker."

George stirred. "Can you talk to her?"

"I don't have permission —"

"Off the record. Just a quick 'hi, how ya doing.' Just to see how she is."

Frankie glanced at her watch and wavered. "Gotta run. I'll … I'll see."

George looked lost as he watched her stride away. "Kaitlyn seemed so happy when she was out with Benson, you know? He wasn't her father, but he was the best she had."

CHAPTER SEVENTEEN

Matthew's phone rang just as he'd packed his laptop into his satchel and was draining the last of his coffee. He glanced at the display: an unknown number with a Toronto area code. He answered with his usual terse "Goderich."

"Are you Matthew Goderich, the lawyer?"

He was about to laugh at the joke when something in the man's apprehensive, almost furtive tone stopped him. It had a faint Spanish inflection. Did he have a Latino source he'd forgotten about? "Who's speaking?" he countered.

"Are you Danielle Torres's lawyer?"

The penny dropped and his pulse quickened. "Yes, I am. Who are you?"

"You said you could help. With documents and … legal things."

Matthew gave up trying to pry the man's name out of him for the moment. "Depends. What does Danielle need help with?"

"Me. I need help."

Matthew rolled his eyes. How many times had the Filipino nannies passed his card around? Had he inadvertently invited every immigrant with a legal problem to contact him?

"With what? Tell me the problem, and I'll tell you if I can help."

"I did some work for a man on his house, and I want to get paid."

"Is he refusing to pay you?"

"No. That's not the problem. He's dead."

"Then go to his next of kin. The estate will pay you."

"They don't know about it."

Matthew sat down again. "If you have a contract —"

"I don't have a contract."

Then you're shit out of luck, Matthew wanted to say, but he restrained himself. "I'm sure if you explain your situation and show them the work you did —"

"It's a secret. The house was a secret. Dr. Benson didn't want his family to know, and if you knew his family …"

Matthew tightened his grip on the phone. "Who did you say?"

"Dr. Benson. Benson Humphries."

"Benson Humphries has a secret house? Not his Rosedale house?"

The man managed a laugh. "No, this is a little house."

"But he owns it? Do the police know?"

"The police?" The man sounded alarmed. "I don't think so. He just buy it. It was a secret."

"So you said." Matthew thought fast. A whole new lead had just broken open! "Look, I may be able to help, but I'm not doing anything over the phone. We have to meet in person, and I want to see this house for myself. See the work for myself," he clarified quickly. Glancing at his watch, he grimaced. Toronto rush hour would be starting soon, turning any trip into a nightmare of red lights. He grabbed a pen. "Give me the address."

The man balked and hemmed and hawed before finally capitulating. Once he'd provided the address and arranged to meet him there in an hour, Matthew hung up and looked up the home on Google Maps. It was north of Eglinton Avenue and west of the core, but still fairly central. Matthew didn't know Toronto well, but in his brief stint as a journalist with the *Toronto Star* decades ago, he remembered the area as rundown and largely working-class.

Curious.

He put in a quick call to Peter Pomeroy, an old university friend of his who was an actual lawyer, specializing by a stroke of luck in property and estate law. Matthew cultivated acquaintances — a journalist could never have too many — and over the decades he had accumulated hundreds. He didn't have much time but wondered if his friend could work his magic and check the title of a specific Toronto property for him. He understood it had recently been purchased. Could Peter find out who had bought it, for what price, and had the deal closed?

It had cost him half the man's outrageous hourly fee plus a bottle of fine Scotch, but a deal had been struck. "If you can give me the answers within half an hour," he added, "two bottles of Scotch."

The half hour was almost up, and Matthew's taxi had worked its way northwest past strip malls and dilapidated shops on Weston Road almost to the cross street when his friend called back.

"You're not telling me the whole truth, Goderich."

"What are you talking about?"

"You know damn well what I'm talking about. Why are you interested in this particular property?"

"I can't tell you that. Journalistic privilege."

"Uh-huh. You're working on a story, aren't you? Digging up dirt."

"As it happens," Matthew said, trying to sound aggrieved, "I'm not. I'm trying to do someone a favour. A worker that the owner owes money to."

Peter Pomeroy said nothing. From the back seat Matthew drummed his fingers on the armrest as the cab waited at the traffic light. Up ahead, he could see a side street lined with an eclectic jumble of tiny bungalows and narrow two-storey homes. Cars lined the curb, and the small, neatly tended yards were taken over by bikes, plastic fences, and overgrown shrubs. *What the hell?*

"Let me guess," he said finally. "It's owned by the recently deceased Dr. Benson Humphries."

"Yes. That's a matter of public record."

"Is the sale final?"

"Yes, it closed last month."

"What day last month?"

"Well before Humphries died, if that's what you're getting at."

"So it's legal and above board?" Matthew said, hanging on as the cab squealed tires around the turn. "His estate owns the house?"

"I'd say so."

"What was the purchase price?"

Pomeroy named a figure that sounded outrageous, but Matthew knew by Toronto standards it was probably modest, as befitted the neighbourhood.

"Is there a mortgage on it? A bank or trust company?"

"Not on the record. He paid for it outright. But then of course he could."

Matthew asked if there were any other relevant details he could share, and Pete chuckled. "For half an hour and two bottles of Scotch, that's what you get. I can look into it further if you or the worker retains me properly."

Matthew thanked him and hung up just as the cab pulled up outside a miniature box of a house wedged into a narrow lot. A rusty pickup sat at the curb out front, and a commercial refuse bin filled much of the postage-stamp yard. Plank walkways crisscrossed the rest of the yard, and ladders, two-by-fours, and buckets of cement were piled on the front porch.

There was no one in sight, but the front door was ajar, and lively Latin music filtered out. Matthew climbed up the wooden steps and pushed open the door, revealing a living room with tarps spread across its gleaming hardwood floor. Cans of paint, cleaner, and rags were grouped in a corner.

A long corridor led toward the back to what Matthew assumed was the kitchen. A young man poked his head warily around the corner. "Mr. Goderich?"

Matthew nodded and watched a smile of relief spread across the man's dark features. Matthew sized him up. A small, compact man with a muscular chest and short-clipped black hair. He was probably in his midthirties, although his smooth skin, high cheekbones, and dark eyes belied his age. He stepped forward to offer his hand.

"Thank you," he said simply.

"I haven't done anything yet. Not till I know what I'm dealing with. And who."

"Julio. Julio Rodriguez."

Matthew hid his excitement behind an intense inspection of the renovation work. He walked from room to room, listening to Julio rattle on about the walls he'd torn out, the supporting beams he'd installed, the new kitchen cabinets, and the electrical and plumbing subcontractors he'd already had to pay out of his own pocket. Now and then Matthew sneaked a surreptitious glance at the man. He was looking for signs of nerves or guilt, of which there were plenty. He talked too fast and flitted from room to room and topic to topic. Benson had paid some of the earlier bills, but by Julio's own accounting, he was still out ten grand on subcontractors and supplies, and now the man who had promised to pay him on nothing more than a handshake was dead.

Matthew doubted the grieving widow would be willing to pay up on a house her husband had kept secret from her. A house that clearly wasn't intended for her. It was a tiny bunga-low in a working-class area tucked up against the railroad tracks, where neighbours lived cheek by jowl, shared gossip across their adjoining front porches, grew vegetables in their minuscule backyards, and parked their second-hand Hondas and Chevies in the street. What had Benson been up to? And Julio. Surely this was the same Julio Benson had hired to work on the Georgian Bay mansion, the same Julio who might have supplied Kaitlyn with the drugs that almost killed her.

Was he also a killer? Amanda thought he might have been involved with Danielle. Just how involved was he in her escape, in the theft of her documents, and in the deaths of Ronny and Benson?

Matthew was standing in the bathroom of the newly fin-ished basement apartment, pretending to admire the tile work around the tub, when he became aware of silence. Julio had run out of words and stood in the hallway, looking at him apprehensively. Matthew could see no guile in his expression, no hint of deception or threat. For the moment he decided to play along.

"It's nice work," he said. "You've put a lot of effort into this."

Julio nodded. "I have no more money. I borrow from suppliers, I put up my truck … if I don't get money, I lose everything."

On the face of it, Julio appeared to have a lot more to lose with Benson dead than alive, and thus no motive at all for killing him. Unless his commitment to Danielle and his desire to help her were stronger. Or Benson's death was an accident.

"But there is no contract," he said.

"I …" Julio shrugged sheepishly. "No. Dr. Benson's word was always good."

"Have you got any records at all? Phone messages, emails,

bank records of the money he's already paid? Anything that proves you had an agreement?"

"It was always cash. Maybe I have texts, but not from Dr. Benson's phone."

Matthew frowned. "Whose phone?"

"I don't know." Julio's gaze flickered, and for the first time Matthew sensed he was lying. "Can you help me?"

"What you need, Julio, is a lawyer who specializes in contracts. I have a friend who does this kind of law. I can put you in touch with him —"

"But I have no money!"

"I'll tell him to charge you a fair price."

Julio stared at him, hope dying in his eyes.

"It's your best chance," Matthew said.

"You tell Danielle's friends you can fix things."

"Not this. Not with no proof. Not when you're hiding things from me."

Julio stiffened. "What things?"

"The phone number. Is it a prepaid phone? Illegal?"

"No! Why do you think that?"

Matthew turned to go back up the stairs, giving a message of dismissal. "Because this makes no sense. Why would Benson Humphries leave no record of your agreement? Why would he buy this house in this neighbourhood?"

"It's a nice house! And a nice neighbourhood."

"But not for the Benson Humphries of this world. He's a wealthy man. If this was all legal and above board —"

"It *is* legal! It's not for him, this house."

Matthew stopped. "Ah."

Julio breathed deeply and shook his head as if to chase away his anger. "You help me or not?"

"Who's the house for?"

"He's a good man. He's only trying to help."

"Who's it for?"

"It's for Danielle."

Chris peered through the open glass doors into the airport terminal. He and Amanda were huddled outside near the departure entrance, as close as Amanda could go with Kaylee in tow.

"I should go," Chris said. "The security line might be pretty long."

Amanda tightened her grip on his hand. Around them, cabs and private cars pulled in and out in a dizzying swirl, and the constant thunder of jet engines ricocheted off the concrete. People poured in through the doors, some bewildered and others striding with purpose, and the clack of footsteps and luggage wheels mingled with the constant drone of the PA.

"There's still lots of time," she countered. "Two hours."

"But this is Pearson at rush hour."

She tilted her head to look at him, and he must have read the hurt in her eyes, for he smiled ruefully. "Sergeant Knotts will kill me if I miss this flight. You know …" He hesitated. "I'm on pretty thin ice as it is. If he ever got word — if Neville Standish ever decided to complain to the RCMP about me snooping around —"

"But you didn't! Well, not really. Trouble just kept falling into our laps."

He didn't laugh. "Because we were snooping around. My career can't take any more trouble right now. Not after Mont-Tremblant."

She laid her head on his shoulder. "I guess I'm a bad influence on you."

He kissed the top of her head. "Very bad. I love it."

She watched a family of six struggling to balance a huge pile of luggage on a trolley while saying goodbye to two other carloads of relatives. The women and girls were wearing bright red and yellow saris with trailing scarves, while the husbands wore standard suits and the small boys sported CN Tower T-shirts. There was a flurry of chatter and hugs before one by one they headed through the doors. Families, struggling with parting.

"So what's next, Officer?" Amanda said gaily.

"When your kayaking trip is over, come to Newfoundland for a visit."

She hesitated. Memories of her ordeal in Newfoundland rose unbidden. Of being lost and terrified in the wilderness. Battling the ferocious surf, pursued by killers, dogged by loss.

Once again he seemed to read her mind. "We'll go to the east coast. Trinity Bay or the Burin Peninsula. They're full of quaint, colourful fishing villages and sparkling coves. It's completely different from the northern peninsula. There's art and theatre and comfy B&Bs."

"How much time can you get away from Sergeant Tight-Ass?"

He laughed. "Come for Labour Day weekend, and I'll take the rest of the week off. Early September is the perfect time to visit Newfoundland."

She gave him a sharp look. How quickly he'd forgotten! To his credit, he flushed. "This time will be different, I promise you."

She sighed. She knew he was right. The island was not to blame for her experience, nor was avoiding it going to erase the fear. Facing it, and laying down good memories, was the best way. Not that she ever intended to go back to northern Nigeria. Some memories were just too horrifying to be written over.

She was about to acquiesce when her phone rang. She glanced at it. "It's Matthew."

He extricated himself and stood up. "I should go."

Kaylee leaped to her feet, anticipating action. Amanda answered. "Matthew —"

"I have news!" Matthew burst out.

"Wait a sec," she said. "I want to say goodbye to Chris." She shoved her phone in her pocket and stood on her tiptoes so she could wrap both arms around his neck. "Despite the craziness ..."

His lips brushed hers. "This week was great."

"You do give a girl a good time. Even if I am a bad influence."

"You're worth it." He enveloped her in a hug and murmured into her ear. "Promise me you won't do anything ... rash."

Instinctively, she stiffened before burying herself deeper into his arms. Now was not the time to take issue.

"This has to last a long time," she whispered instead.

"Matthew's waiting."

"Who?"

They laughed and gave each other one last hug. "Newfoundland, then," she murmured before letting him slip slowly from her grasp. She watched him stride through the doors toward security, all elbows and knees like an inexpertly controlled marionette. When he was out of sight, after one last wave, sadness rolled over her. She took a moment before she fished her phone out of her pocket.

"Where are you?" Matthew asked.

"Just leaving the airport."

"Okay. I've got huge news. Meet me for dinner?"

She glanced at her watch. It was not even six o'clock, but she hadn't eaten since a hasty sandwich in Parry Sound. "Can you give me a hint?"

"Benson's been a bad boy." He chuckled. "The rest can wait until I see you."

CHAPTER EIGHTEEN

Amanda could barely contain herself as she listened to Matthew describe his day. Like a good storyteller, he spun the story out, building suspense, setting the scene, and drawing her through the drama until the final big reveal. They were sitting on the shaded side patio of an Italian restaurant on Queen Street West with Kaylee tied to the other side of the railing beside them. They had ordered, and while they waited for their antipasto, they shared a bottle of wine. A soft, warm breeze filtered through the trees, and the evening sun cast long shadows over the tiled floor.

"Benson was bankrolling Danielle's escape," Matthew concluded triumphantly. "Behind his wife's back! And setting her up in her own place. He paid cash, over six hundred grand, through a private sale. And then there's the renovation costs on top of that, also in cash. We know his family didn't come from money, so it makes you wonder how he paid for the house."

Trying not to jump to conclusions, Amanda ran through possible explanations. The most innocuous; maybe Benson had saved up the required amount of money on his own. He was a successful doctor who'd been in practice for several years. If Janine's money covered most of the family's general living expenses, it was just conceivable that, with personal frugality and a good financial advisor, he could save up that much.

Or maybe Janine had either lent him the money or given him access to her own money. But Janine didn't seem like the type to part with more than half a million without asking questions, unless Benson had lied and invented another reason for wanting it. Maybe he told her he wanted to purchase an investment property. Janine might have seen the little house as a good investment in Toronto's soaring housing market but certainly not as a place for her nanny to escape to. Janine would be furious if she found out.

The third possibility was even more alarming. What if Benson had been syphoning money out of his wife's account without her noticing? Janine didn't strike Amanda as the type who would be easy to fool or the type who would shrug it off if she found out about it.

"Either way," Matthew replied after she'd run her theories by him, "it doesn't matter. It's all degrees of deception. He was going behind her back, actively opposing her wishes by supporting the nanny. We know she didn't want the nanny to leave them and went as far as to lock up her papers. And —" He held up his finger in triumph "— equally important, why did he do it?"

She could tell by the gleam in his eye that he was imagining the worst, but she was reluctant to go down that path. "Maybe he was just a decent guy. He knew Danielle was being mistreated, that in fact her rights were being violated, but she was too scared to cross Janine. Janine would make sure she never got a reference, never got another job, and she'd be on a plane back to the Philippines in disgrace. He knew she was trapped."

He snorted. "Oh, Amanda."

She suppressed her irritation and took a long sip of the cool, crisp Pinot Grigio to marshal her arguments. "I've been giving Benson a lot of thought. I think he felt trapped too, between a selfish, unfeeling wife and three small children who loved and needed him. Kaitlyn, too, for that matter."

"And the money wasn't bad either. The island mansion, the antique boat ..."

She conceded the point. His photos of the bay and his sheer joy at driving that beautiful boat showed how much he loved the place as an escape from the relentless pressures of city life, from the life-and-death challenges of his job, from the foundations, charities, and public engagements that filled many of his free hours.

"But he probably knew that Janine would make life miserable for him and the children if he left her," she said. "She'd use the children against him. It was lose-lose for him."

"But it didn't have to be! My God, he wasn't some penniless housewife. I'm sure he earned well in the six figures. He might have had to come down a peg or two, but he could have walked away and supported his kids quite comfortably."

"For all we know, that might be what he was saving up money for, and then the chance to help Danielle came along, so he ..."

The waiter brought the platter of antipasto and set it down with a flourish. They both fell silent while he topped up their wine. Once he left, Matthew reached across the table to squeeze her hand. "That's what I love about you, Amanda. After all you've seen and all you've been through, you still believe the best of people."

"It's better than the alternative." She flushed. "You think I'm being naive?"

He shrugged. "I just think it's complicated. By your own argument, Benson was a lonely man and starved for genuine affection. Danielle is a pretty young woman, alone in a foreign land, vulnerable, abused by her employer — that same emotionally cold woman. She was caring for his children, very likely providing the love they should have been getting from their mother. Even if we buy the premise that he was a decent man, it's easy to see how feelings could get stirred up. Relationships blurred. He may have genuinely thought he was helping her to get away from an intolerable situation and in the process giving them both a little shot at much-needed love."

"But there's the husband."

He nodded. "And there's the rub. Benson might have been willing to have her as a part-time lover — he had a wife himself, after all — but I doubt Danielle could manage that. Certainly her husband wouldn't."

"Danielle was only twenty-two when they married, and she spent most of the last five years thousands of miles away from her husband. He might be little more than a stranger to her, whereas Benson was there in her life every day."

As she spoke, however, she remembered Danielle had even consulted a lawyer up in Pointe au Baril about sponsoring her husband to come to Canada. Not the actions of a woman who was planning to ditch him and team up with someone else. Doubt crept in, and with it a flare of anger. Benson might be a decent guy; he might even have developed genuine feelings for Danielle over the two years she'd been with them. But was he, deep down, no different from all the other privileged white men who took what they wanted because they could? Danielle would have had little say in the matter without risking her job and her status in this country. Like so many women in her position, keeping him happy with sexual favours might have seemed like a small price to pay for her future freedom and citizenship. Perhaps she'd assumed that when her husband arrived, the arrangement with Benson would be over.

His purchase of a house for her suggested it would not.

Amanda turned the unsavoury idea over in her mind with dismay, for this new twist gave them not one, not two, but three people who might have wanted Benson dead. Janine, the husband Fernando, and Danielle herself.

The waiter had swept away the antipasto platter without her even noticing, and he arrived now with two steaming bowls of penne with scallops in rosé sauce. The fragrance of wine, garlic, basil, and seafood filled the air, and Matthew grinned like a small boy. Amanda banished her dark thoughts with an effort. She didn't know Benson. She didn't know Danielle. Nor did she know the complicated dance between them. She couldn't know how desperate they were or what they were capable of.

Time to put it all behind her and focus on her own life for once. She was halfway through her pasta and was just beginning to accomplish that when Matthew's phone rang. Matthew frowned at the number. When he answered, a high-pitched, agitated female voice blasted through the speaker.

"Mr. Goderich? Mr. Matthew Goderich!"

Matthew jerked the phone away from his ear. "Speaking."

"Who are you? What are you doing?"

The words were muffled by a slight accent. Matthew drew the phone back to his ear. "Danielle?" he ventured.

Amanda bolted upright, gesticulating. *Speaker phone!*

Matthew made the switch, and the woman's familiar voice flooded in. She sounded as frantic and frightened as she had that first time on the lake. "What do you want? I didn't call you. You are not my lawyer."

He sidestepped adroitly. "Danielle, you sound in trouble. Maybe I can help?"

"Who are you? Police? Reporter?"

"No, I work with Amanda Doucette, the woman who helped to rescue you on the lake. She's trying to help you."

"Why?"

Amanda opened her mouth to interject, but Matthew held up his hand. He lowered his voice. "We know you're in a lot of trouble. Maybe for things that aren't your fault."

"Not my fault. No! I didn't do anything! But how can I explain?"

"Where are you, Danielle?"

"I don't know. We are lost!"

"In Toronto?"

"Nooo!" Almost a wail. "In the islands. There are islands and water everywhere. Little houses with nobody home, nothing but bears and snakes, and our boat has a hole."

"So you're still in Georgian Bay?"

"I don't know." A pause. In the silence, the wind crackled over the phone and the waves whispered. After a muffled conversation, she returned to the phone. "Georgian Bay, yes."

"Do you have a map? A compass?"

"No."

"Does your phone have a map function? Or a GPS?"

"It's a cheap phone. Just for phoning."

"Then call the police."

"No police!"

Amanda scribbled on a napkin and Matthew nodded. "Then the coast guard."

"But I have to get out of the country." Danielle's tone sharpened. "I can't stay here. You told my friends you would help me with documents. Can you help me?"

"What documents?"

"Passport. I have no passport."

"Did you lose it in the lake?"

"No, no! It was gone."

"Gone from where?"

"From the safe. When I look ..." She broke off with a sharp gasp.

Amanda shot Matthew a surprised frown and scribbled a hasty note on the napkin. *How does she know?* "How do you know it was empty?" Matthew asked. "Did you look?"

"No! The safe was open."

"When? Before Dr. Humphries died?"

"After. No, I mean before. Someone took it."

Matthew wasn't buying any of it. "Danielle, were you in the room after Dr. Humphries was dead?"

A moan, followed by muttered conversation. Amanda could almost see her scrambling to cover her tracks and think up a new explanation.

"Why didn't you call the police?"

Silence. When she came back on the line, her voice shook. "Please. I need a new passport. New visa."

"Danielle, I can't do that," Matthew said. "Come to Toronto and —"

"No! They will put me in jail."

"Why?"

"It was an accident! He was already dead, but the police will not believe me. I didn't do anything wrong!"

"Are you talking about Benson Humphries? Or Ronny Gifford?"

A stifled cry. The sibilant swish of waves in the silence. "They found Ronny?"

"Yes."

"*Diyos ko po*! Who will believe us? Mrs. Humphries will make sure we go to jail."

Amanda was bursting with questions, but Matthew's calm, soothing voice was drawing Danielle out, and Amanda was afraid she'd hang up in panic if Amanda spoke. She scribbled on her napkin again. *How did Benson die?*

"In Canada, rich people don't control the police," Matthew said, although his expression betrayed his doubts. "There are laws and protections for you. You said Benson's death was an accident?"

"The drugs. He was not supposed to …"

"You gave him drugs?"

"No, no! I think they were not for him." A murmured voice stopped her. "Stop asking questions! I need help. If you can't help me —"

"Okay, Danielle," Matthew said, as if to buy time while he figured out an answer. "I'll help you. But I need some time."

"We have almost no food left. Or water."

"Is there anything around? Cottages? Boats?"

"Nothing."

Amanda wrote. *Catch fish? Build fire?* When Matthew put her questions to Danielle, the woman began to cry. "We have nothing. We are lost. And my little boy is hungry."

"Then you have to call the coast guard."

"No army! No police!" she cried, and the phone clicked dead.

Matthew and Amanda stared at each other for a long time. "Fuck," Matthew muttered.

Amanda fought a familiar sense of frustration. She hated to do nothing. "Let me see that phone."

When he handed over the phone, she studied the number. It stirred a vague memory. "That's …" She paused to check her own phone. "This was one of two numbers made from Ronny's phone on the afternoon he died. The first was Janine, the second was this one."

"Ronny phoned Danielle's phone?" Matthew looked puzzled. "But she was with him."

"This is not her phone. She had no phone when we picked her up. This must be a cheap phone Fernando bought so he could contact her. I think Danielle called him that afternoon using Ronny's phone to tell him where to meet them." Her thoughts raced ahead. It was one small piece of the puzzle explained but another piece shaken loose. Had she phoned her husband before or after Ronny's injury? Ronny would be too heavy for her to move on her own. Had she phoned Fernando in a panic to help her deal with the body?

Amanda shook her head sharply to rid herself of her nagging concerns. All those questions would have to wait. What mattered was that Danielle, Fernando, and a six-year-old boy were stranded on an island with nothing but a dumb phone to communicate. "Maybe I should try to find her. Chris has gone home, but I have to go back up there anyway to finish my tour planning."

He rolled his eyes. The waiter, who'd hovered nearby during the phone call, came to remove their plates. "Dessert, coffee?"

Both declined and thanked him. "It's a big place," Matthew said. "Thirty thousand islands. It'll be a needle in a haystack."

"We do know they were heading south several days ago. Even if they went in circles, they should have covered some distance, but since there are islands all around, they're probably still in the archipelago, not the open lake. I'm guessing they're quite far south of Parry Sound." She paused, warming to the idea as she analyzed the background sounds on the phone. "There was a gusting wind, but the waves sounded gentle. Maybe in a protected bay?"

"Pure speculation. Amanda, we have to call the cops. They have a BOLO out on her. No matter what Danielle said, two people are dead because of her."

"Maybe they *were* accidents, as she said. Ronny could have fallen down the cliff and hit his head. And maybe she's right that no one will believe her. Where she comes from, the police aren't on the side of poor people like her."

He stared at her, shaking his head slowly back and forth. "You're not Superwoman, you know. You don't have to save the world."

"Oh for fuck's sake, Matthew! I'm not trying to save the world. Just help one very scared woman who's backed into a corner. She's been stranded out there for days, without enough food or water, through the storm we had, with a scared little boy. She will hide if she sees the police, but maybe I can persuade her to come back with me and turn herself in."

"Like I said, Superwoman." He sat back. Gave a theatrical shrug. "Do you want company?"

"God, no! You can barely swim. No, I'll find somebody local up there to help me."

"Who?"

"I have some ideas."

"Promise?"

She reached across the table to touch his arm. Inside, she was in knots of apprehension and self-doubt, but she was damned if she'd let him know. The phrase Danielle had let slip — that the drugs were "not for him" — looped around and around in her head. Had the lethal drug been intended for someone else, and if so, who? The most obvious target was the woman who stood in her way, not only by exploiting her and withholding her papers, but also simply by being married to Benson, whose relationship with Danielle was anything but innocent. Janine.

Chris was standing in line at the Air Canada gate, waiting to board. He had spent a restless couple of hours in the departure lounge, ostensibly reading the newspaper but instead thinking of Amanda. Of their week together, which despite the craziness had gone better than he'd dreamed. Of the silk of her skin, the scent of her hair, the taste of her lips. She was fragile but strong. Tender but tough. Playful, prickly, infuriating, and most of all, alive. This week had confirmed what he'd first thought back in Newfoundland eight months ago. He wanted her in his life. Yet his life and hers had their own paths that were not easy to weave together. He doubted she would ever settle for being a Mountie's wife, following him from post to post and finding her own work in the shadow of his. She had a mission of her own, at least as important as his.

But her mission meant even more transient roots than his. She had no place to call home besides her aunt's cabin in the Laurentians. She spent much of her time on the road with her motorcycle and her dog, travelling from coast to coast. If they were going to build a life together, one of them would have to compromise. He loved his job. He was in midcareer with a dream of being a detachment commander some day. Because of some rocky moments in the past couple of years, he had to watch his step, but he was building a reputation as an effective, capable officer in remote postings.

Unlike some of his colleagues who had their eye further up the ladder, he loved being in small detachments, connecting with local communities, and hunting for lost hikers and snowmobilers rather than jostling big-city crowds en route to the halls of power.

A pang of sadness swept over him now as he stood in line, clutching the boarding pass that would take him two thousand kilometres from her. September seemed very far away.

His phone rang. He glanced at it. Matthew. Stepping out of line, he picked up. "I'm about to get on the plane. What's up?"

"Glad I caught you." Matthew sounded frazzled. "I wasn't sure if I should call but thought you'd want to know. Our girl has gone off half-cocked again."

The line was inching past him. "What's she done?"

He listened while Matthew described the phone call from Danielle and Amanda's decision to set off on a search. He glanced out the airport window at the flat expanse of tarmac scattered with planes. Up above, the last blush of sunset filled the sky with lilac gloom. "Oh for fuck's sake! Now?"

"Either now or first thing in the morning. You know how she gets."

Chris thought back to their time on the water in Georgian Bay. It was easy to get lost between two coves, let alone in the whole huge bay. "She probably won't find them," he said. Who was he kidding? This was Amanda, about to move heaven and earth. Again.

"She said she'll get a local to help," Matthew added.

"Well, that's something. Have you called the police?"

There was a pause. Chris could hear traffic revving in the background and the tinny strains of jazz. "Not yet."

"They'll be able to find Danielle faster than Amanda can. They can put out search helicopters with heat-seeking sensors and lots of boats to cover the area."

"I know, but Amanda would kill me if I called them."

Chris gripped the phone in frustration. "Better that than getting herself killed!"

"I hope she's not in danger, at least from Danielle. The woman sounded very scared and said she really wants help."

"What does she think the cops are? Monsters?"

"Probably. Don't forget, her husband's brother was murdered by cops." There was a pause, punctuated only by jazz and by the drone of the airport PA. "I'm not convinced she's as innocent as she claims, but Amanda seems hell-bent on rescuing her. I was hoping you could go with her."

Chris glanced at the gate. The last passenger had passed through, and the attendants were looking at him expectantly. Two thousand kilometres away, Sergeant Knotts was also waiting expectantly, his disciplinary pen poised.

Frustration clashed with fury. "I can't. I'm about to board. Call the cops, Matthew. Neville Standish in Parry Sound. He's not a monster."

Matthew muttered a phrase that sounded suspiciously like "thanks for nothing," but before Chris could counter him, he hung up. Chris held up a finger to the waiting flight attendants as he dialled Amanda's number. If he could reach her, perhaps she'd listen to reason.

But her phone rang and rang. *Goddamn the woman!* Was she already on the road, or was she deliberately ignoring his call in order to avoid a full-blown fight?

CHAPTER NINETEEN

At that moment, Amanda was en route to a cheap roadside hotel in Vaughan on the northern fringe of Toronto. She planned an early start in the morning, and this way the congestion of the city would already be behind her. Her phone was tucked into her pocket, and by the time she rumbled into the hotel parking lot, darkness had fallen, Kaylee needed a walk, and she was dead on her feet.

After completing her chores, she unpacked her pyjamas, washed, and fell into bed. She was awake as the first coral tendrils of dawn were shooting across the eastern sky. Too early for the hotel's dubious self-serve breakfast, she brewed a cup of coffee, packed up, and was about to climb on her bike again before she fished out her phone to check the route to Parry Sound.

Five alerts. Three missed calls — one from Matthew and two from Chris — and two voicemail messages. Maybe one last tender goodbye from Chris. Smiling, she accessed her voicemail.

Chris's voice was anything but tender. "Amanda! Pick up! Matthew called. For god's sake, woman, don't be an idiot! Let the cops handle it. That's our job."

Her irritation flared. She deleted the message after the prompt, and a few seconds later the second voicemail came on. He'd pulled back from the brink. "Where are you? Please call me."

Mollified, she considered calling him. It was an hour and a half later in Newfoundland, so he should be up and on his way to work. But when she ran through the possible conversations in her mind, all of them ended in a fight. He would try to forbid her, and she would refuse. It was no way to maintain the tender but fragile intimacy they had built.

In the end, she decided on a text. *Don't worry, I'm fine and won't do anything rash. Love you.* Her finger hovered over the last two words. They'd been said only jokingly in the past week, which was a start, but not enough. She replaced them with *xox.* The moment she punched "send," she shoved the phone into her pocket, climbed on her bike, and roared off in a blast of fumes.

Chris woke early after a fitful night's sleep. The hotel's ancient air conditioning had rattled on and off all night, and the constant roar of jet engines kept pulling him back to consciousness. He checked his phone and read the cheery but empty words of Amanda's text. *Don't worry, my ass!*

His phone call to her went to voicemail. Fuming, he went downstairs for the hotel's advertised do-it-yourself hot breakfast, only to find the coffee urn empty and the line-up for the waffle iron too long for his frayed nerves. Families who were up even earlier than him occupied most of the tables, cranky babies screamed in high chairs, and sleep-disordered toddlers raced in manic zigzags between the tables.

He stepped out of the hotel into the swirl of early morning rush hour. The breeze was tainted with the smell of jet fuel, and the sun was struggling to poke through the gauze of smog that hung over the horizon. He found a twenty-four-hour diner down the street and ordered a traditional breakfast of fried eggs, sausage, and home fries. Since he didn't know what the day held in store, he decided it would be wise to stoke the fires.

Once he'd downed half a cup of scalding, dishwater coffee, he phoned Matthew. "Have you heard from Amanda?"

Matthew mumbled an indecipherable reply. Belatedly, Chris glanced at his watch. Early, but not criminally so.

"Rise and shine, God."

"Fuck you, Tymko. It's still the middle of the night here."

"No, it's not. And I'm right down the street."

"What?"

"I never left. When I couldn't get a reply out of Amanda, I postponed my flight. I'm hoping you'll tell me she called the whole thing off."

"Well, I can't." Matthew sounded as if he were waking up by degrees. "Let me check if I've got an email from her." There was silence on the line, broken only by the journalist's wheezy breath. Then a quiet curse. "Nothing."

"So she' s off in the Georgian Bay wilderness somewhere, on the trail of a possible killer."

"She did say she was going to get help, but she didn't say who. Probably winging it in her usual fashion."

Chris's blood pressure rose. The waitress arrived with his platter of food, heaped with enough home fries to feed half of Ethiopia. The coffee was curdling his stomach, and the smell made him slightly nauseated. *Goddamn the woman*! he raged as his mind leaped to all the perils.

"I'm glad you're still here," Matthew mumbled.

"Well, I couldn't leave it like this. But I need to get back to my job, or I won't have one. Matthew, I'm calling the OPP."

"She'll be mad as a hornet."

"I don't give a fuck. At least she'll be alive."

"Who will you call?"

"Neville Standish in Parry Sound. He's not in charge, but he'll know who is. He'll be over the moon to get this news, but at least he's already on the ground up there."

"Okay," Matthew said quietly. "You're right. And better you than me."

Chris had Neville Standish's cellphone number in his contacts list. While he waited for the man to pick up, he picked at the sausage that lay congealing on his plate. The taste matched the smell.

"Sergeant Standish, West Parry Sound Detachment," Standish rattled off.

Chris identified himself.

"I thought I'd seen the last of you two."

"Afraid not." Chris gave him a quick summary of Danielle's desperate phone call to Matthew and Amanda's decision to go up to search for her. "She has some cockamamie idea she's going to persuade Danielle to trust the authorities and come back with her."

"And you let her do that?"

"Of course not! I didn't know about it until I was almost on my flight home. Not that I could have stopped her."

Standish let fly with a string of graphic, imaginative curses. "Why the fuck didn't you folks tell us right away! How in hell's name are we supposed to do our jobs with one hand tied behind our backs? Does this Doucette woman think we're a bunch of incompetent morons up here in the sticks who couldn't find our own asses?"

"What's important is that I'm telling you she's up there looking for them."

"And you think we're not? The bay is crawling with cops! We've got helicopters, fixed wing, Zodiacs, plus alerts in every marina and port. Danielle Torres and her husband's photos are plastered in every marina and gas bar from here down the Trent-Severn to Lake Ontario. Every officer in Ontario is on the lookout —"

"But Danielle and her family are not in the Trent-Severn, they're still in the bay, stranded on some island. Can you pull manpower from farther south and step up the search in the bay?"

"Jesus fuck, Tymko! I'm not running this show, ERT and Trenton Coordination Centre are, and they know what they're doing."

"But can you tell them —"

"Every available asset in the air and on the water is already out there! It's a fucking maze of islands and inlets. I warned your girlfriend to back off, so if we have to split our manpower to save her instead of apprehending the killers ..."

Chris clenched his jaw and took a deep breath. It took all his willpower to stop himself from hanging up. Fortunately, before he could fire back something unwise, Standish pulled himself back from the brink. Only the stiff precision of his words betrayed his rage.

"I'll pass this information to Incident Command, Tymko. And if you hear from Amanda, tell her to come back in and talk to me. ASAP."

Chris hung up, his anger and worry now worse than ever, and pushed away his plate of cold, inedible food. He felt powerless and ineffectual stuck in the big city, miles from Amanda and the drama unfolding farther north. Another call to Amanda went unanswered. Where the *fuck* was the woman!

He was tempted to just bail on the whole situation. Give up on Amanda and fly back to Deer Lake, to the peace of his cabin and the job he loved. Amanda had blown into his life like a tornado, carving a swath of chaos and sweeping him helplessly along with her. She had the power to stop, but she didn't. So maybe she didn't give a damn.

He was halfway back to the airport before he calmed down enough to think. He'd done air searches over wilderness and open water before. He knew how difficult it was to spot one tiny boat tucked onto the shore or navigating a narrow inland channel, especially if there were dozens of other small boats zooming about. Even heat-sensing equipment would be of limited use with fishermen and cottagers on the ground. Moreover, if the fugitives didn't want to be found, they had only to shelter in an abandoned cottage to be hidden from the air. He estimated the search area was at least a thousand square kilometres.

Damn it to hell! he thought as he turned the truck around. En route, he phoned Matthew to report. "I'm renting a floatplane," he said. "I can't just leave her out there all alone. What exactly did Danielle say about her location?" He jotted down the meagre details. "I'm going to track down the maps and nautical charts and find a floatplane I can rent. The hell with Sergeant Knotts in Deer Lake." He paused as he heard his own words. "But if Amanda phones you, call me ASAP, so I don't fuck up my whole career needlessly."

The four-lane highway unfurled northward toward Parry Sound in sparkling spring sunshine. The ubiquitous road construction slowed her down, and the summer crowds were just beginning to head out onto the roads. She hummed past RVs lumbering up hills, pick-ups towing powerboats, and Subarus with canoes and kayaks on their roofs. Convoys of transport trucks clogged the lanes on their way to Sudbury, Timmins, and parts farther north.

Two hours later, at barely eight o'clock, she reached the Parry Sound exit and pulled into Richard's Coffee for breakfast. After giving Kaylee some water and a quick pee break, she bought a breakfast sandwich and coffee and chose a curb outside to enjoy the sunshine with Kaylee. While she ate, she studied the map and considered her next move. She needed help from someone with a sturdy boat and expert knowledge of the islands and waterways. Based on the topography of the bay, she guessed Danielle and her family were lost somewhere in the maze of islands between Frying Pan Island and Honey Harbour, a span of about forty to fifty kilometres as the crow flies.

A lot of ground to cover. Although the area had a scattering of island cottages and a couple of boat launching sites as well as a First Nations settlement, most of it was a protected provincial park. There were beaches and campsites in the park, but she doubted there would be many souls willing to brave the bitter May winds and blackflies. An inquiry at the park office would be worthwhile, however.

She had a short list of possible guides in mind. She started with Larry, the fishing guide from the Shawanaga First Nation who had rented a boat to Danielle's husband. The long, winding trek down to his house proved disappointing, however, for when she arrived, she found Larry packing up his truck. He listened to her request quietly before giving a small, regretful shake of his head.

"I'd help you if I could, but I'm on a job. Walleye spawning research. Leaving this morning, going to the Magnetawan River to meet the team up there."

Her heart sank. A few other neighbours collected around Larry's truck, trading possibilities without much luck. While they talked, Larry slipped in and out of his cabin with supplies. After his third trip, he rejoined the group.

"I solved your problem," he said. "I called George Gifford. He's your best bet. He knows the lake almost as well as an Indian."

She hid her alarm. When she and Chris had left George at the hospital the day before, he'd been in no shape to mount a search-and-rescue operation on the lake. Grief and shock had taken their toll. He'd been drinking too much and not sleeping enough. She doubted he'd been eating enough to keep his strength up. And then there was Kaitlyn. She was the reason he got up these days and the hope he clung to. Even if he was willing to leave his hospital vigil, Amanda suspected his thoughts would be back at her bedside rather than focussed on the task at hand.

More importantly, quite apart from his mental state, he'd be unlikely to rush to the rescue of the woman he blamed for Ronny's death.

"But he's got a lot on his plate right now," she said. "He's got Kaitlyn to worry about."

Larry shook his head. "She's in Toronto. Her mother had her transferred last night. Going to put her in rehab down there."

Probably the first wise and caring move Janine had made, Amanda reflected. But not likely to calm George's mood. "George will be upset. And I don't think he'll want to help look for Danielle. After all, she's —"

"Oh ya! He said it gives him something to do. Said he'd meet you down at the Parry Sound dock in an hour."

Amanda pushed the Kawasaki as fast as she dared, leaning into the curves of the twisty road. Her mind raced over possible scenarios. What kind of shape would George be in? How would she assess his mental state without offending him? And if he was drunk, or recklessly angry, how could she gently persuade him to let someone else do the job? If she had to, she'd tell him she wouldn't put both their lives in jeopardy by setting foot in the boat with him.

When she arrived at the dock in Parry Sound, however, there was no sign of him. Thinking perhaps he was still organizing supplies and gear, she waited a while, tossing the ball for Kaylee as they paced the concrete pier. She kept a wary eye on the OPP station next door, hoping she hadn't attracted the attention of Sergeant Neville Standish.

Boats of all sizes came and went, carrying families, fisher-men, and workers heading out to the islands. Right alongside the pier sat a large white cruise ship named *The Island Queen*, sparkling clean and ready for the season. Opening day was only a couple of days away, although the office was still shuttered.

Amanda finally approached a man who'd been working on the engine of his pontoon boat since she arrived. Tools and engine parts were spread over the pier. She asked whether he knew George Gifford, and he eyed her up and down with word-less skepticism. With her lime-green motorcycle and her orange dog, she doubted she looked like a local.

"I'm supposed to meet him here," she added to nudge him along.

"Well, you missed him."

She cursed under her breath. "Did he say when he'd be back?"

"Didn't speak to him. But he didn't look in a mood to be coming back any time soon."

"Which way did he go? Back up toward the highway?"

"Oh no, he was in his boat. Heading out toward the big sound like a bat outta hell."

Amanda drove back up toward Shawanaga, alarmed and frustrated that she had no phone number for Larry. She prayed he hadn't left yet. Halfway along the road, she spot-ted his truck coming the other way. She flashed her lights, honked, and pulled her bike to the side. Larry climbed out, his brow creased.

"Did you tell George where I was planning to search?"

Larry nodded. "He wanted to know, to plan his gear."

A nameless dread shot through her. "He's taken off, to look for her himself, I assume."

"He never said anything about that. Maybe he thought you and the dog would slow him down."

"I don't think that's it. I think ... Larry, I don't like the looks of this. George hasn't been himself since he lost Ronny. He blames Danielle and her husband. I'm not sure what he'll do if he finds them."

"George is a good man." Larry shifted from one foot to the other, avoiding her eyes. "He was upset, yeah, but he'll calm down. The lake will calm him down."

"But what if it doesn't?" She was far less optimistic about his state of mind than Larry was but suspected Larry wanted to believe the best of his friend. She tried another tack. "Or what if he runs into trouble with them? If they've killed once already, he could be in danger by himself."

"Fernando is not a bad ..." Larry shot her an uneasy glance. "Maybe we should call the cops?"

She sifted through her thoughts. She knew Larry was right. If George was headed out on his own, bent on revenge, it was time to call in the professionals. She dreaded the thought of dealing with Standish, who'd be furious and might not even believe her. She tried to pinpoint her reluctance. She owed Danielle nothing. Even if, as Danielle claimed, she was innocent of the actual deaths and was just a scared, vulnerable woman afraid of an imagined police state, she had still persuaded Ronny to desert Amanda and then buried him en route like a discarded bag of garbage.

George was the one she ought to be protecting. He was the one true victim in all this, deprived of his only son and cut off from his ailing granddaughter. She needed to stop him before he got himself in trouble.

"Fine. But maybe we can catch him first if we move fast," she said. "He doesn't have much of a head start, and you know where he's going. Can you spare the day?"

He shook his head.

"I know I'm asking a lot, Larry. But George has been through so much. I'd like to stop him before the police do."

Larry stared at the ground, tracing patterns in the gravel with his boot.

"Just today. Once we're on the water, I'll call the police, and if we don't catch up with him by nightfall, we'll come back."

Slowly, wordlessly, he lifted his shoulders.

An hour later, they were chugging their way through the channel from Shawanaga Landing and heading south past Franklin Island. The sky was a peaceful azure blue, but a stiff westerly wind whipped the water into swells that pitched the boat about. Once they'd set their course, Amanda called the Parry Sound OPP and was relieved to find Sergeant Standish "unavailable." She left a message with the clerk to have him call her.

Larry's boat was not like the sleek, streamlined powerboats that arrowed through the water around them. It was a wide steel tub with an open-topped cockpit and retractable canopy on top and a pair of ancient, rumbling outboard motors on the stern. He had painted the whole thing turquoise, apparently his favourite colour. *The Larry Two* was painted in black along its hull. Amanda suspected it consumed gas like a fiend, but you could stage World War III on board without any risk of tipping.

The boat thumped in rhythm to the waves as it lumbered south. The day was warming up and the sun blazed a swath of silver across the water. Larry sat in the cockpit, steering with one hand and squinting through the scratched windshield. Every now and then, he slowed the boat and stood up to navigate through a narrow trough. The roar of the engines precluded much conversation even if Larry had been so inclined, so Amanda hugged Kaylee close and sat at the bow on the lookout for underwater hazards.

Once clear of Parry Island, Larry stayed between the red and green markers to give the ragged, shallow shoreline a wide berth. He had handed Amanda a pair of binoculars, but with the vibration of the engine and the pitch of the waves, she couldn't focus on anything. Instead, she scoured the shore with the naked eye for the slightest flash of movement or colour that would suggest a boat.

"Go closer to shore," she shouted. "I can't make out anything from this far out."

"Can't."

"Why not?"

"Shoals. Take your propeller out."

"But George will be trying to stay out of sight. He might be in behind these islands."

"He knows about shoals too."

She absorbed this then moved to sit beside him so they wouldn't have to shout for all the lake to hear. Including George.

"But he'll be looking for the nanny and her husband, and they might not know about shoals."

"I told Fernando to stay between the channel markers."

"But they might try to go between the islands to avoid getting caught."

"Then they will be in trouble. Sink my boat." Larry scowled, as if this loss had just occurred to him. He nodded inland toward the barren, uninhabited islands rising out of the water. "Watch out for a turquoise boat. My first boat. The *Larry One*."

Overhead, a floatplane skimmed low, winking white against the sun, and far out in the open water, large vessels lumbered by on their way to and from the cities to the south. Smaller boats buzzed around, following their own logic. From a distance, some of them were brightly lit and looked like police boats.

Larry droned steadily southward, passing islands and hidden inlets. Amanda had the nautical chart spread out on her lap and was using her phone GPS to track their position, but the battery was running low. She remembered Ronny's high-tech aids fondly.

"Do you have a navigational app?" she asked. "It shows exactly where we are."

"I know where we are."

"But it also shows the depth of the water and the possible shoals."

Larry shrugged. "My nephew bought me an iPad with one." A small smile sneaked across his face. "It's still in the box."

She glanced around the boat for signs of modern fishing paraphernalia. "You don't even have a fish finder."

"I advertise the traditional ways."

"Ronny had a navigational app on his tablet, so I'm guessing George has one too." She gestured toward the distant shore. "He'll know exactly where he's going and where the rocks are. He'll be able to search much closer to shore."

He glanced at her and nodded to the bin under the dashboard. "It's in there."

She rummaged in the bin and pulled out the box containing the iPad. She held up the tablet as if it were an alien thing. "I'm not much of a tech wizard," she said, "So I won't promise anything."

That small smile again. She was beginning to like this man. "And I won't promise I'll trust it anyway."

Amanda had just unwrapped the iPad when her phone chimed. She fished it out of her pocket. Another call from Chris. Poor Chris. He'd be in Newfoundland by now and feeling very far away. She hesitated to answer it, knowing that any discussion would end up in an argument, but he deserved better than total silence. Just as she finally answered, however, she heard a single muffled curse and the line went dead. She gazed at the phone in dismay. He wasn't even bothering to plead with her anymore.

She knew she risked ruining the relationship that had just turned delicious. He had always seen her as obsessed with trouble and reckless about her personal safety. He had even accused her of having a saviour complex because she'd been helpless to save the hundreds of children in her care back in Nigeria. He said she'd been challenging death to a rematch ever since.

In her more reflective moments, she admitted there was some truth to this. She did feel the need to protect people and to take on their fights for them. She did put them above herself. She wasn't like other people — Boko Haram had seen to that — but it didn't feel like a choice. Chris wanted her safe, and he'd backed away from the relationship once before when she'd refused to play it safe. He would see this as more evidence of how low he was on her hierarchy of needs.

She sighed, typed, *All is fine, darling. I'm with Larry, but don't worry, no danger. Battery low, so will call back when I'm back on land*, and pressed "Send." Texting was a great invention; it controlled the conversation and pre-empted arguments.

She picked up the iPad again and this time managed to read enough of the start-up instructions to realize the device was useless to them. It needed a mobile account, which Larry did not have, as well as a power source to charge. Reluctantly, she returned it to its resting place under the dash and leaned over to resume her search for water hazards. Only to be interrupted by another call. Matthew. She debated ignoring it, but Matthew knew better than to try to change her mind. He would argue, but it would be pro forma. Besides, he might have news.

"Chris is renting a floatplane," were the first words out of his mouth. Over the drone of the outboard and the slap of the waves, they sounded faint.

Heat spread through her. "He's still in Ontario?"

"Of course he is. Jesus Christ, Amanda, he's ballistic!"

"That's good. The floatplane, I mean. The more eyes we have on this, the better. I'm with Larry, a Shawanaga outfitter, but we're just one small boat in this vast sea of islands. And Larry doesn't even have a GPS!"

"The place is crawling with cops, Amanda. Chris phoned Neville Standish."

Her heart sank. Standish hadn't called her back, probably dismissing her as a flake, and now he'd see her as interfering once again.

"You didn't really expect he wouldn't, did you? He's a cop, after all, and kiddo, this is bigger than either of you. There's been a BOLO out on Danielle for days."

"I know. It's just as well. George Gifford is out there looking for Danielle too, and I'm not sure he has rescue on his mind. George is actually the person we're looking for."

"Does Neville Standish know about George?"

She hesitated. She hadn't given the clerk much detail. "Not specifically."

Silence. Had she lost the signal? The rhythmic roar of the boat made it difficult to tell. "Matthew?"

"Listen," he said. "Call Chris, will you? He's … he's …"

His last words were garbled. She thought he said "He's not the enemy," but she couldn't be sure. "I'm losing you, Matthew. Bye," was all she said before signing off.

CHAPTER TWENTY

When Matthew stepped out of the sunny chaos of Toronto's Bloor Street into the cool hush of the church, he was glad he'd hauled his best suit out of its garment bag at the back of his closet. His decision to attend the funeral had not been a whim; he'd been toying with the idea for days. Amanda — even Chris Tymko — had met the storied Saint Clairs, and after his meeting with Julio, Janine loomed as a powerful central figure in the drama unfolding around her husband's death. She piqued his curiosity. Some people made the news, others *were* the news. In the story he was drafting in his head, she was a pivotal character; whether victim or villain, he had yet to discover.

Despite hanging in his apartment window for an hour, the suit still smelled slightly of mildew, but it was a sedate navy pinstripe that, paired with a conservative white shirt and a blue and grey paisley tie, made it funeral perfect. He was surprised and relieved that it still fit after weeks of excesses at his espresso café, and he tweaked its pocket square with all the flair of a Stratford actor. He would be rubbing shoulders with the elite of Toronto society at St. Paul's Anglican Church, but years on the international diplomatic cocktail circuit had taught him how to play that role.

He walked down the centre aisle at a measured, respectful pace, choosing his seat carefully. Not too close to the family at the front, not so far back as to be inconsequential. He didn't want to be among the hired help and the secretarial staff of the hospital. He wanted to eavesdrop on Benson's medical colleagues and the society crowd who gathered around the Saint Clair flame — friends and admirers Janine might deign to speak with.

The interior of the church was hushed and imposing, a powerful and enduring monument to the upper class that had founded it. Pale limestone arches soared overhead, and stained glass windows flashed in the sunlight. Soft organ music reverberated through the hall. His newly polished black shoes echoed on the stone floor, and his hand touched the dark wood pews as he passed. Heads turned discreetly, and people greeted each other with subdued but barely concealed excitement. Gossip was afoot.

He doubted anyone would question who he was; he had only to behave as if he belonged. He greeted total strangers with nods of recognition and finally chose a pew with a few promising-looking couples. He tuned his ears but heard only snatches of whispered conversation. "Did you know ...? I heard ... Ridiculous! Well, you never know what people ..."

At the front of the church, the nave gleamed of ornate wood and limestone against stained glass, with a discreet array of floral arrangements. Taste and discretion in all things at St. Paul's. The organ struck up a suitable processional hymn — Bach, Matthew thought — and soon the pallbearers were rolling the coffin down the aisle. A blindingly elaborate casket of polished mahogany and brass befitting a prince, his first hint that Janine didn't do anything by halves.

Behind the pallbearers walked the widow, a pale vision in a black suit with satin detailing and a black rose fascinator perched at a tilt on her sleek copper hair. She walked alone, her head held high and her gaze fixed straight ahead. Her make-up was impeccable, and if she had spent the morning, or indeed any time in the last few days, weeping, there was no trace of it.

Behind her, holding the hands of two small twin girls in puffy navy dresses, was a platinum blonde wearing a modest black dress set off by red stiletto heels and a red silk scarf that trailed over her shoulder. Matthew assumed from the pecking order that she was Candace, Janine's sister.

Both women looked stunning. Money could buy a lot of style, but Matthew suspected Janine would turn heads even wearing a potato sack. There was a challenge in her stare and a confidence in her stride that was hard to resist.

A weepy-looking middle-aged couple, hopelessly outclassed in bearing and attire, followed Candace, their anxious eyes flitting over the crowd, possibly in search of a friendly face. Remembering Benson's modest Prairie roots, Matthew surmised these were his parents. He gave them an encouraging smile. Behind them came an assortment of younger couples, presumably siblings, cousins, and their spouses.

The funeral service was mercifully short, with a minimum of religious babble. A few hymns, a psalm or two, a poem read by Benson's brother, the Lord's Prayer, and then it came time for the eulogy. Matthew was astonished when Janine herself rose to deliver it.

She was either a consummate actor who knew her role to a T, or she had a heart of stone. For the first ten minutes, her speech was pitch-perfect. Her voice rose to the rafters, clear and elegant with just a hint of quaver at the right moments. She thanked people for coming to honour her husband. She touched on the difference he made in so many lives through his work and his philanthropy. She talked about his dedication as a father, son, brother, and husband, pausing to look at each family member in turn and her voice quivering on the last. She talked about his humble roots and the values of integrity and compassion his parents had instilled in him. Here, she let a small smile play across her lips.

"Everyone knew that if they wanted anything, it was Benson they approached. He was always ready with a helping hand and always thought the best of people. Perhaps that was his downfall."

It was a throwaway comment, quickly glossed over as she moved on, but Matthew snapped alert. He doubted Janine threw anything away for free. Was she implying something sinister about his death? Did she believe something other than the official party line of accidental overdose? And if so, to whom was she referring?

"The world is a smaller, meaner place without Dr. Benson Humphries," she continued, back on script. "His death leaves a hole in my life, in the lives of my children, and the many people who loved and needed him. But he died in the place he loved best and spent his last day enjoying the peace and beauty of the lake. He will be with us in memory and in spirit always, and nowhere more than in Georgian Bay. Godspeed, my love."

Matthew felt like clapping. All that private schooling had not been entirely lost on the wild child. When she returned to the front pew, she accepted the embrace of every single family member. Benson's parents seemed less effusive, but perhaps it was just their nature.

He had not intended to go to the reception afterward, because he doubted he could pass for a family friend under closer scrutiny, but Janine's performance had intrigued him. Could he use her throwaway comment as a segue into further confidences?

The St. James Club was a rambling red-brick mansion occupying prime real estate on Bloor Street, sheltered from the crowds and press of downtown by a ring of magnificent old trees. Stepping through the wrought-iron gates was like stepping into the cradle of privilege. The St. James Club had been a gentlemen-only club until it was dragged kicking and screaming out of Victorian times into the late twentieth century, but the gentlemen's touch was still evident in the carved panelling and wainscoting of aged oak and walnut, the heavy maroon velvet drapes and the brown leather chairs worn thin by use. Matthew suspected the décor hadn't been changed in decades, and some spots looked sorely in need. Still, to the blue-blooded rich, a touch of shabby lent the weight of tradition.

The reception was being held in a lounge that could easily have passed as a ballroom in Buckingham Palace. It was crowded, and the buzz of conversation created a dull roar that echoed from its fifteen-foot ceilings. Waiters in waistcoats threaded through the crowd with trays of drinks and canapés. Matthew snagged a glass of red wine and drifted through the throng, alert for gossip and hoping no one would recognize him. Former ambassadors or trade attachés might, although perhaps not out of context.

Shreds of animated conversation swirled around as he walked. It seemed the cause of death was an open secret. Expressions of disbelief and outrage mingled with allusions to Benson's darker side. Doctors learn to play fast and loose with drugs during their punishing residency years. Some of them never kick the habit of that instant "on" and "off." You never know....

Whenever he stopped to listen, however, voices dropped and people edged away. In the corner, he spotted Candace, who seemed to have her hands full with the twins. She was immaculately made up, but as he drew near, he noticed the concealer was caked thick around her eyes.

He approached and leaned in. "You seem to have your hands full. Can I get you a drink or a few snacks for the children?"

She looked at him as if he had two heads. He flushed. Women had never been his forte, and she obviously thought his offer was a pick-up line. "Sorry," he mumbled. "Just that I know a lot of this is falling to you."

She didn't look much appeased. "Just send a waiter over and I'll tell him what I want."

He slunk away to waylay a waiter and grabbed a glass of white wine off a passing tray before returning. "He's coming," he said, handing her the wine, "but I thought this might help in the meantime."

She had the good manners to thank him.

"Your sister gave a beautiful eulogy this morning."

"Didn't she, though."

He filed away the irony in her tone. "I was impressed by her composure."

Candace took a sip. "Do you know my sister?"

"Well ... no."

Candace shook her head as if to stop herself and managed a polite smile. "You're right. She was very brave." She tipped her glass toward him. "Thank you for the wine," she said and turned her back.

As a journalist, he was no stranger to rebuffs. He tried to act nonchalant as he strolled in search of another mark. He wanted to snag the grieving widow, but she was still encircled by a crush of people waiting to talk to her. He spotted Benson's parents standing alone in a corner, clutching drinks and looking forlorn. People were drifting by to offer their condolences but seemed to run out of words after a minute or two.

"Mr. and Mrs. Humphries? I'm Matthew Goderich." He offered his hand and hoped his name would be lost in the blur of grief and new faces. "I'm so sorry for your loss. I didn't know your son well, but from what I saw, he was a remarkable man."

Benson's mother nodded vacantly, while her husband muttered perfunctory thanks. *I must sound like every other complete stranger in this room,* he thought. "Janine gave a wonderful eulogy. You must be very proud of your daughter-in-law."

Mr. Humphries said something approximating agreement, but his wife's lips grew tight. Matthew's instincts stirred. He tossed out another feeler. "I especially liked how she said if anyone needed anything, they went to him, not her. That was the Benson I knew. I was a patient of his." Warming to his story, he leaned in as if sharing a confidence. "And she was right. He would give you the shirt off his back, and sometimes, as Janine implied, people took advantage of that."

"Her more than anyone," Mrs. Humphries retorted, as if the dam was threatening to burst.

"Well, I don't know her, but they do seem an unusual match." He hoped that would encourage further indiscretions from the mother-in-law, who clearly had little affection for her daughter-in-law. When none were forthcoming, he pressed on. "Although she certainly is a beautiful woman."

The mother snorted. "More fool him."

"Now, Susan …" Her husband piped up. "It was as much her spirit as her looks, you know that."

Susan cast her husband a withering look. Spirit could mean a lot of things, Matthew thought, but clearly in Susan's view, none of them were good. He nodded toward Candace, who was trying to wrestle the twins out of the room. The little girls were building up a head of steam.

"That's Janine's sister with your granddaughters, isn't it? They seem to have plenty of spirit."

"No discipline. They've been left with nannies all their lives. Benson did what he could to give them attention, but …" She lifted her shoulders in defeat.

"He was busy with work," Mr. Humphries added.

His wife scowled. "*She* had the time."

"I'm surprised the nanny isn't here to help out. To let the sister ..." Matthew waved his hand to encompass the crowd.

"Oh no! She's ... she's ..." The woman almost choked on her outrage.

"Gone," the husband supplied. "And there hasn't been time to find a replacement."

"Oh, that's rough." Matthew nudged them along. "Losing their nanny at the same time as their dad."

"She's the reason he's dead!"

"Susan ..."

She arched her eyebrows defiantly but kept her mouth shut. Mathew debated whether to plunge to the heart of the secret, which would either lose them or open the floodgates. "What? They think the nanny supplied the drugs?"

Susan stiffened. "Benson didn't do drugs."

"But I understood ..."

"Our son would never take drugs," she said coldly. "He's a neurologist. He knows what they do to the brain."

Matthew let the silence lengthen between them, hoping more details would come tumbling out as she defended her son. And sure enough ...

"I know what the autopsy said. Janine says the nanny put them in his drink. She wanted her documents, and now she has them and she's gone. And our Benson is gone." Susan drew herself up with dignity and turned to leave. "Now if you'll excuse me, I'm going back to the hotel. I'm tired, and Janine has an event planned at the house tonight. Henry, are you coming?"

Henry shot Matthew a reproachful look before he scuttled after his wife, leaving Matthew with one last tidbit of family dynamics. Janine Saint Clair had a Rosedale mansion large enough to accommodate a royal entourage, and yet her grieving in-laws were staying at a hotel. Her decision, or theirs?

He scanned the room to see what she was up to now and noticed the informal receiving line around her had dissipated. She was in the corner of the room in animated conversation with an elderly man in a charcoal-grey suit, striped maroon tie, and white shirt with cufflinks. Cufflinks! Who wore those nowadays? His silver hair was so perfectly swept across his brow that Matthew took it for a hairpiece until the man raked his long hands through it shakily.

Janine was leaning in, peppering him with questions. Her voice was low, but her fingers dug into his arm and tears glinted in her eyes. Matthew was just sidling over to catch a few words when she shoved the man and stepped back.

"What the *fuck*, Charlie!" She stormed across the room, scattering well-wishers as she disappeared out the door.

CHAPTER TWENTY-ONE

Matthew was walking along Queen Street on his way back to his apartment when his cellphone rang. It had been a most informative morning, more innuendo than established fact, but it had helped to flesh out his impression of the family dynamics. He'd been hoping for a more nuanced picture of Benson — if not confirmation of his philandering at least some tarnish on his halo — but the halo shone more brightly than ever. Matthew needed a better source.

He didn't recognize the number on his display, but he did recognize the voice once the man uttered two words in his Spanish accent. "Mr. Goderich?"

Ah-hah! Perhaps a source dropped from heaven. "Yes, Julio," he shouted over the roar of the traffic. "How can I help you?"

"I have more trouble. Can you give me the telephone number of that lawyer?"

"What's happened?" Aware of the glares from fellow pedestrians on the busy street corner, he strolled toward the shelter of a building.

"I work on the house today. Finish the tile in the bathroom. I hear the front door open, someone walking around. I call hello, no answer. I come upstairs. Dr. Benson's wife is standing in the kitchen in a black suit and hat. She is opening the cabinet doors and looking at the windows. I say hello, Mrs. Humphries. You tell me she owns the house now, so I think okay, Julio, you better be nice to her."

Matthew rolled his eyes. Out on the street, the noon sun was baking off the pavement and the fumes from cars and buses washed over him. "Julio, what happened?"

"She is very rude. She didn't say hello, she just say Julio, I want you out of my house. I try to explain it's not finished. She says I give you half an hour to take all your tools out of my house. But the tile is half done, I say. I'm bringing my own people in to finish it, she says. It's going on the market next week."

Matthew jumped into the flow. "She's going to sell it?"

"That's what she say. She was very angry. I am afraid to tell her about Danielle, but I say I can finish it for you, I have all the supplies. Then she gets very, very angry. Really, Julio, she says, you think I don't know what you do behind my back? You think I'm going to pay you one cent for all this work? You leave the supplies here, they belong with the house, and you don't show your face here again. You won't get a cent, and she waved her hand at the kitchen, and your little friend Danielle is not going to move in here either."

Matthew groaned. He'd been afraid this would happen. Hell hath no fury ... "How did she find out about the property? Did you approach her about getting paid?"

"No! I was waiting for after the funeral. To show respect."

Well, she didn't waste any time, Matthew thought. She must have stormed directly over from the funeral reception to the little house. Who had told her? Was that the altercation he'd witnessed at the reception?

"It must have been a shock for her to learn all this, just when she's burying her husband," he said lamely. "What did you do?"

"I pack my tools. She watch everything I am taking. And she follow me around, ask questions. How long did I work on the house? Who hire me, Benson or Danielle? Did Danielle and Benson come here together? How long I know Danielle. She think Danielle and me try to trick Benson. Very angry."

Now Matthew was interested. "What story did you tell her, Julio?"

In his heartbeat of hesitation, Matthew had his answer. Julio was hiding something. This innocent façade of just being a hired hand was a lie. At least not the whole truth. When Julio did answer, he seemed to be groping forward.

"Story? It's not a trick. Dr. Benson hire me sometimes. I meet Danielle at his cottage. That's all."

Matthew took a guess. "But you knew her before that, didn't you? She's the one who recommended you to Benson."

Silence.

"Where do you know her from?"

"A friend. One of her friends introduce me."

"Were you her lover, too?"

"No!" Julio sounded genuinely shocked.

"But she was Benson's lover."

"No, no! Miss Janine think that. But is not true."

"As you say, that's how it looks."

"He's a good man. Danielle is a good woman." Julio raised his voice. "Everything is finished for me. I am not a criminal, I don't lie! I just want my money. Please give me that lawyer's number."

After giving Julio the number, Matthew resumed his walk. He was about to phone Peter Pomeroy to give him a heads-up when his phone rang again. *What am I*, he thought, *central switchboard?* It was the number Amanda had recognized the day before. Danielle.

"Did you get the passport?" she asked without so much as a hello.

"Where are you?" he countered.

There was a pause. A cyclist slalomed down the sidewalk, grazing Matthew's elbow. "Still in the islands. Did you get help?"

There was an accusatory edge to her voice that he didn't like. He told himself it was her desperation and her lack of subtlety in English, not hostility or entitlement. But a small voice in the back of his head reminded him that he didn't know this woman or what she was capable of.

"Yes," he said. "There are people looking for you. Amanda and Larry are coming down from Parry Sound."

"Do they have my passport?"

"No, but they can help you get to Toronto. Larry knows every inch of Georgian Bay. So does George, who's also looking for you."

"Who's George?"

"Another outfitter up there. Ronny's father."

She gave an audible gasp. "Ronny's father? He knows where we are?"

"I don't know, but he's out on the bay looking for you."

"Oh no! No, no! *Susmaryosep*! What does his boat look like?"

He stopped at a red light. The bustle of Toronto swirled around him, yet at the other end of the phone line, this woman was stranded on an island in the wilderness, frightened and hunted. "I have no idea," he said.

"I saw a boat. Far away. Going very slow, like looking for something. I didn't know who it was. Maybe police? But the boat had words on the side and a picture of a kayak."

"That's George." Matthew thought fast. "Did he see you?"

"No, we were scared it's police. We hid the boat."

"Okay, listen, Danielle. Don't go out on the lake again. You will get lost. Stay put and watch for Amanda and Larry."

Danielle stifled a wail. "I have my son. He is just a little boy."

"All the more reason to stay put." Matthew heard her whimpering as she brought her panic under control. He debated whether to add to her worry but remembered she might not be as innocent as she pretended. "Your friend Julio contacted me," he said.

"Julio? Julio!" She seemed to flounder. "Why?"

"He told me about the house Dr. Humphries bought for you."

"No, no, no! Why did he call you?"

"Because he wanted my help to get his money for the renovations, and now Janine Saint Clair is not only refusing to pay him, but she won't give you the house either."

"Forget the house! The house is not important now. Tell Julio to stop."

"So it's true? Dr. Humphries bought you a house?"

"He wanted to help me."

"Did you ask him to?"

"No, I didn't ask him!" Her outrage crackled through the line. "He's a nice man. *Was* a nice man. But not Miss Janine! You tell Julio to stay away from Miss Janine!"

"But he's out thousands of dollars."

"Not important!"

"I've given him the name of a good lawyer."

"Lawyer! Aiee! Janine has lawyers, judges, and politicians —" An agitated male voice erupted in the background, speaking in rapid Tagalog, and Danielle dropped her voice. "You don't understand. Julio is illegal. No papers. The big lawyers will send him away."

Matthew was no stranger to the plight of undocumented migrants. During his overseas assignments, famine, war, and ethnic cleansing drove hordes of desperate, penniless people across borders into neighbouring countries or makeshift border camps. A whole underground economy flourished in the tent cities, shantytowns, and back alleys of large cities, where migrants eked out a precarious living under periodic threat of eviction or pogroms. They formed loving communities, raised children, and built schools and storefronts on the dusty streets. Sometimes happy but never secure.

He left Danielle with the promise that he would pass on her message to Julio, but before he did so, he thumbed through his contacts to see if there was any way he could find out more about Julio Rodriguez. What was his status? Was he on a federal list somewhere? Had a deportation order already been issued? He knew thousands of illegals lived happily in the Toronto underground, embraced and shielded by their communities. Many of them had come to Canada under the temporary foreign workers program but had seen their work visas expire under a recent, ill-advised government rule limiting work terms to four years. Just when they'd settled into a life here, they had to leave. Thousands opted instead to go underground.

The largest group was from Mexico, numbers that had swelled since the American president began threatening to deport millions and build a wall to keep them out. Many had sneaked across the nearly nine-thousand-kilometre, largely unprotected border with the United States, even risking death or frostbite by walking across in the middle of winter.

Julio was a Mexican. Had he been a casualty of the four in, four out rule, in which case he would have had some papers of some sort, or had he sneaked across the border?

Matthew didn't want to draw attention to him by contacting anyone in Immigration, Refugees, and Citizenship Canada. He did have one possible trustworthy source, but before he stirred up more embers of trouble, he had to put out the one fire he had already lit.

Peter Pomeroy's cellphone rang six times before flipping over to voicemail. Matthew cursed and left a hasty, cryptic message urging him to hold off taking any action on Julio Rodriguez's claim and to call him ASAP. Next he phoned Julio.

"I called your lawyer," Julio burst in, sounding buoyant. "He says we can fight. Not for the house, but for the money."

"Did you tell Mr. Pomeroy you were undocumented?"

Silence on the phone. Matthew pictured Julio's stunned expression. When he finally spoke, he was defiant. "Who tell you that?"

"Is it true? I want to know what I'm dealing with here. And more importantly, so will Peter Pomeroy before he takes any legal action on your behalf."

"I have documents," Julio said, his defiance fading.

"Are they real?"

A long pause. A muttered curse. Matthew turned the corner onto a side street, leaving the traffic and crowds of Queen Street behind. Peace settled around him. He headed for his apartment in the aging brick low-rise that took up much of the block.

"I have a real driver's license and social insurance number," Julio said. "Good enough?"

"No. Not when Janine Saint Clair's high-powered lawyers get their claws into you."

He sighed. "How did you learn this?"

"I spoke to Danielle. She wants you to back off and forget the house."

"Danielle?" He brightened. "Where is she? Here in Toronto?"

"Not yet. She's having a bit of trouble."

Julio cried out a Spanish curse. "What's wrong?"

"She and her family are lost somewhere in Georgian Bay."

"She is still with Fernando?"

An odd choice of phrase, Matthew thought. "And her son. For now she is safe, but she's very worried about you. She seems to care a lot about you."

"She's … an old friend."

"Friend." Matthew let the ambiguity of the word hang between them. He turned into his apartment building and began up the stairs. "O-kay."

"She is more important than me right now. We have to protect her."

"I have a couple of people looking for her."

"What people? Police?"

"Not police or border agents. Friends. You can trust them."

"Who?"

Reaching the second floor, Matthew was puffing. "Amanda Doucette, the woman I work with, and a local outfitter."

"One woman? One man?"

"Yes. And a big enough boat for them all."

"Do they have a gun?"

Matthew stopped dead on the landing. "I don't think so. Why would they need a gun? Julio, what's going on?"

Silence again. A chill shot through Matthew. "Is something wrong? Is there something you're not telling me?"

"No, no! Fernando is frightened. Tell your friend just ... just be careful. Okay?"

With that, he hung up before Matthew could ask him what the hell he meant. Careful of what? Of Fernando? All his doubts and suspicions about Danielle crowded in. Was there something more going on? Had he inadvertently sent the intrepid Amanda straight into the path of danger?

The heat was sweltering in his apartment when he rushed in. He peeled off his sweaty suit as he jammed his phone in the crook of his neck and phoned Chris, praying the big goofy cop was still around.

"God!" Chris cried. "News?"

"Where are you?"

"Still stuck downtown behind some kind of goddamn parade."

Matthew laughed in his relief. "Welcome to the Big Smoke."

"I'm trying to get to Highway 400 so I can get up north."

Matthew dragged his overnight bag out from under the bed. "What happened to renting an airplane?"

"I am! Well, not renting, borrowing." Against a backdrop of engines rumbling, Matthew heard him sigh. "I wasted all morning trying to find a rental, but they want me to jump through a thousand hoops. I tried waving my RCMP badge, but no dice. My pilot's license isn't enough without proof I'd flown this model of aircraft in the last thirty days. Otherwise I'd have to go up with an instructor and … fuck, I've flown planes all over the north and Newfoundland, flown in blizzards and fog, landed on lakes smaller than postage stamps, but it's not enough. Then I remembered I have an RCMP buddy who retired up near Collingwood. He's got a plane right on the bay, and he's getting her ready as we speak. I just have to get out of this goddamn city!"

"Take me with you."

"What? What for?"

"I can help. Two pairs of eyes are better than one."

"No way! It's not a pleasure trip, Matthew. I can't take an inexperienced civilian —"

"Oh, for fuck's sake, Tymko! I've flown in dangerous missions all over the world. I've been right on the front lines, filed stories from the cockpit of a reconnaissance plane."

"But —"

"Amanda's in trouble, Chris. We both love her. We both owe it to her to do everything we can."

In the background, a motorcycle roared past. A horn honked. Matthew threw clothes into the bag. He waited.

"Do you know something?" Chris asked finally.

"Just that Julio gave me a cryptic warning about Danielle. And we don't really know much about her."

"We don't know anything about Julio, either."

"True." Matthew tossed his toothbrush and washing kit into the bag and zipped it shut. "Look, I'm packed. Ready to go. Tell me where to meet you."

"I don't like it."

"Lump it." Matthew locked his apartment door and ran down the stairs. "I'm grabbing a cab. Where?"

Chris caved in and gave him the name of a street corner just off the major expressway. Matthew was already running toward Queen Street, snapping his fingers at a passing cab, and as he threw himself into the back seat, a huge grin spread across his face.

The old newspaper hack was on the move.

What he hadn't told Chris was that his one and only flight in the combat zone in Afghanistan had nearly gotten him killed, and he'd vowed he would never set foot in a small plane again.

CHAPTER TWENTY-TWO

Chris drove like a rocket up Highway 400. In the middle of the day, the expressway was busy with trucks and commuters, forcing him to weave in and out like an Olympic skier in the Super G. His touch on the wheel was light and his timing split-second, but more than once Matthew felt he was back on the mad highways of Asia. After one such harrowing deke, he glanced over at Chris. Behind sunglasses, the man's expression was grim.

"I assume you guys give each other a pass when you get caught speeding."

Chris grunted. "A pass? I might even ask for an escort!" He reached over to check his phone then swore and tossed it aside.

"Do you want to call her again?" Matthew asked.

"What's the point? She knows my number. If she cared, she'd call me."

Matthew flinched at the bitterness. "When we get in the air, I'm going to phone her and blast her with both barrels for being such a selfish bitch."

"It won't help," Chris said. "When she's on a roll, nothing else matters."

"But there's more in her life than just her and her current mission. Especially now. I can tell her that."

Chris shot him an oblique glance. Matthew knew his face was red, and his voice had more of an edge than he'd intended. He forced himself to pull back.

"You've known her a long time," Chris said. "Was she always like this?"

Matthew shook his head. "But she's always tilted at windmills, ever since I've known her."

"How did you first meet?"

"In Thailand. She was a rookie on her first overseas job, working for a new Canadian NGO start-up called Caring for Cambodia, which was trying to rebuild the country's decimated school system. In the 1970s, the Khmer Rouge regime had assassinated all the intellectuals and professionals, including all the teachers, in an attempt to root out spies and dissidents. So there was no one left to teach the kids. No curriculum or textbooks, either. I was actually covering the conflicts in Afghanistan and Pakistan at the time but was taking some R&R in southern Thailand. It's a small world for the Canadian ex-pat community overseas, especially in Southeast Asia. We met on a beach." He smiled at the memory. "From the moment she learned I was a journalist, she began hounding me to cover Cambodia's struggle to rebuild. The world, of course, was more interested in wars. Iraq was descending into chaos. Afghanistan and Pakistan were both clusterfucks. Pakistan's progressive prime minister, Benazir Bhutto, had just been assassinated. Headline-grabbing shit. The bosses were never going to bankroll a nice feel-good story about Cambodian school children. Boy, did she give me an earful."

Chris floored the truck around a tractor-trailer before taking his eyes briefly off the road. "What was she like back then? Before ..."

"Before Nigeria? More easygoing and upbeat. A great tease. She was still the same shoot-with-both-barrels, go-through-the-mountain Amanda. But the trust ..." He shook his head dolefully. "She sees enemies now where she used to see allies."

"Like the cops."

Matthew shrugged. "In the countries where she worked, they were usually on the wrong side. But in Nigeria she was betrayed by people she thought she could trust. The security guards they hired to protect the village they were working in, for example. They were young men, many still in their teens, some even former students she'd helped. They were hired by some faceless international security firm that uses locals to protect companies and NGOs from thefts, attacks, and terrorists. But the firm's pay is shit and their training less than shit. The kids were easy to bribe and bully. When the Islamic terrorists invaded, the kids all folded like scared puppets. They either joined the terrorists or turned tail and ran."

He paused. Dark memories of Amanda's ordeal crowded in, but he wondered whether she would want them shared. "Has she told you any of this stuff?"

Chris shook his head. "Just broad strokes. We've talked about some of the experiences that just don't let us go. I lost a woman I thought I loved in a botched shoot-out up north. Amanda told me she and her colleague Phil escaped their burning village in the dead of night, but she couldn't save the children."

Matthew nodded. "Couldn't save" didn't begin to describe the horrors. Save from a life of sexual slavery and abuse or a quick death as a suicide bomber or child soldier. "And that's what haunts her the most. Not that she was almost killed. Not that she spent a month hiding in the countryside trying to get to Lagos. It's that she couldn't save the children. They kidnapped the children they wanted and slaughtered the ones who were too young."

Silence. Matthew glanced at Chris, whose face had closed as if a dark cloud had passed over his thoughts. *I've obviously touched a nerve*, he thought. The longer any of us work in the dark halls of human pain, the more black clouds gather in the recesses of our mind. He wondered about the woman Chris had lost and about all the other innocents the Mountie had been unable to save.

"If you're going to be involved with Amanda," he said quietly, "you'll have to understand that about her. The burden she carries is one she can never cast off. But for all that, she's worth a thousand ordinary women."

The dark cloud hung thick as Chris drove on in silence. *You're so fucking lucky,* Matthew wanted to scream at him. *Don't you dare screw this up.* But he'd already said more than he should. Instead, he held his tongue and busied himself with the GPS.

Finally, Chris drew in a deep breath. "I don't know. I don't know if I can handle it."

Whitecaps danced on the waves, catching the afternoon sunlight. Amanda was draped over the bow, her eyes aching from hours of staring at endless water and rock. They were hugging the edge of the islands as closely as Larry dared. He stood at the wheel, studying the land and water up ahead. The engine's low growl carried over the lake and would alert anyone within a three-hundred-metre radius. If George were on a mission of private revenge, he'd keep out of sight. But Amanda hoped Danielle would be looking for their turquoise boat and would make her presence known.

A muffled crack echoed across the water. A snapped branch? A trick of the wind? Kaylee stood up, her ears pricked forward. Amanda signalled for Larry to cut the engine. Together they listened. Waves slapped against the hull and crashed onto the shore. The boat rocked. As they blew toward land, they peered at the shoreline and the inlets nearby.

Nothing.

Kaylee's nose twitched, her ears relaxed, and after a moment she settled back down on the floor.

"Maybe it was nothing," Amanda said, trying to maintain a whisper above the rush of the wind and waves. Voices carried for miles over open water.

Larry shrugged, started the engine up, and revved the boat clear of the approaching rocks. Her phone shrilled, making her jump. She glanced at it. Matthew. *Either answer it or decline it, because this racket will alert the entire bay.*

"Matthew," she whispered.

"Amanda! For fuck's sake, finally. Where are you?" He shouted over the roar of background noise.

"I'm in Larry Judge's boat," she said, still whispering. "We're searching the archipelago south of Parry Sound."

"Any luck?"

"No sign of them yet. We're about twenty miles south, I think."

"Just past Frying Pan Island," Larry interjected. Amanda repeated this. "Where are you? I can hardly hear you."

"Chris and I are just west of Collingwood, on our way to his friend's place to pick up a floatplane. We're going to join the search."

Relief flooded in. She'd been afraid Chris would be furious. "You guys are the best! There have been a couple of planes and helicopters overhead, and boats farther out, but otherwise it's pretty quiet."

"Chris says they'll be doing searches by grid, but air searches over water are tricky, even with the proper equipment. With all the islands and whitecaps, visibility will be poor. We'll fly as low and as slowly as we dare, but Chris says the wind can be wicked out on the open bay."

Amanda strained to catch the gist of his words. "Keep an eye out for turquoise boats. Danielle's and ours are both turquoise."

"Danielle called again."

"What?"

"Danielle called me. She spotted George's boat, but when I told her who it was, she freaked out. So she and her husband have probably gone farther into the islands. She may be even more lost than she was before, but now she's hiding. She'll be hard to spot."

Amanda thought about the distant crack she'd heard. Could it have been a shout for help? Of pain or fear? It had echoed off the granite rocks and reverberated back and forth over the water, making it impossible to pinpoint its origin.

"She's right to be wary of George, because I don't know what he's up to. But can you phone her again?" she asked. "Tell her to be on the lookout for us."

"Amanda, I'm not sure it's safe for you. What do we really know about her and her husband?"

"We've been over this," she snapped. The boat was rocking and pitching in the swell, and she struggled just to hang on, let alone search for shoals and rehash the argument with Matthew.

"I spoke to ..." he said.

The wind whipped his words away. "What?"

"Julio! He kind of implied you should be careful."

"Careful doesn't tell me anything helpful."

"There seems to be a complicated relationship between them all. He's worried about Danielle's safety, and she's protective of him. He didn't really come right out and say it, but I think the husband's the problem. Julio asked if you had a gun."

"Well, we don't." Not in a million years would she hold a gun ever again.

"So all I'm saying is ... approach with caution."

A muffled voice in the background interrupted them. After a brief argument with Chris, Matthew came back on the line. "Chris says if you spot them, don't approach at all. You have a smartphone. Send us the coordinates and let us deal with it."

"How? From the air?"

"Amanda!" Chris shouted in the background. "Trust me, okay? Let me and Neville Standish handle it!"

She wavered. With everyone piling on, Danielle and Fernando might be driven farther into a corner. Trapped and confused, only God knew what they'd do.

Chris's voice penetrated the silence. "Please trust me."

She heard the plea in his voice and imagined the soft crinkle of his blue eyes. She wanted to reassure him, but before she could reply, a loud bang split the air and the boat jolted, throwing her off balance. The phone flew from her hand. Larry cursed and cut the engines.

"We hit a rock," he said. "I need to go ashore to check the propellers. Grab that paddle."

"Amanda? Amanda!" Chris's voice bleated frantically from the bottom of the boat. "Are you okay?"

"We're fine, gotta go!" she shouted, grabbing the phone and shoving it into her pocket. She seized the paddle just as the boat swung perilously close to a chunk of granite. Larry was already paddling hard on the port side. She pushed away from the rock, and together they struggled to paddle the steel tub toward a small, reedy opening in the rocky shore.

Within minutes Larry had laid his toolkit on the flat rock and waded out to inspect the propellers. Amanda paced with growing worry, for the afternoon sun was already low on the horizon.

"Can you repair it?"

He nodded, pulling out a pair of wrenches. "Just dinged the prop. Maybe fifteen minutes."

"Can I help?"

He raised his head and eyed her as one might a two-year-old offering to help with a chain saw. She held her hands up in mock surrender, prompting a faint smile from him. He nodded toward a small hill farther down the island.

"Climb that. Maybe you can see something from the top."

She suspected it was a make-work project, but she dutifully leashed Kaylee and set off. The wind hurled the waves up the granite shore. They foamed at her feet, and she hugged her jacket tightly against the cold. Scudding white clouds crowded the blue sky now, their shadows playing over the silver surf.

The hill barely qualified as a mound, yet when she breached the top, a vista spread out for miles on the other side. Little islands and tongues of land, silver crevices of water, and dark, brooding slabs of evergreen forest. And on a farther island, peeking out of a narrow crack in the wooded shore, two boats. She trained her binoculars and moved them back and forth. One boat was small and turquoise, the other bigger and multi-coloured. As she focussed, she could make out the leaping kayak painted on its side.

Good God. He had found them.

She drew her binoculars over the shoreline in search of movement or the bright colours of life jackets. Nothing. Neither on the granite shore nor in the grass before the dark trees swallowed up the ground.

She didn't dare shout out. Shoving her binoculars back into her knapsack, she raced back down the path, one hand clutching Kaylee's leash and the other arm pinwheeling for balance. Larry looked up in surprise as she leaped across the granite shore. She waved toward the hill behind her.

"They're there!" She gasped for breath. "All of them. George has found them!"

A faint call echoed over the water. Larry chopped the air to silence her and then stood very still, his eyes searching and his nostrils flaring. She suspected every one of his senses was tuned toward the sound.

Another cry, weaker and more drawn out.

Larry picked up his wrench and strode toward the sound. In his heavy, steel-toed boots, he was as agile as an antelope. Halfway around the island, a distant engine roared to life, and within seconds a boat came streaking out between the islands. Its prow rose and its bottom slammed the waves as it accelerated south toward the open water. Amanda could make out the leaping kayak motif and a single person at the helm.

"That's George's boat. I'm going to call Chris." Amanda took out her phone, and as she dialled, she scrambled to keep up with Larry's effortless stride. The line was dead. Amanda swore as she glanced at her phone. Did she have a signal? One bar. And her battery registered ten percent.

Goddamn! She had no power to waste on finding a signal.

Larry had outstripped her, and she leaped recklessly over the rocks to catch up. In order to use her phone, she had let Kaylee go free, and the dog danced along the shoreline, staying close as if she sensed their apprehension.

Bypassing the hill, Larry had circled the island to the inner shore, and soon they were standing on a reedy point, looking across a channel at a barren slab of rock. No narrow creek, no boats.

"I think it's the island on the other side," he said. "We need the boat."

"But —"

"We still have one engine." He must have seen the skepticism on her face, for he gestured toward the channel. "Or we can row."

"Very funny." She turned to head back to the boat. "There's no time to waste."

They had heard no more cries for help from the other island, but she tried not to dwell on the implications. Once they were back in the boat, Larry putted it cautiously around the island. Across the choppy channel, he had to fight hard to keep the boat straight against the brisk crosswind, but once they reached the lee of the second island, they made faster progress. Amanda tried Chris again, and once again was met with empty air.

"There," Larry whispered, pointing. She followed his finger. They had reached the other side of the intervening island and now could see across a second, narrower channel to the large, forested island beyond. The turquoise boat was aground on the reedy shore. There was no sign of movement nearby, but it would be easy to hide in the shelter of the pines. By contrast, she and Larry were sitting ducks out on the water, visible from anywhere along the shore.

She could only pray no one had a gun. As if he had the same fears, Larry revved the engine to cover the short distance to the reedy creek and rammed his boat up alongside the other. They both sat still, listening and waiting. Nothing. If anyone had noticed their arrival, no one was responding.

Larry climbed out to inspect the other boat, which was half swamped from a jagged hole in the bow. His face was grim, but he said nothing as he turned to lead the way along the shore. He had picked up his wrench from his tool box again, small comfort against a bullet but better than nothing. As they jumped from rock to rock, Amanda kept a close eye on Kaylee, who was alert and straining forward on her leash. Her nose was twitching — their early warning system. Amanda gestured to Larry, who nodded and stepped aside to let the dog lead the way. Kaylee's paws scrabbled on the rock as she pulled them along a granite shelf, and an anxious whine bubbled in her throat. The whine grew louder, and she fairly danced as she dragged Amanda on.

At the base of a granite rise, the dog stopped to sniff a smear on the pale pink rock. Then another and another. Amanda touched the smear, and her fingertip came away wet and red. Her scalp prickled. Fuck. *Fuck!*

Larry put his hand on her arm to hold her back then gestured for her to stay put while he went ahead, wrench in hand. She acquiesced gratefully. He was right; he was far bigger and stronger and had a weapon. Moreover, he moved with a cat-like stealth born of years roaming these rocky shores. She would only slow him down.

She led Kaylee toward the shelter of scraggly pines while he continued on the trail of the bloodstains. Crouching down under a large bough, she tried to stifle her breathing. Kaylee was panting, and her eyes were wide with excitement as she watched Larry disappear over a ridge. Soon they were alone in the silence broken only by the swish of waves and the rustle of wind through the trees. Too alone, Amanda thought.

She pulled her cellphone out of her pocket, relieved to see two bars. She accessed her phone map, copied her coordinates, and pasted them into a text to Chris, along with a note that they had spotted both boats. Then she turned off her phone to preserve its battery and drew Kaylee deeper into the shadows to wait.

CHAPTER TWENTY-THREE

Chris and Matthew were weaving through the rolling hills west of Collingwood when Amanda's text came through. According to his GPS, they were still ten minutes from his friend's remote country home. He glanced at the text, stifling his alarm that Amanda was blundering into danger, before handing the phone to Matthew.

"Map that location, will you? I'm going to inform Neville Standish."

Standish's phone went to voicemail, and Chris was halfway through listening to his long, official preamble when Standish himself came on the line with a much more succinct "Standish!"

Chris dispensed with preamble himself. "Amanda has a sighting," he said. "She sent me the coordinates, and I'll forward them to you."

"Gifford or Danielle?"

"Both."

"Did you tell her to stay clear?"

"I didn't talk to her. She sent a text."

"Where are you?"

Chris looked at the map Matthew had pulled up. "We can be in the area in half an hour." Not quite, but good enough to keep him in the game.

"Who's we?"

Chris paused. Glanced at Matthew. Standish would go ape-shit. "I meant me. The plane and me."

"Get on the phone and tell her to get the hell out of the way. You too. I want that area cleared so we can move in."

"Where are you?"

"We're everywhere, Tymko! Now if you get out of our way and let me notify Incident Command —"

In the background, Chris heard Standish on the radio, reporting the latest intel. He suppressed his impatience. Precious minutes were being lost. "We don't know what we're dealing with. I can do a flyover and report back what I see."

Standish came back on the line. "And spook them while you're at it? Drive them deeper underground?"

"My friend's plane has no official markings. I'll just be one more rich cottager heading up to their island."

A muttered string of curses followed by a pause. "Look, Tymko, things just got a whole lot more serious. The post-mortem on Ronny revealed that he hit his head on a rock in a fall, which could have been accidental, but he died of exposure. Traces of dirt were found in his lungs, meaning he was still alive when he was buried. Probably unconscious, but alive. Forensics is trying to pull DNA from the clothes and the shoes and — if we're lucky — fingerprints, but as of now, Ronny's death is officially a homicide. And one of the people your girlfriend is looking for did it."

Chris fought the jolt of fear that shot up his spine. "All the more reason to —"

"To get the hell out. And get off this phone and tell your girlfriend to get the hell out!"

"Will do," Chris replied humbly.

"And update me as soon as you're both clear."

Chris signed off. Matthew had been studying the GPS map, and now he glanced at Chris. "He's pissed."

Chris shrugged. There was no time to explain. He punched in Amanda's number and listened with growing frustration as it rang and rang. "Amanda, don't do this to me!" He tossed the phone at Matthew as he swerved right onto a narrower road. "You keep trying while I turn up the gas."

Rocketing through the country roads, he arrived at his friend's estate in five minutes. He barely registered the expanse of manicured lawn, the ornamental gardens, and the cluster of buildings along the shore as he focussed on the single-engine Beaver bobbing off the main dock. A tall, ramrod-straight man with a white buzz cut and spindly legs strode up as Chris skidded to a stop near the dock. Greetings were kept to a minimum as Chris introduced Vince Sutherland, and within minutes they were all bent over the electronic navigational chart in the man's luxury boathouse. They punched in Amanda's coordinates and then studied the red dot buried deep within a dense maze of islands.

"That's in the middle of Massassauga Provincial Park," Vince said. "It's a maze of bays, islands, and dead-end inlets. Without a detailed map and excellent navigational skills, you could wander around in there for days."

Chris stared at the map with dismay. "How do you even get in there?"

"There's one land access point, here at Pete's Place." Vince pointed to a long, squiggly line through the forest off the highway. "From there, it's by boat."

Chris traced his finger over the maze of straits and inlets leading out from Pete's Place. "Fuck, the cops will never get in there!" he muttered. "Coming by road from Parry Sound to this access point, dragging their boat trailers and search gear, it'll take them at least an hour just to get on the water! But coming in from the lake, even if they have the best navigational apps, they're going to have to crawl through these shoals."

Because he'd done numerous searches by plane over forest and water, he also knew how impossible it would be to spot one tiny boat among the acres and acres of rocks, trees, and silver ribbons of water. Yet the air search was his best hope, and Neville Standish be damned.

"Amanda!" The urgent bellow rose from the trees and echoed across the granite shores. Larry! Holding tight to Kaylee, Amanda ducked out of her hiding spot and hurried toward the sound. She leaped over crevices and scrambled up lichen-encrusted rocks. Soon she spotted Larry in the distance, bent over a prostrate figure sprawled on the rocks. Amanda's breath caught. Not again. *Not again!*

Larry had stripped off his shirt and was pressing it to the injured person's head. The body was too big to be Danielle or her son. Fernando? Had George attacked him and left him for dead? Had he taken off with Danielle and her boy? If so, why? And where?

Only once she was ten feet away, staring at his bloody face, did she recognize the downed man. Larry wiped his blood-stained hands on his pants and looked up.

"He's alive. Bad, but alive."

"George!"

Larry nodded. "Looks like he was hit by buckshot. Grazed his temple. They bleed like a bitch, but it might not be as bad as it looks."

Her gaze shifted to the open channel, where they had seen George's boat moments ago. "Then ..."

"They took his boat."

Amanda knelt at George's side and did her own brief check of his vital signs. His pulse was steady but weak. Judging from the blood pooling around him and oozing over the rock, he'd lost a lot of blood. She turned on her phone, grateful to see a signal but dismayed by the fading battery. She had to make every moment count.

Larry was already fishing out his VHF radio. "You call in the emergency," she said, "911 or the marine OPP. I'll call Chris."

As she was punching in his number, George's eyes fluttered open. "Chris!" she cried the instant she heard his voice. Never had a sound been sweeter!

"Amanda! Where —"

"No time, Chris. No battery. They hurt George and took his boat. Heading southwest into the open channel. Look for his boat!"

"Are you safe?"

"Yes, yes. We're calling for help —" Her phone beeped and powered off. *Damn.* She took a deep breath. Surely the message was enough. Chris and the police could take it from there.

George was shaking his head weakly. "Danielle," he murmured.

Amanda bent over him and checked his pulse again. Still steady. "What about Danielle? Did she do this?"

He kept shaking his head. "Not important. Kaitlyn. You've got to help her."

"Kaitlyn is safe. Don't worry. She'll get the help she needs in Toronto. George, we have to get you to hospital."

Larry reappeared at their side with a grunt. "We're meeting the coast guard at a marina en route to Parry Sound. It will save time. You keep the pressure on the wound, and I'll bring my boat around."

"We shouldn't move him, Larry. Not without a back board and neck brace."

He gave his crooked little smile. "Don't worry, I have a plan. I'll fix the prop too."

As she watched him disappear over the ridge, she became aware of George plucking her sleeve weakly. "No. No!" Spittle formed on his lips in his struggle to speak. "Kaitlyn has disappeared!"

"Where?"

"From rehab. Janine called me. Thought I took her away, because I asked Frankie to talk to her ..." He paused to catch his breath. "But she ran away."

"Do you know where?"

He lifted one shoulder. "In the city? Looking for drugs?"

He was straining to explain. She was so concerned about his agitation that she almost missed a crucial part of George's message. Janine had called.

"Do you have a phone, George?"

"In ... in my jacket."

She rummaged until she retrieved the phone. Fortunately, it had fifty percent battery power. As she started to dial Chris, George clutched her arm again. "Call Janine! Find out about Kaitlyn."

"George, we need to get you to the hospital. Don't tire yourself. The Toronto police will find Kaitlyn."

"No! Janine won't call them." He shut his eyes as if to gather his strength. She waved blackflies from his face. "The publicity ... Janine doesn't want to truth to come ..."

"What truth?"

"About Benson. About the drugs. Call her!" His eyes fluttered shut, and this time they didn't open again. Alarmed, Amanda checked his pulse again and felt its steady beat beneath her fingers. She laid her jacket over him before turning on his phone and accessing recent calls. Janine was the last call, received an hour ago. Amanda pressed the number and waited through half a dozen rings before Janine's voice blasted over the line.

"What, George? There's no fucking news!"

"Janine, it's Amanda Doucette."

Stunned silence, then a steel calm voice, as if Janine had pulled herself back from the brink. "Amanda, I haven't time for a chat. Where's George?"

"He's been attacked, and I don't have time to chat either. I know Kaitlyn has run away. What does she have to do with any of this?"

"Any of what?"

"Benson's death. The drug cover-up."

"That's none of your fucking business."

"There are killers out there, and if she's run away —"

"Kaitlyn doesn't have anything to do with it! She's fourteen years old!"

Amanda switched tacks. "Don't you realize she could be in danger? What if the killer figures out she knows something?"

Silence.

Amanda pressed on. "She does know something about the night Benson died, doesn't she? She knows how he got the drugs. Maybe she supplied them."

"Ridiculous."

"Maybe you supplied them."

"Stay out of it, you meddling bitch! You and George and that freak Frankie! Give us some privacy."

Amanda felt a spike of anger. The girl was fourteen years old. Whatever had happened, Janine's first instinct was to protect her own ass. "Is that it? I know you have some pretty wild parties up there, and who knows what's in drugs these days."

"I don't have to listen to this."

Amanda's anger swept her on. She studied the pale, still figure before her. He was breathing evenly, but she knew head injuries could go south in a minute. How many decent, honest people were going to get caught up in Janine's toxic world? *Keep her talking*, she thought as she scanned the shore for Larry's reassuring figure.

"Then why don't you hang up? Because you want to know what I know. He used your money to buy her a house — *your* nanny, who you thought was your own perfect slave — and all the while ..."

Janine barked a harsh laugh. "Benson was a fool! He got his payback, but not from me."

Amanda held her breath. Had something broken loose from Janine's wall of secrecy? "From who?"

"Who do you think? I've been saying it all along. She's no innocent; she's got a university degree, for fuck's sake, and all kinds of medical certifications. Drugs would be a piece of cake for her. But nobody wants to see that tiny little girl as anything but a victim of us big, bad, rich people. Well, she's playing you all."

With that salvo, she finally did hang up, leaving Amanda wondering who was playing whom. She looked back down at George, who lay so still. She leaned over to check his vitals and shook him gently.

"George, stay with me. George!"

He moaned.

"Talk to me, George. Who did this to you? Danielle? Fernando?"

He opened his eyes but stared into nothingness. At that moment Kaylee growled. In the distance, deep in the woods, leaves crunched. Amanda stood up to stare. She saw nothing but sensed that eyes were watching her. She shivered. *Get a grip, Doucette.* Where the hell was Larry? How long did it take to fix a propeller?

She took George's cold hands in hers. Rubbing them, she leaned down to whisper in his ear. "George, I promise I'll find out about Kaitlyn. Don't worry."

The man was ashen and looked worn out. But he licked his lips and found the strength to speak. "Save her."

Still using his phone, Amanda dialled Matthew. He answered with a cautious, clipped "Goderich." Only when he heard her voice did his warm enthusiasm flood in. Quickly she brought him up to date and asked whether Chris or the police had any news on the search for Danielle and Fernando.

"Not yet. Chris and I are about to take off. But the cops know," he said. "Stay out of their way, Amanda."

"Oh, I will. Larry and I are taking George back to the Parry Sound hospital."

"Why the hell don't you call the EMS!" he exclaimed. "That's what they're there for."

"We did. We're just saving time. Larry knows the way out of these treacherous shoals better than anyone, so we're meeting them en route. Matthew, don't argue with me! I'm glad you haven't left yet. I need you to do something else for me."

"What?" His tone changed from frustrated to focussed.

"Kaitlyn has apparently gone on the lam in Toronto."

"Kaitlyn? I thought she was in a hospital bed up in Parry Sound."

"No, Janine had her moved to a private rehab facility in Toronto."

There was a pause. Over the phone, she could hear a revving engine and distant male voices. "Are you saying you want me to find her?" Matthew asked.

Kaylee growled again. She was standing rigidly now, her gaze fixed on the woods and her hackles raised. Amanda gripped the phone tightly. Where the hell was Larry? "Janine refuses to involve the cops, but you can poke around. Find out where a fourteen-year-old Rosedale kid on the run would go to look for drugs."

"Amanda, there are dozens of street corners!"

She shuddered. "No, I think she'd try to contact one of her sources. Maybe Julio. And that could be bad news, because Julio may be involved in this. He might even have tried to kill her once."

She could sense his reluctance over the phone. She was asking a lot of him to chase after drug dealers and killers. If he poked the wrong hornets' nest ... on the other hand, he'd been poking hornets' nests for decades.

"I still think the cops ought to be called," he said.

The trees behind her rustled. She whirled around and saw a pine bough shift. Kaylee barked. "I gotta go. Do what you think is right. But I think you can be much more effective using your contacts in Toronto than flying five hundred feet over miles of wilderness." With that, she hung up just as a figure stepped through the trees. Short, slender, wearing a black hoodie pulled tight to escape the bugs. In his hand was a battered old shotgun.

Fernando.

CHAPTER TWENTY-FOUR

Their eyes locked. His expression was inscrutable, but the gun twitched at his side. Amanda tamped down all signs of fear as she rose to face him. Kaylee ran forward, barking.

"Fernando" was on the tip of Amanda's tongue before she remembered she wasn't supposed to know who he was. *Play dumb*, she told herself as she called Kaylee back and tried for her friendliest tone.

"Hello. This man is hurt. Can you help me?"

He looked at George, who lay unconscious and motionless on the rock. "He is dead?" he asked in strongly accented English.

"No, but badly hurt."

His gaze softened, becoming almost pleading. "I am lost. You have a boat?"

Once again her mind raced. What was the safest answer? He could be a killer, and if so, he'd shoot her to steal her boat without a moment's hesitation.

"You have no boat?" she countered.

"Broken." He gestured down the shore. As he approached, she saw he was bloody from scratches and insect bites. One eye was nearly swollen shut. Despite the gun in his hand, he didn't look anything like a killer.

But then again, neither did Danielle.

As he approached, she tried not to stare at the gun. She tried instead to hold his gaze. He laid the gun down and knelt at George's side. "He is bad. You have a phone?" He mimicked calling for help.

She edged over, trying to get between him and the gun. Once again she sidestepped the question adroitly. "My name is Amanda. What's yours?"

"Fernando."

"Are you all by yourself out here?"

He nodded, and to her surprise, tears welled in his eyes. "My wife leave in boat. Take my son."

"She left you out here?" She allowed incredulity into her voice.

He nodded, a single tear spilling.

"Why?"

He shrugged. "She say get help." He dropped his gaze as if he couldn't meet hers. Either he was hiding something, or his English wasn't up to a complex explanation. Although English was widely spoken in the Philippines, his wife's mastery of it seemed far greater than his. Janine had said she had a university degree. Another wedge between them?

Amanda nudged the gun aside surreptitiously with her toe. She remembered Danielle had been rescued from the water without a single possession. "Does she have any money?"

Still he didn't meet her gaze, and his reply was barely audible. "She take ... she take man's wallet."

Would she be fool enough to try the credit card? Danielle struck her as anything but a fool. Amanda gestured to George. "Did she do this?"

"No! The gun bang, accident." He seemed to warm to his story. "My wife was afraid. Run away."

"What was she afraid of?"

He searched for words or perhaps a plausible lie. "A bear? Hurt my son?"

"And she left you all alone with this bear?"

He gestured to the gun. "She left me the gun."

She knew he couldn't have brought it into the country, and he'd had little time to go gun shopping. It was a long, heavy shotgun, old enough to be antique, so possibly it had been stolen from one of the empty cottages along the way. She tried for a friendly, nonthreatening tone. "Where are you from, Fernando?"

"Philippines. But stay in Canada now."

"You're a long way from home. Where were you going, out here on the lake?"

"To Toronto. My wife have a house in Toronto."

"But she left you here."

"No. Get help."

Amanda bent to check George's pulse again. He was getting colder, and his pallor had taken on a bluish tinge. She called Kaylee over to lie at his side, and she took off her fleece to place on top of him, leaving her shivering in her T-shirt. *Jesus, Larry, where are you?* In the silence she heard the low growl of a boat. *Thank God!* To distract Fernando, she pressed on. "I don't understand how this man was shot by accident."

"He is shouting at us. Running. We lift the gun up, try to stop him. It go bang." He pantomimed the scene of holding the gun against an assault.

It was a stretch. Credible, but only just. She allowed herself a look of skepticism. "It sounds more like he ran toward you and you shot him."

Fernando's eyes grew wide and he recoiled from her. "No, no! Accident!"

The low growl had stopped. Amanda uttered a silent plea. Was that Larry? "Was it you or your wife who shot him?"

He still stared in horror, once again seemed to weigh the best answer. "My ... my wife."

It could have happened that way, or he could be changing his story to cast blame on the wife who had run off on him.

It occurred to her that although she knew almost nothing about either of them, Danielle was the stronger of the two. She was the one who had gone overseas to support the family, endured years of mistreatment, and fought so fiercely to get a home and papers for the husband and son. Fernando was crumbling under the first real threat he had faced.

"You have a boat?" he asked again, and this time before she had decided on an answer, she saw Larry striding up over the ridge, leaping from one granite slab to the next. In his arms he carried a coil of rope, an emergency blanket, and two long planks. Floorboards from the boat?

A spasm of panic raced across Fernando's face before he broke into a broad grin. "Larry!" he cried.

The big man's face relaxed. Fernando rushed forward, babbling in Tagalog what sounded like a prayer of thanks. "I am lost. Your boat is broken."

Larry nodded, his gaze flitting from Fernando to Amanda, who had dived to pick up the gun. "Everything okay here?"

With a shiver, Amanda hefted the gun's cold, alien weight and broke it open. Empty. She breathed a sigh of relief and only then looked over at Larry. "It is now. But we have to get George to hospital right away. Fernando here says his wife and son took George's boat."

Larry looked alarmed. "Does she know how to drive it?"

"Somewhat," Amanda replied, remembering how Danielle had swamped her escape boat earlier. "Where's our boat?"

"Just over the rise." Larry frowned. "Why did she take off?"

"It's not clear," Amanda said. "It's also not clear how George got hurt."

Larry bent at George's side to check his carotid pulse. His

frown of worry deepened. "We'll leave that to the cops. Let's stabilize his back and neck and get him to the boat fast."

Careful to move him as little as possible, the three of them wrapped him, eased him onto the planks, and lashed his head, chest, and legs with rope. Larry lifted his upper body and Fernando his lower. The injured man was lean but solid, and the Filipino staggered under his weight. Setting down the gun, Amanda moved to help Fernando, and together they inched their way over the uneven rock and down into the narrow crevice where Larry had secured the boat. When they laid him out on the padded bench, Kaylee leaped in beside him and nuzzled him like an anxious mother.

The waves bumped the boat against the rocks, and George's face contorted with pain. *At least he's aware of pain,* Amanda thought as she stuffed extra cushions around him. "We've got to get moving," she said.

Fernando hovered. "You take me with you?"

"Sure," said Larry. "Hop in."

"No," Amanda countered, the words out of her mouth before she'd even thought about it. Both Larry and Fernando looked at her in surprise. "I'm sorry, Fernando. George has to come first. I don't know how he got hurt —"

"Accident!"

"Maybe, but we can't be worried about you while George is so sick."

Fernando looked to Larry for support, but the guide busied himself wrapping a PFD cushion on George. His head was bowed. Fernando's face began to crumple as he recognized defeat. "You leave me on the island? Alone? With bears?"

"Bears won't hurt you," Larry mumbled.

Amanda's heart ached. "We'll notify the Coast Guard that you're here. They'll come for you."

"Coast Guard?" Fernando's face scrunched in confusion.

"They rescue people. They're like the police."

Fernando's jaw gaped. "Police?" He shook his head in fear, the same reaction his wife had had to the mention of police. But this time Amanda knew he had good reason to fear the police. Dead bodies, illegal escape, and lots of questions.

"I have a friend in the police," she said. "He's looking for you by plane. You can trust him."

Fernando's chin trembled, and once again a single tear spilled.

"He's a good guy," she said gently, on the verge of relenting. "We'll leave you food and blankets until he comes." She reached for the storage boxes under the seat.

"You leave the gun?"

In the split second of Amanda's hesitation, Larry nodded. He had been silently sorting through his equipment box, and now he offered Fernando a boat repair kit.

"You can try to patch your boat. It's not a big hole."

Fernando didn't move. As Larry laid all the supplies down on the rocks, he merely watched in helpless bewilderment. Larry glanced at Amanda. She saw the silent plea in his eyes, but she forced herself to shake her head. They didn't know whom to trust and what story to believe, but one fact was beyond dispute; Ronny's injury may have been accidental, but his burial was not. The two of them had tried for a respectful, Christian burial, but the truth remained that they had buried him alive. Panicked, careless, or ruthless?

None of them spoke as Larry poled the boat off shore and turned it into the waves. Fernando remained a forlorn figure at the water's edge as they roared away. All Larry's attention was directed toward avoiding the treacherous shoals, but once they were safely free, he continued to ignore her. She pulled out George's phone to report in to the EMS. Once she'd reported their coordinates and George's condition, EMS decided a hand-over at Frying Pan Island would be the most efficient. It was out of the worst of the shoals and had a marina. Meanwhile, she would keep them updated on his status so they could provide assistance.

Larry was staring impassively out over the water, and she didn't think he'd been listening, but after a while, he spoke. "Fernando is a good guy."

"I didn't like leaving him there either, Larry, but we couldn't take the risk he'd try to take over the boat."

"You don't know him. He was so happy to come to Canada and so excited to meet his wife again. He just wants to be a family again. He is a good father, held his little boy in his lap the whole trip in the truck, showing him things out the window. He said they saved money for years for this chance to come to Canada and give their son a good life."

It was the longest speech she'd ever heard from him. "I know that. Believe me, I know how he felt. I've seen that same hope in so many faces overseas. 'Can you help me get into Canada, can you sponsor me, can you get me a visa?' But it doesn't change the facts. Ronny is dead and George is badly injured. That's desperation, Larry. Desperation makes good people do bad things. Do you want to be out on the open water when he decides he doesn't want to go back to town where the cops are waiting? That he'd rather hijack the boat, toss us overboard, and go south toward Toronto instead?"

Larry snorted. "Fernando couldn't throw us overboard. I weigh twice what he does."

"Maybe, but he had a gun."

"No ammunition. And we would have left the gun behind."

"I'm not happy he has a gun now. If he's that desperate, anything could go wrong when the cops come to rescue him."

Larry was silent a moment. "He was a good man trying to make an honest living in the Philippines, working for pennies a day in a shoe factory. Canadians don't know what being poor is like. Being scared to walk the streets. He talked about police killing people in the city at night. No trial, no proof, just shot. Even his brother. This was his hope. That's all I am saying."

Amanda could scarcely believe she was taking the side of law and order over that of a poor man who had suffered enough. She glanced at George. If they didn't have him to protect, she would have taken her chances.

"It's not our call to decide if he's innocent, Larry. This is not a police state, and he will get rescued. Whatever else happens depends on what he's done."

He grunted. "And not who he is? Not the colour of his skin?"

She felt a twinge of shame. She walked on the privileged side of the fence, and she had seen how different it could be on the other side. "I hope not, Larry. If he's innocent, I'll do everything I can once this is over."

"Innocent." Larry grunted again, as if that too were a privilege accorded to her side of the fence. When people scrounged a living in the dirt of poverty and crime and prejudice, innocence was an early casualty.

"I'll help. Chris will help."

"I talked to him. Whatever he did, he was in over his head. What does he know about our laws and rules, the way we do things? He got a call from his wife. She said come right away. She had a house for them and a job in construction for him, but he had to get a visa fast. He spent a lot of his money getting a visa from a guy his wife told him about. She's the one who knew the ropes and told him what to do. She means everything to him, and now she's dumped him like a bunch of garbage." Larry set his jaw and squinted against the sun slanting off the lake. "If anyone is guilty in all this, it's that wife of his."

CHAPTER TWENTY-FIVE

Chris eased the yoke forward and dropped the plane another two hundred feet. Below him, the lake wove silver threads through islands that shimmered like pink, black, and green opals in the afternoon sun. Although the vast canopy looked the same for miles, his GPS told him he was approaching the coordinates Amanda had sent.

He'd been keeping an eye out for George's boat, but even from five hundred feet it was impossible to tell one boat from another. The lake was streaked with long ribbons as boats made their way across it.

The tiny Beaver was a dream, more than half a century old but still as solid as a tank. She was noisy as hell, and the control wheel throbbed beneath his hands, but she would probably fly forever. Despite the gravity of the task at hand, he smiled at the sheer joy of being in the air again. How he had missed this! The sun played across the windshield, and the clouds whipped by in streaks of pink and gold. He dipped and turned playfully to get the feel for the plane.

Soaring high above the miniature world always restored his perspective. Now his frustration and anger melted away, and problems that had loomed large seemed trivial. He was glad Matthew wasn't with him and suspected his friend felt the same.

The poor man had paled at the sight of the pockmarked little plane bobbing in the water, and his voice had quavered when he asked how old it was. His pallor had taken on a greenish tinge when Vince said it was fifty-five years old. "Probably older than you," the man had laughed, "but in better shape. I do every bit of the maintenance on her myself."

Vince was also a vintage car freak and owned an entire stable of more-or-less drivable cars. Matthew had borrowed one of his classic British sports cars and roared off with a huge grin on his face and a trail of fumes in his wake. By now he'd be halfway to Toronto in pursuit of Amanda's latest cockamamie idea.

While here I am, floating over Georgian Bay in search of an elusive boat, and both of us in heaven.

His phone rang, an unknown number. He linked the phone to his earphones and microphone. Amanda's voice came through, thin and reedy. "Everything all right?" he shouted above the din of the engine.

"More or less. Where are you?"

"Somewhere over the islands. Where are you?"

"Larry and I are taking George up to Frying Pan Island."

Chris felt a wash of relief. "How is he?"

"I think he'll be all right, but we're going as fast as we can." She paused. He could hear the roar of the engine. "Is Matthew with you?"

"No." He chuckled. "I don't think he trusted my piloting skills. He got a better offer — 1969 MGB, dark British racing green — and he's on his way back to Toronto to look for Kaitlyn. So you can reassure George on that score."

"I bet he's loving that!"

"He was really holding out for the Lotus."

She didn't laugh. Instead she dropped her voice. "I have a favour to ask of you."

His joy evaporated. "Of course you do."

"Chris …"

"What's the favour?"

"We left Fernando behind on the island —"

"Fernando? I thought you said they took off in George's boat."

"Danielle did, with their son, but she left Fernando behind. It's not clear why. A lot of things aren't clear —" The wind snatched her voice away.

"What?" he yelled. "I can hardly hear you."

"Fernando is all by himself. I didn't want to take him with us because … well, he might be a killer. He also has a gun."

Fuck! He gripped the control wheel and took a breath to calm his voice. "What kind of gun?"

"An ancient-looking shotgun. It's not loaded, but you should know, in case he has more shells. We left him some supplies too. I told him I'd call the cops or the coast guard to look for him, but …"

"But what?"

"The idea of cops freaked him out."

"With good reason. He's in a shitload of trouble, and he better not point that gun at them."

"That's what I'm worried about. It could be a mess. But what if he's innocent? What if Danielle set it all up?"

"That's not for us to figure out, Amanda."

"But maybe she dumped him and took off with her son so she could meet up with her lover in Toronto."

"Oh, she has a second lover now?" The sarcasm was out of his mouth before he could stop it, and predictably, she flared.

"I don't know! Who the hell is Julio, and why is he renovating a house for her? I'm just saying Fernando needs to be rescued!"

"Then we should call the cops. I'll call Standish, and I'll warn him about the gun."

Silence, punctuated by the roar of engines, the roar of the boat, and the rattle of wind. Had he lost her? "There's not much help I can give him except fly over him and wave."

"This isn't funny!"

He shut his eyes and gave his head a shake. "I'm sorry, Amanda. I'm not trying to be a jerk. But you said yourself that we don't know what's going on, and things could get ugly. We need to let the cops do their job and let the chips fall where they may."

More silence.

"Please, honey, I know you want to help, but this is the best solution."

When she finally spoke, her voice was so soft, he could barely hear her. "I know. You're right. I just feel bad."

After he hung up, Chris sat quietly for a few minutes, peering down at the water and trees skimming below him as he tried to sort out his thoughts. Amanda's impulses always came from the heart, and as infuriating as they sometimes were, that's what he loved about her. Furthermore, her instincts about people were often on the mark. Fernando's welfare was in her sights right now, and she'd asked for his help.

As a police officer, he'd seen a lot of struggle and misery. He knew most people were not bad at their core, just messed up. Bad choices or bad luck made good lives go off the rails. But that didn't earn them a free pass. People had to follow the rules, or society fell apart.

He focussed his gaze on the endless, squiggly patchwork of islands and water. On the impossibility of the task. Then he reached for his phone again to call Neville Standish.

Standish had already passed on the coordinates Amanda had sent, and Incident Command had assigned two marine teams and a helicopter to the manhunt. The teams were just heading out into the southern channel below Parry Island.

"Wait a minute," he shouted, suddenly alert. "You're saying Fernando Torres is by himself?"

"Correct. With no means to get off the island. He has a firearm, however —"

"What kind of firearm?"

"A shotgun. Maybe not loaded, but —"

"Got it." Standish's voice was curt and impatient. "You're sure Danielle is not with him?"

"She's not!" Chris yelled over the roar of the plane. "She took off in George Gifford's boat, heading south, Amanda said."

"When?"

"I'm not sure. An hour or two ago?"

"Shit," Standish exclaimed. "George's boat is fast. She could be reaching the south shore any minute. I have to update Incident Command. The teams watching the southern ports need to know."

"Okay, but —"

"Hang on!"

Abruptly, the line went dead. Chris waiting, watching the golden ball of fire settle over the western bay. The whole lake shimmered gold and rose. But beyond the beauty, Chris knew the sunset meant trouble. Soon, visibility on the water would be nil. If the boat ran without lights, Danielle could slip ashore anywhere and fade into the countryside. Moreover, no one would be able to navigate the shallow shoals to rescue Fernando.

"Tymko? You still there?"

Chris snapped back.

"We've pulled the search teams off Fernando and redirected them toward the south shore."

"What about Fernando?"

"He can wait till morning. There's an incident on Lake Huron that's taking some of our resources. Fernando's stuck on an island, you said? So he's not going anywhere. But we're running out of time to catch Danielle. And she's top priority."

The suppressed excitement in Standish's voice rang a bell with Chris. He recognized the thrill of being on the hunt. "You've got something, don't you?"

"Yeah. This lead."

"I mean, you've got something on Danielle."

Standish didn't answer. Chris strained to hear over the droning engine. "Come on, like it or not, I'm in the middle of this."

"We just got the tox results back on Benson and the girl. Traces of a new synthetic fentanyl analog, much more powerful than fentanyl or even carfentanil. It takes a shitload of naloxone to treat it, and Benson didn't stand a chance." Standish was winding up, worry fuelling anger. Chris pieced together his words through the racket. "It's not local. It's brand new on the market in the big cities, so some bastard brought it in. The Chinese are making new opioids faster than we can figure out what they are, dealers are cutting their product with it because it's cheaper, and people are overdosing by the hundreds in the US and Canada. No way in hell I want this shit in my own backyard!"

"Any idea how Benson got hold of it? Was it mixed with something else he was taking, like cocaine?"

"Forensics found traces of it in the Scotch he drank as a nightcap, but there were no other drugs detected, so no, it doesn't look like an accidental overdose. The nanny was working the party that night, serving and clearing up, and the cook remembers she took the Scotch to Benson."

Chris absorbed the information with surprise. What had been Danielle's motive for killing Benson? Janine was her adversary. "Are you sure the drink was meant for Benson?"

"The cook says Danielle was really upset about having to work the party. There was a big fight, and she demanded her passport and papers. Maybe he was just in the way. But you can bet we'll be asking her the minute we find her. We've issued a Canada-wide warrant for her. This is murder, Tymko, no matter how you cut it. No one dumps a lethal dose of this new drug into a drink by accident. They had to know it was killing people. Look what happened to Kaitlyn!"

"Wait a minute! Kaitlyn overdosed on the same drug?"

"Yes, it took a while to identify the exact match, but forensics confirmed it. So we've got a warrant out on Julio Rodriguez too. We think he and Danielle are in this together. He supplied the drug and she administered it. Half of Toronto Police Services are out looking for him. We need this stuff off the streets. So if you see anything at all from up in the sky there, you call me ASAP!"

The MGB was humming along the expressway at an effortless one hundred kilometres an hour, turning heads wherever she went. Despite the chilly evening air, Matthew had the top down, savouring the thrill of the wind. He would have loved to open her up to get the full power of the experience, but he'd seen the anxiety flit across Vince's face when he got behind the wheel. Besides, he had no wish to attract the attention of the boys in blue.

His phone rang when he was just approaching Vaughan. He could barely hear Chris shouting over the ear-splitting racket of his plane.

"News from Amanda?" he yelled back.

"She's fine. On her way to town with George. But there's been a development."

He struggled to hear as Chris filled him in on his phone conversation with Neville Standish. "This is a clear-cut murder inquiry now, Matthew, of both Ronny and Benson. Danielle and

Julio are both in the frame. So watch your step and stay well away from Julio."

"Does Amanda know this?"

"No, and I don't plan to tell her yet. But it's possible Kaitlyn could be in danger. She might know something about the night Benson died. Maybe she saw something or knows where the drug came from."

"Did you tell Standish she's on the lam in Toronto?"

A pause, punctuated by the roar of the wind and the engine. "It didn't come up," Chris said. "But listen, both Julio and Danielle could be a threat to her. Danielle ditched her husband and was last seen making a beeline for Toronto. There are arrest warrants out on both of them. The Toronto cops and the OPP are all over this. If you get any leads on Kaitlyn, get her some place safe and let the cops know right away. And for fuck's sake, watch your back!"

After a hasty promise to do so, Matthew hung up and called up Julio's number on Siri. As the phone rang, he formulated a plan of attack. Head-on, he decided. Julio did not strike him as the deadly drug dealer type but rather a bit player in over his head. And easily intimidated.

"Julio! Matthew Goderich," he snapped as soon as he heard the man's wary hello. "I'm looking for Kaitlyn."

"Kaitlyn who?"

Matthew rolled his eyes. "I know you know Kaitlyn. You sell drugs to her. She overdosed on those drugs and ended up in the hospital."

"I didn't do that!"

"She nearly died."

"Not my drugs!"

"Cut the bullshit, Julio. The cops are way ahead of you on this. Kaitlyn went to your cottage, and that's where she got the drugs."

"I was in the city! You know I was, you met me there."

"But the cops found traces of the drug at your cottage, and Kaitlyn went there. Why?"

The line went quiet. Through the wind roaring in his ears, Matthew thought he heard a whimper.

Then finally, "I need your lawyer."

"Did you supply her with drugs?"

"I need a lawyer."

Matthew upped the ante. "And I need answers! My good friend, the woman I love most in the world, is in the middle of this! Talk!"

"I ... I gave her weed and E, that's all. She ..." His voice cracked and grew plaintive. "She found me having a toke on my break one time, and she asked if I could get some for her. Just weed. She said I could make a little money. It's almost legal, right?"

"For fuck's sake, Julio! She's fourteen."

"I need money. You know that. I had big expenses on the little house. Mr. B couldn't get my money right away."

Matthew laid the disgust on thick. "How long have you been dealing to Kaitlyn?"

"Just a few times! Danielle got very mad at me when she find out."

"Wait a minute. Danielle knew you were selling to Kaitlyn?" Matthew's mind raced. If Danielle knew about Kaitlyn's drugs, it would be a simple matter for her to substitute a lethal opioid for the more innocuous ecstasy. "How did she find out?"

"Kaitlyn came to the Mahoney Avenue house one time last month with Danielle. They were out shopping."

"You mean Kaitlyn knew about the house? The one Benson was fixing up for Danielle behind her mother's back?"

"Yes...." Julio paused as if realizing he'd gone too far. "But Danielle made her promise not to tell anyone. Kaitlyn — she understand that. She like Danielle. She not like how her mother treat her. She would never tell."

Matthew pondered this surprise twist. Kaitlyn might have genuinely sympathized with Danielle's plight and wanted to see her get her dream house. But all that might pale in a clash with her mother. That piece of information was a powerful weapon in a fight. Who knew what she would do with it in a fit of vengeful adolescent pique?

"Julio, we know Kaitlyn is in Toronto looking for drugs. The time for covering your ass is gone. Where is she?"

"I don't know! It's a big city."

"You're in deep shit. The cops have a warrant out for your arrest."

Julio stifled a wail. "I need a lawyer. But your lawyer not call me!"

"Okay, listen. If you want my help, or Mr. Pomeroy's help, you call me ASAP if you hear from her! Then you'll get your lawyer."

CHAPTER TWENTY-SIX

Chris knew he was running out of time. He estimated he had an hour of daylight left, which should be enough to get to the floatplane base in Parry Sound, but only if he left soon. According to his navigational app, he should be flying right over the island where Amanda had left Fernando. He banked, circled, and dropped as low as he dared. The wind buffeted the plane, forcing him to hold on tight.

He rubbed his aching eyes and peered out the window at the water skimming below. At the islands topped with scruffy pines that clung to the granite shelves. Which island was it? He did another pass but could see nothing. Maybe Fernando was hiding from him; a sinister thought, for if he was innocent, he would surely want to be rescued. The Beaver had no official markings, so Fernando had no reason to fear he was from the police.

The sky took on a lavender hue as the last rays of sunset flamed out, leaving nothing but embers glowing in the west. Chris hesitated, dropped the plane still farther, and banked around the pointed tip of the largest island one last time. Down below, he spotted a wink of turquoise in the shelter of a small inlet.

He swung around to get a better look, and the turquoise boat came into full view. Tools lay spread out on the rocks beside it, and cowering under partial cover of a nearby pine was a man.

Chris pulled up abruptly. Fernando was there, apparently trying to repair the boat. More importantly, he seemed to be trying to hide. Not the mark of an innocent man. Amanda would protest that maybe he was just scared, but Chris was not quite so optimistic. Ten years on the job had taught him otherwise.

If Fernando managed to repair the boat, would he be foolhardy enough to make a run for the south shore in the dead of night? If he did, they'd lose him in the teeming crowds of the city, and they might never know what part he played in the deaths. Moreover, the man had a firearm, and an armed man running scared on the streets of Toronto could be lethal.

In a split second, Chris made the decision to pick him up. After years in the north, he'd learned to land on narrow rivers and tiny lakes barely larger than a swimming pool. The trick would be taking off afterward, but he'd face that when the time came. He circled around to size up his options, picked an open channel in the lee of the island, and headed back out to make his approach.

The plane kissed the lake as delicately as a butterfly landing on a flower. Chris taxied toward a sliver of sandy shore, killed the engine, and allowed it to wash in on the waves while he climbed down onto the pontoon with the paddle and ropes.

The swell was rougher than he'd thought from the air, and for a moment he feared his friend's beloved plane would be bashed on nearby rocks. He leaped out into the frigid water and quickly wrapped the ropes to trees on both sides. Once he was sure the plane was secure, he grabbed the .308 hunting rifle that Vince had stowed behind the seat and set off along the shore in search of Fernando.

After about ten minutes of squelching over rocks and mossy bogs, he came upon the turquoise boat. No sign of Fernando. The state of the scattered tools and the half-submerged boat suggested that Fernando was never going to fix this one.

He slipped behind the shelter of a boulder and scanned the trees and shore. The woods were nearly black with night, but nothing moved. "Fernando!"

No response.

"Fernando, I'm Chris, a friend of Amanda. She sent me to get you."

Still nothing.

"I'm a friend. I won't hurt you."

A slight rustle in the darkness of the woods. Chris waited. Mosquitoes whined in his ears, but he willed himself not to react. Another rustle as boughs moved. A twig snapped. Then, finally, a pine branch swept aside and a short, slight man emerged, gripping a battered old twelve-gauge, break-action shotgun with both hands. His liquid eyes glistened in the purple light, and Chris could almost smell his fear.

Chris rose from behind the rock. He aimed his own rifle, all his reflexes ready. "I won't hurt you. Put the gun down."

The man didn't move. "Put the gun down," Chris repeated. "No one wants to get hurt here."

Instead, Fernando lifted the gun marginally. Chris estimated the weapon was at least nine pounds and four feet long — a lot for a small man to hang on to — and Chris doubted he could hold it steady enough to hit the broad side of a barn. He rested his finger on the trigger but kept his voice as calm as he could. "Fernando, I don't want to hurt you. I want to help. You look cold and tired. Put the gun down and we'll build a fire."

For a moment they stared at each other through the gloom. Finally, the man leaned down and laid the shotgun on the ground.

"Thank you. Now move back. Step away from it."

Mesmerized, Fernando backed up. He began to whimper as Chris approached. Chris held out a soothing hand. "I won't hurt you. I'll just ..." He bent over, and with slow movements so as not to spook the man, he picked up the shotgun. Broke it open.

And breathed again. Empty. Within seconds he'd emptied his own rifle and set both firearms on the boulder. Only then did he approach the shaking man to lay a gentle hand on his arm.

"It's too dark to go anywhere tonight, but I need to dry off, and we can at least get warm and get rid of these bugs."

Half an hour later, they had a healthy campfire blazing from driftwood they scrounged along the shore, and orange flames leaped into the descending darkness. Overhead, stars winked to life in the midnight blue sky, and the lake glistened like onyx. Chris returned to the plane, taking the firearms with him, and uttered a prayer of thanks to Vince's RCMP training. Stowed in the small cargo section were emergency supplies: a tent, sleeping bag, water filter, and some packages of dehydrated stew. These, combined with the snacks Fernando had been given, were enough to make a passable dinner.

Also stored in the back was a bottle of Glenfiddich single malt. Chris laughed. No emergency supplies were ever complete without a bottle of Scotch.

Fernando said little during the meal preparations, but his face lit up at the sight of the bottle. They passed it back and forth a few times until Chris, mellow and warm to the tips of his toes, figured Fernando was relaxed enough to talk.

"Where did you get the gun, Fernando?"

The man shivered, pulled his knees up to his chest, and hid his face. "We hide in a cottage for some days. Lost. We eat food. Take the gun."

"Have you ever used a gun before?"

He hesitated. Shook his head dolefully. "Danielle shoot George. Accident."

Chris reached out to pat the man's shoulder. "We'll sort it out. Tomorrow morning at first light we will fly out of here and down to Blue Mountain. We'll leave the plane there. My truck is there, and we will drive to Toronto." He had no intention of doing that, but he needed to build Fernando's trust. "Are you going to meet Danielle in Toronto?"

Fernando's face closed. "I don't know."

Chris tried again. "Is she in Toronto?"

Fernando paused. Was it a language problem or a reluctance to confide? Finally, Fernando gave a faint nod.

"Why did she leave you here?"

"George hurt bad. She tell me take care of him. She get help."

"But she took his boat and left you. Why didn't she take all of you back to Parry Sound?"

Fernando blinked rapidly and shook his head, frustrated at his lack of English. "She worry about a friend. In Toronto."

"What friend? Julio?"

Fernando's eyes widened. "Julio? No! A girl. From the family."

Chris passed the Scotch bottle back to Fernando and watched him gulp convulsively. "Is her name Kaitlyn?"

Fernando coughed and shrugged his ignorance. "Don't know. Danielle worried."

Chris tried to think through the spreading fog of Scotch and fatigue. Had Danielle rushed down to Toronto to meet Kaitlyn, and if so, why? And why was she worried about her? Was it because Kaitlyn had nearly died or because she knew something she shouldn't?

"Do you trust Danielle, Fernando?"

Fernando looked startled. Puzzled.

"Is she a good person? You haven't seen her in a long time."

"She is a good person. A very good person."

Some interviewer you are, Tymko. "But people are dead. Benson Humphries."

"She not do that!"

"Ronny Gifford."

"An accident! We fight. He fall down."

"What did you fight about?"

Fernando's eyes grew haunted. "He find out the doctor is dead. He not want to take us ... he want to call police. Danielle try to run but he ..." Fernando reached out to grab Chris's arm. "He stop her like this. Accident!"

Chris disengaged himself carefully. The man had a surprisingly strong grip. "But you dragged him into the bush and buried him."

Fernando's breathing grew ragged. His hands shook, and he thrust the bottle away. "Scared. Our son. Our life. Danielle say no one find."

Chris leaned closer. His eyes, like his heart, were heavy. "Do you know Ronny was still alive when you buried him? He died in the cold and rain. You could have saved him."

A howl burst from Fernando's throat, deep and wrenching, as if it had been dragged up from the pit of his soul. He gripped his head. "Danielle check ... check ..." He groped for his wrist. "Nothing. Dead."

"Did you check?"

He whipped his head back and forth.

"So Danielle said he was dead, and it was her idea to bury him."

Fernando's eyes were brimming, and if he understood what Chris was hinting at, he gave no sign. "We make Catholic prayers ..."

"And now she's left you behind on this island, and she took off with your son." He leaned over to touch the trembling man's arm. "Who's Julio, Fernando?"

Fernando lifted his head. He looked haggard and broken. "Julio? Julio is a friend."

"Danielle's friend, you mean? Her lover?"

Fernando jerked back as if shocked. "Lover? No, no! He is not her lover!"

"How do you know? She's been here for two years without you."

"He is her brother."

Now it was Chris's turn to snap back in surprise. "What are you talking about? He's Mexican."

"Mexican, yes. I'm confused. Not good word. Like her brother." He lay down on the hard granite. "I go sleep."

Chris helped him into the tent, gave him the sleeping bag, and took his own blankets back out by the fire. For a long time, despite fatigue, the long day, and the Scotch, he couldn't sleep. An hour later, when he heard the snores from inside the tent, he slipped over the rise and down to the water's edge to give Amanda a call.

Amanda had spent two hours being hauled over the coals by Neville Standish, and her patience was as exhausted as her body. Now that George was safely in the care of doctors, she didn't care about procedures or evidence or formal statements. She cared about Chris and Danielle and Kaitlyn. And right now she wanted to talk to Frankie. A question nagged at her.

By feigning near collapse, she finally persuaded Standish to postpone further questioning until a later date. Finding a bench on the deserted dock beside the police station, she phoned the social worker. It was nearly midnight, but it couldn't be helped.

Frankie answered on the second ring, sounding wide awake and ready for any crisis. Amanda suspected that was her permanent state. Too tired for a long preamble, Amanda gave her sketchy details about George's assault before cutting to the chase.

"George is worried about Kaitlyn. I remember he asked you to talk to her. Did you?"

"I can't tell you that. You know that."

Amanda rolled her eyes. "Yes, I know that, but this is urgent. Maybe even life-and-death."

"I don't see how."

"Kaitlyn has run away from the rehab centre in Toronto. Her mother is refusing to call the police. If you know anything about why she ran away or where she's gone, please tell me. That's all I need to know."

"Damn," Frankie muttered, and her voice softened. "Amanda ... I wish I could help. I don't know where she's gone, and even if I did, I'm still bound —"

"Oh, for God's sake, she's fourteen. A child!"

"Which might give that useless mother of hers some rights, but not you."

Amanda gripped the phone. Out in the channel, the crescent moon glistened off the water and a distant boat chugged by. Across the water, lights winked in the darkness. She took a deep breath and reached for peace. "Okay, let's back up. She's a child at risk, and her mother's refusal to call police could be putting her life in danger. Can you report what you know to the cops?"

Frankie hesitated. "It's still 'you said he said she said.' The reality is the cops aren't going to act on it without Janine's express request. Another reality is Kaitlyn didn't get a chance to tell me anything."

"Didn't get a chance?"

There was a long silence. Amanda could almost hear her wrestling with her conscience. Finally, Frankie sighed. Her voice dropped, as if the words had to fight their way out. "You're right, I dropped by while she was in the hospital. George was worried about her drug use, but frankly I was worried about sexual abuse."

Amanda said nothing, not wanting to break the spell.

"There were some signs, and I'm kind of primed. When a stepfather gets cosy with an adolescent daughter, it's a big red flag for me. But Kaitlyn had something far different on her mind. Right away, she started to cry. I could see she was tormented, not by anything being done to her but by something she had done. Something she said she couldn't undo. So big and so horrible, she wasn't sure she could live with it." Frankie lapsed into silence.

"What was it?"

"That's what she didn't get a chance to tell me. Janine stormed in, screaming about me traumatizing her daughter. Threw me out, and next thing I knew, Kaitlyn had been transferred to Toronto. And I thought, well, at least she'll get some help."

"But now she's on the run."

"And that's why I'm breaking this confidence. Because frankly, I'm worried about her. If she's not co-operating with rehab, and her mother still has her head in the sand ... I'm worried about what she might do."

Amanda's phone vibrated in her hand. She glanced at it. Chris was calling. She needed to talk to him, but it would have to wait a few minutes.

"You mean to herself?" she asked.

Frankie didn't answer, but her silence seemed answer enough. Amanda skirted around the thought she was dreading. "Do you think ... she's referring to her part in Benson's death?"

"Jesus, I hope not. But yeah."

Matthew was jolted awake by the thunder of a motorcycle that seemed to be right below his window, sputtering and roaring. He groped for his phone by the bedside. *Three-fucking-forty a.m.*

Goddamn morons, revving through the deadened streets at this hour of the night.

He had barely finished that private curse when boots thumped up the stairs and a fist hammered at his door. For an instant, he was back in Africa with officials banging on his door. The next instant, "Matthew!"

It was a hoarse, urgent whisper, as if she hadn't already woken the dead with her motorcycle and her boots. He staggered up to let her in. Kaylee burst through the door, her whole body wagging, and immediately snatched up a sock lying on the floor. Amanda followed and stepped into his arms with relief. He held her close, inhaling the dusty, oily, windblown scent of her.

"I'm dead," she said. "I figured I'd never get a hotel room at this hour of the night, looking like this and with a motorcycle and a dog. Then I remembered you had a sofa." She was already peeling off clothes as she headed toward the bathroom. "Pretty please, can you give her some water?"

Ten minutes later, still damp from the shower, she was crammed into the little chair by his desk, sipping a hot cup of tea. Kaylee was lying with the sock between her paws, hoping for a playmate.

"You could have waited to drive down in the morning, you know." He had thrown some jeans and a T-shirt over his boxers, but he still felt like a grubby old man.

She shook her head. "I'm worried about Kaitlyn. Chris called. He found Fernando. He told me about the lethal opioids and the murder charges against Danielle and Julio." She glowered at him over the rim of the cup. "You guys should have told me that yesterday, you know. Chris is worried Danielle may be after her, because Kaitlyn knew about the little house, and I'm worried about her state of mind. She's apparently carrying a whole load of guilt about something. Any luck finding her?"

He shook his head. "I've got feelers out. I figure she'll contact Julio, so I'm leaning on him. We may learn more soon. How is George?"

The change of topic seemed to dissipate her tension. She glanced up at him and smiled. "Sorry to wake you. Thanks for the tea. It really hits the spot. George is in intensive care. Hairline fracture of his skull where some buckshot grazed him, and some swelling of the brain, but the doctors say he was incredibly lucky. They won't commit, of course — the next forty-eight hours are critical, blah, blah, blah — but the nurse told me he'll be okay. They all love him up there because of his charity work, and half the women want to marry him, so he's in good hands. Larry's staying with him, and he promised to keep me posted. What a sweetheart Larry is. Beneath that gnarled exterior, he's a marshmallow." She stopped for breath. "So first thing in the morning ..."

He took her hand in his and caressed its soft warmth. "Never mind the morning. Now, we'll sleep. You take my bed, and I'll take the sofa."

"Matthew ..."

"No arguments. You've been roughing it for days. At least the bed has no springs poking through it."

The same could not be said for the sofa. Long after she stumbled into bed, he lay awake on it, trying to arrange his body to avoid the worst of the sags and lumps. Just when he thought he'd found a manageable position, Kaylee leaped up and claimed the bottom half of the sofa, pinning his legs up to his chest. She was a dead weight, not budging as he tried to squeeze his legs beside her.

God, they're a pair, he thought before he drifted into unconsciousness.

His phone ripped him from sleep at eight o'clock, although to his befuddled brain it still felt like the middle of the night.

Instead, daylight seeped in through his sooty window, barely lighting the interior, and the morning rush hour belched fumes below. He groped for the phone.

Julio's voice came through, furtive and hushed. "Mr. M?"

He snapped awake. Amanda appeared in his bedroom doorway, wrapping one of his shirts around herself.

"Yes, Julio."

"Kaitlyn called me. She wants to meet."

"What did you arrange?"

Julio dropped his voice further. Began to whine. "I don't ..."

"Did you arrange to meet her?" Standing there with his gut hanging over his boxers and his comb-over on end, Matthew was all business. The old reporter quizzing a source.

"Yes."

"Where?"

"Not a good idea."

"What's not a good idea?"

"That you come."

"Julio! Cut the crap!"

Beside him, Amanda began to wave her arms around in protest. "I need to see her!" she whispered.

Matthew waved her to silence. Something had spooked Julio, and he didn't want him to get any more nervous. "Where is she meeting you?"

"You will bring police."

"No, I will not bring police. Julio, trust me! I want to help her."

Julio moaned and muttered a few words in Spanish, possibly prayers, possibly curses, before spitting out the name of a coffee shop on Danforth Avenue. "Her idea," he said, and then he hung up before Matthew could get in another word. When he and Amanda Googled it, it turned out to be an obscure little spot with a two-star rating on the east Danforth, tucked between a kick-boxing studio and an auto-body repair shop, far from the trendy, gentrified shops of Greektown.

Certainly far from a Rosedale girl's normal stomping ground.

Amanda scooped up the clothes she'd tossed on the floor, gave them a quick sniff, and shrugged. There was no time to waste on niceties; they had to get there ahead of Kaitlyn or at least before she left again. Amanda was still tugging on her sweatshirt as she bolted out the door with Kaylee for her quick morning pee. Back upstairs, she threw some dog food in a bowl.

"Sorry, princess, but this time you stay here. Guard the fort."

Kaylee was too startled to protest as they slammed the door in her face and thundered down the stairs. Outside, Amanda stopped beside her motorcycle with dismay. On the street, the morning traffic inched from red light to red light.

"We could hail a cab," she said.

"Forget it," he said. "We'll be much faster on your bike."

"There's not much room."

"Since when has that stopped us? In most of the world, a family of six would fit on this thing. With all their belongings."

She grinned as memories flooded in of mothers balancing babies on handlebars while kids and garbage bags of clothes hung from every spare inch. "Okay, but hang on tight. I'm going to go really fast!"

After digging out her extra helmet, she locked the trailer to a post and broke every rule in the book trying to get across downtown Toronto in morning rush hour. She wove in and out of traffic, grazing bumpers, running orange lights, and even jumping onto the sidewalk at one particularly clogged inter-section. On the Danforth, driving east against the traffic, she gunned the engine as fast as she dared, praying there were no cops along the way. Matthew, bless him, leaned with her and didn't say a word.

They reached the dingy little coffee shop in less than half an hour and spotted Julio sitting at a corner table on the patio with his back to the wall and a view of the street in both directions. To her astonishment, a dark-haired little boy sat with him, perched on a chair with his feet swinging and a large ice cream sundae on the rickety table before him.

The patio was otherwise deserted, although a steady stream of men in work boots and grimy jackets went in and emerged with take-out coffees. Julio half rose from his seat at the sight of Matthew but froze as Amanda joined him.

"What's this?" Matthew demanded. "You brought a kid into the middle of this? Drug dealers, potential killers?"

"Who is this?" Julio countered, pulling the child close to him. Fortunately, the boy didn't seem to understand a word of the talk of drugs and death.

Amanda stepped forward and offered her hand. "I'm Amanda Doucette, and I'm guessing this is Raoul, Danielle's little boy?"

At the mention of his name, the boy looked up and gave her a broad smile. He had mischievous eyes and a shy grin that made him the spitting image of his father. Amanda leaned down to shake his hand solemnly.

Matthew was less charming. "What the hell, Julio!"

"Danielle leave him with me!" Julio exclaimed. "She bang on my door this morning. No clothes, no food —"

"Was this before or after Kaitlyn called?"

"Just now. She say she come from the bus from Collingwood. She is very, very angry at me. She say my drugs kill Dr. B and almost kill Kaitlyn. She ask where I buy them, did I know they were bad? I tell her my drugs are always safe, always clean. I only buy from one man."

Julio's voice was rising as he got into his tale, and he waved his arms for emphasis. Sensing his distress, little Raoul tugged at his arm and said something in Tagalog. Julio replied, patted the boy's head, and rose to take the boy inside. Amanda was so focussed on the drama of the tale that she almost missed the crucial detail. Julio had spoken Tagalog. He and Raoul returned a moment later with a muffin and orange juice for the boy.

"Julio, you speak Tagalog?" Amanda said quietly.

He blinked then glanced from Amanda to the boy. "It is a lot like Spanish. Many words are the same."

Amanda let it slide. "So where is Danielle now?"

He shrugged. "I told her it wasn't my drugs. I say remember when Kaitlyn come to the house? I promise you I will never hurt her? Danielle stops yelling. She goes all funny and she says, '*Diyos ko po!*' and she takes off."

"Where?"

"Down the street. I don't know where. She just tell me to take care of Raoul."

Amanda's mind was racing. Had Danielle suddenly remembered a crucial clue? Or seen a connection she'd previously missed? Something about bad drugs? Or Kaitlyn?

At that moment she glimpsed a figure slouching up the Danforth from the direction of the subway. Pale, haggard, and so thin she barely cast a shadow. Kaitlyn.

Amanda caught her breath. The drugs, grief, and guilt of the past week had almost killed the girl. Kaitlyn looked up and her bruised, hollowed eyes registered Amanda's presence. She froze. Her mouth formed a silent "oh," and she turned to flee, stumbling at the abrupt movement.

The girl was in no shape to outrun Amanda, who closed the gap in a dozen strides. She took her thin arm and kept her touch gentle as she steered her to the nearest chair. "I'm Amanda, the one who helped save your life. I'm not here to hurt you or to give you grief. I want to help."

As if in slow motion, Kaitlyn turned accusing eyes on Julio. "You *called* them?"

Julio lifted his shoulders in weak defeat.

"You're all bastards! The whole fucking world is nothing but bastards! You made me kill Benson. He's dead because he took the drugs you sold me!"

"No, I didn't! I swear on … on my mother's grave. I only sell E and weed. That's what I bring to the island!"

Kaitlyn was glaring at him, her steely rage fading as doubt crept in. Amanda sucked in her breath as some pieces of the puzzle tumbled into place, forming a diabolical alternative. Who else might have brought drugs to the island? She gripped Kaitlyn's hands and wouldn't let her pull away. Willed her to listen.

"They were not your drugs, Kaitlyn. It wasn't your fault. Someone put a powerful drug in his drink. Way more powerful than fentanyl. And you found the rest of it in Julio's cottage. I think it was planted there on purpose to implicate him, or with luck to kill him. Either way, to close the circle."

Beside her, Julio recoiled, but Kaitlyn didn't move.

Amanda kept her gaze locked on the girl. "I have one very important question for you. Did you tell your mother about the little Mahoney Avenue house?"

Kaitlyn stared at her through her hollow, haunted eyes. "No," she whimpered.

"Kaitlyn, I need the truth."

The girl seemed to have no voice. No words. As if a huge well of grief and disbelief and horror were rising up inside. But she managed a faint nod.

With an effort, Amanda kept her grip tender and her voice soft as she fought the alarm that shot through her. This was what Danielle had realized. This was what had sent her racing out into the street earlier. Racing, very likely, to confront a killer.

"Thank you, Kaitlyn. I know that was hard." She took a deep breath and stepped away from the patio. "Matthew, may I have a word with you?"

In a few rapid words, she sketched out her fear. "Call 911," she said, already strapping on her helmet. "Send them to Janine Saint Clair's house. Tell them Danielle, the woman they are looking for, is there."

"I'm going with you."

"No, you're needed here to deal with the police and help Kaitlyn." When he opened his mouth to protest, she held up her hand. "I won't do anything stupid. If you call now, the cops should get there ahead of me." She shoved him back toward the patio. "Go! Text me her address and then take care of Kaitlyn."

CHAPTER TWENTY-SEVEN

Matthew's further protests were lost in the roar of her motorcycle as she took off. Hunched over the handlebars, she barrelled west along the Danforth, her mind racing to plan the route ahead. For a brief moment she wondered whether, in a bid to keep her safe, Matthew would neglect to send Janine's address, but as she was crossing the Bloor Street Viaduct, her phone chirped in her pocket. Waiting at a red light, she fished it out. The text from Matthew provided the address and also a note. *I think cops on way but dispatcher skeptical.*

She punched the address into her map and had a quick look before revving away from the light. One-handed, she shouted at Siri to phone Chris. Voicemail. *Goddamn!*

"Chris," she yelled over the Bloor Street torrent of trucks, cars, and buses, everyone impatient. "Call Toronto 911. Tell them Danielle is heading to Janine's house for a confrontation. Not sure they believe me. Use your cop influence." She hesitated. No time to fill him in or explain reasons. "Remind them Danielle is a murder suspect."

She thrust the phone back into her jacket pocket and grabbed her handlebars just in time to slew around the corner north onto Glen Road. Rosedale was a secretive maze of streets that was easy to get lost in, so she was forced to slow down. As she drove deeper into the wealthy enclave, the streets grew hushed. No sirens, no screaming or sounds of attack. Only her motorcycle blasted through the genteel silence.

She made two wrong turns but finally rounded a corner to see two cruisers parked outside a red-brick mansion at the curve of the crescent. Their engines were idling but their roof lights were off. The house looked quiet and the driveway was empty, with no white Lincoln Navigator in sight.

One officer was sitting in his cruiser, writing on his computer, while two others were conversing on their radios as they checked out the exterior. All of them looked up in surprise as she rumbled up to the curb and switched off her bike. The closest officer approached her sternly as she was clambering off.

"Is this your residence, ma'am?"

"No, I'm Amanda Doucette. I'm the one who requested you."

The officer asked for ID and gave her driver's license a thorough inspection before handing it to the officer in the cruiser, presumably to check whether there were any alerts out on her. Amanda's reflexive flash of annoyance died as she realized that might save her the trouble of long explanations.

It did not.

"Why did you request assistance, ma'am?"

Amanda launched into an abbreviated version. "I recently learned that Danielle Torres returned to Toronto this morning. There is a warrant out for her arrest in connection with the death of Janine Saint Clair's husband. I believe Danielle may have been coming here to confront Janine."

The officer's face was as impassive as a stone. She had no idea whether he believed her or thought she was an utter nutbar. "There is no one here, ma'am."

"Have you checked inside?"

"We rang the doorbell and looked in the windows. The house appears empty."

"Appears? But —"

One of the officers who had been patrolling the perimeter approached. "Neighbours report no unusual activity," he said to Officer Stoneface. "The owner of the property left in her vehicle about an hour ago."

"Who?" Amanda jumped in. "Janine Saint —"

Stoneface headed her off. "Thank you for your concern, Ms. Doucette. We'll take it from here."

Stoneface faced her down, blocking her view of the house. She tried to peer around him for signs of movement inside. A twitching curtain or fleeting shadow. Danielle might still have a key to the house, or at least the access code, and she could be hiding in the house, waiting for Janine's return.

"Will you be sticking around for a while to make sure there's no one inside?"

"We have no grounds for suspicion, Ms. Doucette. As you can see, Mrs. Torres is not here." Belatedly, Stoneface reached into his pocket and handed her his card. "If you have any further information pertaining to this case, please give this number a call."

It was done with diplomatic flourish, but it was a "buzz off" order nonetheless. Amanda returned to her bike and felt three pairs of silent, skeptical eyes on her back as she climbed on. She was frustrated and on edge. She was sure Danielle had been on a mission to confront someone, and who else other than Janine? Only minutes earlier Danielle had learned that Janine knew all along, even before her husband's death, that Benson had bought Danielle a house.

Now Janine had gone out. There were two women loose in the city on a collision course that could be deadly.

As she wove back through the genteel, leafy streets, her mind wrestled with the puzzle, but it wasn't until she hit the noise and hustle of Bloor Street again that the answer came to her.

She fished out Stoneface's card. It might not be as fast as 911, but at least she would not have to explain all over again and risk complete disbelief this time. She was caught at a red light with little time to get the whole story out.

"This is Amanda Doucette, Officer St—" she checked herself and babbled on. "I got the location wrong. I thought Danielle Torres would go to Janine Saint Clair's house, but she may have gone to another property of Janine's on Mahoney Avenue in the west end. They have a dispute over that house."

"Ms. Doucette —" She could hear the doubt in his voice.

"I'm not a flake, and I'm not trying to waste your time. Two people have already been murdered, and the killer has not been found. Things are unravelling fast, and I'm worried."

The light turned green, and cars behind her honked. She waited through a long silence before the officer said, "I'll pass it on."

She thanked him and hung up. *Pass it on when?* she wondered. And with what kind of "crazy lady" caveat? She fed Siri the new address and told it to pick the fastest route, which unexpectedly took her through the heart of Forest Hill, perhaps even more staid and exclusive than Rosedale. She felt grim satisfaction at the racket of her lime-green motorcycle echoing off the stately stone mansions.

Soon she nosed into the stream of cars inching along Eglinton Avenue and ducked in and out of lanes until she reached Weston Road. No sound of sirens. A short hop took her to Mahoney Avenue. Unlike Rosedale, the street was crowded with little houses pressing up against the street. The street had a scattering of modest cars but no police cruisers. However, among the aging

Civics and Fords, as out of place as a panther among barn cats, was a white Lincoln Navigator.

Amanda tucked her bike down the block behind it. The instant she took her helmet off, she heard shouting, indecipherable with rage. Shielded by the cars, she slipped up the street until she could see the house clearly. The door was open, and Danielle was standing on the front porch, wearing a man's leather jacket that came down to her knees. She was carrying nothing, not even a purse, let alone a weapon, and her fists were clenched at her sides. She looked impossibly tiny.

She was facing the open doorway, beyond which Amanda could make out a shadowy figure in the interior gloom. The screaming was coming from inside, and even pitched high enough to shatter glass, Amanda recognized Janine's voice.

"Did you think you could walk into my life and steal it all from me? Did you think you could have my husband, a new house, and a shitload of my money too?"

"I don't want your money," Danielle shouted back, matching her pitch for pitch. "I didn't want your husband! All I want is a little house in our new Canadian home. Your husband lend me the money for Fernando and me to move here."

"Oh! And what did you do to persuade him to do that?"

"Nothing!"

Janine's voice dropped, quivering with contempt. "You just crooked your little finger and asked pretty please?"

"I didn't ask. He want to do it. I told him Fernando and I will pay him back every little bit."

"Really? And why would my husband want to do that?"

Danielle's reply was inaudible. Amanda took out her phone and crept along the neighbour's hedge to get closer.

"What the fuck did you say?" Janine roared.

"He was a nice man!" Danielle retorted. "He talked to me.

He knew I have a dream — our own home in Canada for me and my husband and our children."

"This dump?" Janine snorted. "Well, guess what, bitch. You're not getting it! With all this shit Julio carelessly left around, this place will go up like a torch."

A flame flared in the darkness. Danielle shrieked and plunged through the doorway, arms flailing. All Amanda could see were shadows dancing in the darkened room. She rushed toward the porch, holding down the emergency button on her phone. *Where the hell is Officer Fucking Stoneface?*

Abruptly, Danielle's voice cut through the chaos, steely soft.

"I know what happened. You killed Dr. B, the only nice person in your whole family. The only person who cares."

"About you?"

"Yes, about me. And your children. You put drugs in his drink and you told me to give it to him. You thought you could make me pay."

"Of all the …! You think the police will believe that crap?"

Amanda had one foot on the bottom step, ready to react if Janine struck another match. Danielle's response stopped her short. "I don't want the police. I want my little house. I won't tell anybody what you did if you give me my house."

Another match flared, illuminating the two women squaring off in the living room. Janine circled, waving the flame in Danielle's face to force her farther inside. When the nanny stood her ground, Janine barked an angry laugh. "Honey, you're way out of your league. The police think it's all you. And this house? You burned it down because I wouldn't give it to you." She raised her free hand and waved a small booklet in Danielle's face. "Oh look, the police will even find your passport half charred in the rubble. Too bad you don't know anything about setting fires. They kill so fast, often the arsonist doesn't escape."

She lunged forward, thrusting the match into Danielle's face, causing her to shriek in panic. Amanda burst through the doorway and shoved Janine aside as hard as she could. The startled woman tripped on loose cloths and went sprawling. The match flew from her hand, dying just as it hit a pile of rags in the corner. Flame smouldered, and Danielle rushed to put it out.

"Don't!" Amanda flung out her arm and caught Danielle's wrist. She spun the tiny woman around like a top and sent her spinning back down the front steps. Janine was thrashing around on the floor, tangled in drop cloths and screaming with rage. In that instant, a can of solvent exploded in flames, flooding the room with an eerie orange glow.

Amanda froze as memories crashed in. The stench of smoke, orange flames leaping, fleeing shadows on the wall, the howls of terrified villagers....

"What the fuck, bitch!" Janine screamed at her.

Amanda blinked and saw Janine's eyes locked on hers in disbelief, the drop cloths on fire around her. Through the searing heat and pain, she reached down to pull the woman free. A second later they were both out in the cool, soft air, coughing and sputtering. Danielle was standing on the lawn, watching as flames blew out the windows and raced up the siding to the roof. Tears gathered in her eyes and seeped down her cheeks.

Amanda bent over, breathing deeply to beat back the dread of the past. Someone put a blanket over her shoulders. Time blurred until in the distance she heard the clamour of sirens. Within seconds the first responders flooded the scene, shouting orders and ushering her to an EMS van.

When next she looked for Danielle, the tiny woman in the oversized jacket had melted away into the crowd.

CHAPTER TWENTY-EIGHT

It was late afternoon by the time Amanda trudged up Matthew's stairs and used her foot to kick at his apartment door. Her hands, swaddled in bandages, still throbbed, but it was the gruelling police interrogation at the hospital that had truly worn her down. They had grilled her on her 911 call and challenged every word she said about the fire. *How far away did you say you were? How much traffic was there on the street? Did you at any time actually see Janine Saint Clair light a match?*

She lost her temper a couple of times, which didn't help her case, and by the end she suspected they didn't believe a word she'd said.

Kaylee greeted her at the door with an ecstasy that brought a smile to her heart, however fleeting. She let Matthew fold her into his arms for a moment before pulling away and turning to his laptop.

"Is there anything in the news yet?"

He blocked her view. "You don't want to know."

"Fuck," she muttered, shouldering him aside and clicking on a news website. There it was. House in Weston Road area destroyed by fire, significant damage to adjoining property, the owner of the house, a wealthy Rosedale widow and prominent philanthropist, tried to put it out at great risk to herself, but it was too late. Arson suspected, police and fire marshal's office investigating. Police are interested in talking to the former nanny, Danielle Torres.

A headshot of Danielle filled the screen, followed by a juicy video clip of Janine standing on the front lawn against the backdrop of the smouldering house. Her hair was in disarray, her clothes torn and sooty, and her face smudged with black. Effective cinematography.

"The house was being renovated by my late husband as a thank-you gift to our long-time nanny," she said, "but when I realized she'd murdered my husband, I withdrew the gift. This —" she swept her hand over the devastation "— was her revenge."

"Double fuck," Amanda repeated. "No wonder the cops don't believe me."

"She didn't waste any time," Matthew said.

"And I probably made it worse with my 911 call. I wanted them to take it seriously, so I implied Danielle was out for revenge." She sank into a chair and stared at the screen blankly. The news had gone on to other topics. "Danielle doesn't stand a chance. Where's Kaitlyn?"

Matthew nodded toward his closed bedroom door. "Asleep. Poor kid is done in."

"Thank you for —"

The door opened, framing the girl in the doorway. She sagged with fatigue but her eyes sparked. "That bitch is a total fucking liar."

"Danielle?"

Kaitlyn snorted. "No. My psycho mother."

Amanda hesitated in search of diplomatic words, but Matthew had no such qualms. "Very true. But she holds all the cards. Danielle is on the run, and she's got not one but two murder charges hanging over her."

Kaitlyn crossed her arms and thrust out her chin. For the first time Amanda glimpsed the spirit that ran through the Saint Clair line. Her eyes narrowed. "You know something, don't you?"

"Danielle might have given Benson that drink, but Mother was in the kitchen when it was poured, and she ordered Danielle to take the tray to him. Practically shoved it at her. Gave her the evil eye and said, 'Don't screw up this time. This is eighteen-year-old Scotch.'"

Amanda's anger mixed with hope. "Did you see all this?"

"No, Edith told me. It's weird, because Mother never goes in the kitchen."

It was plausible. Amanda remembered her encounter with the fiercely territorial cook. "Do you think Edith will tell all this to the police?"

"I don't know." Kaitlyn's face fell. "Edith doesn't like my mother, but she keeps her mouth shut. I know she wanted a cabin on the island for when she retired, so ..." She shrugged and left the hint dangling. Janine wielded all the power, and there were not many willing to risk their future by standing up to her.

"But to save Danielle?"

Once again, Kaitlyn shrugged. "Like I said, if she pisses my mother off, what's she got?"

In the distance, a door slammed and footsteps thudded up the stairs. Even before the knock on the door, Kaylee's tail began to wag.

Matthew stepped up to let Chris in. The tall, gangly Mountie stooped as he entered what was by now a crowded room. But he seemed to see nothing but Amanda, and within two strides he wrapped her in his arms.

She knew she must look a sight. Hands bandaged like boxing gloves, face singed red from the fire, hair and clothes smelling of smoke and paint thinner. But all her doubts evaporated at the gentleness of his touch.

"What am I going to do with you?" he asked as he kissed her softly.

She tilted her head up. "Just this."

He grinned before looking around and taking half a step away from her in embarrassment.

"You heard?" she asked.

"About the fire?"

"Yes, and about it all being laid at Danielle's feet."

"Yeah. I just came down from Incident Command in Parry Sound. The team up there is comparing notes with the lead arson guy here in Toronto. It's a multipronged, multijurisdictional case, so it's going to take a while. Plus Border Services have their oar in, because of Fernando."

"Where is Fernando?"

"Still up in Parry Sound. When I left, he was being booked into a holding cell."

In spite of herself, Amanda flinched. "The poor man."

"I had to take him there, Amanda. He's a wanted man. And now there's this arson accusation against Danielle...."

"But that has nothing to do with him."

"Even so, it's part of the picture police are acting on right now. You forget, honey, I *am* the police."

"I know," she grumbled, knowing he was right but hating it. Hating this commitment to duty that divided them.

"What he should get," Chris continued as if she hadn't resisted, "is a good lawyer. I'm going to ask Tight-Ass Knotts for one more week's personal leave so I can get him a good lawyer and testify at his show cause hearing when it comes up."

Amanda felt a surge of affection and shame. Silently, she squeezed his hand. He really *was* one of the good guys. And this meant one more week! Matthew had been very quiet, and she wondered whether he had witnessed the subtle shifts between them. "What about your friend?" she asked to distract him.

Matthew shook his head. "Peter is property and estate law. But I can ask him to recommend a good criminal and immigration rights lawyer."

Chris nodded. "There's not a lot of hard evidence to implicate Fernando in anything more than buying the wrong kind of visa."

"What about Ronny's death?"

"I actually think he's innocent. Fernando told me Ronny fell during an altercation and hit his head, which is consistent with the autopsy findings. It was Danielle who told him Ronny was dead. He seemed genuinely upset when I told him he wasn't." He paused. "I get the feeling Danielle runs the show in that marriage. I'm not sure how far she'd go."

Amanda remembered the fierce woman shouting down Janine outside the little house she'd dreamed of. Making a bargain with the devil for the sake of her family. That thought brought her up short. "Where's their son?"

"I left him at the coffee shop with Julio," Matthew said. "I wanted to get Kaitlyn back here. Julio seemed to be taking good care of him, and the kid was happy to be with him."

Amanda recalled the intimacy of the two at the coffee shop. The obvious affection Julio had shown for the boy, who should have been a total stranger. "Julio speaks Tagalog," she said quietly.

Matthew met her gaze.

"What did you say Danielle's full name was?" she asked him.

"Danielle Rodriguez Torres."

"In some cultures," Amanda said slowly, "the woman keeps her maiden name as a middle name."

"Her brother," Chris said. "Fernando let that slip, and then said it was his poor English."

Matthew's expression betrayed no surprise, as if he already knew. "Do the police know Julio and Danielle know each other?" he asked.

Chris and Amanda shook their heads, and they were all startled when Kaitlyn spoke from the corner, where she'd been patting Kaylee. "You can bet the Bitch-in-Chief will tell them. Anything to make it look like they were all in this together."

"She's right," said Amanda. "Janine is going to kill as many birds as she can with this stone."

"They'll all need good lawyers," Chris said.

"If they're ever heard from again," Matthew muttered.

Chris studied him in silence for a moment before turning back to Amanda. "Right. Well, for now let's focus on the important things. I for one could use a good steak and a pint! Then we need somewhere to sleep, and not all in this tiny place."

Kaitlyn's teeth were chattering so violently, the entire front seat of the car vibrated. Amanda was tempted to intervene and tell Venetia to call the whole thing off. Barely a week ago, the girl's life had been hanging by a thread, and here she was, sitting in Venetia's Subaru outside the police station in Toronto, preparing to betray her mother. It was a great deal to ask of any fourteen-year-old, let alone one who'd just had her world blown apart.

Amanda knew it was what the girl wanted, however. Deep down, it was her first step toward putting her life back together. She had at her side the solid, steadfast support of her Aunt Venetia, technically a second cousin rather than an aunt, but the bond was just as strong. No sooner had Amanda phoned her than Venetia had thrown some clothes and a toothbrush into an overnight bag, climbed into her aging Subaru, and made the trip to Toronto at breakneck speed.

The three of them had spent two days walking in High Park, strolling along the waterfront, and hunched over take-out in the spacious hotel suite Venetia had splurged on. For two days they had talked. Venetia was unequivocal. "This is a lot to ask of you, honey," she'd said, gripping the girl's hands. "But I want you to know that no matter what you decide, you have a home with me. And remember, you didn't do this. This was all Janine's doing."

Kaitlyn had been quiet a long time before giving voice to her deepest, darkest fear; that it was she who'd put the fateful chain of events in motion. She and her mother fought all the time, each inflicting small slashes that had ceased to have any effect. A couple of weeks ago, during a particularly spectacular argument, she had wanted to draw blood. She'd been hoping to go sailing with Benson, but Janine had insisted she stay with the baby while Danielle took the twins out with him instead. "Benson wants to spend some time with his girls," Janine had said, a subtle reminder that Kaitlyn was not.

"Oh, like Danielle's got nothing to do with it," Kaitlyn had retorted, and in a fit of jealous hurt, she'd blurted out the news about the little house.

If she hadn't, Benson might still be alive. She'd probably expected her mother to be hurt and angry, but how could she possibly have predicted the woman would resort to murder? It was a guilt that would haunt her for a long time.

If blame could be placed elsewhere, it could be with Janine's ongoing mistreatment of Danielle, or maybe even more accurately with Benson's decision to go behind his wife's back. Perhaps out of the goodness of his heart, perhaps as one small attempt to stand up to her, perhaps a bit of both. But as unwise as that decision had been, the true blame lay squarely with Janine, who had turned a family feud into murder.

After two days, Kaitlyn reached her own decision. She would tell the police that she had informed her mother about the little house a week before her husband's death. She would tell them her mother had much more sophisticated drug sources than either Julio or Danielle because she was a party user of custom drug cocktails that mixed MDMA and cocaine to achieve the perfect edge. Kaitlyn would also tell them that although Danielle had served the Scotch, the cook claimed Janine was in the kitchen when it was prepared and had ordered Danielle to serve it.

It wasn't much, especially stacked up against Janine's social standing and her powerful lawyers, but it might be enough to broaden the police investigation. If the cook corroborated Kaitlyn's story, it created a plausible alternative to Danielle's guilt.

Venetia had already had a private phone chat with Edith, who fiercely denied Kaitlyn's version of events. "That girl just wants to get back at her mother," she'd insisted, but Venetia could hear the fear in her voice. Edith didn't want to go up against the power of the Saint Clairs either. She'd dedicated her whole life to their service and would have nothing if that were taken away.

"I suspect Janine has already laid that on the line," Venetia said to Amanda later than night. "She may even have sweetened the deal with a subtle bribe. I know Edith had her heart set on the little retirement cabin that Janine's father had promised and Janine had scuttled. If Janine put that back on the table ..."

They were sitting in the small hotel living room, unwinding at the end of the second day. Kaitlyn had finally fallen asleep, and the two women were sharing a bottle of Merlot. The wine wrapped Amanda in a warm glow, and she felt as if she'd known this generous woman for years.

"We'll just have to find a way to appeal to Edith's conscience," she replied. "I think she liked Danielle and sympathized with her plight."

"She also despises Janine. Janine has made a lot of people angry over the years."

"Then maybe her famous social standing won't protect her as much as you think," Amanda said. "Once people start speaking up, others will join in. Edith seems like a woman with strong ideas about what's right and wrong. Once the police start pushing her to do the right thing ..."

In the cold, stark light of the next day, parked outside the towering pink cubes of Toronto Police headquarters, Amanda's confidence wavered. Set amid soaring glass skyscrapers in the city's downtown core, the building screamed of power and privilege, of secret deals and old boys' understandings. This was Janine's world, not that of a drug-using teenager or a family cook. Certainly not of a foreign nanny on the run. But Venetia, with traces of Saint Clair blood pulsing through her veins, circled the car and took the girl's hand.

"This is going to be sweet payback," she said with a smile as she strode toward the glass doors.

CHAPTER TWENTY- NINE

Kaylee spotted him before Amanda did. She snatched up her ball and raced gleefully up the hill toward the path. Through the trees and dappled sunshine, a figure strode into view, his long limbs all akimbo and a Montreal Canadiens ball cap perched crooked on his head. A potential lynching offence here in Toronto Maple Leafs territory, but Chris had joined the legions of Canadiens fans who cheered from the bars of Newfoundland.

Kaylee bounced in circles around him. He tossed the ball and raised his hand to wave at Amanda. Instantly the sun shone more brightly and heat welled within her. He'd been in Parry Sound less than a week, but it felt like a year. She left the blanket and picnic lunch to run into his arms.

"How did it go?" she asked when they came up for air.

"Lots has happened, for sure! Is that ours?" He pointed to the picnic cooler on the blanket. When she nodded, he grabbed her hand and headed down toward it. "I'm starving! Standish just called me on my way back — we're on our way to becoming best buds — and he says the Toronto cops are closing in. They've been rounding up drug dealers across the city to try to get to their sources. This opioid crisis has everybody spooked, especially the politicians, so the word from on high is throw as much money at it as you need and clean it up.

ASAP. So deals are being offered, and a few of the lower-level guys are starting to sing."

He broke off to fold himself down onto the blanket. He peered into the cooler, grinned, and reached for a beer in a brown paper bag. "You're so bad for me, woman."

"I try. But I don't think any of your comrades are fooled for one minute."

He laughed. They were in Toronto's High Park, an oasis of woodlands, trails, and meadows in the heart of the city's west end. Like all city parks, alcohol was banned except under specific circumstances, so coffee cups and paper bags were popular. Chris paused to take a deep, appreciative sip of the craft beer Amanda had brought.

Amanda swatted him impatiently. "And?"

"One of the canaries had Janine Saint Clair on his client list."

Triumph mixed with the disgust that shot through her. No matter how much she learned about Janine, each new level of depravity came as a fresh shock. "The noose is tightening."

"Let's hope so. So far they don't have nearly enough to sew up a murder charge. They're going to have another go at the cook now that they have this new information, but meanwhile Fernando and Danielle are still in the frame."

"And has Fernando had his show cause hearing?"

"This afternoon. It was postponed and postponed, so I finally had to leave. The wheels sure grind slow up there in the country. Matthew and his pal Pomeroy hired this whiz of a Toronto criminal defence lawyer. I don't know the guy, but Pomeroy says he eats cops and Crowns for breakfast. But he has his work cut out for him getting Fernando out on bail. For now, the charge is second-degree murder in the death of Ronny Gifford, but the shark lawyer is trying to get that downgraded. It's a serious charge, so even with a fancy defence lawyer, bail is unlikely."

A little joy seeped out of the afternoon as Amanda contemplated the poor man languishing in a jail cell far from home, alone, unfamiliar with the language and customs, and rightfully frightened of the police. To make matters worse, Danielle had not been seen or heard from since her little house burned down. Jullo too had dropped out of sight, no doubt into the secretive, protective underworld of the undocumented. Without Danielle's testimony, there would be nothing to corroborate Fernando's claim that Ronny's injury had been accidental and he'd believed the young man to be dead when they buried him.

"What about George? No charges there?"

He took a bite out of his curried-chicken wrap before shaking his head. "I visited George again before I left this morning. He's on the mend, and he told Standish he came on like a raging bull when he found Fernando and Danielle on the island, and they freaked out. Danielle was carrying the shotgun, but it was way too heavy for her and it just went off. That's more or less what Fernando told me. George doesn't want to press charges. He even took some comfort from the care they showed burying Ronny. The cross and the prayers." He paused for another bite and Amanda picked up her own wrap. "He's set his sights in a new direction anyway. He's going for custody of Kaitlyn."

Amanda stopped with the wrap halfway to her mouth. Her eyes widened. "That's a stretch."

"Not if her mother goes to jail. And if DNA testing shows he's the grandfather. Effectively next of kin."

"But still, he's a stranger."

"He plans to change that."

Amanda frowned. "Kaitlyn is a fragile girl. She needs familiarity and love. Her Aunt Venetia will be taking her in."

He gave a mischievous, Cheshire Cat grin. "Yeah. And just as I was leaving this morning, Venetia popped in to see him. She was smiling ear to ear, and I can't say he was unhappy to see her. I think something will work out."

Amanda pictured practical, back-to-the-earth Venetia and the grizzled outfitter together. Both were used to running their own lives, simple, unadorned, and rooted in their own interests. But maybe both had room in their hearts for another like-minded soul.

"Wouldn't that be cool," she said. "And Kaitlyn would be out of that toxic, drug-infested environment in Toronto. Fresh air, open water, the slower pace of country life." She wondered how the restless, urban girl would adjust, and hoped she wouldn't get bored. Maybe a stint as a junior counsellor on the Fun for Families kayaking trip this summer was in order. Kaitlyn would learn a lot from those struggling mothers and kids and even more from Frankie.

She tilted her head to look at him, drinking in the charm of his crinkly blue eyes and ski-jump nose. "Have you run out of excuses for staying here?"

He nodded. "The shark lawyer wanted me to stick around for the show cause hearing. Fernando doesn't have any character references — Larry and I are it — but Sergeant Knotts is finally out of patience. I tried to persuade him the OPP still needed my input, but he is not buying it. He booked me on the night shift tomorrow."

Her mood plummeted. "So this is our last day?"

He shook his head. "I booked the airport Comfort Inn for one last night. If I fly out tomorrow morning ..."

"King-sized bed?"

"Two queens. One for us and one for the princess here."

"Ever the optimist, that's you."

In fact, Kaylee left them alone until eight thirty the next morning, when she crawled up between them, inching forward as if unsure of her welcome. Amanda opened her eyes languidly and reached over to stroke her head. The bed vibrated with the wagging of her tail.

Chris brushed Amanda's tumbled hair from her eyes and kissed her nose. "You stay in bed. I'll take her out and make us coffee."

How did this angel fall into my life? she wondered, barely aware of him moving around. Some minutes later, he woke her again with a fragrant cup of coffee by her bedside.

"Newfoundland is so far away," she murmured.

He slid in beside her, balancing his cup. "But beautiful in late August, don't forget."

A shadow passed over her heart. Newfoundland, despite its charms, still held frightening memories. She sipped her coffee to centre herself. "I know. But it's not a solution."

"It's a start. You can organize your trips just as easily from Deer Lake as you can from your aunt's cottage in Quebec. It can be as temporary or as permanent as you like."

She started to draw away, but he caught her arm. "Just think about it. You have no home, Amanda."

She felt the sharp pain of his words. He was right. How often had she thought the same thing? But before she could think of an answer, his cellphone rang. When he answered it, he snapped instantly alert. "Standish," he mouthed as he turned away.

From his brief, cryptic replies, she tried to piece together the conversation. Standish's voice, even muffled by the phone, was sharp and angry.

"No ..." Chris replied. "What? Oh fuck ... No, I haven't heard from him ... No idea ... Today ... Of course I will. Keep me posted."

When he hung up, he turned to her grimly. "Fernando has skipped town. That defence lawyer shark apparently persuaded the Crown to reduce the charge to manslaughter and then persuaded the judge to grant bail over the furious objections of Standish and the Crown. I don't know where the bond money came from. Some mystery fund that the lawyer signed for. Fernando wasn't supposed to leave Parry Sound, but Standish didn't trust him an inch, so he checked the rooming house this morning. Gone. Packed up all his stuff and left the place clean as a whistle."

Amanda muttered a soft curse. Danielle and Fernando were digging themselves in deeper and deeper.

Chris stood up to pace. "They went for the manslaughter charge, but I'm amazed he got bail all the same. That judge must have known he'd be a flight risk. What's there for him in Parry Sound? He's going to come here to Toronto. Or take the first route he can out of the country."

"He's pretty scared. And he'd have no trust in our justice system."

"But still. Goddamn! Somebody must be helping him. And what's this mystery fund that paid his bail? Any ideas?"

She pretended to inspect her coffee cup so he wouldn't see the evasion in her eyes. She remembered Matthew's vague answers when she quizzed him about the whereabouts of Julio and the little boy. She also remembered how effortlessly Danielle had melted into the crowd after the fire and how all the resources of the Toronto Police had failed to find her.

Danielle knew Matthew and had even asked him to get her false papers. Would she have contacted him for help again? Would he have facilitated the reunion of the family? Julio was already managing a comfortable living in Toronto's underground world. Would Matthew have helped the rest of them slip underground as well?

She had no doubt it was possible. He'd seen too many innocents caught up in webs of injustice in dangerous parts of the
world to have much trust left. As a journalist he always avoided
personal entanglements, but in this case, on his own home turf,
he might have let his objectivity slip.

She had no intention of asking him, however. She didn't want
to know the answer, because then she would have to lie to Chris.
Secrets and lies were very poor foundations for a relationship.

"That lawyer may have some powerful connections," she
said, which was probably true. "It's not difficult to disappear in
a place as big and ethnically diverse as Toronto if you've got the
contacts and the money."

Chris shook his head incredulously. "But why would he risk
his license and reputation by breaking the law? Besides, how
would Fernando even get to Toronto? The man has zero contacts
in Parry Sound."

Not exactly true, Amanda thought; Fernando knew Larry,
who had a soft spot for him. But she said nothing. No point in
drawing even more people into trouble.

Instead she shrugged. "However he managed it, I think it's safe
to assume we'll never see Fernando, Danielle, or their son again."

Chris swung on her, his eyes narrowing. "Are you *glad* about
this? They're in a hell of a lot of trouble! If they'd stayed around
to have their day in court, especially with this shark lawyer,
they might have been cleared and then applied for Canadian
citizenship in the future. This way, they'll be looking over their
shoulders their whole lives."

She cradled her coffee, still avoiding his gaze and his unerr-
ing faith in the system he represented. She was far less optimistic
about their acquittals, for there were two additional facts she had
no intention of telling him. Facts that a well-informed Crown
attorney would certainly reveal at the trial. First, that Danielle had

tried to blackmail Janine Saint Clair into giving her the little house in return for Danielle's silence about Janine's role in Benson's death. With a few choice words whispered in the Crown's ear, Janine would get that ploy on the record as evidence of Danielle's moral bankruptcy.

Secondly, Danielle claimed she'd checked Ronny's pulse and determined he was dead before they'd buried him. Although conceivable, Amanda had a niggle of doubt. Danielle was an educated woman. In addition to her teaching degree, as a nanny she would have been trained in first aid and should know how to take a pulse. Either she chose not to take it, so as not to be faced with an untenable choice, or she'd lied to Fernando because she was desperate to get on with the escape. Saving Ronny would have slowed them down.

Neither of these facts would go down well with Chris, her straight-as-an-arrow policeman. Danielle had stepped, by choice, into the murky world of moral expediency. She didn't have the luxury of righteousness; she was a survivor. She had made her first choice five years ago when she left her homeland, her husband, and her young son to find work abroad to support them. Her ultimate dream had been a little home in Canada, in a safe neighbourhood, to give her son a chance at a better life. She had survived by keeping her sights on that goal, and threatened with its loss, she had doubled her fight.

That determination, born of a hardship unknown to most Canadians, had made her ruthless. In a world where self-serving power, corruption, and greed were the guiding principles, the powerless learned early to take care of themselves. Amanda had known thousands like her in her work overseas; at their core, good, caring people faced with appalling choices.

Danielle had made such a choice. Not trusting the system to believe her and give her voice equal weight to that of the

Saint Clairs, she'd chosen not to risk what little freedom she had. She'd chosen instead to live in the shadows. In that, she had plenty of company.

When Amanda didn't reply, Chris came to stand over her. "You *are* glad about this."

She finally raised her eyes to meet his, for on this score, she had nothing to hide. "I'm not glad about it. I wish they had trusted our system, but I understand why they didn't. Guilt and innocence are fragile concepts, and the justice system sometimes takes a sledgehammer to them. I'm not even sure I trust our system in this case, and I was raised here."

He gave her a long, thoughtful look. She bit her lip and tolerated the silence. It was a silence filled with unspoken clamour.

"Are we going to be all right?" he asked softly.

"I hope so, Chris. If we try. If we can bend."

His lips twitched. "I'm not as rigid as you think, you know."

She cocked her head, crooked her finger, and watched as his beautiful crinkly blue-eyed smile lit up his face.

ACKNOWLEDGEMENTS

For me as a writer, research is at the core of credibility. If I get the little things wrong, how will the reader trust the truth of the larger things I have to say? Before I even begin a novel, and at virtually every page along the way, I check my facts. Luckily for writers today, the internet has made a wealth of information available from our armchairs at the click of a mouse, and books, newspapers, and maps can supply even more. But there is no research more powerful than being in the place, filling the senses, and asking the simple, everyday questions that enrich the scenes and draw both writer and reader deeper into the story.

I made two research trips to Georgian Bay, and during the last visit my sister and I rented a cottage for a week so that I could follow Amanda's journey through the book, hiking the trails and kayaking in the bays. I would like to thank the many people who answered my questions along the way, including the staff at White Squall Paddling Centre, Killarney Outfitters, Katawoda Cottages, Payne Marine, Gilly's Snug Harbour Restaurant and Marine, and many others. Back at home, friends George Pike and Guy MacLeod provided much-needed expertise on boats and outboard motors.

As always, I'd like to thank my long-time friends and masterful critiquers Sue Pike, Joan Boswell, and Mary Jane Maffini for helping to fashion the rough, ragged story into the best it could be. I've been fortunate to have the same editor for many of my books over the years, and so a special thanks goes to Allister Thompson for his thoroughness, his professional insights, and most of all his calm, unflappable advice, leavened by his dry wit. I'd also like to thank Laura Boyle, the cover designer, who once again has done a brilliant job; and Michelle Melski, my publicist, who shepherds me and my books through the promotional maze with enthusiasm and good cheer; and the rest of the Dundurn staff who work behind the scenes to make the book a success. Last but not least a heartfelt thank you to Dundurn's publisher, Kirk Howard, and former vice-president Beth Bruder — champions and advocates of Canadian stories — for their continued support and belief in my work.

The biggest thanks goes to my sister, Pamela Baillie Currie, to whom I have dedicated this book, for always being there and for providing a sounding board, willing companionship, and a helping hand, whether it's caring for my dogs while I was away or coming with me on my location scouting adventures. And most of all, for that steadfast affection and support perhaps only a sister can give.

BOOK CREDITS

Acquiring Editor: Shannon Whibbs
Project Editor: Jenny McWha
Editor: Allister Thompson
Proofreader: Tara Quigley

Cover Designer: Laura Boyle
Interior Designer: Jennifer Gallinger

Publicist: Michelle Melski

DUNDURN

Publisher: Kirk Howard
Editorial Director: Kathryn Lane
Artistic Director: Laura Boyle
Director of Sales and Marketing: Synora Van Drine
Publicity Manager: Michelle Melski

Editorial: Allison Hirst, Dominic Farrell, Jenny McWha, Rachel Spence, Elena Radic
Marketing and Publicity: Kendra Martin, Kathryn Bassett, Elham Ali

dundurn.com
@dundurnpress
dundurnpress

dundurnpress
dundurnpress
info@dundurn.com

FIND US ON NETGALLEY & GOODREADS TOO!

DUNDURN